PRAISE FOR

"Romance, danger, rebellion, exploration...and it's all delivered with the intricate sensory details and historical research readers have come to expect from Stewart's work."
—Julie Cantrell, *New York Times* and *USA Today* bestselling author of *Into the Free* and *When Mountains Move*

"Rich and complex...In A FLYING AFFAIR, the world is just opening up to women aviators, and Stewart does a beautiful job of capturing the exhilaration and anxiety of the era."
—Judy Christie, award-winning author of *Wreath, A Girl*

"Deftly written, with a keen eye toward history, Carla Stewart's latest is sure to delight!"
—Lisa Wingate, national bestselling author of *The Prayer Box* and *The Story Keeper*

"From a 1920s horse farm to the exciting world of women aviators, Stewart combines adventure, romance, and faith in a truly compelling story."
—Myra Johnson, author of *When Clouds Roll By*, historical fiction winner of the 2014 Christian Retailing Best Award

"Carla Stewart has written a novel to remember...With a plot that kept me turning pages from engaging beginning to exhilarating end, A FLYING AFFAIR positively soars!"
—Karen Halvorsen Schreck, author of *Sing for Me* and *Broken Ground*

"A FLYING AFFAIR is more than a great read—it's an experience!" —Ane Mulligan, author of *Chapel Springs Revival*

"Tons of adventure and a sprinkling of romance...It's a journey you won't want to miss."   —Anne Mateer, author of *Playing by Heart*

"[A] breathtaking tale of love, ambition, and self-discovery."
                        —Camille Eide, author of *Like There's No Tomorrow*

PRAISE FOR *The Hatmaker's Heart*

"Stewart has once again written a rich and delicate novel that readers will love. Nell is a beautiful person with a heart of gold. Her resilience and determination to succeed and help others is refreshing, while her struggles are relatable."   —*RT Book Reviews*

"Fans of Carla Stewart's work won't be disappointed with this Jazz Age tale. With lush sensory details, Stewart brings us deep into this historical setting...readers will savor the sweet escape."
                        —Julie Cantrell, *New York Times* best-selling author
                        of *When Mountains Move*

"Carla Stewart captures this time period with amazing accuracy... When choosing 'never-to-be-missed' writers, put Carla Stewart at the top of your list."
     —Kim Vogel Sawyer, best-selling author of *What Once Was Lost*

"Fans of the Jazz Age will cheer Nell's journey and treasure this richly rendered taste of the Roaring Twenties."
                        —Lisa Wingate, national best-selling author of *The Prayer Box*

"*The Hatmaker's Heart* contains love, betrayal, and family secrets—all the elements that delight fans of *Downton Abbey*."
                        —Kellie Coates Gilbert, author of *Mother of Pearl*

PRAISE FOR *Sweet Dreams*

"*Sweet Dreams* is an inspiring novel and one that is heartfelt. Readers are sure to savor every page of this wonderful story."
—Michael Morris, author of *A Place Called Wiregrass*

"Carla Stewart is masterful at creating characters you care about—and places that seem so real you feel like you've gone for a visit."
—Judy Christie, author of the Green series and *Wreath*

PRAISE FOR *Stardust*

"[An] enjoyable, worthwhile read." —*RT Book Reviews*

"*Stardust* is told with heart and skill and obvious love for her characters. A gripping story line that is inspiring and unforgettable."
—Julie L. Cannon, best-selling author of *I'll Be Home for Christmas* and *Twang*

PRAISE FOR *Broken Wings*

"While the story is heartbreaking, there is much more to this book... Stewart skillfully entertains and engages the reader with each character's private pain and survival skills." —*RT Book Reviews*

"With apt descriptions and artful prose, Stewart delves into the vibrant, jazzy 1940s, at the same time creating a true-to-life present."
—Christina Berry, award-winning author of *The Familiar Stranger*

D0170537

PRAISE FOR *Chasing Lilacs*

"Coming-of-age stories are a fiction staple, but well-done ones much rarer. This emotionally acute novel is one of the rare ones."

—*Publishers Weekly* (starred review)

"A warm, compelling tale."   —*BookPage*

A FLYING AFFAIR

Heartfelt Fiction from Carla Stewart:

The Hatmaker's Heart

Sweet Dreams

Stardust

Broken Wings

Chasing Lilacs

Available from FaithWords wherever books are sold.

A FLYING AFFAIR

A Novel

CARLA STEWART

New York • Boston • Nashville

Copyright © 2015 by Carla Stewart

Carla Stewart is represented by MacGregor Literary, Inc., Hillsboro, Oregon.

FaithWords
Hachette Book Group
1290 Avenue of the Americas
New York, NY 10104

www.faithwords.com

RRD–C

Printed in the United States of America

First edition: June 2015

10 9 8 7 6 5 4 3 2 1

FaithWords is a division of Hachette Book Group, Inc.

The FaithWords name and logo are trademarks of Hachette Book Group, Inc.

The Hachette Speakers Bureau provides a wide range of authors for speaking events. To find out more, go to www.hachettespeakersbureau.com or call (866) 376-6591.

Library of Congress Cataloging-in-Publication Data

Stewart, Carla.
 A flying affair / Carla Stewart.—First edition.
    pages ; cm
  ISBN 978-1-4555-4999-3 (softcover) — ISBN 978-1-4555-4997-9 (ebook)
1. Women air pilots—Fiction. 2. Nineteen twenties—Fiction. 3. Man-woman relationships—Fiction. 4. United States—Social life and customs—20th century—Fiction I. Title.
 PS3619.T4937F59 2015
 813'.6—dc23

2014036043

For Sandra Bishop,
whose guidance is the rudder that keeps me
flying on course.

Acknowledgments

It's a sacred privilege to write novels, and I'm reminded once again of both the joy in exploring new topics and ideas and the debt of gratitude to so many good folks who've come alongside.

My thanks first of all to Sandra Bishop, my agent to whom this book is dedicated. She set my feet on this path of writing about the Roaring Twenties the moment she whispered two words to me: Kentucky Derby. While the story was never meant to be about horse racing, her inspiration led me to explore the wonders of Kentucky, which birthed both *The Hatmaker's Heart* and *A Flying Affair*. "Thank you" is inadequate to express my appreciation for your encouragement and love of great stories.

Ideas, of course, lead to research and, if I'm lucky, road trips. Thank you, Max, for indulging me once again. I know this wasn't what you signed up for when you said, "I do," but there's no one on earth I'd rather travel the highways and byways with. You have my heart today and always.

Special thanks to Hoppy Bennett, owner of Undulata Farms in Shelbyville, Kentucky, for sharing your passion for American Saddlebred horses and for your kindness in letting me observe firsthand the training of this magnificent breed.

A bushel of thanks to Thirza Peevey, horsewoman extraordinaire, for the many "horse" talks we had and for being a first reader. Your expertise helped me more than words can say.

To Bobby Walker, who challenged me to write a "completely true fictional story" about him and his mad skills as a pilot and flying instructor. Any similarities between the Bobby in *A Flying Affair* and the real Bobby are coincidental.

Christina Boys, you continue to amaze me with your insights and careful attention to every detail. You've earned your "wings" for sure! Thank you and the entire team at FaithWords: Virginia Hensley, Laini Brown, JuLee Brand (the cover art is swoon worthy!), Katie Connors, and all of the sales, marketing, and production staff. What a blessing you all are!

My thanks to the many writing friends who travel this road with me. Your encouragement, hugs, and prayers mean the world to me. A very warm thank you to Kathy Murphy and the Pulpwood Queens, whose ongoing support I cherish. Your gift at bringing authors and readers together is unparalleled.

Heartfelt thanks to Melanie Benjamin (*The Aviator's Wife*) for sharing your writing experience and teaching me the value of "discovering the story you want to tell."

To my family—Max, kids, grands, my sisters, and my dad—you've been asked to carry the load and revere the deadline a lot this past year. Your love and support are the glue that's held me together through long days and mountains of research papers and books. I love you!

Thank you, dear readers, for taking this journey with me. I pray you will find the courage to soar toward your own hopes and dreams.

And to the One who makes it all possible—thank you, Jesus, for the gift of words and for your Word that is the spirit of truth and love and boundless joy.

A FLYING AFFAIR

CHAPTER 1

Summer 1927

In the early rays of morning, three-year-old Gypsy's bay coat shimmered like liquid gold, her raven mane waving as Mittie Humphreys took her through the paces. Even through the saddle that separated the two, Mittie felt the ripple of anticipation, the inner surge of fire Gypsy couldn't contain. When they got beyond the paddock to the bluegrass hills, an unspoken communication passed between them. Time to do what they both really wanted. Time to fly.

Mittie leaned forward and whispered, "Let's go, girl!"

The filly twitched her ears and broke into a canter. The wind rushed past, lifting Mittie's long hair into a sail behind, her heart quickening as they raced toward the red emblazoned horizon, the sky above streaked with tangerine and pink. Gypsy's muscles rippled as she ran, her hooves scarcely touching the ground.

Her daddy called Mittie a natural when it came to horses, but every time he said it, Mittie winced. While she adored Gypsy with a fierceness that sometimes scared her, her dreams went beyond the bounds of Morning Glory Farms. Beyond the hills of Kentucky.

One day she'd soar and bank and roll, performing the stunts she'd read about the barnstormers doing—someday when Daddy was stronger and there were fewer demands with the horses and the trainers *and* when she'd convinced her parents there was nothing more in all the world she wanted.

A slight tug on the reins and Gypsy responded with the same ease as the bi-wing plane at Bowman Field. "Aviatrix!" she shouted into the billowing dawn. "Someday, Gypsy, you're going to see me flying above you. Just you wait."

Someday.

She gave an involuntary shudder as she pulled Gypsy up into a trot, then a walk as they headed for the stables, giving them both time to cool down. Toby, her favorite trainer, met them at the barns. Mittie dismounted and handed the reins to Toby, who had a handful of carrot nuggets ready for Gypsy. They exchanged pleasantries, and then Mittie gave a final nuzzle to Gypsy and headed to the house. She skirted a pool of mud and nearly bumped into Moses Roper, the groundskeeper and dearest man in six counties. He greeted her with a nod of his woolly head. "Everything all right with you this fine morning?"

"Better now that I've seen you, Moses. You coming in for breakfast?"

"Not this morning. Miz Sarah got herself worked plumb to a tizzy when I checked with Mr. Eli for my job list today. Best if you square your shoulders and keep that smile on your face." He nodded toward a shiny late-model automobile with sleek running boards sitting on the front drive.

"Gosh, I bet it's Iris' friends—her bridesmaids. I didn't think they were coming until later on."

Moses shook his head, his eyes never leaving the ground. "Not Miz Iris' friends."

"Someone I know?"

Moses shrugged, then shuffled off toward the gardening shed without answering.

Mittie took the servants' entrance and back stairs up to her room for a quick wash and to change from her jodhpurs. Might as well make herself presentable for the mystery guest.

Once she'd freshened up and dressed in a skirt and blouse, she gave her hair a quick brush and went to the dining room. Her parents were alone at the table, her mother sipping tea, her dad his usual coffee. No guest in sight. She gave her daddy a peck on the cheek and helped herself to bacon, eggs, and grits from the chafing dishes on the sideboard. She set her plate down and went back for a side dish of biscuits and gravy, which brought a scowl from her mother.

"Gracious, you eat like a farmhand." The familiar pinched lips graced her mother's face.

"I'm starving. There's nothing like doing the chores and a quick ride to work up an appetite." She winked at her dad. "Gypsy enjoyed it, too. You know I think she secretly believes she's a Thoroughbred and not a show pony."

Her daddy sat erect, aided by the brace the doctors in Cincinnati had fitted for him. A gentleman's corset, he called it. "She's full of spunk all right. Like someone else I know. What kind of high jinks have you two been up to?" His smile was warm, his eyes twinkling.

Mittie's mother set down her tea cup. "Honestly, you don't have to encourage her, Eli."

"Good grief, Sarah. We all know Mittie's only doing her duty here until I get back in the saddle. We ought to be grateful she's willing to do that."

"She's our daughter. Why wouldn't she?"

Mittie waved her hand. "Hey, I'm here. You can talk *to* me, not *about* me." She gulped down a long drink of sweet milk. "So, tell me—who was your morning visitor? Anyone I know?"

A look passed between her parents that Mittie couldn't decipher. Mittie drummed her fingers on the linen breakfast cloth and looked at her mother. "Well? A surprise for Iris? Don't tell me Hayden Wainwright's shown up early and decided to elope with my dear sister?"

"Forevermore, Mittie. Where you come up with these preposterous ideas is beyond me."

"It's what you did with Daddy, and you didn't think it preposterous then."

"They're not eloping. It wasn't even Hayden who came. But speaking of the wedding, I hope you haven't forgotten your fitting for the bridesmaid's dress this morning."

"I haven't forgotten. But I'll have to meet up there. I'm off to Bowman Field right now."

"This is certainly not the day to be traipsing off and taking another one of those horrid airplane rides."

"No, Mother. I'm not going up in a plane today. The Lindbergh Committee is meeting. Social responsibility—that's what you've taught me. Serve the community."

Excitement bubbled inside. Even if her own dream of flying was light-years away, she could at least say she'd met the pilot who'd conquered the Atlantic—a true aviator and not just Mr. Weaver, the Bowman Field manager who gave her rides here and there.

She rubbed the goose bumps that had popped out on her arms. "It's going to be the event of the year, if not the entire decade. Charles Lindbergh flying the *Spirit of St. Louis* into Louisville. Won't that be grand?" She pushed her half-eaten breakfast away, not surprised that her mother didn't share her enthusiasm. "I'll meet you all at Martha's shop. Eleven o'clock, right?"

"And not one minute past."

"Where is Iris anyway?"

"In the drawing room, embroidering the hostess gifts for the bridesmaids' brunch." Mittie sighed. Her twin. The perfect bride. Beautiful, talented, and everything Mittie wasn't. Not that Mittie minded that Iris was having the wedding that everyone who was anyone between Louisville and Birmingham would be attending in less than a week, but already she dreaded losing Iris and her moving to Alabama. With her twin married off to a man of means and social standing, Mittie was in line to be their mother's next project. Heaven help her.

Mittie gulped the last of her coffee, then remembered the car in the drive. "Daddy, you never said who your visitor was. Whoever it was must not have stayed long."

The muscles in her dad's strong jaw clenched. "Buck Lamberson doesn't believe in social lingering. He came straight to the point."

Mittie held her breath, her breakfast eggs turned to stone in her stomach, but she kept her voice light. "Was Dobbs with him?"

"No, Dobbs needs a new bone operation. One that will lessen the limp."

Mittie closed her eyes and wished she hadn't asked. She rose from the table, went to her dad, and pressed her lips against the top of his head, the thick salt and pepper hair as soft as Gypsy's muzzle. "I'm sorry, Daddy."

Eli Humphreys took Mittie's hand in his and gave a gentle squeeze. "I know you are, sugar. Now run on or you'll be late for your meeting."

Mittie gripped the wheel of her roadster and took the curves at speeds that made her heart race, pushing thoughts of Buck Lamberson away. It was ancient history, and she wasn't going to let the unfortunate incident with Dobbs ruin her mood for the Lindbergh meeting.

Committee work didn't normally suit Mittie, at least not the sort her mother nudged her toward. Putting on silk stockings and heels, a Sunday hat, and a fashionable afternoon dress to sit in a stuffy room and sip tea from china cups might be all right if you wanted to get your name on the society page. Mittie had no interest in that and no talent for the pretense that went along with it.

And she usually made some gaffe that embarrassed her mother. There was no doubt Mittie wasn't the ladylike debutante her mother had hoped for, but maybe being on the Lindy Committee would prove more to Mittie's liking and gain her mother's approval at the same time.

She pulled her berry red roadster into a spot on the gravel parking lot and swung her long silk-stockinged legs out of the car. For once, it didn't chafe to dress the part of a civic-minded socialite. She sidestepped a puddle left from rain during the night and hurried toward the meeting room in the terminal.

Mr. Weaver, the airfield manager, was on the committee as well as Victor Booth from the Aero Club. Their expertise would be valuable to the mayor, who would oversee the planning for the whole of the Louisville community. Weaver waved for Mittie to come in and took his seat near the head of the table next to Gordon Chase. Gordon, a pasty-faced bachelor in his midtwenties, had come to all of Iris' debutante balls, and Mittie had heard he got a job as an aide for the new mayor. Perhaps the mayor had sent Gordon in his stead. When he saw Mittie, Gordon rose and walked on pigeon-toed feet across the floor to greet her with a handshake and peck on the cheek.

"Mittie. You look quite fetching, as usual." He needed a peppermint for his sour breath, but she shook his hand and gave him an air-kiss before taking her spot next to Weaver. One by one, a half dozen others trickled into the room as coffee from an urn brought in from the airfield canteen was poured into stout ceramic mugs. Not a hand-painted teapot or china cup in sight.

Gordon rustled some papers, his doughy cheeks twitching when he cleared his throat. "Mayor O'Neill asked me to preside since he's still getting settled into his office. And we have a lot of work to do today. The August eighth date has been confirmed for the Lindbergh Goodwill Tour, which starts on the East Coast in a few days. Louisville is most fortunate to have received the honor of hosting him for an overnight stop."

He paused when a well-dressed woman came in late and slipped into the empty seat beside Mittie. Gordon plunged on. "We'll have a ticker tape parade, of course. And we'll need advertising and a welcome committee."

A volunteer said, "Police officers. We don't want any violence, and you know the crowd will be monstrous. Bigger than Derby Day, I suspect."

Others nodded. Everyone in America wanted to lay eyes on the Lone Eagle, as the papers had taken to calling Lindbergh.

The latecomer leaned over and asked Mittie what organization she represented.

"I'm an airfield volunteer. Maybe I'll be the one to present the rose bouquet as a symbol of our great city."

The woman sniffed. "It's not a horse race, darling."

Gordon's eyes brightened. "That's a peach of an idea, Mittie. I'm sure the mayor will agree. And by the way, would you mind keeping minutes of our meeting?" He shoved a steno pad across the table to her. Someone provided a pencil.

"What about speeches?" Victor Booth of the Aero Club wanted to know. "As president of the organization for promotion of flight, I'd like the honor of doing the welcome."

Gordon shook his head. "I'll have to check. Seems like that's a job for the mayor."

Victor blew a puff of cigarette smoke. "Seems like he would've bothered to show up if he's of a mind to give the speech." A few murmurs of aye and nay went around the table without a consensus, and Gordon looked to Mittie for help.

Mittie cleared her throat. "I tend to think it's the mayor's job, but Victor, you've got that swell open-touring Silver Ghost that would be perfect to transport Colonel Lindbergh along the parade route. With you and that lovely wife of yours beside him, of course."

"I'd be honored as long as it comes with a spot at the head table at the banquet."

Gordon scratched his head. "The mayor didn't say anything about a banquet."

The representative of the Downtown Louisville Women's League nearly danced in her seat. "We would be remiss not to provide a formal meal and evening of entertainment for an occasion of this magnitude." Heads bobbed like mares at the grain trough as she continued. "The Crystal Ballroom at the Brown Hotel would be the wise choice. A formal dinner by invitation only. And a band. Every woman in town will want to dance with Colonel Lindbergh." Hands went up to volunteer for the committee.

Gordon looked like he was lost at sea. He cleared his throat, unable to offer any direction about which politicians to invite, whether to hire a celebrity jazz band or someone local, what the best parade route would be, and what local sites Colonel Lindbergh might want to see.

Mittie was starting to feel sorry for Lindy. All that attention being foisted upon him. Thrust into the limelight day after day, expected to perform like a circus pony and sit elbow to elbow with people he'd never laid eyes on, then dance with their daughters. She wasn't even sure the poor fella liked to dance.

Mittie scribbled until her fingers cramped, fully aware that nothing was being decided. Gordon was hapless at organizing and giving direction. Mittie glanced at the clock on the far wall and groaned. She was due at Martha's in half an hour.

She held up her hand for silence. "Gordon, I think we've got a good start here. I suggest we divide up the various duties, let each committee member gather pertinent facts and figures, and come back here next week to share our information."

Gordon's face flushed purple. "Yes, I was getting around to that point, Mittie."

Victor huffed, a plume of smoke making phantom curlicues. "You bet he was. Just not in this century."

Mittie read off what she had and told Gordon she'd bring a type-written copy of the minutes to the mayor's office the next morning.

Gordon adjourned the meeting, and as Mittie was nearly to the door, Weaver asked to have a word. "Nice job of keeping things under control." He jerked his head in the direction of Gordon. "Poor sap got in over his head. Thanks for stepping in."

"My pleasure, but I hope I didn't speak out of turn."

"Don't concern yourself with that, my dear girl. Give me a call when you want to take another jaunt in the old Canuck."

"It'll be a while, I'm afraid. Iris' wedding is just around the corner."

Weaver nodded. "Ah, yes. Give her my best. With your charm and good looks, I'm sure it'll be your turn soon."

She glanced at the clock, which told her she was going to have to floorboard it to make it to the fitting. She offered her apology for having to run and sailed out the door, chuckling at Weaver's remark. The last thing she wanted—or needed—was a husband.

Low clouds hovered over the airfield, the air heavy with the promise of another storm. Mittie strode to the end of the walk, but at the edge of the gravel, her heel sunk into the soft earth, causing her to teeter off-balance for a moment. When she put her foot on solid ground, a sharp pain shot through the ball of her left foot—a piece of gravel had slipped into her shoe and lodged there.

She winced, plucked off her shoe, and shook out the offending pebble. When she looked up, a man in an aviator helmet and leather flight jacket offered his hand while she slipped the shoe back on.

She muttered her thanks and hurried on.

"Wait, miss!" The pilot fell in stride with Mittie. "Don't I know you? You look terribly familiar and gorgeous to boot."

Mittie stopped. The voice was familiar, perhaps someone who'd given her a come-on before. She gave him a quick glance, thinking she might slap him if he said something fresh. The chin strap of his leather helmet swung unfastened along a strong jaw, flight goggles resting atop his head. On his forehead, a black lock of hair had escaped, grazing a raised eyebrow. One raised brow that invited a response. Her stomach lurched with recognition.

"Ames? Ames Dewberry?"

"In the flesh. And if I recall, you're the lass from Long Island that begged me to take you up in that old Curtiss of mine. Musta been what—three, four years ago?"

"Four years next month." *Ames Dewberry*. How she'd dreamed one day he'd step into her life the way he had when she and Iris had gone to that garden party with their cousin Nell. Ames Dewberry, mystic and intrepid, swaggering onto the lawn that night, leaning on one elbow on the backyard bar. He'd matured a lot in four years, but there was the same cleft in his chin. Same dark eyes that, when Mittie wasn't dreaming about flying, drifted into her sleep and uncountable waking hours.

"Mattie, wasn't it?"

She snickered. "Close, but no. Mittie. And I didn't beg." She had begged. Pathetically. And scribbled her address on the back of a calling card she found in her evening bag. "I spent months thinking I hallucinated the whole thing since I never heard from you."

His brows converged into a *V* between simmering coal eyes. "I lost the card you gave me—thought I put it in my pocket, but never could find it." His hand rested on her forearm, searing through the voile of her afternoon dress.

"So what brings you to Louisville?"

"Barnstorming across the river in Indiana, scoping out some new spots and crowds to entertain." He nodded toward the runways. "The setup here would be a good place for home base. And getting reacquainted with you if you're not spoken for, although I fear I'm probably too late for that. Dolls like you don't stay unattached for long."

Mittie shrugged noncommittally. "I'd love to chat with you and hear what you've been doing, but I'm in somewhat of a rush. Perhaps soon."

"How soon?"

"Well, not today. The next few days are swarming with things I have to do." *Those eyes.* Sympathetic. Hopeful. Pleading. Clouds drifted past, the minutes ticking away. She was already dreadfully late.

"Rotten luck for me, then." His smile made the sun pale in comparison when he offered his hand for a shake. "In case you change your mind, I'll be around at ten in the morning. This joint have a coffee shop?"

"Canteen. But don't wait around. Like I said, I've got loads of things going on." She turned and ran to the car, and when she glanced back over her shoulder, Ames Dewberry hadn't moved, his wide shoulders and narrow hips everything she remembered. Her hands trembled on the steering wheel all the way to Martha Vine's Dress Shop.

CHAPTER 2

Mittie hoped to sneak into Martha's salon for the fitting, but Caroline, her feisty nine-year-old cousin, met her in the anteroom. She twirled, her tea-length dress of palest lavender swishy above shiny buckled shoes. "Aunt Sarah! Mittie's here!"

Caroline planted a hand on one hip. "How do I look?"

"Like a princess. I'm sure you'll have every male at the wedding vying to dance with you."

"Ick. If you mean boys, then no thank you. Dancing is splendid, but why ruin it with boys?"

Mittie tweaked her cousin's nose. "That's rather the point, sugar. You'll change your tune someday."

"That's what Mama says, but Aunt Sarah says I should quit being a tomboy and be more ladylike. Like Iris. Will you take me for a ride in your roadster when we're done here? There's a big ship docked on the river, and I'm ab-so-lute-ly dying to get a closer look."

Poor kid. She'd come along when Aunt Evangeline, Mittie's mother's sister, was nearly forty. Her daddy died on a British Royal Navy ship during the war before she was born, but still she was obsessed with anything to do with water—swimming, sailing, riverboats. Caroline tapped her toe in expectation of an answer.

"Not today, I'm afraid. Your aunt Sarah's booked a table at the Brown for lunch later. No sense ruffling her feathers."

"When has that ever bothered you?" Mittie's mother strode from one of the fitting rooms and told Caroline to scoot, that the seamstress was ready for her. She leveled her gaze on Mittie. "Look at you. Late and such a fright. You've splatters on your dress, and it looks like you've crossed a field with the mud on your shoes. What happened? Did you get a tire puncture and have to change it yourself?"

Too many questions, and no answer would suit her mother, who'd donned her Mother Superior cap relegating Mittie to aberrant child status. She half-wished she'd stayed and talked to Ames.

Mittie pecked her mother on the cheek. "Nice to see you, too. Where do I need to go for my fitting?"

"Over here." Iris waved her over to the large room at the back where the other bridesmaids—two of Iris' college chums—were already dressed and being nipped and tucked by Martha and her assistant. Their gowns, exquisite in whisper-soft pink and baby-blue organza, were a veritable rainbow of pastel that Mittie's mother had insisted would be the talk of all Louisville for months to come.

Mittie knew different. Iris' wedding would get a flashy write-up in the Sunday edition of Louisville's *Courier-Journal* and no doubt in newspapers in Alabama where the Wainwright family had a firm clasp on the steel industry. By marrying Hayden, heir to the dynasty, Iris would be breaking the hearts of every hopeful mother in Birmingham. But Lucky Lindy would be who people were talking about for months to come.

Iris' cornflower-blue eyes darkened to deep azure—the please-don't-make-this-difficult look that Mittie knew all too well. Her twin carried the burden of keeping things smoothed over in the family—always patching things up between Mittie and their impossibly interfering mother, calming the house staff when they'd been scolded, and offering apologies to complete strangers who felt slighted when their mother spoke her mind. Iris had agreed to the pastel wedding, the guest list, and even the menu for the reception. Iris, though, was no doormat. She simply had the finesse Mittie lacked and was, in fact, brilliant. She said and did the right things on cue and was witty and engaging, but not coy. Mittie was happy for her. Thrilled, really. As their eyes locked, Mittie knew she wouldn't do anything to take away from the joy of this day for her womb mate and dearest friend.

She took the frothy frock from Iris, all billowy and yellow, a color that would give Mittie's complexion a waxen pallor, and said, "It's even snazzier than I remembered. And sorry for being late. The meeting ran long, and I—"

"Don't worry. Mother hasn't even worked herself into a lather yet. And the adjustments so far have been minor. It's more to reassure Mother that this is going to be all she imagined." Her voice trailed off in a wistful tone, and for a fraction of a second, Mittie wondered whether Iris had regrets over the future she was choosing. Soon, Iris would enjoy life in her Alabama colonial where she could make her own decisions and welcome her adoring husband each night with a glass of sweet tea and a kiss. The very thought made Mittie want to hightail it to the Kentucky hills. It wasn't a startling discovery. Everyone knew she and Iris were as different as midnight and dawn—Mittie the dark unknown and Iris like a pat of butter on a warm biscuit.

The yellow frock wasn't all bad. Mittie turned this way and that, getting the full effect in the cheval mirror. Nice straight lines through the torso with a swingy gored skirt that would work well on the dance floor. The lace ruffle framing the V-neckline, though, drew attention to her long neck.

Her cousin Nell, who was Caroline's older sister, stepped inside the fitting room, hat in hand. "Oh goodness—don't you look fabulous!"

Mittie wrinkled her nose. "I look like a giraffe."

Nell cocked her head and laughed. "Only you would think such a thing. What I wouldn't give for your height and long neck." She held out the hat she'd brought in. "I think you'll be surprised when we get your hair done and you wear this."

The hat was a dream, like all of Nell's creations—airy gold netting over a silk cloche with rhinestones in the same lemon color as her gown, and a narrow velvet ribbon in deep chocolate. Nell fluffed out Mittie's dark curls, tucking a few wisps behind each ear before arranging the hat at a flattering angle.

"What do you think?"

Mittie gasped at her reflection. "I think you're a living doll—that's what!" Simple, yet elegant. Perhaps she wouldn't feel like she was the object of a safari after all. In the mirror, she saw her mother approach and nod in approval.

"I simply do not know how Louisville survived without you, Nell. Every one of the bridesmaids' hats are perfect. Just think: someday you'll be making Mittie's bridal veil." She dabbed at the corner of her moist eye.

"Mother, don't start getting sappy. Let's get Iris married first."

Her mother waved a hand. "Your day will come." She draped an arm around Nell and said she had some questions about Iris' trousseau.

Mittie thought of her visit to Nell when she lived in New York, the visit where Mittie had met—and flown with—Ames. Heat rushed to her cheeks. Four years, and Ames had shown up in Louisville. Her skin was still tingling with the thought when Martha Vine declared the fittings complete and said the dresses would be delivered by the following afternoon.

Cornelia Humphreys, Mittie's paternal grandmother, in a suit the color of a new buffalo nickel, greeted them when they arrived at the

Brown Hotel. She patted the chair next to her for Mittie to have a seat. Her marcel-waved hair beneath a charcoal silk hat matched her outfit exactly. A tuft of netting at the front skimmed her thin, arched brows. Mittie idolized her—her no-nonsense manner, the way she didn't give in to the conventions of style but still managed to pull off a surprisingly fashionable look, even at age seventy-four. Widowed since Mittie was three, she lived in a grand but small stone home at the back of Morning Glory Farms property—one with a view of her beloved saddlebreds and in the perfect location to keep an eye on everything that went on.

Her grandmother leaned in and whispered, "You and Gypsy were having quite a frolic this morning." She patted Mittie's hand, liver spots dotting the weathered hands that had handled horses and weren't afraid of hard work. Hands that offered a firm shake when sealing horse agreements and yet were tender enough to caress Mittie and Iris when they'd come to her with strawberries on skinned knees, bee stings, and broken hearts.

While Mittie and her grandmother talked about Gypsy and how she'd progressed with her gait training, conversation bubbled around the table. They nibbled on shrimp "fresh from the gulf and trucked in special for y'all," the waiter had said.

Mittie's gaze caught Nell's, and she thought her cousin looked a bit wan. Perhaps the wedding trousseau questions from Mittie's mom had been too much, the pinch of last-minute changes. Nell bit off a corner of cracker, her shrimp cocktail untouched.

Soup followed and then the main course: a luncheon portion of Hot Brown, the chef's specialty that had caught on like wildfire with the locals. Mittie took a bite and wondered if they would serve it to Charles Lindbergh at his Louisville banquet. She would suggest it on the typed notes she took to Gordon at the mayor's office tomorrow. Tomorrow. She'd told Ames Dewberry she was too busy to see him, but if she worked it just right, maybe she could squeeze in a stop at Bowman Field after seeing Gordon. She wanted to know more about the barnstorming. She'd read about it in the papers, how planes buzzed over farms and put on shows with aerial tricks, but she hadn't ever met anyone who actually did it. Her skin tingled.

"Mittie!" Her mother's voice drew her out of her rambling thoughts, and from the look on her face, it wasn't the first time her mother had said her name. "Mittie, dear, as the maid of honor, wouldn't you like to propose a toast for Iris?"

"Oh, sure. Don't know what got into me." She rose and hoisted her water glass. "To Iris, the best sister in the world. I'm going to miss you terribly. Here's to the perfect wedding day and a lifetime of love." A lump filled Mittie's throat.

Iris chewed on her bottom lip, her eyes misting, as she whispered, "Thank you."

Caroline wiggled in her seat. "I have a sister toast, too." She stood and lifted her glass, drawing smiles from around the table. "Nell and Quentin, sitting in a tree. K-I-S-S-I-N-G. First comes love, then comes marriage, then comes Nell pushing a baby carriage."

Nell's eyes grew round, her face flushed. "Caroline! Where did you hear that?"

"School, girls teasing, but I'm not teasing—not even a tiny bit. I heard you and Mama talking." She giggled and pronounced, "Nell's going to have a baby!"

Aunt Evangeline placed a firm hand on her young daughter's arm. "First of all, young lady, you don't eavesdrop on conversations. And you also don't go blabbering things you know nothing about."

All eyes were on Nell, who now looked green instead of just pale. She glared at her little sister. "Mama's right, Caroline." To the rest of the guests, she shrugged. "I'm sorry; I didn't want to say anything until after Iris' wedding. This is her big day, and we have worlds of time to talk about the baby."

Questions came from around the table in a flurry about when the baby would come and if they were hoping for a boy or a girl.

Nell sighed. "We think January, and I'm hoping for a boy." She gave Caroline a narrow-eyed look. "Boys aren't so nosy and wouldn't be blabbering."

Caroline tucked her chin to her chest. "I'm sorry. I thought it would make you happy." Tears filled her eyes. "I always wanted a baby brother or sister..."

Nell rose and went to Caroline and hugged her. "I know; I always did, too, and then when you were born, no one was happier than me." She kissed her cheek and then thanked her aunt for the lunch. "I am feeling a little peaked and think maybe I should go." She turned to Iris. "Don't worry. I'll have everything ready for your trousseau. For now, I just need a bit of rest."

The party lost some of its glow with Nell gone, but Mittie was grateful that her mother didn't say anything about her sister Evangeline becoming a grandmother before her. Under normal circumstances, the competition between the two of them might have surfaced, and really, there was no harm done. If anything, it was another reason to celebrate.

When the chatter resumed, Grandmother leaned over and whispered to Mittie, "Your father called and told me about Buck Lamberson."

Mittie wanted to spit. Just the mention of his name coiled like a snake in her belly. "Rotten timing with the wedding." It was the best she could muster.

"I'm sure the operation won't be cheap and is perhaps necessary, but it gives me pause. I think he planned his visit with a touch of malice in mind—coming on the eve of Iris' wedding and knowing that finances might be somewhat stretched right now."

Mittie kept her voice low. "And that Mother has spared no expense, you mean."

"I just thought his request untimely—that's all."

"Dobbs deserves the best, to be able to walk normally. And if there was anything at all that I could do to repay Daddy, I would. There's not a day goes by that I don't wish the accident hadn't happened."

"No one blames you. Certainly not your dad. It wasn't even your fault."

The familiar panic swelled in Mittie's chest. No, her grandmother and father didn't blame her for the incident with Dobbs. But Dobbs did, and so did his parents. A broken leg that left him a cripple was a big price for Dobbs to pay.

Mittie's lunch soured in her stomach.

CHAPTER 3

Mittie dreamed she was flying. Clouds above, rolling hills below. Soaring on an air thermal with the wind eating at her cheeks, her right hand numb from gripping the stick. Above her, a clap of thunder shook the bi-winged plane followed by a funny feeling in her stomach as, one with the machine, she nose-dived. The verdant meadows below rose faster and faster, the horses in the paddock just specks a moment before, now so close she could see their nostrils flaring. The pace of her heart inched upward, her breath trapped in her chest. A cramp clenched the calf muscle of her right leg as she kept her feet steady on the rudder bar, trying to decide whether the impact would be greater if she stayed level or tipped the wings right or left. Where was the lever for the flaps? *Pull back. Pull back on the stick!*

A flash of blue blinded her, and Mittie startled from her sleep. Had she crashed? Another flash followed and with it a boom that shook the windowpanes of her upstairs bedroom. A torrent beat the glass behind lace curtains, and somewhere in the distance, a banging noise beat a steady rhythm. A shutter on a window in the servants' wing? The rusty-hinged door to the garden shed? She shook the foggy sleep from her head, her muscles still taut from maneuvering the Canuck in her dreams.

The horses. They would be spooked and that furious wind might've damaged the pens. She leaned over to switch on the lamp, but the storm had knocked out the electricity. She stumbled in the dark to the chifforobe and fished around until she came up with jodhpurs and a riding shirt. She dressed quickly and retrieved a kerosene lantern and matches, then felt her way to the banister of the staircase.

"Mittie? Is that you?" Her mother's voice drifted from the end of the hall.

"Yes, Mother. I'm going to the barns. Tell Daddy not to worry."

"He's already got himself worked up. Hasn't had a wink of sleep all night and now this." Her mother had made her way to Mittie's side, blackness between them as the rain beat the roof over their heads. "You can't do anything in the rain. Let Ogilvie take care of the horses. That's what we pay him a king's ransom to do."

"It's my responsibility, Mother—you know that. Besides, Daddy will want a full report. Was it his back bothering him all night or did the storm keep him awake?"

"Muscle spasms. I just gave him that new miracle powder the doctor gave him. Maybe it will help." It had been three years since her daddy's accident, the broken back that had kept him bedfast for two years and left her to shoulder the operation of Morning Glory Farms. He'd made great strides, and only in the past few months had Mittie dared to hope that one day she'd be free to sort out her own dreams for the future.

At the base of the stairs, the grandfather clock chimed. Mittie waited to hear the hour. Five o'clock. "It will be light as soon as the storm passes. Tell Daddy to rest, and I'll be in later to give him any news."

Mittie didn't wait for an argument from her mother and took the lantern to the mudroom behind the servants' kitchen where she wriggled into riding boots and a slicker. She removed the globe from the lamp, adjusted the wick, and lit it. Then, clutching its wire handle, she braced against the wind and made her way to the stables.

Mittie found Parker Ogilvie, their stable foreman, in the big barn where six stalls flanked each side of the center promenade. As she suspected, the horses were in a tizzy, neighing, pawing the sawdust and straw mix over the earthen floor. Like worker bees in a hive, the half dozen grooms who lived in the bunkhouse worked by lantern light, cooing to the horses, tethering a couple that were more high-strung, bringing in pitchforks of fresh straw. And in the midst, Ogilvie sat in a straight chair in the center of the promenade barking orders, whittling on a stick.

His head jerked up when Mittie called his name. "Morning, Miss Humphreys. Anything I can do for you?"

"I came to check on the horses, see if there was any damage from the storm."

"None that I can see. Got us a few frisky ones, but the boys'll get 'em right in no time."

"And the other barn? The one with the broodmares? Are they all right as well?"

"I woulda heard by now if they weren't."

"You didn't go and check yourself?"

"Not yet." He leaned back and stretched out long legs, crossing his boots at the ankle. "First rule of management—hire reliable help. Surely your old man taught you that when he was schooling you in the finer points of not sticking your nose in where it don't belong."

Mittie's face flamed as she bit back a retort to the cutting remark—the one meant to put her in her place. It wasn't the first time he questioned her authority. Cheekiness was one of his not-so-endearing qualities. As a matter of fact, Parker Ogilvie wasn't her choice for foreman when Whitey Munce, their beloved and long-time overseer, dropped dead of a heart attack. Ogilvie had good credentials, but she was afraid Daddy's laudanum for his back pain had fuzzed his brain when he hired him on the spot eight months before.

"What about the paddock? Was there any damage?"

"Like I said, it don't concern you. Matter of fact, you coming in here with a hitch in your fancy pants don't set all that well with me. I take my orders from Mr. Humphreys, not some female who don't know her behind from a porcupine." He went back to whittling.

"I expect a report in an hour. I don't need to remind you that we have valuable stock that we can't afford to have injured if they come in contact with broken rails." A hush had fallen except for soft snorts from the horse bays as the grooms needled her with bug-eyed looks. *The second rule of management: Don't chastise an employee in front of his underlings.* Mittie shuddered. Her daddy would have been more tactful.

Ogilvie sneered and yelled at the nearest groom. "You heard the dame. Get your fat, lazy butts out there and check the fences." He smirked at Mittie. "Happy?"

"I'll be waiting on your report." She spun on the heels of her riding boots and went to check on Gypsy herself.

The airfield canteen was empty when Mittie arrived, the attendant having put a Return in Ten Minutes sign on the counter. Mittie sat on the round barstool, hooked her boot heels over the lower rung, and drummed her fingers, berating herself for giving in to the temptation to take Ames up on his offer to meet. She didn't need another interruption in her life, but the tingle under her skin when she thought about Ames—and flying—told her it might be just the distraction she needed from the nettled encounter with Parker Ogilvie.

An hour after their heated exchange, Ogilvie had knocked on her daddy's office door and told her the damage to the paddock was minimal and assured her that repairs were already underway. While not repentant, Ogilvie was cordial and they parted with a handshake.

She caught her reflection in the Coca-Cola-etched mirror above the soda fountain that sported such flavors as chocolate, wild cherry, and sarsaparilla labeled on silver levers. Mittie moistened her lips and patted her hair, then flipped up the collar of the short-waisted flight jacket she'd worn in case Ames had flying on his agenda. She sighed. He might already be in the air or have decided to skip the canteen altogether. A brilliant blue sky followed the morning rain, and Mittie felt it a shame to waste a perfectly fine day waiting indoors. She gave her hair a toss and took a final glance in the mirror. Maybe Weaver was around and could take her up in his Canuck.

"Hey, doll! Do you always spend that much time primping in front of the mirror?"

She whirled around, almost eye to eye with Ames, his hair tousled without the aviator helmet, his body so close she could smell fresh soap and feel the warmth he radiated.

"A lady always presents herself in the most favorable light. How long have you been watching me?"

"Just breezed in for a cup of joe before taking my sweet girl up for a spin. How about a hug for your old friend?"

Mittie extended her hand and offered a half grin. "Nice try, but since this is only the third time we've met, I hardly qualify as an old friend. Or as your sweet girl."

His shake was firm, his hand warm in hers as he sandwiched it with both of his. "Sorry. The sweet girl I was referring to was my little Curtiss Oriole parked on the other side of those hangars, and it was presumptuous of me about the friend remark. Thing is, seeing you yesterday did my lonely heart good. I'm glad you were able to stop by."

Mittie couldn't help but laugh. "My apologies, too. Is this your first time in Louisville?"

"First time in a coon's age."

"That doesn't sound like something a fella from back East would say."

His laugh was throaty as he turned to greet a plump woman with a hairnet who'd taken her station behind the bar and asked what they'd like.

"Coffee. Black," Mittie and Ames said at the same time. He tossed a few coins on the counter, and they took steaming hot cups to a table by a window with a view of the hangars.

"I just had my first look around yesterday. Some nice aircraft here, and it seems progressive. How about you? Have your own little plane out there?"

"I wish. I've only flown in Weaver's Canuck."

He eyed her aviator jacket, his brows inching up a fraction. "Natty dresser, I'll give you that. Maybe you can show me the ropes. Give me a tour of the countryside?" His voice was warm, inviting.

"I'd be honored, and I'd love to see your plane, but the tour will have to wait until after my sister's wedding. You might remember her from Mrs. Benchley's party."

"Mrs. Who?"

"Mrs. Benchley—the one with the summer home on Long Island."

"Oh, right. I'd forgotten her name. May not have ever known it—I was acquainted with some of the sports who were there. Last-minute invite and all that."

"Sort of like Iris and me. Serendipity that day was meeting you and falling in love with flying all in one afternoon."

He grinned and gave her a sidelong look. "So this Weaver—is he someone you're sweet on?"

"No, he's the airfield manager. He's taught me a few basics and takes me up once in a while. What I'm really hoping for is a flight instructor when the time is right."

"You're a dabbler then."

It did sound pathetic. "I've been otherwise engaged."

"College?"

"A semester, right after I met you. But it's more of a family situation."

"Don't tell me you've gotten yourself into a hopeless marriage." He looked at her hand. "No ring. Something that didn't work out?"

She laughed. "Do you always jump to conclusions like that? First Weaver, now some stranger you've invented. It's actually much less scandalous than all that."

"Now I'm intrigued."

"My family has a horse farm, and I've been filling in for Daddy. Three years ago he took a nasty fall from a frisky stallion and broke his back."

"Ah, the doting, responsible daughter."

"I suppose. Things are on the upswing, though. And I hope to be flying more, like I said."

He rose and offered his arm. "Have time for a test ride? My rigging's not new, but with the proper care and modification, I have swell plans for *Trixie*."

"You named your plane *Trixie*?"

"Just wait and you'll see why." They walked outside toward the hangars and a line of bi-wings shimmering in the summer sun. "Here she is."

Trixie was cherry red with narrow white stripes along the sides and on the struts separating the wings, her name painted near the tail.

"She's beautiful." Mittie ran a hand near the nose, stroking it like she did Gypsy. "I'd love to see what she can do."

Ames jumped on a wing and leaned into the cockpit. He pulled out two leather helmets and goggles, handing her one of each. "Unless you have your own."

"These will be fine. Nice paint. I'm guessing the shorter wing-span gives you more flexibility with stunts." She twisted her hair in the back and tucked it in the helmet, anticipation rushing through her blood vessels.

"Among other things." He nodded and told her the lower wings had undergone modifications. "Less drag on the struts and wires in case I need more speed. An engine upgrade has also helped with that." He waved at another fellow dressed in flight gear, then offered her a hand up on the wing. Ames showed her the controls, one arm around her waist holding her steady, then said, "Let's give it a whirl."

It was an easy step into the front passenger seat, and the next thing Mittie knew, they were soaring two hundred feet, three hundred, four—higher and higher as the plane curved gently away from the airfield and the town of Louisville toward open country. Below them were creeks like ribbons, black tobacco barns like postage stamps, patchwork farms like a velvet crazy quilt. And Mittie felt just as crazy as she had the first time she'd flown with Ames. Giddy and reverent at the same time, she sat tall in the seat and inhaled deep in her lungs. If paradise had a scent, this was it.

The wind caressed her cheeks as she got her bearings and realized they were right over Morning Glory Farms. She pointed to the rolling green beneath them, the toy-sized horses in their paddock honeycomb.

Ames nodded and banked sharply to the left, apparently unaware that she was pointing out her home. He nosed up and put the engine in a stall. Mittie's stomach lurched upward one minute and plummeted to her toes the next with the sensation of free fall. It was the same feeling as her dream, but with adrenaline sending starburst pulses of joy through her. Ames prolonged the stall, then opened the throttle and in one smooth motion rolled the Oriole in a complete revolution. Laughter bubbled in Mittie's throat as Ames spiraled again and again, then eased the plane upward to a safe altitude and onto an even keel. She turned to nod her approval. Ames pointed to her and mimicked steering navigation, his eyes wide as if inquiring whether she wanted to fly. She nodded and checked the gauges. She wouldn't do anything fancy—she didn't even think she could if she knew how—but with her feet steady on the rudder and hands gripping the wheel, she flew over trees and farms, past limestone cliffs and sorghum fields, over lush valleys lined with bluegrass.

"Can you find your way back?" Ames' voice carried on the wind, above the engine's roar. She nodded and flew in that direction until Bowman Field came into view. She held up her hands and thumbed back for Ames to take over the landing. Moments later, the wheels touched down as smooth as silk, bumps jolting them like a series of hiccups only when the tail came in contact with the ground to act as the braking mechanism.

Both feet on the ground and Mittie's heart still pounding, they fell in step together.

"*Trixie*'s wonderful, and so was the flight. Thanks."

"You're a natural," he told her. "Any thoughts of doing a little barnstorming with me?"

"I'd love to, but not anytime soon. Iris' wedding is this Saturday, and we've loads of work left to do. I shouldn't have even stayed away from the farm this long. Did you see the place I pointed to?"

Ames let out a whistle. "*That* was your place?"

"Home, sweet home." She gave him a quizzical look. "Tell me more about barnstorming."

"Not an exact science, but we look for barns near small towns and buzz down to see if we get any interest. If we do, we land and ask if we can use their field for a demonstration. If they're agreeable, we put up flyers in a few local businesses with the particulars. Folks come from miles around, happy to pay the admission for a chance at seeing the planes and the stunts we do."

"It sounds like the berries, but you said *we*? You work with someone else?"

"Couple of buddies. We're thinking about making Bowman Field our base of operations." He swiped the back of his hand across his brow, the sun glinting from his raven hair. Dark eyes peered intently into hers. "So your sister's getting hitched?"

"The event of Louisville's social season."

"Big doin's, huh?"

She nodded. "You've no idea. I do hate to rush..."

Ames held up his hands. "I know. See you later." He touched his fingers to his lips and blew her a kiss.

Mittie hurried toward the parking area, but a dozen paces later, a thought came to her. She turned around and shouted, "If you're not from back East, then where are you from?"

A few long strides and he caught up with her. "Iowa. Not the city that bears my name, but a little place you've never heard of."

"Oh. All right then. Ames from Iowa, would you like to be my guest at my sister's wedding on Saturday?"

It wasn't totally clear to her if the squint in his eye was from the sun or trying to figure out what she'd just said, but a smile parted his lips when he said, "All I can promise is that I'll try."

She told him when and where. "I'll be easy to find—just look for the gal who's a ringer for a giraffe."

When Mittie got back to the farm, she found Toby in the arena taking Gypsy through her paces. Ogilvie stood next to her daddy at the rail, arms crossed, a smoke dangling from his lips. A Bull Durham pouch bulged in his chest pocket.

Mittie nodded to both of them. "Daddy, good to see you up and about."

"Taking it slow, but thought it was high time I came to see how our Gypsy was progressing."

Parker Ogilvie nodded and gave her two thumbs-up. Maybe her insistence that he do his work was paying off.

Her dad looked at Toby and asked him to reverse direction with Gypsy. "She seems off just a hair on the rack."

"Yes, sir, I noticed that. She's trying to rush it, I think." Toby was a treasure—an aspiring jockey in his teens, but when his head brushed the tops of the doorframes and he filled out like a lumberjack, he said so long to his dream and came to Morning Glory Farms looking for a job. In two years, his intuitive nature with horses and youthful energy made him valuable as both a trainer and showman of saddlebreds.

Toby reversed as requested, his pink-palmed dark hands holding the reins with just the right amount of tension, his own bearing erect yet relaxed.

"She's better that direction. Give her another couple of laps, then call it a day." Mittie's dad turned to Ogilvie and asked about a couple of horses that belonged to a man in West Virginia.

"They're due in the ring momentarily. Heck of a pair, Gingersnap and April Showers. Look to see 'em both do well when we go over to the July meet. Sure would be a pleasure if you could make it."

They talked about the entry classes for the horses and moved on to another section of the fence. As they drifted off, Mittie's dad turned and said, "Hey, sugar, your mother was looking for you earlier. Something about the flowers or maybe it was the guest list. I can't keep all these wedding doin's straight."

"Oh, right. Guess you don't need me, then."

"Best not to get your mother riled up."

"I'm sure she's got it all under control."

"Not to hear her tell it. Maybe I'll just give you the money to elope when your time comes." He turned to Ogilvie. "You got any daughters?"

"No, sir. Not even a wife. Works out better that way." The two of them talked as they ambled past another two sections of the fencing away from Mittie.

An odd sensation welled up in her chest. While it was good to see her dad up and around, she felt shut out somehow. Maybe she would elope. If she had any prospects. Ames with his broad shoulders and slim hips slipped into her thoughts. If Ogilvie hadn't been there, she might've even mentioned Ames. She kicked a rock. She wasn't sure what got into her inviting him to the wedding on a whim. Her mother would have a fit no doubt over Mittie's rash decision.

Still, a tingle danced up Mittie's spine as she went in search of her mother. She found her in the ladies' parlor downstairs along with Iris and Bertha Stone, their housekeeper, who popped out after a cheery hello.

"Daddy said you were looking for me."

"Indeed I was." Her mother blew out a puff of smoke from her ever-present Chesterfield, then stubbed out the cigarette in a crystal ashtray. "I meant to ask you to take the final guest list by the Brown Hotel while you were in town. They need it as soon as possible."

Iris looked up from the netting, flowers, and ribbon scattered on the sofa and her lap. "I offered to go, but Mother wanted me to finish these nosegays for you bridesmaids."

Mittie got a look of exasperation from her mother. "I had no idea you'd be frittering away half the day just delivering your notes to the mayor's office. Where, pray tell, have you been all this time?"

"Here and there. I just came in from the barns. It was good to see Daddy getting some fresh air."

"Poor man's going mad stuck here in the house. I just hope he doesn't overdo it."

Iris patted their mother's arm. "He'll be fine, Mother. I've almost finished here and will run the list into town."

"You have guests to entertain. Where are your sweet bridesmaids anyway?"

"They've gone to a matinee and to do some shopping."

How Iris kept her voice so serene and managed to keep a smile on her face was beyond Mittie's comprehension, but a twinge of guilt pierced her. She had to give her mother her due: Mittie *had* frittered away precious time with Ames. Not that she was sorry; sometimes one has to seize opportunity when it arises. "Let me go to town for you. And by the way, I ran into an old friend today, so if it's not too late, I'd like to add his name to the guest list."

Her mother stopped midstride on her way to the morning desk and turned back. "Oh? I was certain we'd invited everyone we could think of."

Hesitation lolled on Mittie's tongue, but she waved a hand like it was nothing. "Actually, this is someone you've not met, but he's a swell fella, an entrepreneur, and so handsome even you will swoon, Mother."

Her mother riffled through a sheaf of papers in the desk. "Are you mocking me?"

"Not at all, but I do think it will be nice to have his name on the list so the maître d' doesn't think he's a party crasher."

Her mother sat poised with a fountain pen, waiting for the answer. "Well? Who is he? I can't read your mind."

Mittie swallowed and glanced at Iris, who was also eyeing her now with curiosity.

"Ames. Ames Dewberry."

Iris' fair brows twitched in concentration. Then her face paled, her eyes as round as the flow-blue saucers on the coffee table. But, bless her, her twin sister—the one who would go to the moon and back for Mittie—picked up a scrap of netting and said not a word.

Mittie took the list and dashed out the front door.

"Ames Dewberry? The one you took that absurd plane ride with on Long Island? You called him?" Iris waited until after dinner and her college friends were tucked in the guest room before coming into Mittie's bedroom. Although Iris kept her voice barely above a whisper, emotion buzzed like a deranged mosquito in her words.

"I ran into him, like I said. *And* I went up in his new plane. Of course I didn't want to mention where I'd been to Mother. Keep it mum and I promise I'm your slave from this moment until you say 'I do.'"

"I'm not worried about whether you're around to help or not. I just wish I had a place to escape to like you always seem to have time for."

"You're not getting cold feet, are you?"

"Gracious, no. I'm just ready to get through this wedding. Every night when I talk to Hayden on the telephone, I fall in love with him all over again, and that's what I want for you. A guy who flips over you and can take care of you."

"Sweet pea, there's not a man alive that meets that criteria. You know what my dream is, and if romance happens along when I'm a licensed aviator, then I'm game. I want to love and laugh and dance and maybe even get married someday. Just not anytime soon."

"You'll be a spinster by then."

"But I'll be a happy spinster. And besides, Mother already thinks I'm past my prime. Daddy, too, although he thinks he's holding me back by letting me manage the farm while he's ailing."

"Is that what you think?"

"It's immaterial. I love the horses—"

"And bossing people around. You and Mother are more alike than you realize. Being away at Vanderbilt made me see that when I came home."

"I'm *not* like Mother. Not in the least." Fingers of realization massaged a deep place within her. Bossy? Yes, but she had to be assertive with the grooms and trainers or they'd slough off their work. Like Ogilvie. The reputation of the farm had to be upheld, a task

she owed to her dad, not just as his daughter but also for his standing by her through the ordeal with Dobbs. "Okay, maybe a tiny bit
bossy. What does that have to do with me running into Ames?"

Iris rolled her eyes and flopped back on one of the bed pillows.
"I'm suspicious, that's all. You've been flirting with this flying thing
and your obsession with Lindbergh, and now Ames Dewberry
shows up out of the blue."

"A divine coincidence." Warmth flooded Mittie's chest.

"You didn't orchestrate it? Call him? Call a friend who knew a
friend?"

"No!" Mittie grabbed the other pillow, propped herself up, and
told Iris everything. Before long, they were both lying flat on their
backs the way they'd done since they'd graduated from their cra-
dles, giggling, interrupting one another, completing each other's
sentences.

"So, on a whim, I invited him to your wedding and the reception. If Ames' dance moves are anything like his prowess in the
cockpit, it will be a night to remember." She closed her eyes, wondering if Ames was more the Charleston type or a cheek-to-cheek
romantic. She hummed "Japanese Sandman" off-key, then shifted
and looked at Iris.

Tears tracked across porcelain cheeks, Iris' chin quivering.

"I know I can't carry a tune, but it's not wretched enough to
make you cry."

Iris sat up and backhanded Mittie on the forearm. "It's not that.
Something just came over me. Here we are, you and me..." She
gulped in a big breath. "I...I'm...this..." She sniffled.

"What? What did I say? Don't you want it to be a night to remember?"

Iris shook her head. "It's not that. Don't you see? This may be
our last chance to lay in here and talk and giggle. In a few days I'll
be married and sharing Hayden's bed."

"You're letting the wedding jitters get to you. It's not like we won't be sisters. And anytime you're home, we'll have time to talk. We haven't shared a womb and a lifetime to have it stop just like that."

"But you know it will be different."

Mittie didn't want to think about it. "Different, but better. And just in case he doesn't know it, Hayden Wainwright has me to contend with if he doesn't treat you like a queen. He should be scared. Very scared."

"I'm petrified just thinking about it." Iris swiped the wet from her face. "Promise me this—let me have one dance with Ames at the reception."

"Only if you promise you'll say sweet and flattering things about me."

"Always, dear Mittie. Always."

CHAPTER 4

Iris radiated happiness on her wedding day, a perpetual smile on her face, her lace gown simple with a scalloped hem. She wore a single strand of pearls, a gift from Grandmother Humphreys.

Mittie's mom appeared and told them it was time for the processional. She carried the pastel theme into her own gown as well, a dusty lavender silk Jeanne Lanvin dress with sheer lace sleeves. A jeweled cluster of lilacs adorned her matching cloche. Mittie swallowed a gasp when she saw her mother and Iris side by side. Except for the lines etched around her mother's eyes, the two could pass as sisters. Cupid lips and startling blue eyes glistened as they regarded each other.

St. Andrew's Church had been chosen for its capacity to accommodate the massive guest list. Their quaint and serene village church in Rigby was "simply inadequate," according to Mittie's mother. Indeed, the larger church in Louisville overflowed by the time the wedding party had filed in and taken their places. Spotting Ames in the crowd would be impossible. Instead of trying, Mittie willed away the itch caused by the yellow ruffle at her neck and kept her eyes on the bridal couple.

Quentin Bledsoe—Nell's cute British husband who'd just finished seminary—assisted the rector with the wedding vows. *Do you take this man?* A frog lodged in Mittie's throat as she blinked back threatening tears and felt stupid for allowing herself to get sappy.

Chimes from the church tower rang as the organ recessional swelled, and Mr. and Mrs. Hayden Wainwright clutched hands and swept down the center aisle where her daddy's Bentley waited to whisk them to the Crystal Ballroom for the dinner and dance.

At the hotel, Mittie kept an eye out for Ames—not an easy task in the throng of women in drop-waist gowns of silk and chiffon and men in tuxedos with wide lapels and satin bowties. Like a vast golden melting pot, the room swirled with Saddlebred Association members, her parents' friends, a host of people from Alabama, classmates from days gone by. Bankers and politicians were easy to spot as they clumped in smoky circles, clapping each other on the back. Mittie nodded and greeted people she knew, people she didn't, and people she would never see again. But she didn't find Ames.

A jazz combo played as the dinner courses were served, steam rising from domed platter covers toward faceted crystal chandeliers and ornate plaster relief ceilings. Mittie's dad sat on her right with Caroline on her left. When the toasts were offered, both fathers gave their blessing to the couple, and when her dad sat down, he whispered, "I do believe the groom's best man has his eye on you."

"That stuffed shirt? I've heard he's left three girls at the altar."

"Well, I wouldn't want you to be next, but don't fret. Your time will come, sweetheart."

"It's all right, Daddy. I'm not in need of sympathy. I'm looking for adventure—you know that. Like you and Mother."

"Your Mother's an adventure for certain." He winced as he changed position.

"Is your back bothering you? I don't want you to miss out on your dance with Iris."

"Nah, it'll be fine. Looking forward to it, in fact." He signaled
the waiter for a coffee refill. "Speaking of adventure ... I've invited
someone to dinner tomorrow night that I think you might like."

"I hope you're not trying to set me up. For one thing, you can't
afford another wedding anytime in this decade."

"It's not that at all." He winked and turned to her mother, who
was pulling on his coat sleeve.

"Dear, the dancing has started." She nodded toward the center of
the ballroom where Iris and Hayden kept perfect step to the "Vi-
ennese Waltz." Paul Whiteman's band couldn't have made a sweeter
sound than the one on stage. Mittie tapped her feet and craned
her neck, still looking for Ames. She caught the eye of the best
man instead, who made a beeline for her when the band picked up
the tempo for a rousing Irving Berlin number and the dance floor
flooded with merriment.

She flashed him her most dazzling smile. Why not? Dancing
might erase the disappointment biting at her, and there were plenty
of eligible men in the room. While she believed that flirting and
turning on the charm were highly overrated, this was her sister's
wedding and she would have a grand time if it killed her. The best
man, who told her his name was Bernard, trampled on her feet and
attempted conversation, but Mittie only nodded and pretended the
music was too loud for her to hear. When the dance was over, she
handed him off to Caroline, who had decided she wanted to dance
after all if Mittie would find her dancing partners. Maybe Bernard
would be gentler with a child who scarcely came to his chest. Mittie
didn't lack for ready partners herself as she twirled and danced with
all of the groomsmen, her daddy, the secretary of the Saddlebred
Association, and a courteous gentleman who told her he was the
governor of Alabama.

Iris floated by in Hayden's arms and said, "I haven't seen Ames.
Is he here?"

Mittie shook her head. "Guess he couldn't make it." Then while the soloist crooned "The Sheik of Araby," she found herself getting her toes mangled by Bernard once again and was ready to holler uncle when a new partner cut in. Strong arms encircled her waist and clasped her right hand. She blinked, her breath trapped in her chest. Ames.

Rakish and handsome, Ames looked for all the world like a white knight in a cream tuxedo with a black bowtie and cummerbund. She leaned in close and said, "It took you long enough."

"You didn't give me much time to get my wardrobe organized."

"Looks like you must've gotten that from some dandy."

"Anything for the lady."

"Well, you're the nattiest guy in the room—I'll give you that. And thanks for rescuing me."

"And you're the foxiest giraffe I've ever seen."

The music had ended, and they stood with eyes locked, both of Ames' arms now dropped to her waist. A tingle traveled up her spine as she lost herself in the warmth of his gaze.

The band announced a short break, so Mittie grabbed Ames' hand and threaded her way back to the table, pulling him along with her.

"Daddy, Mother, I've someone for you to meet." She introduced Ames, and when her dad asked what line of work he was in, Ames startled her by saying, "Aeronautical design and development."

Raised eyebrows from her daddy. "I hear that's the up-and-coming thing."

"Certainly is, sir."

"What corporation are you with?"

"I'm independent, trying to garner interest for a new carburetor intake mechanism that will increase fuel efficiency."

Mittie had to remind herself not to gape. Here she thought Ames was just a barnstormer with Casanova good looks and a fresh line.

Her dad nodded. "Guess you met Mittie out at Bowman Field, then?"

"You might say that. Sure was a stroke of good fortune on my part."

Mittie's mother eyed her curiously and leaned in to whisper in Mittie's ear. "So *this* is the one who's supposed to make me swoon?" The down-turned corners of her mouth were assurance there was no possibility of needing to call for smelling salts for her mother. With a firm hand on Mittie's elbow, her mother steered them a few paces away from the conversation between Ames and her dad.

"Do you know his family or even one single thing about this man?"

"I know that he's accomplished at what he does, intelligent, and I rather like him."

"Pedigree, my child. Pedigree." She waved at a state senator and a woman who looked too young to be his wife. "You would do well to take a page from Iris, Mittie."

"Oh, look. Mrs. Wainwright is coming this way. Hurry on, Mother. You don't want to keep her waiting."

The band was tuning up again onstage, so her dad told Ames to enjoy the dancing. "It's been a pleasure meeting you."

The first number was a cheek-to-cheek song, "Someone to Watch over Me," and Ames smoothly swept her across the floor. Although there were no stalls and spin maneuvers in his steps, every time Mittie gazed into Ames' dark eyes, her stomach did a dive.

Three dances later, Mittie felt a tug on her arm. Caroline stood tapping an outstretched toe and said, "Is it proper for girls to cut in or does it always have to be the boys who do the asking?"

"Oh, I think you'd be safe if you didn't make it a habit." She took Ames' hand and put it in Caroline's. "Your next dance partner. I'm off to get some punch."

The song was a lively number that drew a host of young couples to the floor, and after finding a waiter with a tray of drinks, Mittie grabbed a punch for herself and another for Ames, then stood and watched Ames and Caroline. Caroline swung her arms and kicked back her heels, then burst out laughing when Ames twirled her around and around.

When Ames returned to Mittie's side with his young partner, Caroline said, "Mr. Dewberry, you are the cat's pajamas."

"And you, my dear, are full of malarkey, but you're a swell dancer."

Mittie shook her head and smiled.

Ames asked if they might get some fresh air, so they carried punch cups into an alcove where filmy curtains fluttered in the breeze of an open window.

Mittie spoke first. "So what were you really doing that you couldn't get here on time?"

Ames ran a weathered finger along her cheek. "Our first date, and you're already grilling me."

"Sorry, I usually speak my mind. I thought perhaps you were flying."

"I did take a short hop into Indiana today. An investor is interested in my idea."

"Is that what you meant by design and development? You get an idea and then sell it?"

"Not exactly. I'm mechanically inclined, so I try my ideas out first. *Trixie* has been the guinea pig for quite a few of them. Some pan out; some don't. The one I'm working on now shows great promise."

"I like the hands-on approach. It's Daddy's philosophy with the horses, too."

Ames asked about the farm and Mittie's involvement. Words flowed like warm honey between them, and Mittie wondered if she was flipping over Ames. The notion was ridiculous, of course.

She barely knew him, but the way he trapped her gaze with his, laughed in all the right places, and made her feel what she had to say was worthwhile made her think that possibly this was a relationship worth pursuing.

When his full, moist lips grazed hers and the sweet taste of punch lingered, she closed her eyes, hungry for more. Instead, Ames gave her a peck on the cheek. "We should go back. I don't want you to chance your mother's disapproval, and something tells me she may be less than enthralled with me."

Her mother certainly had strong opinions, but when a chill danced down her spine, Mittie couldn't tell if it was because she herself was enthralled with Ames. Or terrified.

CHAPTER 5

Mittie's parents were too bushed to attend services in their village church on Sunday, so after checking on the horses and consulting with Ogilvie, Mittie changed and drove the three miles to Rigby.

She sat down next to Grandmother and inhaled the aroma of the newly waxed wooden pews, the scent of time and a warm embrace. Even after the exhausting wedding day, her grandmother looked fresh as she wrapped her gloved hand in Mittie's. While they sang the first hymn, sharing a songbook, Mittie smiled. Grandmother would've liked Ames. She was sorry her grandmother had begged off from the dancing and had Moses drive her home early.

When the service was over, Mittie declined her grandmother's invitation to lunch and said she'd see her at dinner that evening—the dinner to which her dad had invited a stranger that was to be Mittie's ticket to adventure. More like a consolation prize for not being the one who got married. She hoped it wasn't some balding, paunchy guy with wads of money. She shivered. Her mother might attempt such a coup, but not her dad.

Mittie retrieved two baskets from her car that held arrangements she'd rescued from the reception tables, compact clusters of roses in gold urns. The summer sun warmed her as she pushed open the iron gate to the churchyard and went first to her grandfather Elias Humphreys' grave and placed an urn. Behind his simple stone rested a trio of graves marked by flat stones and inscriptions with the birth and death of Mittie's three brothers. All were stillborns who'd come in the early years of her parents' marriage, before the miracle arrival of Iris and Mittie. A gift, Grandmother often said—a baby girl for each of their parents. What she didn't say was that neither was a son who would carry the Humphreys' name.

Mittie carried the unspoken mantle, though—a lifetime of trying to prove to her daddy that she could do anything a boy could. And then some. She'd shadowed his every move. Said clever things. Learned how to spit and climb fences. And ride like the wind. Still, the part of her that was her mother—yes, she'd come to grips with the truth of that—itched for something more. Not the capers her mother was fond of bringing up, but to follow a calling and throw her whole self into it. Her mother had fled her dismal life in Yorkshire and the house of her drunkard father to marry a man from Kentucky. That Elias Humphreys had turned out to be such a fine man was no doubt a stroke of fortune, but it had taken courage, a stubbornness that Mittie knew she, too, possessed. It would be irreverent to disregard her heritage, the life of privilege it had given her, and the last thing she wanted was to disappoint her parents. Or burden them. She couldn't be dependent on them forever, especially now that her daddy was itching to get back to running the farm. Would her penchant for aviation disappoint them or be something that would make them proud?

The memory of dancing with Ames and flying with him flitted in and out of her thoughts. Maybe Ames showing up when he did *was* providential as she'd told Iris.

Mittie placed an urn of roses on each tiny grave and then strode briskly back to her roadster. A new determination coursed through her.

She spent the afternoon in the arena, working with three client horses and discussing them with Toby. A chalkboard in the training barn listed the horses, their primary trainer, the events they would qualify for, and the dates of the shows.

"It looks like we're on target for the show in West Virginia," Mittie said. It was too far for her dad to travel in his condition, but clients liked their trainers to be there. "I'm thinking about attending this one myself. I'll check with Mr. Ogilvie to see if he has the transport arrangements made."

Toby nodded. "Ogilvie's taking a half day off. Said he had a personal matter to attend to."

"He didn't mention it this morning, and I'm certain that was his truck by the bunkhouse."

"Some fella picked him up."

"All right, then. I'll talk to him tomorrow. And thanks for doing a good job, Toby."

Mittie's folks and her grandmother were already chatting with the surprise guest when Mittie breezed into the formal parlor, hoping she could get through dinner and remain aloof without being rude. Her sleeveless crepe dress with simple beading was one of her favorites—not stuffy, and it swung easily when she walked. She abandoned summer gloves and wore a dinner ring with an oversized topaz and a matching necklace that stopped just short of the cleavage of her V-necked dress.

"Ah, here she is now." Her daddy spoke and lifted a glass—sherry, most likely, since he didn't like to have anything stronger in the house in case a revenuer stopped by. With Prohibition still the stickiest topic in political circles, one could never be too careful. And sherry could always be passed off as a kitchen ingredient.

"I hope I haven't kept you waiting." She kept her gaze intentionally away from the gentleman between her parents and helped herself to a lemonade from the beverage tray before joining them. She raised the frosty glass and smiled. "Daddy said we'd have a guest. Let me introduce myself. Mittie Humphreys." She extended her free hand.

"Bobby York." His voice was deeper than she expected with his slim build, but as their hands clasped and their eyes met, she was pleased to see that he was also taller than she first thought. And not gray or balding or paunchy. Rather, he looked to be in his midtwenties, and his ice blue eyes had a touch of merriment. "Lovely to make your acquaintance."

"Likewise." *Was that a trace of a British accent?*

Her mother said, "Bobby is here from England, and it was a stroke of good luck that we found out he was in the States, wasn't it, dear?"

Mittie's dad nodded. "Bobby's dad, Robert Sr., sent me a wire that got misplaced in the wedding correspondence. Luckily your mother ran across it last week, and I was able to track him down."

"Then that is truly fortunate for us." Mittie kept her voice light. It was too soon to tell what her dad was up to, but Bobby York had an interesting look about him. Reserved. Polite. Refined, if the dashing suit and silk tie were any indication.

Her mother said, "We've just been telling Bobby about the wedding, that he would've enjoyed the dancing and meeting some of the members of the Saddlebred Association."

"Oh, so your family has saddlebreds as well."

"No, we've stayed with Thoroughbreds. Flat races and a few jumpers."

Her dad explained. "Bobby's dad is an old friend with a stable in Newmarket. We met the first time I went to London. I've been trying for years to get the old rascal to consider putting his money in saddlebreds. Maybe I'll be able to convince his son instead."

Ah, the *adventure* mystery was beginning to clear. *Robert York?* Mittie tried to place the name, trying to recall if she'd met him when her family had gone to England, but nothing came to mind. Perhaps her daddy wanted to send her to England on his behalf and thought that by teasing her with an eligible suitor, her interest would be piqued. She saw no harm in playing along.

"And what brings you to Kentucky? Horses, I presume. Are you shopping?" One dazzling smile wouldn't hurt, but before he could answer, Ruby, their cook and the wife of Moses, announced that dinner was ready.

Heaping platters of fried chicken, mashed potatoes and gravy, and baby collards were already on the table, but Ruby had retreated to the kitchen. She made it plain that she cooked and washed up, but she didn't serve.

As the food went around and the first bites were taken, Bobby said he didn't believe he'd ever had fried chicken.

Mittie's mother, in one of her fawning moods, said, "Oh Bobby, I'd never had it before I married Eli, either. And greens? Puh-leese." She took a sip of water. "Like a true Southerner, though, I've come to adore both the chicken and the collards."

"Yes, ma'am, these are quite tasty." He lifted a forkful of greens. "The flavor puts me in mind of our cabbage."

"Now that you mention it, you're right—we Brits did grow up with our bubble and squeak." She waved her fork. "It takes me back to supper tables I'd just as soon forget." Her voice faltered as it often did when she remembered her childhood, but she recovered in a flash. "Enough about food. I'm curious about you. Eli says you've brought some horses over."

"A pair of mares for a buyer in Elizabethtown."

Mittie's dad said, "Breeding stock?"

A nod from Bobby. "Nice on the track. Both had jolly good runs in the Falmouth and Guineas Stakes. Champions four generations back."

"Introducing new blood into a lineup is always good, something Mittie and I discuss on a regular basis. She outsmarts me every time we get in a verbal debate on pedigrees."

"You've no one to blame but yourself, Daddy. From the time I could crawl into your lap, you read bloodstock catalogs to me instead of Mother Goose." She knew about crossbreeding, inbreeding, and linebreeding, and the benefits and dangers with all of them.

Mittie's grandmother arched an eyebrow at Bobby. "Even though our saddlebreds spring from the Narragansett Pacer, the English Thoroughbreds have been bred into virtually all lines, so I suppose it's possible some of your family's horses could be kissing cousins to the ones here at Morning Glory Farms."

"Not sure about kissing cousins, but both breeds are highly developed, just different."

"Variety is the spice of life." Her grandmother gave him a teasing look. "I've met your dad, and your mother, too. Lovely people. Your father has other endeavors as well, if I remember correctly."

Bobby shrugged. "A few. The horses are his recreational outlet."

Mittie was starting to feel sorry for Bobby. It was like a grand inquisition. What do you do? Who are your people? And branded in the back of her mind was her mother's mantra: *Pedigree. Pedigree. Pedigree.* She would bet her best pair of riding boots that Bobby was from some titled family with an estate in the country and a town house in London and a few other important connections thrown in, and that her family was trying to pawn her off on someone of British nobility since their efforts had fallen short with eligible American suitors.

Time to get the poor fella off the hook. "So, Bobby, how long are you in the States?"

"A few months, give or take."

"Traveling, then? Visiting some of the American racecourses?"

"Not precisely. While I fancy a good race and a place at the rail, I'm not the horse expert. My father is. What I'm most interested in is aviation."

Mittie's mother choked on a drink of water.

"You okay, Mother?"

"I'm fine, dear." She smiled at Bobby. "I don't believe your parents ever mentioned that."

"Not likely. They would have preferred I go into finance or shipping or one of my father's other specialties."

Mittie's dad raised an eyebrow. "Small world. Mittie's a budding aviatrix herself."

Her mother scowled, and Mittie detected a motion akin to a kick in the shins to her daddy under the table. "I'd hardly call her an aviatrix. A rather uppity word in my opinion for such a dangerous sport. Mittie dabbles, that's all—just a passing fancy until she settles into a more conventional lifestyle."

"Mother means like marriage. Like my sister, Iris. And I do understand; I truly do. She's just never had the thrill of seeing the world from the air."

"So you fancy aviation yourself?"

"I can tell you that Lindbergh first flew in a Lincoln Standard 'Tourabout,' that a mere five years later, on May twentieth of this year, he took off from a muddy runway in New York in the *Spirit of St. Louis* with four hundred and fifty gallons of fuel, and that thirty-three point five hours later he landed in Paris, France. And that someday, I'd like to be a qualified competitor."

"You're smitten, I'd say."

"In the worst way you can imagine. As a matter of fact, I'm attending my first barnstorming event in Indiana next weekend with a pilot friend of mine." When Bobby raised his eyebrows in question, she explained what Ames had told her.

"Ah, an air display. Clever name you Americans have for it."

Mittie was treading treacherous waters, inviting the rebuke of her mother and possibly her dad, by mentioning the show Ames had invited her to, but they were the ones who asked Bobby York to dinner. Why not be truthful? If Bobby was meant to be a setup from her well-meaning parents, he deserved to know what he was getting.

Mittie leaned into Bobby and bumped shoulders with him. "Maybe I could take you out and show you the horses and you could tell me about your flying experience."

"That sounds lovely."

Her parents exchanged a look, but her daddy's was one of amusement. Her mother's, not so much. Clearly she didn't know that Bobby, the pedigreed boy from her homeland, harbored an interest in flying. He intrigued Mittie more than she would dare admit, but Mittie also had a feeling her dad knew more about Bobby than he'd let on.

Her dad smiled. "Bobby, this dinner may have been providential. Mittie's acquainted with the manager at Bowman Field. Perhaps she can give you an introduction so you can see what they have to offer."

Bobby nodded. "I actually have an appointment with him tomorrow in response to an advert in last week's paper."

Mittie's mouth dropped open. "What advert?"

"They need someone to give flying lessons, so I thought I'd see if I fit their criteria."

Mittie's grandmother nodded. "A sharp young man like yourself should have no trouble. And if you need a reference, I'd be happy to offer one."

"That would be most kind."

A wooden smile graced Mittie's mother's lips. This was obviously not the direction she intended for the conversation to go, but she gathered her wits and asked if anyone cared for strawberry short-cake.

Mittie gave Bobby a tour of the barns and the paddock when they'd finished dessert. As they reached the last of the pens, Bobby leaned on the rail and gazed across the meadow.

"I didn't expect to find Kentucky so beautiful nor to remind me so much of England."

"That's what my aunt Evangeline said when she first came. She hailed from the Cotswolds and came over after her husband died on a Royal Navy ship."

"It does evoke a certain feeling of home, but different, too. More vast, like the sky."

"I believe you were being rather modest about your flying experience."

He seemed lost in thought, but then he turned to her. "One never knows how much to reveal. I do have my international license and instructor's permit."

Her heart did a crazy skip. "Did my dad know this when he invited you to dinner?"

"I hadn't told him, if that's what you mean. My father might have at some point."

She chuckled.

"You find it humorous?"

"Not that you're a pilot. It's funny because I thought Daddy invited you to dinner to console me because Iris married before me."

"And that was a concern to you? To find a husband?"

She shuddered. "Do I look like I'm shattered by the fact?"

His smile was wide, his lips full when he answered no. He had slightly irregular teeth on the bottom, and somehow that made her glad. Bobby wasn't perfect, after all—close, but not completely, which made her wonder if there were other parts about him that weren't perfect, too.

"So what's your real story? Why did you come to Kentucky? And don't feed me a line about your love of your daddy's horses."

"Actually, I do love the horses, but I didn't grow up among them like you did. We were weekend warriors, going to the cottage in Newmarket. When my father needed someone to make sure the mares had a safe passage, he asked me."

"I thought grooms usually did that sort of thing."

"This was an important sale, and my father had other obligations."

"If you only went to Newmarket on the weekends, where did you live the rest of the week?"

"Boarding schools mostly. I took my A-levels at Harrow and went to Pembroke after that."

Her eyebrows shot up. "And studied what?"

"Veterinary science at first, since my father suggested it. We'd had a run of horses going lame from this, that, and the other. I switched to anthropology when I discovered the sight of entrails made me woozy. Then I decided to race cars and went to Brooklands in Surrey, which is where I discovered aviation and myself. And there you have it: the abridged version of the life of Bobby York."

"And now world traveler. Until you get a new itch."

"No, aviation is it. So, tell me about this barnstorming. Do you fly?"

"Not yet. I'm just observing. And someday I'd love to take lessons and get a license."

"Bowman doesn't have an aviation academy, do they?"

"Not that I know of. Is that what the advertisement was for?"

"An instructor, but it didn't give many details."

"It sounds like you're planning to stick around for more than a month or two."

"We'll see what happens tomorrow. May I call you and let you know?"

"I'd be furious if you didn't. You have our number."

"Thank you—for the grand tour...and the conversation." Bobby's hand lay nearly weightless on her arm, his touch gentle, his blue eyes softened in the fading light of day.

A spidery warning zipped up her spine. Bobby might be just the person to help her with her license—a nice turn of events if her parents meant him as a consolation prize. But the air of mystery that lurked behind those startling blue eyes told her to be careful. Very careful.

CHAPTER 6

Mittie parked her roadster between a Model T and a sagging pickup truck and followed a stream of people to the demonstration field where a man in a dusty suit collected the admission fee in a tin bucket. Her neck prickled with heat and the excitement that buzzed in the air. She wove through the crowd of young boys with cowlicks and farmers in overalls and women in housedresses clutching toddlers by the hand or holding babies to their breasts. All of them kept looking up like it might be the Second Coming when, in fact, Ames and *Trixie* and the two other performing planes sat in full view straight ahead. The Flying Patriots, the team was called. Ames with his red Oriole with white stripes, a brilliant blue Canuck with stars that glittered in the bright sun, and a white Curtiss Jenny with an American flag painted on the tail.

Mittie stopped short of a row of barrels that served as a boundary to keep people from getting too close, but when Ames looked her way, she waved. He flashed a smile and went back to strapping a leather helmet on a boy with pants that stopped four inches short of his ankles. He adjusted the youth's goggles and jumped on the wing, then gave the boy a hand up. The engine was idling, but when Ames revved it up, the propellers sputtered to life, spinning like the blades on a window fan.

A gentleman with a butcher's apron tied around his middle shooed the crowd back as the berry red Oriole moved in an arc and then bumped along the field in the opposite direction and slowly rose over the distant trees. The crowd cheered, Mittie along with them. It wasn't a stunt but an airplane ride, which Ames had told her was the bread and butter of the operation.

"Third time my boy went up this morning," a man in a dusty gray suit beside her said. "I told him I'd spend my life savings if that's what it took to make him the next Charles Lindbergh."

"So your son wants to fly?"

"Do geese fly south in the winter?" His eyes were on the sky. His boy's dream. He wrapped his arm around a reedy woman with a bun atop her head. "Mother, that boy of ours is going places."

Mittie wished the couple and their son well before she moved along in the crowd. A ten- or twelve-year-old boy with carrot-colored hair carried a cardboard sign that said Airplane Rides: Five Dollars.

Mittie did a quick calculation. Three planes. Three or four rides per plane per hour. Forty-five to sixty dollars an hour. Of course there were fuel costs and giving a dollar or two to the helpers in the crowd.

Ames had explained the routine to Mittie when she'd seen him after her most recent Lindbergh Committee meeting, and he'd given her directions to the air show. He'd said they liked to arrive at their destination a day or two early for advance publicity—buzzing low over the streets of downtown, dropping flyers with the time and location of the demonstration. They encouraged people to bring picnic lunches and arranged for a local business to bring soda pop to sell. The town of Crawley, Indiana, had not let them down.

An airplane ride or two later, Ames cut the engine on *Trixie* and announced that the show would begin in fifteen minutes. He took the bottle of root beer offered by a pigtailed girl in her early teens and told her she was an angel. Then he came to the barrel where Mittie stood and offered her the first swig and asked if she was having a good time.

"Wonderful. The only thing that could make it better is if I were flying with you."

Ames signed an autograph for a freckle-faced boy in short britches and took a sandwich the boy's mother handed him.

"Regular price five dollars, but for you"—he wiggled his eyebrows at Mittie—"I'll make an exception and only charge ten." He inhaled half the sandwich as a bead of sweat tracked a line from his temple to his jaw.

Mittie swiped it away with the back of her finger. "Spoken like a true businessman."

One of the pilots hollered for Ames.

"Be right there, Lester." He took the last bite of the sandwich and said, "You're in for a thrill you've never experienced before."

He turned and, with a long stride, joined his team.

Mittie found a spot on the grass and sat down, eager for the show to begin. Ames was right—once the performance started, her heart did stalls and rollovers and spirals right along with the Patriots. Once, she counted four revolutions before Ames pulled *Trixie* out of the spin and nosed her upward as the crowd erupted in a cheer and hollered, "More! More!"

The three planes headed away from the crowd, and when they returned, it was only the Oriole and the Canuck, flying so close together it looked as if their wings could kiss. Ames circled away from his partner plane as a man dressed head to toe in a light-colored tuxedo that looked remarkably like the one Ames had worn to Iris' wedding emerged from the forward seat of the Canuck. He grasped the strut separating the wings of the plane and, with the agility of a gymnast, swung himself up to the top wing. He took a bow, then inched along the wing toward the outermost tip. The crowd held its breath as the stuntman waved, then raised his hands in a victory stance.

Yes, it was the same tuxedo. Before Mittie had time to ponder, though, Ames in his cheery red Oriole appeared alongside the wing walker, the two pilots lining up their wing positions. Then for a moment, the man in the tuxedo seemed to float on air as his feet went from one plane to the other.

"Did you see that?" A woman sitting next to Mittie fanned herself. "I don't know about you, but I think those guys up there are plain nuts. If God meant for people to walk on air—"

A gasp went up from the crowd. The man in white teetered, his body whipping like a cornstalk in the wind. His feet slipped as if on ice until all Mittie could see was a pair of legs dangling over the Oriole's wing. She jumped to her feet and shielded her eyes, her heart in her throat. The swath of legs moved frantically through the air, the upper body obscured from view.

"He's falling! He's not going to make it! Catch him!" Shouts reverberated in the air. Then as the crowd flooded the field below the plane, arms outstretched, the wing tilted and Mittie detected the stuntman's hands on a bar or handle of some sort, hanging on like tiny leeches. In the next instant, legs heaved onto the wing, the man in the light suit erect, one hand on his heart, the other waving an American flag.

A woman swooned and dropped to the ground as men, women, and children streamed past, cheering with shouts of "God bless America" and "Best dadburn sight I've witnessed in all my born days."

Mittie's own chest felt as if it would explode, the heat of the day and the terror of what might have turned into a disaster meshed together in a volcanic swirl.

As she explained her reaction to Ames after the last airplane ride had been given and the sun glowed crimson and peach and violet on the horizon, he draped his arm around her and said, "That's the general idea—give people what they came for."

"But slipping off the edge of the wing was surely not intentional."

Ames just smiled and raised one brow. "Buster likes to ham it up—not a timid bone in his body. You should see what he does with the ladder we sometimes drop from the underbelly of the plane."

"Seriously?" A chill raced over Mittie's bare arms. She'd seen jockeys who took terrible chances, and if they were skilled, it paid off. Her eyes met Ames'. "I want to learn to do that. Can you teach me? Or get Buster to show me?"

"Would love to, doll, but we're headed up to French Lick this evening."

"Going to take the healing waters at the mineral springs?"

"No, meeting someone interested in my air intake invention."

"Well then, how about next week?"

Ames shook his head. "We'll be in Wichita by then."

"Ah, Amelia Earhart's state. If she were joining you, I'd hop on the next train."

"Don't think she's from Wichita, but you'd be welcome if you showed up."

"What kind of death-defying acts are you going to do there?"

"Stunts, my sweet, not acts. And it depends on what the others have lined up. We aim for variety. You serious about coming?"

"Next time, maybe, if I had a little advance notice." It was tempting. The whole day had been exhilarating, but Bobby York had danced in the back of her mind as well. Weaver had hired him to give lessons at Bowman Field, and Mittie had asked if she could be his first student. She wanted to surprise Ames with her skill when he returned.

"Like you gave me for the wedding." His voice teased the air, and when she offered to take him to town to his hotel or wherever he was staying, he shrugged.

"My night to sleep under the stars and watch the planes. Could use your company."

"And with that line, I'm leaving. Don't be a stranger, okay?"

A chime sounded when Mittie pushed open the door to the Nightingale's Song Hat Shoppe. Her cousin, Nell, was busy with a customer and said she'd be with her in a tick, her British accent reminiscent of Bobby York.

"No hurry. I'll make myself at home." Mittie tossed the togs she planned to wear to the horse show in West Virginia on a nearby chair and ambled about.

Nell had made improvements to the little shop on Bardstown Road. A settee covered in a divine cabbage rose print was angled in the corner. *Vogue* and *Everylady's* magazines fanned out across a coffee table that had once belonged to Nell's grandmother in England—not the grandmother they shared, but Lady Mira, who had bequeathed Nell and her sister some of her things when she died. The shop could pass as a British cottage, which was probably why it was one of the most popular salons in Louisville. Nell's talent for putting people at ease was almost as remarkable as her millinery skills. The latest hat designs were scattered throughout the shop, and on the far wall a glass jeweler's case displayed fashion baubles everyone was raving for—tasseled brooches, over-the-elbow gloves, beaded bags, long ropey pearls.

The door chimed as the customer left, leaving Mittie and Nell with the shop to themselves.

"So business is still good, I see."

"Lovely, as a matter of fact. Once the newspaper ran the story about the Lindbergh visit, I've had a flurry of clients."

"See and be seen—the mantra of every fashionable woman in America." Mittie pointed to a mother-of-pearl cigarette case in the glass display. "Mother would love that. She's been mopey lately with Iris gone and not having to wait on Daddy so much. Can you wrap it?"

"Absolutely. Nice choice." She asked about Iris.

"All we've had is a postcard from Niagara Falls."

"I know you miss her."

"More than you can imagine. I'm thrilled for her, but it's not the life for me."

"You said you needed a couple of hats for next month."

"The horse show in West Virginia. I'm driving Grandmother over. Daddy wants to go in the worst way, but Mother had a conniption when he mentioned it."

"Actually, your grandmother came by and picked out the most adorable hat to go with a heather suit she's wearing. Let's see what you have."

Mittie held up a boxy chocolate-colored dress with a short fawn jacket piped around the cuffs and collar with the same chocolate. "There's a scarf, too, which I forgot to bring. Coral and turquoise, and I have shoes like the ones Clara Bow wore in *Dancing Mothers*. Did you see that?"

"No, there's not much time since Quentin has taken that little church."

"And you've been busy making babies. You doing okay?"

"Better than at first. Still dragging around by evening, but Mama says that will soon pass and I'll be a mass of energy." She eyed Mittie's dress and pulled a cloche from a stand. "How about this in the jacket color, and I'll add a tiny MG Farms insignia in the coral and turquoise? Your grandmother was pleased with the one I did for her."

"Perfect." Mittie tossed the dress aside and held up the other outfit—a navy trouser suit.

Nell's eyes widened and she inhaled with a sharp intake of air.

"Go ahead and say it. You think I've flipped. Mother thinks so, but I wear jodhpurs for riding and flying, so why not elsewhere? I've heard Coco Chanel is mad about wearing trousers herself. Who knows? Maybe they'll catch on and everyone will be dashing out to get them."

Nell sighed and shook her head. "Oh, Mittie. Only you would be so bold."

"Brazen is what Mother said."

"So that's really why you're getting her a present?"

"You know she drives me mad."

"And you do things to exasperate her."

"How else would she know I love her?"

Nell put a hand on her hip. Truly, to be so mild-mannered, Nell had a way of getting to Mittie that neither Iris nor her mother could do.

Mittie pressed the linen trousers against her body and held up the jacket. "So what do you think? A navy bowler to match the jacket?"

Nell scrunched her lips. "No. If you're going to make a statement, then let's go with scarlet. It would add a patriotic touch."

"That's me—the all-American troublemaker."

"That's what makes people love you."

"Ha! Ames loves me so much he went to Kansas. Goodness knows when he'll be back."

"But you've still got that cute newcomer from London, Bobby something."

"Grandmother must've talked about more than the horse show. York. His name is Bobby York, and while he's charming, I'm convinced it was a setup, a little ploy by Mother and Daddy to push me toward a proper suitor like you Brits are so fond of saying?"

"You're a fright, Mittie Humphreys. His name has a nice ring to it, though. Are you going to see him again?"

"As a matter of fact, I am, but not like you're thinking. It turns out he's a flying instructor with all the credentials, and I'm going to start taking lessons from him when he gets it all set up. Maybe as soon as next week."

"Just what you've been wanting."

"It is." Mittie checked her watch. "Gotta dash." She turned to leave as the door chimed, and Wilma Lamberson waltzed into the shop.

Mittie swallowed hard and kept the smile on her face. "Mrs. Lamberson, how nice to see you. How's Dobbs?"

Wilma, a stout woman with mousy hair and a dour disposition, blinked. "Oh, well, if it isn't Mittie Humphreys. I'd heard that some kinfolk of yours had this shop."

"My cousin Nell, and you will love her. She can do anything you can imagine with hats."

"The way you do with pony carts, I suppose."

Mittie's neck burned with the insinuation. And she probably deserved it, but she wouldn't let the woman get to her. "No, Nell is patient and gentle and kind as well as talented." She turned to Nell. "I'm not aware if you two have met. This is Wilma Lamberson. Her son Dobbs took horse showing instructions from us when he and I were fifteen."

A flicker of understanding crossed Nell's face. She extended her hand. "I'm Nell Bledsoe. Welcome to my shop."

Mittie waved and started toward the door, but Wilma reached out and clamped her forearm, ignoring Nell. "Rumor has it your daddy's still suffering from that back injury."

"He's doing better, thanks."

"Must be quite enlightening for him to find out what it's like to be a cripple like my Dobbs."

Mittie smiled through clenched teeth. "You know I'm still just as sorry today as I was seven years ago about what happened to Dobbs."

"But your life goes on. Every day I have to watch my boy struggle, limping like a lame dog. He'll never attract a nice girl or provide me with grandchildren." Her fingernails bit into Mittie's flesh like a chicken hawk hanging onto a rabbit for dear life.

"Dobbs is a swell fella, Mrs. Lamberson. He can do anything he sets his mind to." *Like persuade the stable owner's daughter to let him go flying down a hill in a cart pulled by a novice horse.*

"That's easy for you to say. You weren't maimed."

"You're right—I wasn't. But I'm still sorry about what happened. Would it help if I came to see Dobbs?"

Mrs. Lamberson drew herself closer so they were nose to nose. "You stay away from my boy." She shoved Mittie away.

"You have my word. And while you're here, you might want to check out the jewelry in Nell's collection. There are some nice chokers."

CHAPTER 7

Mittie spent the remainder of the week lamenting her choice of words to Wilma Lamberson, but even more, she deplored letting the woman get under her skin. Poor Dobbs. It had been seven years, but what hurt the most then, and now, was that Dobbs was her friend... and the first boy she let kiss her. The farrier's son had tried, but he got a kick in the shins for his efforts. Dobbs was different. He was full of fun, and she later realized it was his reckless streak that attracted her. Even when she'd cautioned him about keeping the horse's pace under control with the cart, he'd egged her on, faster and faster, laughing and whooping it up until the wheel had hit a rut and sent Dobbs flying. The cart had overturned and pinned Dobbs beneath it. His leg had been broken in two places, and when his parents arrived, he blamed Mittie.

Her daddy had paid for the operations that followed and all the hospital bills—plus a tidy sum to keep Buck Lamberson quiet when he threatened to bring a complaint before the Saddlebred Commission. Her face flamed at the memory. Dobbs wasn't the only one with scars.

The following Monday, Mittie peeked around the corner of the door into the classroom at Bowman Field. Butterflies flapped in her stomach like it was the first day of school. "I'm early. Mind if I come on in?"

Bobby waved her in. "Mittie, lovely to see you, and I'm glad you're early. You can help me get these diagrams tacked up."

A US map was already tacked on one wall with red pins showing airfields across the country. A chalkboard covered the opposite wall with an oak table centered in the room. Bobby unrolled a chart and asked her to hold it while he put thumbtacks on the corners. It reminded Mittie of a gilded-framed print in her daddy's study showing the anatomy of the horse, only this time it was a bi-wing shown in three perspectives: above, head-on, and a side view, each segment labeled. Two other charts were of an instrument panel and one with arrows in different directions that she couldn't figure out.

"Atmospheric layers and wind currents," he explained when he saw her tilting her head and frowning.

Just as they finished, three young men, hardly out of their teens, came in and Bobby asked them all to have a seat so they could get started.

The one on Mittie's left said, "I thought I signed up to get in a cockpit and fly, not sit in a stuffy room."

Bobby did a slow pivot and faced the class. "Right you are, chap. But you wouldn't want a bloke off the street to start fiddling about in your mouth with a drill or a tooth extractor if he didn't have some prior knowledge about dentistry. The same is true of airplanes. While some of you may have already had the chance to sit in a cockpit or take a flight or two, perhaps even man the controls, a true aviator is one who knows his subject from the inside out and what to do should an engine falter. Your name, chap?"

"Delbert McCombs, sir."

Delbert's ears were the color of spiced apples, and Mittie was certain hers were, too. Weaver and Ames had both let her take the controls when she knew nothing but to watch the altimeter and the compass.

"Stay with me, mate, and you'll be flying aces in no time. While a license is not required to take to the skies, it does qualify you for competitions and the growing number of jobs in aviation."

With that, he launched into the anatomy of the plane and what each part was made of and its purpose. Delbert sat tall in his seat and took notes. They all did. The classroom instruction would last eight hours per week for two weeks before they were allowed to begin the actual flight training in the cockpit. But Mittie's heart was already in the clouds.

When the session ended, the other students exited quickly, and Bobby asked if he could have a word.

"Certainly, but I don't want anyone to think I'm getting preferential treatment."

"You needn't fret. I'm tough, but fair. And I do believe you show a tick more promise than the others, although it's always hard to tell at first. May I buy you a cup of tea?"

"I'd prefer coffee."

They sat in the canteen together, Bobby and his tea, Mittie with her coffee.

He spoke first. "I owe you an apology and a word of thanks."

"For what? You're the answer to my prayers."

"The apology is because I was hoping to call earlier and perhaps take you to dinner, but once things got rolling, there was a plane to purchase and applications to process."

"No apology needed. I've been rather busy myself with the horses." She told him about the upcoming show and prattled on about nothing. Truthfully, she was a little jumpy. Not only was Bobby everything she'd imagined in the way of expertise, but he was cute to boot. She hoped to keep their friendship on a purely platonic level. And looking across the table at him, she realized it was going to be harder than she thought. Much harder.

She took a sip of coffee, but it had grown cold. "You said earlier you wanted to thank me, but you didn't say why."

"You and your grandmother—you for entrusting me to be your instructor and your grandmother for putting in a good word for me with Weaver. He was reticent at first, but when I mentioned her name as a reference, he warmed up right away."

"My grandmother does have a fine reputation. And as for me— I'm still pinching myself over my good fortune."

He drained his cup and held it suspended. "To many happy hours and blue skies."

Mittie recited what she learned to Gypsy the next morning on their ride across the hills. Sometimes the best friends were the ones who just listened and didn't answer back or give advice. So Gypsy listened as Mittie told her about wingspans and struts, how to compensate for crosswinds, and how to utilize a tailwind to the best advantage.

It became their routine—Mittie taking instruction from Bobby York, Gypsy being privy to it all. As the gray-green fog of morning thinned into a milky haze, Mittie's recitations rode on the wind. "Remember this, Gypsy: a plane can rotate in three dimensions depending on the axis. Just wait until Ames comes back and I throw some pitch, yaw, and roll at him. You think he'll be surprised?"

Gypsy answered by twitching her right ear. Mittie laughed and leaned in, giving Gypsy permission to do her own version of forward thrust. As they topped the highest of the hills of MG Farms, the sun broke through the clouds, scattering golden glitter like fairy dust.

Mittie pulled Gypsy into a halt and let the moment settle. A low rumble came from behind, a sound she first took for the gnawing hunger in her belly, but as the rumble became a roar and filled her ears, she knew different. Mittie shielded her eyes from the glare. The flash of red could only mean one thing—Ames was back in the Oriole. The plane swooped until it was only a few hundred feet above the ground, then passed and disappeared over the distant trees. Mittie waited, hoping he'd circle around or even touch down on the open meadow.

When the air stilled and nothing appeared, she reined Gypsy hard to the right and let her gallop, both their hearts wide open.

Mittie was tempted to hop in her roadster and drive straight to Bowman Field, but Toby wanted her to watch the horses for the upcoming show as he put them through their paces. They both performed at top level, and she was pleased when her daddy joined her and nodded his approval.

"You had a phone call earlier—that bright young man from the wedding. Ames Dewberry, I believe."

Her heart leapt. "I think I just saw him fly over. Did he leave a number for me to call back?"

"No, but I invited him to come for lunch. Told him we ate around one."

"Does he need a ride?"

"No, he said he'd borrow a car from someone."

"What did Mother say?"

"Nothing. She's gone for the day—over at the church putting together boxes for the Mississippi flood victims."

"I'm glad it will just be the three of us. I'd like you to get to know Ames better."

"Me, too. I consider it my duty to keep abreast of the gentlemen my daughter is sweet on." He regarded her with raised eyebrows.

"Gentlemen? Is there someone I don't know about?"

"Well, there is young York as well."

"He's my flight instructor, but I have a sneaking suspicion you knew more about Bobby than you let on when you invited him here."

"A bit."

"Did you know he was a pilot?"

He shook his head. "I wasn't certain, but after I invited him, I remembered Robert Sr. mentioning that his son was interested in flying. I didn't know he was an instructor."

"And Mother? Did you tell her?"

"I thought it best to see if my memory was correct. What's important is that you're showing an interest in young men. You will keep an open mind, won't you?"

"That sounds like a trick question, but thank you for inviting Ames. And for agreeing to my taking lessons from Bobby."

"My pleasure."

Ames wore linen trousers and a white open-necked shirt with a gold-and-black-patterned cravat at the neck. "Thank you, sir, for inviting me."

Her daddy clapped Ames on the shoulder like they were old friends and invited him to the gentleman's parlor, nodding for Mittie to join them. "Mittie tells me you've been barnstorming in Kansas."

"Yes, sir. I tried to get Mittie to join us, but she's quite dedicated to her work here."

"That she is. It's our busy season with training and upcoming shows."

They chatted about it being the peak for flying as well, taking advantage of the long summer hours and giving folks good, clean entertainment.

Mittie asked if anything new had been added to the show.

"Every show is different. You get a bead on the crowd, what you think they'd like. In Kansas, Buster jumped from the back of a moving car onto the ladder I was telling you about. He's quite an aerialist, and the crowd couldn't get enough."

Mittie's dad chuckled and offered Ames a sherry.

"No, thanks. I like to keep a clear head."

"Smart boy." Her daddy nodded when Ruby appeared in the doorway and announced lunch.

After saying grace, Mittie's dad said, "You mentioned you were in aeronautical design. Anything I might have heard of?"

Ames swallowed his bite of meat loaf. "Depends on how well you know engines and carburetors."

"Not much, I'm afraid. I leave the maintenance on our vehicles to Moses or the mechanic in town. But I'm always interested in how young people today are contributing to the future."

"You can be sure aviation is going to play a big role."

"Ever since Mittie learned about Lindbergh visiting our fair city, I've heard nothing else."

"You exaggerate, Daddy." She turned to Ames. "Daddy's afraid that since I'm taking flying lessons, I'm going to fly off into the wild blue yonder."

Ames asked, "What flying lessons?"

"Oh, I haven't had a chance to tell you. Bobby York is a friend of the family and just here from England, but he's hired on at Bowman Field to give lessons. Isn't that grand?"

Ames blinked. "Shucks. I was hoping to have the privilege of teaching you."

"I need all the help I can get."

Her dad smiled. "Fair warning, Ames. Her enthusiasm can be overwhelming, but there's nothing I like more than seeing the excitement that lights up both of your eyes when you talk about aviation."

It was all new to Mittie, too, but gaining her daddy's admiration was a bonus. She might have her mother's impulsive nature, but the competitive spirit came from her daddy. Hard work. Honest sweat. Winning when it mattered.

When her daddy suggested that Mittie show Ames the stables, Ames said, "I've fond memories of my grandparents' farm. I'm game whenever you're ready." He wiped his mouth on his napkin. "And I must say, this was one of the finest meals I've had in a long while."

"I'll let Ruby know. Please join us anytime."

The July heat bore down as Mittie led the way to the barns, the farm's border collie trailing after them. Ames offered the back of his hand for a sniff, and when Skipper licked it, Ames crouched down and let the dog slurp his tongue on his face.

"Good boy. What's his name?"

"Skipper. Official watchdog and general nuisance."

Ames rose and draped an arm across Mittie's shoulders. "This is quite the place. I've flown over a few times trying to get a glimpse of you."

"Get out. You think you might catch me in my dressing gown?"

"That would be a treat. Truth is, I'd look at you no matter what you're wearing."

The heat rushing to Mittie's face wasn't from the sun. "Guess Daddy might have something to say about that. He'd prefer to keep me under his watchful eye until he's pushing daisies."

"Your dad's swell."

"He is. And I think he liked you, too."

She took him on the grand tour, chatting the whole time while Skipper kept to Ames' heels, hoping for a pat on the head. She saved the best for last: Gypsy.

Mittie handed Ames a handful of carrot nuggets. "This is Gypsy. She'll be your best friend if you feed her."

"This is some magnificent horse. Is she yours?" He offered Gypsy a nugget and tangled his fingers in her dark mane.

"She is. A gift when I turned nineteen. She was born right here at MG Farms."

"What a beauty—nothing like the nags I grew up with . . . the ones at Granny's place." His voice drifted off like he was trying to capture a memory.

"Do you ever go back?"

"We lost Granny and Papaw both in the flu epidemic."

"I'm sorry. For you and your family."

He shrugged. "Such is life." His face brightened. "Now there are skies to conquer. You up for a ride this afternoon? Buster said he'd be willing to show you the ropes on wing walking since you were keen on it last time."

Her heart thundered in her chest. "Give me five minutes and I'll grab my things."

Mittie flew with Ames to a field west of town where Buster, the stuntman who'd worn the tuxedo, gave her basic directions while they were on the ground. He showed her how to climb from the forward seat of the Oriole when the plane was aloft and how to use the wires for balance when walking toward a strut.

"Balance and making no sudden moves will keep you from getting killed."

"Not getting killed would be nice."

He shrugged. "It happens. Keep your legs slightly bent in a crouch like you're going to jump." He demonstrated. "Stay loose and use the wires to steady you. Once you're comfortable with that, we'll have Ames take you out for a ground run."

Buster was graceful and limber, something Mittie was short on, but her legs were strong, and as a child, she'd been scolded for walking along the top rails of the fences. She'd never fallen, although she'd been yanked down by her daddy plenty of times. When she stepped out onto the wing, she faced forward as instructed and shuffled sideways to the strut nearest the cockpit. Easy. Buster met her there and showed her where to grasp the upper wing, using the strut as a leg up.

"The better aerialists roll up using their arm muscles, but I usually just shimmy up by the strut."

Mittie practiced a few times and found the leg up and over, like mounting a horse, worked best for her. Once she was on top, though, there weren't any struts to hang on to. She swallowed the hunk of fear in her throat, held her arms out, and looked down. She'd jumped off barn roofs that were farther off the ground, but the wide, smooth surface of the wing felt amazingly different. And she knew that when the Oriole was two hundred feet in the air, it would be even more thrilling.

Buster, hanging on to the upper wings with his elbows, grinned. "Good work. Ready?"

She clambered down and told Ames to start the engine. Ames told her he would signal when to climb onto the wing. Buster would watch from the ground and take notes.

Mittie climbed into the training seat and gave Ames the thumbs-up that she was ready. He taxied across the field and lifted off. At the signal, Mittie unfastened her belt and pushed herself up from the seat and onto the wing. The wind slammed against her, stronger than she expected, but she leaned into it and took a deep breath, a prayer on her lips. When she had her bearings, she nodded at Ames. He nosed down gradually. She couldn't risk looking at him for directions again, but when she felt they were at a safe altitude, she inched her way across the wing to the strut and did the ascent onto the upper wing. She crawled on all fours to the center of the wing and waited. Ames couldn't see her now, so she had to make her own best judgment for when to stand.

On the count of three, she stood up, legs quivering but a current sparking through her limbs. Like a tightrope walker, she used her arms for balance as she strolled from one wingtip to the other, then raised her hands in victory at the precise moment that Ames nosed the plane up. She lost her footing, and just as she'd always heard, her life flashed before her, and she envisioned her body being hurled into space where it would plummet to eternity.

It wasn't eternity that met her, but the painted canvas of the wing and a bracket that held one of the struts. She grabbed hold, and with no grace whatsoever, lowered herself from the upper wing and to safety.

When they'd rolled to a stop, Buster hollered up at her, "Nice recovery."

Mittie hopped off the wing, trembling. She leaned over, hands on knees, to catch her breath, and when she came up, she tossed her head and shouted up at Ames, "I'm ready. Let's give it another try."

They practiced until Mittie was sure she had grown feathers and wings and said she needed to get back and check on the horses. What she really wanted was a long soak in the tub, but Ames had another suggestion.

"How about we celebrate Mittie's maiden voyage as a wing walker with a night on the town—say, over at the Hen's Nest?"

Mittie said, "The dance club over on Bardstown?"

"Unless you have another suggestion."

"None that I can think of. But I can't go like this. I need to change into something more suitable."

"That's the trouble with women. Always thinking they have to get dolled up."

She punched him on the arm. "And just who do you think we get dolled up for?"

"When you go out on the barnstorming circuit, you're going to have to mend your pampered ways, sweetheart."

"Pampered? Hardly."

He draped his arm over her shoulder. "You run on then, pretty yourself up, and we'll meet you there."

Live Music Tuesday, Friday, and Saturday.
The sign filled the window of the Hen's Nest, and the advertising had drawn a lively crowd. Mittie's quick bath and putting on a silky green dress with a handkerchief hem had rejuvenated her—and brought a raised brow from her mother when Mittie found her in the parlor and told her she was meeting Ames in town.

Her mother blew out a puff of smoke. "In my day, it was considered good manners for a young man to call on his date and pick her up."

"Ames would be the first to agree with you...if he had an automobile. He flies everywhere he goes, and it would be impractical, if not impossible, to have a vehicle ready in every town where the Patriots stop."

"He managed to find one to come to lunch today."

"Yes. One of the mechanics at the airfield loaned him a car for a few hours."

"Oh, very well. It is nice to see you dressed in something other than jodhpurs. Have a good time."

Ames was already seated with the Patriots in the Hen's Nest. A smoky haze blanketed the room as she sat with them and ate and laughed and sang along with the music, talking about the day's practice. And they danced. The band played lively jazz tunes, and when they returned to their seats to catch their breath, Lester pulled a flask from his pocket and offered to jazz up their drinks.

Mittie shook her head. She didn't want the effects of Lester's bathtub gin, or whatever it was, to ruin what had been a perfect day. She raised her root beer. "To good friends."

Ames, who had taken Lester up on his offer twice already, swayed a bit in his chair and held up his glass. "To you, sweet Mittie, and you, Lester, and you, Shorty, and to my pup back home. May we all enjoy posterity...prosp...plus...oh blast it—may we all get rich!"

Buster snorted and held up his glass. "I believe this dear boy may be a bit pickled."

Ames widened his eyes. "A gentleman knows when he's been insulted, but to prove my sobriety..." He held out his hand to Mittie. "I'd like to have the next dance, if you please."

"Such gallantry." Buster held the back of his hand to his forehead.

"What a bunch of cutups. I accept your offer." But Ames was already on his feet, arm outstretched. She took the hand he offered and let him lead her to the dance floor. He tucked his thumbs in his armpits and moved his elbows up and down to the beat of the "Darktown Strutters' Ball." Mittie matched him move for move, their arms and legs akimbo with the tricky Charleston steps. Ames' hair fell across his forehead as he gave Mittie a twirl then bumped hips and changed steps, his joints loose, feet light. Other dancers parted to give them room, then stopped altogether and ringed the dance area, watching. Mittie threw back her head and laughed. She and Ames kicked their heels up for a few measures, then leaned over, hands on knees, and crossed their hands back and forth. Long after the song should have ended, the band played on as Ames and Mittie tapped and reeled and whirled.

Bravos and cheers filled the Hen's Nest when at last the music stopped and they returned to the table breathless, their clothes drenched.

Ames mopped his brow with a handkerchief and laughed. "We make a good team. Agree?" He grabbed his drink and drained the glass.

Lester held up the flask, but Ames waved it away. "You ask me, you don't have hooch in there but some kind of evil potion."

A waiter appeared with two glasses of water and told Ames and Mittie they'd be welcome anytime. Ames thanked him and said, "Sure, boss."

Strains of a slow waltz drifted through the air, the saxophone notes mellow and sweet. Ames led Mittie once again to the dance floor, his arm firm around her waist, the heat of his body melting into hers. He leaned in and nuzzled her neck, sending a tingle through her. She missed a step from his lead, and for a moment, they teetered awkwardly, trying to get back into rhythm. Instead Ames stepped on her foot, sending a fiery jolt up her ankle.

When he apologized, she leaned back and looked into his dark eyes. "We've had a long day. Why don't we call it a night?"

"The night is still young." He tilted her chin with one finger and brushed her lips with his.

Although her insides ached to return his kiss, she didn't. "That may be, but I have early morning duties at the farm."

"You're not sore because I had a shot of Lester's whiskey, are you?"

She wasn't sure. He'd refused her daddy's sherry, but a drink or two wasn't unheard of. Heaven knows, she'd seen a lot worse among her rowdy friends from high school, but other than the occasional sip of wine, alcohol had never really appealed to her. She shrugged, her answer noncommittal. "It's not like I have any right to say what you do or don't do. Now if we were an item, and last time I checked, we weren't . . ."

"We're not?" His dark eyes searched hers. "I was hoping . . . well, guess I'm the fool then."

"You've just given me one of the best days of my entire life, so I wouldn't say the possibilities aren't there."

By way of reply, he drew her close, their feet having somehow found their groove as they now moved smoothly to the one-two-three beat of the music.

She relaxed in the glow of tavern lights and strong arms, the warm mix of body odor and aftershave, cheap cigars, and forbidden whiskey.

CHAPTER 8

"Gracious sakes, Mittie, would you stop fidgeting? You're making me a basket of nerves."

"Sorry, Grandmother." She uncrossed her legs and rose from the ringside seat at the West Virginia horse show. Not a whisper of air stirred in the sweltering July heat. Mittie was beginning to regret wearing the trouser suit, wishing she'd opted for a day dress with sheer sleeves. "I don't remember it taking so long between events. I'm going for a lemonade. You want one?"

"A lemonade would be nice, dear." Her grandmother waved a silk fan, looking every bit the grand matron of horse owners and breeders. "And if you see the Fords, you might invite them to join us."

In the show ring, attendants scrambled with a shovel and bucket, clearing the ring of horse dung and raking it for the next event. Toby would be riding Jake Ford's chestnut, April Showers, in the five-gait championship, having taken first in the four-year-old class the day before. Gingersnap had faltered in the three-gait class and not placed, but Mr. Ford had taken it well. Mittie was glad she'd brought her grandmother over, and bless her, she was right. Mittie was fidgety.

The week had flown by as she'd practiced twice more with Ames while still giving attention to April Showers' and Gingersnap's training, but Mittie had an itch she couldn't explain. Now that the world of flying was opening up before her, it consumed her every thought. Wing walking. Flight lessons with Bobby. Even her own plane someday so she could compete. She didn't want to get ahead of herself, but she was having a tough time reining in the excitement that skated along her bones.

She scanned the crowd for the Fords to no avail. They were most likely in the holding area with April Showers or already on their way to their seats in her grandmother's box. Mittie nodded at several people she knew and strode toward the refreshment area. A familiar figure at the end of the counter stopped her. Buck Lamberson was having a heated discussion with someone.

Drat. What's he doing here? She paused, mentally going over the list of contenders at the horse show. She would have remembered if the Lambersons had an entry. An uneasy feeling settled in her stomach, and she thought of returning to her seat, though she was still as parched as if her mouth were filled with soda crackers. Then, before she'd decided what to do, Parker Ogilvie spun around and stormed away from Lamberson. His head jerked up when he saw her.

"For pity's sake, Mittie, what are you doing following me around? Checking to see if I'm doing my job?" He glared, his look as bristly as the whiskers of his sideburns.

"Not at all, although I'm surprised that you're not in the holding paddock with April Showers getting ready for the final event."

Mr. Lamberson strode up beside Ogilvie. "Well, well. If it's not the farmer's daughter. Had to take a second look, though, since you're wearing those trousers. Wearing the britches in the family now that your dad's all crippled up, eh?"

"Good afternoon, Mr. Lamberson. And Daddy's doing much better, thank you."

He tipped his hat. "So you say."

"Is Dobbs here with you?"

He scowled. "Guess you hadn't heard. He's in Cincinnati with his mama, seeing a doctor about a new operation."

Mittie's gut clenched. *The operation Daddy's paying for.* "Yes, Daddy mentioned it. Give him my best, will you?"

Lamberson snorted as Ogilvie gave him a sidelong look and an almost imperceptible shake of his head, warning him off, it seemed. A voice over the loudspeaker announced that the next event was about to commence.

Mittie ran her tongue over bone-dry teeth. "I'm sorry I can't visit. I was just coming after a lemonade." She turned to Ogilvie. "You're welcome to join Grandmother and me with the Fords in our box."

"I wouldn't want to impose."

Mittie ignored the sarcastic edge in his tone, aware that he hadn't given a reason why he wasn't at his post with Toby. She wished them both a good day and went to the refreshment table.

The first entrant was already in the ring when she handed Grandmother the frosty drink, but the Fords were still absent. She settled into the wooden folding chair to watch the show. April Showers entered the arena fifth, head erect, mane and tail in their full glory. The horses were judged on animation of movement as well as showmanship, both of which April Showers excelled in. The horse pawed the dirt, resisting Toby's reining as he took her through the walk and park trot, never quite getting the rhythm or the crowd's enthusiasm.

Her grandmother whispered, "Looks like the old girl has lead in her feet. The judge will dock points for lack of spirit." And neither were surprised when the six horses were brought before the judge for a final look and April Showers was dead last.

As the cup was presented to the winner, Jake Ford appeared in their box, his face florid, his lips set in a line of disgust.

Mittie offered her hand. "My condolences. She had a fine showing yesterday."

"Not when it counts, though. I was a fool to throw away good money on a trainer who didn't bother to show up."

"Daddy is grieved by that, I assure you. He hoped having Grandmother and me here to represent MG Farms would make up for that."

"I was counting on a win today."

"I'll talk with Toby, see if he noticed something amiss. It could have just been the stress of travel and sleeping in an unfamiliar stall. You have my word that we will continue to do our best to help April Showers perform well in future events."

"Tell your old man I'll be in on Monday." He strode off, not even bothering to stop at the rail and have a word with Toby.

"You handled that well, dear. No one likes to think their horse was the ugly baby in the lineup." Her grandmother patted her hand.

Mittie did understand Mr. Ford's disappointment. Mittie had been the *ugly baby*, the one people overlooked when they went on about how cute Iris looked in her latest frock or what a smart little cookie Iris was. Their mother's mantra that Mittie would outgrow it was a laugh. She'd outgrown it all right, standing almost eye to eye with her father and shoulders broad enough to pass for a dockworker. Thankfully, her long, slender legs managed to get her enough wolf whistles to make up for it.

Mittie scowled. "She didn't deserve last place. She's a better horse than that. And I will check into it . . . for Daddy's sake and the reputation of MG Farms."

"Sometimes you just have to take the hits. And I'm sure the farm's reputation's not too badly damaged. Your grandfather and I had many disappointments in the ring, but character is built by what is done in spite of it."

"Sounds like Daddy's version of 'Get back in the saddle and try again.'"

"I suppose. Jake Ford reacted the way many owners do when the wounds are fresh. He'll come to his senses before Monday."

"Let's hope so." Mittie told her grandmother she would meet her in the car. It was Ogilvie's job to check that the horses were loaded, but in her gut, Mittie knew the ultimate responsibility was hers. And Ogilvie was a loose cannon—"yes, ma'am" one minute, then sneering the next. The respect she thought she'd gained from him was as thin as her sister's wedding veil.

Mittie found Toby brushing down April Showers, talking gently to her, telling her she'd have her place in the winner's circle another day. He looked up and sighed when he saw Mittie.

"Tough day, Toby?"

"Beats all I ever seen, Miz Mittie. April Showers was fine this morning. I would've sworn she'd be in the top three, if not the winner."

"Did you change her feed or give her too much water? That could have thrown her off." Mittie wished for a ready explanation, trying to quell the growing knot in her gut that the conversation she'd observed between Ogilvie and Lamberson played a part.

He shook his head and offered April Showers a treat from his pocket.

"Were you with her all day?"

"Right here in the paddock with her or feeding Gingersnap." He thumbed to the adjacent enclosure. "The groom's already loaded her, and Mr. Ogilvie just left, told me to take April Showers to the horse trailer soon as she's cooled down."

"She seems all right now."

"Not as chipper as usual, but I've gone over every inch of her and didn't find a nick or a hair out of place."

"We'll sort it out. Thanks for doing your best."

His hangdog look mirrored that of the horse. And for the present, all Mittie could do was brush it off and hope her suspicions were unfounded.

While Mittie and her grandmother dined on ham steak with red-eye gravy, Mittie asked if she knew why Buck Lamberson was at the West Virginia show.

"Like a bad penny, he just keeps turning up. He's a mean old cuss if you ask me."

Mittie smiled at her grandmother's crudeness, but it was one of the things she loved about her—her ability to cut to the heart of the situation.

"I saw him with Ogilvie—arguing, it seemed. Ogilvie seems a little slippery to me."

"He's just cut from a rougher cloth than you're used to. And I suspect he's not too keen on taking orders from you, but things will smooth out with your dad being more involved."

They ate in silence while Mittie stewed about the day's events.

Her grandmother finished eating and folded her napkin. "You've not been yourself the last few weeks, and I know you only came to the show to placate me. For that I'm grateful, but I think your daddy is right. It's time for you to spread your wings. If your heart's desire is to jump in an airplane or out of one, then you need to pursue it. Heaven knows, I'll wear out my knees praying with you up in the air, but you'll never be happy if you don't give it your full attention."

"I'm working on it. I'm just afraid I'll disappoint Mother and Daddy."

"The least of your worries. My parents thought I'd lost my mind when I married your grandfather and moved from Boston to be with a man who had a wild idea about raising horses—show animals at that. Best decision I ever made."

"And your parents? Did they forgive you?"

"I gave them your darling father. How could they not?" Her laugh was throaty and warm.

Mittie squeezed the age-spotted hand of her grandmother and let her grandmother's unspoken blessing pour over her.

CHAPTER 9

On Sunday morning, a fine mist rose from the lush green of the paddock, a thin veil of sweetness that would burn off before it was time for church. Mittie stopped first in Ogilvie's office and found him reviewing feed orders.

After exchanging pleasantries about their return from West Virginia, Mittie asked about April Showers.

"Happy as a tick on a coonhound."

"About her performance yesterday—did you notice anything unusual about her?"

"Nary a thing. It happens, you know. An off day here and there."

"Still, I wonder if we should give a call to the veterinary service and see if they can send someone out."

"I've already arranged for them to come this afternoon."

"Excellent. And thank you."

The look he gave her was smug. "Now, beg your pardon, but I have work to do." He tapped a pencil on the form before him, and Mittie left to check the barns. She couldn't help it—Ogilvie still annoyed her. She believed he only told her what she wanted to hear. And yet, April Showers showed no signs of illness or sluggishness when Mittie checked her box, which was confirmed by Toby as well.

After church, she spent the rest of the day studying aviation manuals in preparation for her first flight with Bobby on Monday, and going over newspaper articles she'd been saving about the splash Lindbergh was making across America. When she rode Gypsy after dinner that night, she practiced what she would say to him. *How did you know you wanted to be an aviator? What was the most difficult part of the flight to Paris? What advice would you give to fellow aviators?*

The katydids in the gingko trees around the house had begun their evensong by the time they returned to the stables, and since Toby was busy, she unsaddled Gypsy and grabbed the sweat blade, running it in long strokes over Gypsy's dark coat. A lantern hung outside the stall, illuminating Gypsy's space when the top of the Dutch door was left open, but Mittie didn't need the light. She knew every inch of Gypsy as well as she knew herself. When the excess moisture had been removed, Mittie looped her hand in the strap on the back of the grooming brush and, with rhythmic motion, rubbed until Gypsy's coat shone. As she ran the brush over her withers, Gypsy responded with a low grunt of a contented sigh.

Chunky shadows cast by the lantern played scenes on the heavy beams and slatted walls of the stall, and Mittie was transported to the icy April morning when Gypsy made her entrance into the world. She was to be Mittie's birthday gift, the first foal born at MG Farms that was wholly hers. Their foreman, Whitey Munce, had been alive then and kept a careful eye on Rosella, the one whose belly had grown pendulous with the foal she carried. On the final round of the barns the evening before, Whitey said it was time to move Rosella to the loafing shed, her udder tight, the teats waxing tiny beads of colostrum that would nourish the foal. A groom was assigned watch for the night, but Mittie had been as restless as Rosella, crawling from bed and going to the barn to check her every hour.

In the inky part of the night just before dawn, she found the groom and Whitey in the shed, their frosted breaths like puffs of smoke from her daddy's pipe. Rosella lay on her side, her neck slick with the damp sheen of labor.

Whitey nodded when Mittie entered. "Won't be long now." As he said it, Rosella grunted and writhed, hoisting herself to her feet. She pawed the straw and nipped at her flanks as if trying to rid her body of the source of pain. Her coat lathered from her efforts, glistening in the lantern light.

Mittie had witnessed other foalings, but this one was different. It would be hers from the moment it drew breath. That the foal came from champion bloodlines was of no consequence—Mittie knew she would cherish it no matter what the pedigree said.

They gave Rosella space, and presently, she lowered back onto the straw, extending her extremities, her nostrils flaring with effort.

The foal's forelegs came first as they were meant to do, the head tucked between them. The coat was dark without any visible white, slimy with the amniotic fluid and the lubricant of the birth passage. The shoulders and hips followed quickly, the foal squirming on the stable floor. Rosella stood and nuzzled her offspring, her tongue washing over the dark, wet coat. The foal responded, rising on wobbly legs before nosing back down. Rosella's head prodded, and the newborn gave a soft snort and tried again. This time, the stilt-like legs trembled and held. A quick jerking movement severed the umbilical cord.

"A fine filly! And a frisky one at that." Whitey moved to Rosella's rear to watch for the afterbirth, but Mittie's eyes were locked with the shiny orbs of the foal, who stretched her neck and pranced, awkward for sure but vigorous and independent, promising to live up to her heritage. She would be a champion.

Mittie named her Gypsy for the wild black mane that was luxurious from birth. Five months later, Gypsy was feistier than ever and had weaned herself from her mother's milk. Rosella, though, was sold to pay for new leg braces for Dobbs Lamberson. Mittie's hand gripped the brush, her strokes now short and hard. Gypsy craned her neck and nudged Mittie's arm, the unspoken affection between them thick. Mittie rubbed the soft muzzle and let her hand linger on the jawline. "You were born for great things, dear Gypsy. Just you wait." Even as she spoke, Mittie wasn't certain if the words were for Gypsy or herself. She could hardly wait for morning to arrive, and with it, her first lesson in the cockpit with Bobby York.

"Remember your checklist?"

Mittie nodded and surveyed the instrument panel. While Weaver and Ames had pointed them out to her and she'd asked questions, her knowledge had been shallow, not built on mechanical understanding. The classroom sessions with Bobby had opened up an entire new universe to her.

"Controls, check. Instruments, check. Gas, sufficient for flight. Attitude"—she noted the aileron and rudder positions—"check." She did a run-up for the engine check and, above the roar, shouted, "All set! Just need the flight instructor to take his seat and get strapped in. We are headed for blue skies."

It was comforting to know that Bobby could override any mistakes she made from his position behind her, but Mittie wanted to get everything right the first time. She bumped the plane across the grass, her neck tense, the muscles in her arms quivering from gripping the control wheel. Bump. Bump. *Nose up. Steady on the rudder. More throttle. Easy.* She braced for another bump, but it didn't come—just air between the earth and the wheels. Adrenaline swept through her. Her first takeoff! The exhilaration that pulsed through her equaled that of standing atop the Oriole's wing.

Time lost all meaning as she climbed higher and led with the rudder to bank. And when she nosed up, the wind was like a kiss on her cheeks. She kept an eye on the instruments as she went through the maneuvers she and Bobby had discussed. Unexpected pressure on the right rudder and an adverse yaw sent a momentary ripple of uncertainty through her. Either the ailerons or air currents around the tail were the cause, if she remembered correctly. She centered the rudder, and the plane leveled as wind played the wires leading from the struts. To Mittie, it sounded like a harp, the music of angels an arm's length away. She banked right and left, the biplane cutting through the sky with the ease of an eagle in flight. This—this!— was what she dreamed of... riding the wind currents, feasting on atmospheric manna. Bobby tapped her on the shoulder, the signal for descent and landing. She wasn't nearly ready but ticked off the landing checklist in her head and began the descent, her eyes peeled for the runway. When she found it and checked her bearing along with her speed and altitude, she said a prayer and approached the earth.

It came up faster than she expected, with the first contact a bounce that would have ejected her if she hadn't been strapped in. A few more bounces while she cut the fuel mixture and kept the rudder centered. When the tail skid touched down, the plane slowed, thrusting her forward, and she nearly choked the engine. Poor Bobby. She'd no doubt rearranged his insides by now.

They rolled to a stop, and she puffed out her cheeks, releasing the breath she'd been holding. She closed her eyes and leaned back.

"Jolly good for the first go." Bobby's voice was inches from her ear. "Cut the engine and come down to talk about it."

They strode shoulder to shoulder, Bobby in his natty black leather flight jacket and her with collar turned up, helmet and goggles in hand—two aviators coming in from a day's work. She wasn't sure if her feet ever touched the ground.

In the classroom, Bobby commended her on handling the takeoff and adverse yaw caused by airflow on the tail. "You reacted with good instincts, but your landing is in need of some practice."

"You sure you're not bruised from that bumpy ending?"

"I've encountered worse. I could have taken over and smoothed it out, but since the only danger you posed was the possible loss of my breakfast, I let you ride it out." He went over the approach to landing—recommending elevation and speed—and fuel mixtures again. He consulted a black memo book he pulled from his pocket. "How about every Monday and Friday for the next few weeks, if you're free?"

"I'm free. What I'm worried about is whether you'll have time to recover by Friday."

When he smiled, the blue in his eyes was deeper than she remembered. "I have nerves of steel, which is fortuitous since I have three more students today."

That evening, her dad asked about her flying lesson at the dinner table.

"In a word, spectacular—all except the landing, which Bobby assured me would improve with time."

Her mother raised her eyebrows. "You know I'm still worried about your flying—"

"Which you never fail to remind me of, Mother."

"You didn't let me finish. What I wanted to say is that I hoped you were getting along well with Bobby. He's such a nice young man and from an upstanding family. Any romantic sparks between you?"

"You know I'm not interested in that sort of thing. He's polite and professional. And part genius, I think." Admitting that she found him attractive would only encourage her mother, and Mittie's priority was flying, not walking down the church aisle.

"Perhaps you should invite him to dinner again. He's surely lonely being new here and not yet acquainted."

"Honestly, Mother. I don't need a matchmaker. Or a match. I do, however, need a couple of dresses for the Lindbergh visit—one for the greeting reception and a gown for the dinner at the Crystal Ballroom."

"Our invitation just came in Saturday's post, so I'll need something, too."

Her dad cleared his throat. "Before you go clearing out the bank account on a shopping spree, there's something I should mention. And before I do, I want you to know, sugar, that I'm not placing blame on you."

Buck Lamberson. Her fists curled into knots as she waited for her daddy to give her the latest blow.

"Jake Ford paid me a visit this afternoon. He's taking April Showers and Gingersnap to another trainer."

Relief and horror swirled into a cocktail of emotions. "No! Did he give a reason?"

"Apparently he wasn't keen on Saturday's performance. I assured him we're looking at every angle, but he was quite determined."

"Have you talked with Toby and Ogilvie? What do they say about April Showers?"

"I have, and I'm completely satisfied with their answers. The veterinarian gave a clean bill of health. Ford will send someone with a horse box to transfer the mares."

"I'm dumbfounded. Mr. Ford was upset at the show, but I thought he would cool down. It seems sudden and rather mean to me."

"I know what you are saying, but I've been in this business long enough to learn that owners of show ponies have big egos and pocketbooks to match. Winning is the only thing that matters to them."

Mittie wanted to ask how he could be in such a business, but she already knew the answer. He liked winning as well. And in her gut, Mittie knew she did, too.

Her dad smiled. "Not that you two shouldn't have new dresses, but we may have to watch the finances more closely for a while."

"Daddy, I have scads of things in my closet. I'll make do."

Her mother let out a soft sigh. "I suppose I will, too."

CHAPTER 10

"That's it, then." The driver latched the trailer when April Showers and Gingersnap were loaded. Mittie was disappointed that Mr. Ford hadn't come himself so she could have one last chance to persuade him to change his mind.

Regret lolled in her gut. Losing one client wasn't the end of the world, but it felt like she'd let her daddy down somehow. "Yes, that's it. If you don't mind my asking, who will the new trainer be?"

"Reckon that's none of your concern. My business is with Ford." He stepped around her and up into the cab of the truck.

All right, then. It wasn't like she wouldn't find out. The trainer was always listed in the show programs. She stalked off and nearly bumped into Toby.

"Sorry. I didn't see you. Were you looking for me?"

"Yes, ma'am, I was. Just checking to see if you wanted to watch Gypsy in the ring today."

"Nothing I'd like better."

"I'm sorry about Mr. Ford's horses."

"No need to be. You did a good job. Now let's see what a real champion looks like."

While Toby took Gypsy through the paces, Mittie offered encouragement and asked to see the slow gait again. Like the faster-paced rack, where no two hooves touched the ground at the same time, the slow gait was a beautiful four-beat rhythm to watch, mesmerizing in its effect. Adoration welled up in Mittie's chest. The hard work and patience had paid off. Gypsy yielded well to the commands yet was showy when she needed to be. Refining her underlying talents and practice—worlds of practice—had paid off.

The same things Mittie needed if she was going to succeed as an aviatrix.

She called Weaver at Bowman Field when she returned to the house and asked if he could take her up in his plane.

"I'm on a tight schedule today, but there was a fella asking about you earlier. The one with the stunt show."

"Ames Dewberry? Is he still there?"

"That's the one. Hang on; I'll check and see if his plane is still here."

When he returned and confirmed that the Oriole was indeed there, she asked him to send a message to Ames that she'd be right out.

Half an hour later, she found Ames, Lester, and Shorty in a hangar playing poker.

"Hey, Mittie. Give me a kiss and I'll deal you in."

"You'd be sorry. I'm wicked with a deck of cards. Never met a barnstormer I couldn't beat. What are you betting?"

"High stakes. Ante up for a nickel."

"Go ahead with your game, fellas. I wouldn't want to take all your money. You might not take me up in *Trixie* if I did that."

Shorty looked at his cards and folded. "Smart girl. These bums cheat."

Ames tossed a nickel out and told Lester he called. "Shorty, I don't cheat. The problem, as I see it, is that you don't know a straight from a rattlesnake."

"I know I got a hole gnawed in my stomach from starvation. I'm going to find something to eat." He disappeared through the wide doors of the hangar, swallowed by the sunlight.

Lester laid down his cards. "A pair of aces."

Ames smiled. "You're beat, sport. Two pair. Queens over deuces." He raked in the pile of nickels and turned to Mittie. "I'm glad you showed up. We're making a run over by Fort Knox next weekend for some barnstorming. Think you're ready for your debut on the wings?"

Her heart stopped. Was she ready? How would she know if she didn't try? But it was the weekend before Lindy's visit. Her questions must've shown by the challenging look Ames gave her—so much for the poker face.

She jutted her chin up and smiled. "Gotcha. You thought I was going to say no, didn't you? When do we leave?"

She had a lesson with Bobby scheduled for Friday, the day the Patriots would leave to "rattle the bushes" and get people enthused about the show on Saturday. "Is it all right if I meet you on Friday evening? I have a flying lesson that morning."

Ames gave her a curious look.

"You remember; I told you about Bobby York, the flight instructor here—"

"Guess it slipped my mind. Think you can get out of it?"

"Probably, but I need the flight hours to get my license. If it's a problem..."

"No, no problem." He winked at her. "This time."

Mittie sidled up to him. "I'm ready when y'all are."

Mittie woke with sore muscles the next day. Her arms and legs were achy from hoisting herself onto the top wing of the Oriole a dozen times, but every time she stepped out onto the wing and looked up, the breath of heaven kissed her. A warm buzz carried her through the days that followed as she made phone calls for the Lindbergh publicity committee and updated the newspaper on the details of Lindbergh's visit—all of which Mittie worked in between her morning duties at MG Farms, flying sessions with Bobby, and wing-walking practice with the Patriots.

She was almost grateful that she and her mother hadn't scheduled a shopping trip for a new gown for the Lindbergh dinner. On the Tuesday before Lindy was due in Louisville, her mother asked if she'd decided what to wear.

"I was hoping you could rummage through the wardrobe with me—you always have good instincts."

The scent of cedar wafted in the air when her mother opened the wardrobe doors and started riffling through the dresses. She pulled out one Mittie had worn to a friend's wedding the summer before.

Her mother handed it to her. "I don't remember this, but it must be yours. No one else wears red quite the way you do."

She reminded her mother of the occasion and held it against her as she looked in the cheval mirror. It was still stylish with a drop waist and rhinestone band that circled her hips. The tiered skirt was made for dancing and would be perfect for the dinner at the Crystal Ballroom.

She slipped out of her clothes and wriggled into the dress. "Maybe I'll entice Mr. Lindbergh onto the dance floor."

Her mother fanned her fingers before her face. "He would be quite the catch, but let's not get our hopes up. There's quite the competition for landing him, you know."

"I'm only hoping for a single dance, not a marriage proposal. And it's flying I want to discuss if I get the chance." She took another look in the mirror. "This will work fine. Maybe Nell has a headpiece that will go with it."

"Speaking of flying, have you perchance thought to invite Bobby to dinner like we talked about? We've hardly entertained at all since the wedding."

"I don't think he needs us to help him out socially. He seems quite capable of that."

"We owe it to his parents to extend our hospitality. You seem to have lost that sense of propriety since you've been running with those circus performers."

Mittie burst out laughing. "And before you know it, I'm going to be the painted lady who parades around with a live boa constrictor around my neck."

"Why do you do that?"

"Do what?"

"You know what. You bristle at every suggestion I have and then taunt me."

"I was only teasing you. I sought your opinion for what to wear to the dinner, didn't I? And you've gotten the wrong impression about the Flying Patriots. An air circus is not like the Ringling Brothers, although the atmosphere is quite festive. No animals. No freak show. Just good all-American fun."

"Dangerous fun. I read the newspapers."

"Yes, there is some danger involved. I won't pretend that there's not. But there was a time when people scoffed at motor cars and the dangers with them. In a few years, you'll be able to ride an airplane to New York City and be there in half the time the train takes. I find it exciting and exhilarating to be a part of aviation history."

"If only you would pour that passion into something more suitable, I would rest better at night."

"Maybe it would be a good idea to invite Bobby over. Perhaps he can put your mind at rest."

"This Sunday would be lovely, dear. We'll have Delores and George Porter and Evangeline and Granville. That would be a lively mix. Perhaps Nell and Quentin, too."

She groaned inwardly. A quiet dinner had grown into a full-fledged party, and it was the evening before Lindbergh flew in. Mittie would be a mass of nerves, but the pleading look on her mother's face told her it was more than just having Bobby to dinner. Her mother missed Iris, whose letters were filled with news of the home Hayden was having built for her and her whirling social calendar.

"Bobby's giving me an extra lesson tomorrow. I'll see if he's free Sunday evening."

After her flight with Bobby the following day, Mittie said, "I believe I owe you a cup of tea. Would you care to join me in the canteen?"

"As luck would have it, I do have some time. The mechanic needs to do some routine checks on the plane and would probably appreciate if I didn't peer over his shoulder."

In the canteen, Bobby nodded toward one of the Lindbergh flyers on the wall. "Quite the excitement for Louisville. You'll be there, I would imagine."

"Actually I'm on the welcoming committee and will be presenting him with roses that represent our fair city. Are you coming?"

He nodded. "Weaver gave me a ticket to the dinner and said he would give me an introduction. Lindbergh's a very humble man, I hear. One of few words."

"I'm hoping to get an audience with him, too." She laughed. "Sounds like we're talking about the Pope, doesn't it?"

Bobby sipped his tea, then leaned in and said, "I've been meaning to call your parents. My father's asked if I'd done my duty and paid them a visit."

"Funny you should say that. Mother's been after me to ask you to come to dinner. She specifically asked about this Sunday. Are you free?"

He ran his tongue over his lower lip. "Your mother's idea, is it?"

"And mine, of course. I didn't mean to imply—"

"Of course not; I was giving you a bit of a tease."

She wrinkled her nose. "Well, then, can we count on you for dinner? Mother is asking a few others as well and thinks it will be a lively evening."

"I'd be delighted."

"Mother will be, too." She rose and Bobby followed suit. "Sunday, then, around seven?"

He nodded. "May I walk you to your motor car?"

"Thanks, but I need to ask Ames a question about the barnstorming on Saturday. You should come and watch; it's my first attempt at wing walking," she said as they walked to the door.

"There's nothing I'd like more, but I have plans on Saturday." Bobby held the door for her. Once outside he said, "I did a little wing walking myself when I was at Brooklands in Surrey."

"Really? How did you like it?"

"It's quite the sport, but it upset the girl I was with at the time, so I gave it up. Sort of wish I'd kept at it."

"This girl—someone special?"

"She was." And with that he strode toward the parking area. Mittie would have loved to know more, but something told her she'd learned all she was going to from Bobby York.

CHAPTER 11

People arrived early for the barnstorming, streaming in from all directions like ants gathering for a picnic. Mittie wore jodhpurs and a lightweight flight jacket as she circulated, answered questions, and helped gather money for the airplane rides the Patriots were giving. The activity kept her from thinking about the tangle of nerves in her stomach.

When Ames signaled her that it was time, Mittie dashed to her car and changed into a pair of white trousers and a body-hugging red blouse dotted with rhinestones. She strapped on a pair of low-heeled shoes that would give her traction on the wing and help her stay balanced.

She waited out of sight until Ames picked up a megaphone. "Ladies and gentlemen, not only will you see some heart-stopping stunts with the planes, but we've a special treat for you today. Please welcome our wing-walking wonders."

Buster ran up from one edge of the crowd as Mittie approached from the other. The throng whooped and hollered, wolf whistles shrill above the sound of the cheers. Five minutes later, they were high above the rolling bluegrass where rivers meandered and converged and splintered off again. Ames started with a few easy rolls to get the crowd warmed up, then made a wide circle out of view as Lester and Shorty did their first stunts. Stalls and spirals followed, and like kittens at play, the planes raced and frolicked, slowed and then sprinted again.

Ames nosed up toward silver-bellied clouds that shifted lazily, breathing it seemed and bloating a bit more with each inhalation. The roar of the engine filled her ears, the thrill of the skies too much for her heart to hold.

Ames tapped Mittie on the shoulder to signal that it was time for her to get ready. She checked their altitude, then released the strap across her shoulders and took a deep breath. A cloud shadow passed them, creating a small updraft that rocked the plane. When Ames smoothed it out, Mittie crawled from the cockpit and onto the underwing. At the right altitude, she shuffled toward the strut, the simple maneuver that had her heart in her throat two weeks ago now familiar as she moved effortlessly toward it and made a bow. The wind tousled her hair, but she leaned into it and counted to twenty under her breath. Now for the top wing. She pulled up and over to the count of three and waved to the crowd. Her steps were light as she strolled from one wing tip to the other, then back to the center where she raised her hands in a victory gesture. Still facing forward, she made a last-minute decision to add a few dance steps. She kicked her heels back and waved her hands in synchronized rhythm as Ames descended further. She inhaled and moved to midwing, swinging her hips, arms outstretched for balance until she was over the mark where she would lower herself and take a final bow.

A shadow appeared in her side vision, startling her. She whipped her head in that direction, a squawk splitting the air, as flapping black wings aimed straight for her face. She screamed as her feet rushed from under her, and there was nothing but air between her and the bluegrass below.

★ ★ ★

When she opened her eyes, she expected to see Saint Peter, but it was her daddy's face that leaned in close to hers. Her eyelids fluttered as she tried to focus, but it took too much effort. The next time she opened them, a stranger had one hand on her wrist and a stern expression on his face.

"Looks like she's out of the woods. Lucky for her she's alive at all."

She shut her eyes again. She was alive, but a pounding pressure inside her head and an ache in her left shoulder told her something wasn't right. Sleep overtook the pain.

Doors opened and creaked closed. Shoes shuffled across the floor of her mind. Whispers. A sea of black again claimed her.

Fingers pried her eyelids apart, and an intense light filled her head. "Good pupil response." She didn't know whether that was good or bad.

A butterfly brushed her forehead, soft as a feather. She opened her eyes to see it and peered into bottomless dark eyes. She smiled and whispered, "Ames."

"Yes, doll, it's me. And right over here's your mom and dad."

She blinked and found her mother's face. "Mother. You okay?"

"Of course not. How could I ever be okay when my daughter has tumbled from the sky like a sack of potatoes?"

"Sarah." Her daddy's voice was gentle but firm. He leaned over and smiled. "We're just thankful it wasn't more serious."

It was serious enough. Mittie drifted back off. When she awoke again, her daddy called for the doctor, who told her she'd broken her left collarbone and had a mild concussion.

"You'll have to remain in the hospital under observation tonight, and we've strapped your arm to your chest to keep the broken edges of your clavicle from grating against one another."

She moved in the bed and winced, determined not to let the pain show on her face. "I can go home tomorrow, then?"

"Only if there are no complications." The doctor's gray pock-marked face offered dismal expectation.

"I'll be fine." The stormy look from her mother kept her from saying she'd be home in time to see Lindbergh.

That evening Bobby popped in and brought her a box of pecan clusters.

"How did you know they were my favorite?"

"I didn't. The lady at the counter picked them out." He had a sheepish look. "Actually, I bought one for you and your mother and was going to bring them to dinner tomorrow night."

"I guess I upset that royally."

"There will be other dinners. I'm just glad you're going to be okay."

The door creaked open, and Ames entered. "Sorry—hope I'm not interrupting."

When Mittie turned, a pain shot through her shoulder. "Ouch." She blew out a breath through pursed lips, then smiled. "No, you're not interrupting." She looked from Bobby to Ames. "Have you two met?"

Bobby extended his hand. "Bobby York."

Ames shook his hand and introduced himself. Mittie closed her eyes to will away a sharp spasm that had come with the pain. Bobby asked if she needed anything.

"I'll be okay in a bit. The nurse gave me an injection right before you came in."

Bobby said he needed to be going and told Ames it was a pleasure to meet him. Ames nodded and waited until Bobby left before lean-ing over and kissing Mittie on the cheek.

"I'd have been back sooner, but I had to make a couple of phone calls. I hate to leave you, doll, but the Patriots and I are pulling out tomorrow. The folks in Nebraska asked if we could come early."

"I guess you'll be looking for a new stunt girl while you're gone."

"Nah, I like the one I have, but it looks like the next show will be short one wing walker."

"As long as you keep my spot open."

"Mittie Humphreys, you may be a grown woman, but you're still my daughter, and I forbid you to even think of such a thing."

"Hello, Mother. I didn't hear you come in."

"I've never left my station outside the door."

"What? Are you afraid I'll sneak out and do something foolish?"

"You've already done that." She looked at Ames and lifted her chin. "I appreciate your concern for Mittie, and you seem like a nice young man, but I hope this has been a reminder for both of you about the danger of airplanes."

"Yes, ma'am. I'm sure Mittie will have plenty of time to think about that. She's lucky to have a mother who's concerned for her welfare."

"Not just her welfare. Her life."

"Yes, ma'am. And no one wants to keep her alive more than I do." He leaned over and gave Mittie another kiss. "I'll give you a call when I'm back in town."

"I miss you already."

"Don't take any wooden nickels." He offered his hand to her mother, and it was clear that it took all the propriety she could gather to shake his hand. "Take care of her, Mrs. Humphreys."

"I will do precisely that."

Mittie let the morphine take her into dreams where winged creatures flew at her and carnival barkers waved bystanders into a tent to see the woman who could fly.

★ ★ ★

Mittie awoke with beads of sweat dampening her skin and a gnawing in her stomach. She learned if she kept her eyes closed, she
didn't have to face the anxious eyes of her parents, the ones who'd
given her life and indulged her every whim. She'd repaid them time
and again with impulsive actions that had brought nothing but grief.

Her daddy caressed her arm, and when she looked at him, the
deep tanned lines of his face broke into a half smile.

"I'm sorry, Daddy, to cause you so much trouble."

"There's no need to apologize, sugar."

"But there is. My whole life I've done nothing but disappoint
you with my foolishness when all I truly wanted to do was make
you proud of me, of who I am."

"Is a fish sorry for having scales and not fur? You have to be true
to the way God made you, and when I see your eyes light up when
you talk about flying, I am proud."

"But Mother..."

He winked. "She'll come around."

On Sunday morning, a nurse handed her a glass medicine cup
and a tumbler of water. "The doctor says if this takes care of your
pain, we can send you home this afternoon."

A shiver cascaded down her arms as she put the medicine cup to
her lips and let the bitter liquid slide down her throat. *Laudanum.*
The elixir her daddy had taken for his back. It burned a bitter path
to her stomach.

Home had never looked so good as it did when her daddy drove
the Bentley through the stone pillars of Morning Glory Farms on
Sunday afternoon. Her mother guided her up the stairs to her
room where the table by the velvet wingback held an assortment of
amusements in easy reach—fashion magazines; writing paper, ink,

and a fountain pen; an embroidery hoop with a stamped linen tea towel and skeins of thread.

She turned to her mother. "Bertha thought of everything, didn't she?"

"I gave her a few suggestions, but I know how restless you can get, so I wanted you to have alternatives when you got bored."

"It's sweet, although embroidering with one hand might be a little tricky with my arm strapped to my chest like this." Even dressing had proved a challenge since her blouse wouldn't button over her immobilized arm. "How long did the doctor say I had to wear this mummy contraption?"

"Four weeks. And your left hand is free, so I don't see why you couldn't hold the hoop with it and work the thread with your right hand."

Mittie nodded. Since she'd never taken to embroidery when she had two good arms, she doubted she would attempt now. Her mother was trying to be helpful, but it was an odd dance between them. A mother in control, desperate to be needed. Mittie, the daughter who wanted to do everything herself. Four weeks? She wasn't sure she could survive a single day.

Her mother folded back the summer coverlet and sheets. "Ready to get in bed?"

"Not yet."

The dance continued.

"Ring for Bertha when you are, then."

Mittie sat in the chair and peered at the sky—the one that would deliver Charles Lindbergh in less than twenty-four hours. An ache coiled in her chest, different from the grating bones of her clavicle. Deeper. An ache that laudanum couldn't fix.

Tears welled up in her eyes, her throat constricted with sobs she refused to relinquish. She only had herself to thank for missing Lucky Lindy.

The door of her room squeaked. She turned to see who'd come but saw instead the hem of her mother's dress retreating before the door clicked shut.

Apricot rays filtered through the lace curtains of her bedroom window. Mittie shifted positions and nearly screamed when a fiery pain pierced her clavicle. She counted slowly to ten. Then with a gulp of air, she sat up and swung her legs over the edge of the bed. Another count of ten to recover, then she rose and padded barefoot to the window.

Figures bustled this way and that, some taking horses to the paddock, others carrying buckets of rations and water. And in the arena, Toby, his face the same dark as Gypsy's mane, sat erect in the cutback saddle, reins held with just the right amount of tension. Gypsy lifted her forefeet high with grace and precision. Mittie rested her chin on the rail of the lower window sash and looked heavenward. Not a cloud in the sky.

"Mittie." Her daddy's voice behind her. "Just coming to check on you, sugar."

Mittie turned to face him, her face wet with tears. "Morning, Daddy."

"I didn't expect to see you up."

"I'm usually in the barns by now. Old habit of mine."

"Can I send you up a cup of coffee? Have Ruby fix you a tray?"

"Nope. I'm coming down. You think Mother will mind if I'm not dressed?"

"It will be a relief to her just to see you up and about."

"I don't see any reason to lie about all day. Or busy myself with needlework." She pointed to the untouched things beside the chair. "I'll read horse journals or go over the books with you. A girl has to earn her keep, you know."

"Oh, Mittie." He shook his head and left.

Ten minutes later, she'd brushed her teeth, pinched her cheeks to put some color in them, painted on Clara Bow cupid lips, and made it to the breakfast room.

Her mother's eyes grew round. "If you don't look wide awake and smart today. How did you sleep?"

"Like a lamb. I'm starving."

Her mother pushed her chair back and went to the sideboard. "Here, let me fix your plate."

Mittie finished off bacon, eggs, grits, and toast and said she'd like some oatmeal.

"You're going to have to watch your figure, since you're not going to be as active for the next few weeks."

"I don't know about that. I think Ogilvie will take great delight in finding chores for me."

Her daddy cleared his throat. "I'm sure he would if he were still employed here."

"What? When did this happen?"

"He submitted his resignation Saturday. Effective immediately."

"Did he say why?"

"He got a better offer." He kept his head lowered and shoveled in a forkful of eggs.

"What aren't you telling me?"

Mittie looked at her mother. Pinched lips. Nostrils flaring.

Her daddy swallowed, his knuckles white from gripping his fork. "He's gone to Buck Lamberson's stables. Same place as April Showers and Gingersnap."

Mittie threw down her napkin, the sudden movement sending an electric jolt from her collarbone to her toes. "I knew it! I knew something was going on in West Virginia."

The furrows in her daddy's forehead deepened. "You had knowledge of this?"

"It was just a suspicion. When I went for a lemonade, I saw

Ogilvie talking to Mr. Lamberson. Arguing, I thought. But when Ogilvie saw me, he left Lamberson and made a crude remark about me checking up on him. He was no doubt trying to deflect me so I would forget who I'd seen him with."

"Was this before or after April Showers went in the show ring?"

"Right before. And then when April Showers placed dead last in her class, Mr. Ford came charging over and accused me...us...of doing a poor job."

Her mother said, "We believe Mr. Ford's made a grave error and was intentionally led to believe our stable was inferior. We don't know what all transpired, but it appears that Lamberson and Ogilvie have colluded to lure Mr. Ford away."

Her dad nodded. "By rigging April Showers' performance most likely."

"Drugging?"

A big sigh from her daddy. "That would be my guess."

"But Toby was with the horses all day, and I'm sure they couldn't have convinced him to go along with their scheme."

"Your daddy talked to Toby again. He said Ogilvie offered to spell him for a few minutes while he went for a hot dog. He said it was ten minutes at most."

Mittie nodded. "Plenty of time to inject the horse or slip the horse a treat with something in it."

"I've called the vet to review the report he gave us."

"The vet that Ogilvie called." Mittie's appetite vanished, replaced by a sick feeling. "The question remains: Why?"

"The same reason Lamberson does everything. He won't rest until he's brought your father to his knees."

"For which you have me to thank."

Her daddy shook his head. "No, sugar. It was never your fault. Nor Dobbs' really. He was a harebrained teenager who thought he was invincible. Like someone else I know."

Mittie shrank from his gaze. Whether he placed the blame on her or not, Dobbs' accident still weighed heavily on her.

But it didn't alter the matter at hand. "As long as we let him badger us, he'll just keep right on."

"I know it's not a popular concept, but I do believe that turning the other cheek is the right thing to do in this case."

A knot twisted in Mittie's gut. "For once, I disagree completely."

"Which is your choice, sugar."

Her mother patted her arm. "We didn't want to tell you at all in your condition."

"My condition is fine, Mother. Or at least it will be. I'm going to lie down for a while."

"Sounds like a good idea. Your mother and I thought that we might go for a drive later. We'd like you to come if you're feeling up to it."

"I'll see."

A drive with her parents. On the day she was missing the *Spirit of St. Louis* and the chance to see Colonel Lindbergh in the flesh. If this was going to be the new norm for her, Mittie knew she would go mad. But staying in the house would be worse.

Two hours later, she'd borrowed one of her daddy's shirts that was roomy enough to fit over her arm anchored to her chest and pulled on a skirt. A breeze came through the open windows of the Bentley, and as she gulped in buckets of the fresh air, her head cleared.

Instead of rumbling over the country roads, though, her daddy declared the highway would give a smoother ride. They went through Rigby, then turned west toward Louisville. Mittie rested her head against the back of the seat and when her daddy turned onto Taylorsville Road, she knew what the intrigue was. A wave of gratitude flooded her chest.

"Daddy, you sly fox," she said as they took the turnoff to the airfield where Lindy was due within the hour.

A security officer stopped them, and when her daddy told them his name, the man directed them to park near the runway.

"How did you get such plum treatment?" Mittie asked.

Her mother turned and smiled. "Your daddy called Mr. Weaver. Seems he thinks you're pretty special."

"I don't know how to thank you. Both of you."

Her dad turned off the motor and said, "Thank your mother. It was all her idea."

The crowd cheered when it was announced that Lucky Lindy was due in any minute. Mittie, pitifully unfashionable in her daddy's shirt and a skirt that had seen better days, let her dad help her from the car.

When the *Spirit of St. Louis* was a mere speck, no larger than the bird that had upended Mittie from the Oriole's wing, people went mad with shouts, their arms extended upward, pointing to the most famous man in the universe.

A cloud of dust roiled up as the wheels touched down, but the landing was as smooth as fresh cream. Mittie couldn't take her eyes from the door where Lindbergh would emerge. A set of steps was rolled to the silver beauty of a plane, and almost at once, Lindy stepped out and waved to his eager admirers. At the foot of the steps, the welcoming committee greeted him. Victor Booth and his wife waited in the Silver Ghost at the end of the path that Lindbergh, bareheaded and taller than Mittie expected, now walked.

A few dozen feet from the plane, Lindbergh stopped and bent his head toward Weaver, who was no doubt informing him of the day's plan. Lindy nodded and stroked his chin with one hand. Then rather than continue on the expected path, he veered off and came straight toward Mittie, Weaver at his side. Her heart bounced from her chest to her throat, its beating that of horses' hooves at full gallop.

Weaver spoke first. "Colonel Lindbergh, Mittie Humphreys, one of your greatest fans."

Lindy offered his hand. "My pleasure. I'm told you had a small accident with an airplane."

"Wing walking, actually. I apologize for my appearance; I didn't think I would make it out today, but then my parents surprised me, and well, here we are." *What a babbling idiot.*

"I'm glad you came out. Do you fly as well?"

"I'm a novice, but yes, I hope to be in the cockpit again soon. Thank you for making Louisville part of your tour and especially for greeting me."

"My pleasure." He nodded at Mittie's parents and turned to go.

"Colonel Lindbergh, may I ask you a question?"

He swiveled back around and raised his eyebrows.

Mittie blurted out, "To what do you owe your success?"

"Dedication, of course, but more than that, being willing to take a risk. Without risking our very souls, we miss out on the greatest joys of life."

"Thank you, sir. I'll remember that."

"You might also consider changing from wing walking to parachuting. The landings are much softer."

Mittie stood, feet planted to the ground, as he walked back to the laid-out path and stepped into Victor's Silver Ghost. She watched him perch atop the back seat and wave to the crowd as the Rolls crawled past the onlookers. Then the man who risked everything by strapping himself into the seat of an airplane and flying the Atlantic disappeared over the horizon.

CHAPTER 12

Autumn 1927

The Kentucky State Fair featured six glorious days of variety shows with trick bears and jugglers, canning demonstrations, acres of quilts and garden produce, carnival rides, and the sweet smell of cotton candy that promised a taste of heaven at only a quarter a box. And it was home to the World's Championship Horse Show, the premier American saddlebred event in the country.

Mittie stroked Gypsy's neck, her coat groomed to perfection, her full mane and tail vibrant. "I'm counting on you, Gypsy. You've got it in you; I know you do. Today, you'll strut like the beauty you are." She didn't want to let on how much a win today would mean, but she thought Gypsy could sense it. Toby, too. She'd been unable to sleep after their win in the three-year-old class the day before and unable to tear herself away from Gypsy today. But it all boiled down to the next hour. If Gypsy won—and there was a good chance of that since she'd done well in several local shows—the prize money would enable her to pay her daddy back for Dobbs' latest operation and contribute to the family coffers.

Mittie had wrestled for a month with her embarrassment over

the wing-walking accident and the straits it put her parents in. If anything good had come of it, it was that she had time to focus on what she really wanted. In her gut, she knew she couldn't give up flying over one stupid incident any more than Gypsy could forget she was a saddlebred meant for the show ring. And Colonel Lindbergh's words were never more than a heartbeat away. *Risk.* She'd done that with wing walking, which ended poorly. And she'd come to the conclusion that risk was twofold: that of a fool and that which was calculated.

It was a blessing of sorts that Ogilvie had gone. It gave Mittie the chance to smooth things out with her dad by taking over the foreman office and the duties she could do with one arm. As she'd long suspected, Ogilvie had been a careless manager. In four weeks, she'd let two grooms go who were loafing and stirring up trouble in the barns, and she'd found discrepancies in the feed orders— money paid out without inventory to match. She and her dad surmised Ogilvie had pocketed more than his salary. The one thing she hadn't been able to find out was how April Showers had been tampered with. The veterinary service stood by its claim, and since Ogilvie had engaged them, there was really nothing else to do outside of calling them liars. It niggled, but she was too busy to dwell on it.

Ames surprised her one weekend when he'd shown up in a secondhand runabout he bought with the proceeds from Nebraska. They'd taken a long drive across the river and eaten in a little café in Indiana where she'd told him about Lindbergh's visit and her decision to give up wing walking.

"A little gun-shy, are you?"

She pointed to her still-immobile arm. "Skittish, but not about flying. If anything, I'm more determined than ever to pursue my pilot's license and start entering some of the challenge races the newspapers report."

He scratched his head. "The only problem I see is that you're stuck running your daddy's farm—"

"Temporary, my dear Watson. Daddy's put ads in the journals and spread the word that we're looking for an overseer. Hopefully by the time my collarbone is mended and I'm out of this straightjacket, we'll have found one. How about you? Any more barnstorming shows lined up?"

"A couple. It's not the same without you, though, doll."

"It's nice to know I'm missed." She tucked her chin toward her shoulder and puckered her lips. She smacked the air and whispered, "And I've missed you terribly, too."

Gypsy nickered, pulling Mittie out of her daydream about Ames. Mittie scratched under her chin and Gypsy responded by running her muzzle along Mittie's cheek. When the announcement was made for the horses to take their places for the warm-up, Toby took the reins from Mittie and led Gypsy to the mounting area. Mittie's palms sweated.

"Go get 'em, Toby!" No last-minute instructions or change of tactics. Gypsy knew what to do.

With a knot in her throat, Mittie went to the section her daddy had reserved for the family. They were all there—Grandmother, Aunt Evangeline with Granville and Caroline, Nell and Quentin, her parents.

"Everything all right with Gypsy?" her dad whispered when she slid into the seat next to him.

"She's in fine spirits. Ready to go."

"That's what I like to hear." His chin jutted up and he waved someone over. Bobby York. "I hope you don't mind that I offered him our spare seat."

"No, I'm glad you did." She greeted him, and after a round of introductions, Bobby sat beside her mother. Behind him, Caroline chattered and leaned over to ask if he'd like some of her cotton candy. Mittie didn't hear what he said as organ music ushered in the beginning of the show and the welcome by the announcer.

Mittie kept her eyes riveted on the first horse and its rider, a contender they'd seen at the Lexington show in the spring. Her daddy leaned over, elbow on knee with his hand cupping his chin, mentally calculating each point the judges would be looking at. Mittie relaxed into her seat. A beautiful stallion, but no match for Gypsy. The same for the next two entrants, but the fourth sent a chill down her spine. April Showers.

She nudged her dad. "Did you know about this?"

"Just found out when they posted the finalists. I didn't want to upset you while you were with Gypsy."

He was right—she would've had kittens if she'd known. The qualifying list wasn't posted until scores of the morning and early afternoon classes were tallied. Mittie had known April Showers was showing, but since she'd not left Gypsy all day, she hadn't heard the results. She wondered if Toby knew.

And April Showers was not performing like a horse who'd been dead last in West Virginia. Instead, the mare circled the arena in complete command. And the crowd loved her. Mittie's stomach twisted, her limbs growing numb as she waited for Gypsy to enter. She locked her fingers together in her lap and sat up straighter, determined not to let the queasiness in her belly show.

"Gypsy. Morning Glory Farms."

Toby sat tall and elegant astride Gypsy, the tails of his riding tuxedo resting on Gypsy's point of hip as he rode on the walk around the rail. His long gloved fingers held the reins taut but relaxed enough to let Gypsy do the work.

When all the horses were in the ring, the judges put them through the three natural gaits as a group—walk, trot, canter. Mittie knew that any moment, the judges would call for the slow gait and rack—the trained gaits Gypsy had taken to like it was child's play.

When the time came, Gypsy's muscles rippled, her head and tail erect, her heels lifting high. She made it seem effortless, the spirited nature she'd had from birth.

The horses were directed to change directions and repeat the gaits. Each time Gypsy passed a section, the crowd responded with enthusiasm. But clearly, April Showers was a favorite as well. The judges milled about the center of the ring, looking first at one entrant, then another and then called for the conformation check. Each rider removed the flat English saddle and held the reins while the judges ran their hands from the withers down the shoulders in front, moving along the sides and then to the back where the hindquarters were examined for form and proportion.

With a slight break in the action, Mittie chanced a look at her dad. His expression remained calm, stoic. Poker-faced. She wished she could hide her emotions as well. He looked at her momentarily and winked, then turned his eyes back to the ring. Her mother's hand rested on his leg, her fingers gripping his trousers. Mittie ached from the bones out, wishing she could jump from her seat and pace the aisles. But composure was expected.

She crossed her legs at the knee, then uncrossed them when her mother shot a frown her way. The wait was excruciating as minutes dragged like hours until at last the judges came together in a huddle. Decision time. Excitement vibrated like current down a wire. One by one the horses who weren't in the top three were pulled to the center of the ring until at last only Gypsy, April Showers, and a bay gelding remained.

Great silver bowls rested on the table in the center of the ring. When the judges went to collect them, the audience knew a winner had been chosen.

"First place and the 1927 Five-Gait World's Championship prize goes to April Showers of Lamberson Stables." Mittie didn't hear the rest. The smell of sawdust and horse sweat and defeat swirled in her head. And the next thing she knew, her daddy had his hand on her elbow, guiding her to the award box to receive the trophy for second place. She lifted her chin, a smile fixed to her face as she and her dad received the bowl together and thanked the judges. A stone smile graced her mother's lips as well. As Mittie waved to the spectators, a smirking figure in the front row locked eyes with her. Buck Lamberson. And beside him was Ogilvie with the sneer on his lips she knew too well. Her smile never wavered.

"More punch?" Bobby held up his empty glass. Bless him, he'd joined them for the reception that followed the show. She hadn't wanted to go and almost stayed at her Aunt Evangeline's house where they'd changed into evening wear. But her mother's insistence that she had been raised better than that won out.

She'd put on the flirty red dress meant for Lindbergh's dinner and the rhinestone headpiece that rested on her forehead. For all the rotten luck the dress had brought, she had half a mind to burn it. Thank goodness she had Bobby to keep her company for the dreadful evening.

"No more punch for me, thanks. I need to find Mr. Ford and offer my congratulations on April Showers' win."

"Bugger of a deal, but I know it's expected. Off you go, then, and I'd be honored if you'd spare me a dance before the night is over."

"I will. No, wait—I adore the song the band's playing now. I accept your offer." She was grateful for the excuse from having to face Mr. Ford.

He offered his arm and led her to the dance floor.

A few spins and Mittie lifted her eyebrows. "I didn't know you had such smooth rhythm."

"Comes from all those boarding school dances at Harrow when we had to button up and put on bow ties for the girls' school soirees."

"Don't you miss it?"

"Miss what?"

"England? Your life back there?"

"Now and again I'd like to pop in the pub and have a pint, but..." He hesitated like there was more he wanted to say, but the music ended and he thanked her for the dance. "I believe there was someone you needed to find." He smiled and drifted toward the circle where her dad stood talking with his colleagues. Rehashing the evening, no doubt. Mr. Ford wasn't among them.

She was sorry she hadn't been asked for another dance. She felt as rudderless as Bobby seemed at times. He was always obliging and proper, but other than talking about flying, they couldn't hit quite the right chord to get a conversation off the ground. Mittie ran her tongue across her bottom lip and with leaden feet went to find Mr. Ford.

She found her grandmother instead sitting at a table with a man with wavy silver hair and strong hands clasped before him. He had an oddly familiar look—a new distraction for her grandmother? Honestly, she was getting as bad as her mother, but there was no doubt: her grandmother was a handsome woman with a youthful sparkle about her.

"Mittie, you know Rex Kline, I believe."

"I don't believe we've met, although you look familiar."

He rose and pulled out the chair next to her grandmother for her. "Someone pointed you out at the show in West Virginia. I've been friends with your father and Cordelia for some time."

"You have a horse farm, then?" The name still wasn't one she knew, but then apparently her parents and grandmother had friends everywhere that she'd taken no notice of.

"Not my own, no."

Her grandmother cleared her throat. "He was with the Evans Farm in West Virginia. Mr. Evans passed recently, and his wife has decided to sell the farm and move to Atlanta to be near her grandchildren."

"So you're interested in buying the business."

"If that were possible, yes, but I can't afford it."

"Rex was their foreman, sharp as they come. I'm trying to talk him into putting in his application with us."

Mr. Kline twiddled his thumbs. "You are quite the temptress, Cordelia."

Her grandmother smiled. "I like to think I'm more a woman of sensible persuasion. Eli would jump at the chance to have you, and I'm sure Mittie would agree."

"Don't you just know it? If you're going to be in Louisville for a few days, please come out and at least look around."

"With both of you twisting my arm, it looks like I have no choice."

A shadow fell to Mittie's left. She turned to see Mr. Ford standing beside her. She jumped from her chair and extended her hand for a shake. "My apologies, sir, for not coming to find you earlier."

"Whatever for?"

"To congratulate you. April Showers was stunning in the ring today. You must be pleased with how things are going with Mr. Lamberson." She might as well lay it on thick.

"I only came to tell you that you'd dropped this on the dance floor." He handed her a rhinestone bauble that must have come detached from her headpiece.

"Why, thank you. I hadn't noticed it was missing."

He spun on his heels and strode away. So much for the art of being gracious. Or maybe those rules only applied to women. One thing she knew: a single defeat wasn't the end of the world.

Runner-up to world champion was nothing to sneeze at. Gypsy would have other chances, and if things worked out with Mr. Kline, she might be spending a lot more time in the sky instead of the stable. Her steps were light as she went to see if Bobby might give her another spin on the dance floor.

CHAPTER 13

Two weeks later, Rex Kline moved into the foreman's cottage. By mid-October, three clients from his former place of employment had sent their horses over, saying they'd rather stay with Kline than face uncertainty with the turnover of the West Virginia farm. It was the ebb and flow of the saddlebred industry but a nice windfall for Morning Glory Farms—and breathing room for Mittie as well. Gypsy was put on an off-season training program, maintaining her morning exercise but without the rigid pace of the show season.

Ames and the Patriots took their barnstorming act to Oklahoma, deeming it the most successful venture yet. Every time Ames called, Mittie hoped it was to say he was back in Louisville. The three-minute calls that cost him precious money were never long enough, and she spent hours recalling the taste of his lips, his hands circling her waist, the way the wind ruffled his hair. His latest news was that his air intake invention had been awarded a patent and garnered the interest of a manufacturer in Kansas City.

Mittie's mother left for Alabama to visit Iris, cheerful about the prospect. She invited Mittie to join her, but it was a half-hearted attempt. When Mittie declined, saying she'd rather resume her flying lessons while she still remembered what Bobby taught her, her mother seemed relieved. When she and her dad took her mother to the train, all her mother could talk about was shopping and the social occasions Iris had planned.

Mittie progressed through her training with Bobby and made her first solo flight without a hitch. She was only a few hours short of qualifying for her license when Bobby met her in the canteen one day and handed her a newspaper.

"Something that might interest you." He pointed to an article near the bottom of the page.

Aviation Competition Announced

An air rally sponsored by the joint aeronautic clubs of St. Louis and Kansas City will be held the last weekend in November. The two-day competition will feature several categories, including altitude records and fastest round-trip between St. Louis and Kansas City. Separate categories for women. Prize money to top finishers.

Questions snapped through Mittie's head like electricity. "Well, fiddlesticks. That's only a month away, and I'm still short on solo hours. Is it possible for me to qualify in time? And what about a plane? Do you have to own the plane you fly?" She could hardly ask her daddy to buy her one since she still felt indebted to him for Dobbs. She had the trust fund from Grandfather Humphreys—a tidy sum—but she wasn't sure she was ready to part with it just yet.

"Slow down. Let's take this one chunk at a time. I see no reason we can't get the rest of your solo hours in this week. We've covered everything that is likely to be on the knowledge test. There will be an oral exam by the examiner and the air test."

"But do you think I can pass?"

Bobby gave her a crooked grin. "I have every confidence you

will. If not, then I'm in the wrong line of work. I'll check on the plane ownership, but it's not unusual for pilots to borrow planes or secure a sponsor. The question is, do you want to try?"

"Get out! You know this is what I've been waiting for. *If* I'm considered."

"The competition may be tough—you do understand that, right?"

"Competition I can handle. And I don't even care if I win; it's taking that first step. You know how it is with horses. You train and groom them and set them up for their first outing to see how they do. You don't expect a first or even a second because you're building experience, giving them credibility. You take calculated risks."

Bobby's expression changed from thoughtful listening to one of amusement as she talked. She stopped and tossed her hair back. "What? Are you laughing at me?"

"Not at all. You remind me of the way I was when I discovered that flying was my passion."

"Why don't you enter, too? I could learn from you, and we could compare notes."

He shook his head. "Not my ball of string."

"I wonder if Ames would consider it."

Bobby stilled, his eyes narrowing. "He doesn't strike me as the type, either. He's flush with experience, but—"

"The prize would interest him. It doesn't say how much is being offered, but it's got to be better than what he makes barnstorming."

"Why don't you ask him, then? It does say it's an open competition." There was a brusqueness in his tone that told her to drop the subject.

Ames breezed into town on Friday, the Oriole slipping from the sky and onto the runway while Mittie was doing her postflight check. Bobby signed off on her flight and told her he'd learned more about the air competition. Because of the high level of interest, there would be a limit to the number of contenders based on when the applications were filed. Lindbergh's campaign to promote aviation was apparently working.

"I talked to my parents. Mother still thinks I'm putting my neck in a noose by flying, but Daddy's come around. Now I just have to qualify with the license so I can send in my application for the women's race."

"How does next week sound? An examiner will be here on the tenth."

Mittie blew out a long breath. "Perfect. Where do I sign up?"

"I've already put your name on the list."

Mittie threw her arms around Bobby's neck and kissed him on the cheek. "You're the berries, Bobby York!"

Behind her, someone cleared his throat. "I thought I was the berries. Guess that'll teach me to stay away so long."

"Ames! I thought I saw you coming in, and it's high time you got back." She leaned into him, waiting for a kiss.

Instead, he bumped shoulders with her and held up his hands. "I didn't mean to interrupt."

"Don't be daft. Bobby has the most wonderful news. Tell him, Bobby."

"Not sure which news you mean."

Ames took off his leather helmet and swiped the back of his hand across his forehead. "Looks like this could go either way. Good news for the two of you could mean bad news for me."

Mittie said, "The news . . . our news is that I'm so close to qualifying for a license I can taste it. The examiner comes next week." She took in a deep breath. "And if I pass that means I qualify for a competitive air race in St. Louis in three weeks. Isn't that grand?"

"Really? That is swell news." He clapped Bobby on the back. "Good work, man." He kissed the tip of Mittie's nose. "Wanna tag

along while I put *Trixie* in the hangar? I need to check a couple of
knocks I heard."

"I'd love to." She thanked Bobby, who said he'd see her on
Monday. His tone was pleasant enough, but Mittie detected a momentary narrowing of his eyes when he told Ames to take it easy.
It might have been the sun that caused the squint, but it appeared
more like a challenge.

They celebrated Ames' return with a late-afternoon drive along
the Ohio River. Ames pulled his runabout off on a patch of dry
ground and asked if she'd like to take a walk. Mittie took his arm
when he offered it, the grassy slope along the water a carpet beneath
their feet. She gazed at his stubbled chin, memorizing the creases
around his eyes, letting the gentle slosh of the river pull her into the
quixotic moment.

"It's good to have you back. You can't imagine how I've missed
you."

"I wasn't sure when I saw you with York earlier."

"He's been swell about finding out the details for the rally. Then
he caught me by surprise, taking care to get me on the examiner's
list so I could qualify. I'd have shown you the same appreciation."

They stopped and watched as a tugboat chugged along, a foamy
brine lapping its edges. Upriver, a steamboat whistled like a sour
note on the church organ.

Ames encircled her in his arms, her back to his chest, his breath
warm on her neck. "I know you would have, doll. No fella likes to
have his thunder stolen."

She tilted her head back and asked what he meant.

"I just learned about the rally myself a few days ago and was going to surprise you. I stopped in St. Louis yesterday so I could get
you an entry form in case you got your license in time."

Warmth rushed over her as she turned to face Ames and wrapped
her arms around his waist. His lips found hers, soft and gentle, then

firmer as broad hands splayed across her back pulling her closer. When his mouth released hers, she whispered, "You're the berries, Ames Dewberry."

They both chuckled at the echo of her words and found the other's lips again.

Mittie was the first to pull back. "You know it would be fun if you entered, too."

"And who would be your mechanic, making sure everything was tip-top? It's the least I can do for you, doll." He stopped, a decided pucker in his forehead. "Unless you'd prefer York."

"Of course not. I even thought Bobby might enter, but he's not keen on the competitive side of aviation. Or the prize money."

"And I'm the poor sap who could use it. Is that what you're saying?"

"Heavens, no...well, I did think you could, but I also thought it might be something you'd like to do. And why are you so prickly about Bobby?"

"I wouldn't call it prickly. Only keeping track of the competition. You should know that from the horse showing circuit."

"The competition isn't Bobby. It's not even a person."

"You lost me with that."

"It's not something I can really explain, but most of my life I've been waffling about never living up to anyone's expectations— even, quite frankly, my own. Maybe someday I'll find out who I really am."

"I know you're different from anyone I've ever known. And not just the gorgeous part. You are fierce and talented and drive me mad."

The whistle of the steamboat sounded, closer this time. Ames grasped her hand in his and lowered himself onto the bluegrass, pulling her with him. She sat with her arms wrapped around bent knees while he reclined on his side, propped up on one elbow. He traced a finger along her arm as she watched the fading light play on the river. Ebb and flow. It was the stuff of life, too, and having Ames beside her filled a spot that had been empty for a while. Maybe her whole life.

She stretched her legs before her and leaned over for another taste of Ames.

CHAPTER 14

The day after Thanksgiving, Mittie and Ames flew to St. Louis. The two-day race—five hundred miles round trip—would take them to Kansas City on day one, where the competitors would spend the night and then fly back to St. Louis the following day. When Weaver had mentioned the competition to the Aero Club, Victor Booth offered his plane, a silver and white Swallow. Mittie's early practice in it had been both exhilarating and humbling as she knew Victor was as proud of it as he was of his Silver Ghost. Although her skin tingled with excitement, Mittie reminded herself that this was just a trial, a way to dip her toes in the world of competition. It would help her gain experience using map navigation and test her endurance abilities under pressure.

They arrived at Lambert Field midafternoon and were directed to the hangar housing the air rally headquarters—a table where a gentleman with a cigar checked her in, told her she was number six.

The man yelled across the dusty hangar. "That's the last of the ladies." He nodded at Ames. "Next." Recognition spread across his wide face. "I remember you from the day you picked up an entry form. Which category did you enter?"

"I'm not entered. I'm with Miss Humphreys."

"So you'll be flying with her. Excellent idea to have a man on board in case the little woman gets into trouble along the way."

Mittie stepped forward. "He won't be in the plane with me for the race. That wouldn't seem quite kosher for it being the women's category."

The man blew out a puff of smoke. "I see. You're one of those, are you?"

"One of what?"

"Pretty gal that fancies herself capable."

"No offense, sir, but I *am* capable. You'll see."

He laughed. "I reckon you are. As long as you have some mechanical skills and are familiar with the route, you should be okay. Guess this isn't your first rally."

"Actually, it is, but Lord willing, it won't be my last."

"Good luck. If you're not taking a mechanic on board, should I alert Kansas City to be on standby in case you need anything?"

"Thanks, but no. My flight instructor, Bobby York, will meet me there."

Ames had originally told her he'd have Lester meet her in Kansas City at the end of the first day of competition, but Bobby had volunteered the same afternoon. He said he'd been wanting to see a bit more of the country and would make a week of it, taking his Morris Oxford that his father shipped from England to try out the American highways. It was a spiffy little automobile, a brilliant blue a few shades darker than Bobby's eyes. And it fit him. Sporty and solid.

It was a kind offer, and she'd readily accepted. Even Ames agreed—he didn't want her stranded without help if she needed it.

The man at the table made a note of Bobby's name and called for "next" again.

Pilots and mechanics greeted one another like they were at a fraternity party. Contentment rode along Mittie's bones as she breathed in the scent of engine grease and hangar dust and cigar smoke.

Above the chatter, a female voice rang out. "Ames Dewberry. As I live and breathe, I didn't expect to see you here."

A willowy woman in a slim skirt and chiffon blouse that ruffled at the neck swept across the floor and threw her arms around Ames' neck.

"Peach." A husky whisper escaped from Ames' throat as he returned her embrace, and with one arm still around her narrow shoulders, he said, "What's so unexpected? The last time I checked, this was an airfield, and I am a pilot of some note."

"You've got that right, Ames darlin'."

Ames turned to Mittie. "This is Calista Gilson, better known as Peach on the stunt circuit." In a grand gesture, he presented Mittie as "the new girl in town who's going to turn the aviation world on its end."

"Hey, that's my line." Calista offered her hand to Mittie. "Ames knows I'm kidding, at least halfway. I'm tickled pink to meet you." She was tall, like Mittie, but fine boned with high cheekbones accented by bobbed hair the color of sunlit honey.

Mittie shook her hand. "Likewise."

Calista had an air of femininity about her that made Mittie, still in her flight clothes, look like a galumphing twit. "Are you here with someone in the competition?"

"Oh, no, I'm flying in the competition. Just here by my lonesome. My mechanic couldn't make it, so one of the boys back there said he'd check *Peaches* over for me and swing the prop for me tomorrow."

"Peaches?"

"My little Curtiss. The one I'm flying in the race."

Mittie did a double take. "I guess I didn't understand that part. So that's where your nickname comes from—your plane."

"No, flip it the other way. Fellas call me Peach, so my wings are my namesake."

"Your skirt...is that what you fly in?"

Calista laughed. "It's a little trick I learned from one of the other gals on the circuit. I did a quick change in the cockpit before I hopped out. Girlish charm and all that." She had that by the bushel.

"You look like you stepped from the page of a magazine, not out of an airplane, and I mean that in the most complimentary of ways." Mittie looked from Calista to Ames. "So how do you two know each other?"

Ames rocked back on his heels. "Peach was flying with a group in Kansas when the Patriots were there. Picture, if you will, an angel in a flowing white dress balancing on the wing of an airplane."

It wasn't difficult at all to imagine. Calista was winsome and ethereal, her cheeks rosy beneath gray eyes as pale as water. "I can see that. You're a wing walker, then. I thought maybe you two knew each other from Iowa."

Calista nudged Ames. "I didn't know you were from Iowa. I thought you said Louisville." She had a way of drawing out the syllables like someone from the Deep South. Definitely not Iowa. When the corners of her mouth tilted up, her face glowed.

Ames stepped back and held up both hands, palms out. "I don't recall you ever asking." To Mittie he said, "We need to get going while there's still daylight and do that engine check."

"Good to meet you, Calista. Guess I'll see you tomorrow."

"Lord willing. Y'all take care now." She backed up and gave a little wave, then turned and slipped through the crowd. If her moves in the sky were as smooth as her hip movements, Mittie was in for a stiff competition.

The day of the rally dawned with overcast skies that were expected to clear by midmorning. Victor Booth and Weaver had driven over the day before, both to cheer Mittie on and meet with the aeronau-

tic club members in Kansas City to discuss new ideas in aviation—
hobnobbing, her daddy would call it.

As the clouds thinned and the skies opened up, the planes with
the women pilots were instructed to line up. Ames did a final engine check and told Mittie he'd hang around the airfield until the
reports of the first day came in.

Weaver said, "Stick with the roads if you can, although that
might be tricky if you're over a forested area. Remember the Missouri River will be to your south all the way to Columbia but to
your north after that."

Victor agreed and told her to keep her altitude high enough to
avoid brushing the tops of the trees. "Two hundred feet would be
best, but whatever feels right for the air current."

Ames joined them just as the announcer told the contestants to
board their planes. He pulled Mittie into his arms and kissed her
softly. "That's to remember me by until tomorrow."

"As if I could forget." She took a deep breath and wiped damp
palms on her wool jodhpurs that would keep her warm in the nippy
air. She pulled on leather gloves and hopped on the wing, then slid
into the cockpit. Chin strap snapped, she slid the goggles resting
atop her head into place. Although the preflight check had already
been done when she'd pulled the plane into the sixth position—
her number in the race—she checked the gauges again and put her
hands on the wheel.

Calista Gilson was in fifth position, and when Mittie looked
her way, she gave a friendly wave. Her pale orange Curtiss had
"Peaches" in a broad script on the side, a bi-wing that oozed the
same charm as its owner. Adrenaline pulsed in Mittie's neck and
temples as Calista moved forward at the signal and taxied toward the
open field. When the flagman waved at Mittie, she followed, everything she'd learned up until this point doing laps inside her head.

And then the sky was hers. She climbed higher and higher, her hours of training taking over. A short five months ago, this had been only a dream, and now she soared, banking to the left and finding the ribbon of highway that snaked across Missouri, taking her toward Columbia, the halfway mark, on wings of silver.

Her eyes burned even with goggles, the rush of air cold on her cheeks, but she'd never felt more glorious. She kept one eye on the compass and altimeter, the other on the landscape below. Feet on the rudder, hands on the wheel, she tended Victor's Swallow with the same precision as she did when training Gypsy. The wind whistled by, catching her at times in its currents, giving her heart a momentary start until she leveled out and checked her position. Below her, the highway was the hand that guided her. Obscured from view for minutes at a time, the road wound through hilly terrain, then straightened and beckoned her to follow. An hour, then almost two, and she passed a small lake that blinded her with its reflection of the sun and mounds created by Indians centuries before. The splendor of creation and the work of man converged in wonderment beneath her. Mittie sent a prayer of gratitude heavenward and moments later saw the sprawl of Columbia on a plateau above the Ozarks. She corrected her direction and circled to the north and the plains where the airfield waited.

An official of the race met her at the end of the runway, stopwatch in hand.

She jumped from the wing, eager to know how she'd done and to stretch her legs while the ground crew added fuel. When the timekeeper didn't offer the information, she asked if the others had touched down yet.

"You're the fourth one to check in. Any trouble?"

"None at all."

"Good luck, then."

She slipped back into the cockpit, took a swig of water from a canteen, and prepared for the next 125 miles. Ten minutes later, she crossed the Missouri River and made a decision to follow it rather than the highway. It took her a bit off course to the north, but she could fly at a higher altitude and go faster.

Fourth place. It wasn't bad. Maybe she could advance her position before Kansas City. Mittie opened the throttle and stayed the course. When she arrived at Kansas City's Sweeney Airport, the first person she saw after the official was Calista. She stood, flight helmet in hand, the hem of her skirt riffling in the breeze with a man on either side. One looked an awful lot like Bobby. Mittie wasn't sure why, but irritation bubbled up.

Mittie taxied to the area where the official pointed, cut the engine, and crawled out. Bobby stepped away from Calista and came to greet her, his smile wide, arms open.

"I made it." Her muscles trembled when she hugged him back.

"Never doubted you for a minute. Three of you so far. And record times, from what I hear."

"Get out. How did you find out?"

"One of the contestants sweet-talked the timekeeper."

"Girl with a Southern accent?"

"Could be. All you Yankees talk funny to me, but if you're talking about the comely blonde over there, then yes."

"So you've met Calista."

"We weren't formally introduced. One of the chaps called her Peach."

"That's the one. Sweet girl, and from the looks of it, quite a competitor."

"As are you. How was the flight?"

Mittie closed her eyes, the feel of the wind still on her cheeks. "More than I ever imagined. You know, there was this moment when it felt as if I were suspended in time, that the only things around me were the heavens and the breath of God. I was almost sorry when the airfield came into view."

Bobby wiped a strand of hair away from her cheek. "It's what I call divine affirmation—that feeling that comes from the soul." His eyes, when they peered into hers, were as deep as the ocean—mysterious, as if more dwelt beneath the surface of Bobby York than he was willing to share.

The roar of an approaching plane broke the trance. Another entrant had made it.

Dinner for all of the contenders and their teams was in the hotel dining room that evening. After changing in her room, Mittie went to the lobby to wait for Bobby. Calista waved her over to join her and two of the other girls from the race and made introductions all around. Her enthusiasm was contagious with a constant string of *darlin'* this and *bless your heart* that peppering her conversation. When the other girls drifted off to meet their companions, she asked Mittie about the handsome devil that had driven her from the airfield.

"You mean Bobby? He's my flight instructor."

"Lucky you. A fella in every port."

"I wouldn't say that. I'm just fortunate that Bobby wanted to see more of the country. He's not been in the States that long, so it worked out for him to drive over and meet me here."

"He's British, isn't he?" When Mittie nodded, she said, "He seems more your type than Ames."

"I wasn't aware that I had a type. I've barely even met you, and you're sizing me up?"

"Trust me—I know these things."

"And how, pray tell, have you come to this conclusion?"

"I've been around, seen things. That flight jacket you had on cost more than Ames makes in an entire weekend."

What nerve. She wanted to ask what, if anything, she'd seen about Bobby while she'd *been around*, but Bobby sauntered up at just that moment.

After the introductions, Calista gave him a coy look and said it was a joy to meet him. "And please, my friends call me Peach."

"Peach it is. May I escort you lovely ladies into the dining room?"

He held out the chair for Calista and the one next to it for Mittie, then sat on Mittie's right. The atmosphere was lively with much talk about the day's race as plates of roasted chicken with potatoes and green beans were set in front of them.

And it seemed that Calista—Mittie refused to think of her as Peach—knew everyone. "See that fella over there?" She pointed to one of the men in the race. "He's got a rose tattoo on his bicep for the gal he met in England during the war. And Barb—she's the one that finished first today and is sitting with her daddy—she works as a fashion model in Dallas. I call her Venus—you know, the Roman goddess of beauty. Fits her, don't you think?"

"I suppose. She is cute as can be, but how do you know all this about people?" A fleeting thought about what Calista might say about her zipped through her head.

Calista's pale eyes grew round, innocent. "Just curious, I guess." She leaned in and looked at Bobby. "Like I'm curious about that sweet little roadster I saw you driving. Any chance you'd give me a ride sometime?"

Bobby swallowed what he was chewing and said, "I suppose, but time is rather short with needing to be at the airfield in the morning."

"The night is young."

"Did you have a particular destination in mind? Someplace you needed to go?"

"Not right offhand. Of course, I don't want to infringe on Kentucky here's territory if you've already made plans."

A flicker of irritation nipped at Mittie. "Kentucky? Do you give everyone pet names?"

"Sorry. It's a terrible habit I've picked up trying to remember all the people I've met on the barnstorming circuit. Mama says I should mind my manners in a way that's befitting the Georgia raisin' she bestowed upon me. What would you like me to call you?"

Mittie smiled. "How about Mittie? So you're from Georgia?"

"Yes, *Mittie*, I'm from Atlanta. Born and bred. My granddaddy rebuilt half of the city after those damn Yankees burned it to the ground." She clapped her fingers to her lips. "I have to be careful when I'm in a big crowd like this that I don't step on some damn Yankee's toes."

"It's all right. Bobby calls everyone in the States Yankees."

Calista pointed her fork at him. "I'll be happy to set you straight on the difference between the North and the South when we go for that spin. How about when we finish eating?"

Bobby cocked his head at Mittie with a questioning look.

"Oh, don't mind me. I want to call Mother and Daddy and take a steaming hot bath." The sudden chill she'd developed wasn't from the weather.

"If you're sure you don't mind."

They decided on the time to meet the following morning.

As she lay staring at the ceiling two hours later, Mittie's thoughts swirled. She was in third place after the first day, but a remnant of disappointment ate at the fringes of her heart. Calista was in second place and had monopolized the conversation with Bobby—time that Mittie had hoped to spend telling him about her flight and discussing strategy for the return trip to St. Louis. As she drifted off, it came to her that perhaps Calista wasn't the innocent she pretended to be. Perhaps the chatty blond banter and making eyes at Bobby was to distract Mittie and put her on edge. And as the evening's events replayed in her head, Mittie pressed her palms against the sheets to keep her hands from curling into knots. Seeing Calista prance off with Bobby bothered her more than she was willing to admit.

CHAPTER 15

Mittie and Bobby arrived at Sweeney Field early the next morning, having had a quiet, uninterrupted breakfast where they did get to talk about the previous day's flight. They looked over the maps, and she asked if he was driving to St. Louis for the end of the race or if he was still touring the country.

"I'll be in St. Louis—maybe not by the time you land, but soon thereabout."

"Thanks. Did you and Calista have a nice drive?"

Bobby swallowed his coffee, his eyes clouding just a bit. "Calista? Oh, you mean Peach. Yes, we did. The river's got quite a nice view at night."

"Did she set you straight on the differences between the North and the South?"

He rubbed the side of his neck and chuckled. "Guess the subject never came up. She was curious about Brooklands, where I trained, and what I'm doing in the States. Have you talked to Ames?"

"I left a message for him with the desk clerk at his hotel. And for Victor as well. I do appreciate your coming. It was nice to see a friendly face when I stepped out of the cockpit yesterday. How can I ever thank you?"

"Just finishing the race today is all the thanks I need."

Although the skies were a brilliant blue on takeoff, a thin black line of clouds threatened on the northern horizon. Sudden updrafts and air instability kept Mittie's feet riveted to the rudder for control the entire way to Columbia. She lowered her altitude, looking for a pocket of smoother air, but she knew she was sacrificing speed. And this time, when she stopped for fuel, she didn't ask how the others were doing.

The flight from Columbia to St. Louis was equidistant to the first half of the trip, which she'd done in two hours and forty minutes if her calculations were correct, but it was also more difficult to fly because it was more wooded and what few leaves were left on the tree branches played with the light in a dizzying effect. Her neck ached from stretching to keep on course, and her mouth felt as if it were full of sand. She fished in her pocket for a piece of Beech-Nut gum just as an updraft rocked the plane. *Steady. Feet on the rudder.* She didn't need an adverse yaw when she was this close. Another wind pocket bounced her again. She gripped the stick, her muscles taut.

Stay calm. Check the compass. She nosed down to get a better look at the countryside and discovered she was directly over Lambert Field and going too fast to land. She would have to circle back, losing precious time, but relief swelled within her. She'd made it.

After the postflight check, Mittie jumped from the wing as photographers and male reporters with pencils poised scurried onto the field toward her. Mittie braced herself to give a word about the flight, but the press reps streamed past her straight for Calista, who stood by her little plane. A short, filmy skirt whipped around her legs, her smile that of a film starlet.

Mittie popped the piece of Beech-Nut in her mouth. She'd come to check out the competition, and it couldn't have been more clear had it been written across the sky. She pulled off her leather helmet, tossed her head to let her hair fly free, and headed to the hangar to find Ames.

The temperature had dropped considerably since the day before, but there was still a nice crowd of onlookers. They gave Mittie a hearty round of applause as she stepped into their midst. A small boy with two front teeth missing tugged on her arm and asked for an autograph.

She patted his cheek as she'd seen Ames do at barnstormings. "My pleasure, young man." She scribbled her name on the scrap of paper he thrust at her, and when she handed it back, she gave him a stick of Beech-Nut and winked. "It's a secret weapon for aviators."

"Thanks, lady; I'll remember that."

"There you are." Victor approached from her left before she made it to the hangar's open doors. He waved Weaver over. "So glad to see the Swallow dip out of the sky with you in it. I worried a few years off my life when the wind shifted with that cold front."

"I think I hit it about ten miles out."

"Did you have any trouble?"

"Not really. I hit a few air bumps, but the Swallow got me here."

Weaver gave her a fatherly hug. "I couldn't be more proud than if you were my own daughter."

"I'm just thankful for both of you. Have all the women made it?"

Victor said, "Last report was all but one. We've stayed close to the officials' table just inside the door to keep abreast of any news."

A wave of apprehension sloshed in Mittie's belly as Weaver said, "Hope she didn't have trouble. I don't like the looks of those dark clouds."

The air buzzed with worry as people watched the sky. Mittie looked around for Ames and caught snatches of conversation.

I'd rather get caught up in a tornado than a blue norther.

Heard it dropped thirty degrees in an hour over in Columbia.

Sure hope the hail don't hit before we get out of here.

She turned to Weaver and Victor. "Have you seen Ames?"

Victor said he was inside earlier but thought he'd seen him going out to the plane.

"I must've missed him, then. Any idea how we all placed in the finish?"

Weaver shrugged. "Don't expect they'll announce it until everyone's accounted for." His eyes stayed riveted on the sky.

The wind, brisk when Mittie landed, now gusted, sending hats sailing and kicking up dust on the runway, pelting them with grit.

Victor held his hand on his hat and jerked his head toward the hangar. "Let's get back inside."

Mittie followed, her head turned, still hoping to catch sight of Ames. She tugged on Victor's sleeve. "I think I'll go over and see if Ames is with the Swallow. I bet he's tinkering with something, maybe putting the cockpit cover on in case it starts raining."

She didn't wait for any objections and turned, bracing herself against the wind. Calista and the entourage of reporters had disappeared, leaving only the flagman and a few men in coveralls on the field. She sprinted to the Swallow, but no Ames. And since she was there, she felt she owed it to Victor to protect the jewel he was so proud of. She grabbed the canvas from the baggage compartment, hefted it up on the wing, and jumped on after it. Bending her knees to get leverage, she threw it up into the cockpit. A gust of wind nearly threw her overboard, but determined, she climbed into the rear passenger seat, dragging the cover with her. It landed splayed open, saving her from wrestling with that at least. She took the bottom rope, threaded it through the slot on the rear right of the open seat, and knotted it. The same for the rear left. Working the fanfold, she threw her leg over into the next seat, pulling the canvas with her. She stopped to take a breath, the effort bringing tears to her eyes. Leg up and over into the cockpit. The canvas felt like it weighed five hundred pounds. As she fished for the right front rope, the air gusted. She struggled to hold the tarp down, but the force of the gale was stronger. The canvas flew up, snapping like sheets on a clothesline as it whipped around beneath the upper wing. She hopped back toward the rear where she started, her arms and legs quivering. Her fingers clutched an edge; then from behind, strong arms reached over her, two beefy hands pulling the canvas into submission.

Ames.

He pointed for her to move to the cockpit, and together, they hauled the unruly cover into place. As Ames knotted the last rope, the first icy rain fell from the sky.

"Let's go!" he yelled above the roar of the wind. He grabbed her hand, and they raced toward the hangar and slipped inside, just missing the downpour of hail that hammered the roof of the metal hangar.

They leaned over, heaving to catch their breath as people gave them room. Mittie glanced sideways at Ames and said, "Thanks." It was all she could manage with the strength she had left.

When she straightened, soaked to the bone and wrung out, the first person she saw was Peach, delicate hands on either side of her face, her water-pale eyes as big as twin moons. Next to her stood Bobby York.

By evening, a pilot named Marie still hadn't returned. Sandwiches from the Lambert Field canteen were passed around with paper cups of bitter coffee that at least chased the chill of the storm away. Bobby congratulated Mittie, who smelled of damp wool and had only run her fingers through the tangles of her hair. She wished she'd grabbed her duffel from the baggage compartment when getting the tarp. It didn't really matter—she'd been wet before, and it was trivial in comparison to what Marie might be going through.

When seven o'clock arrived, the man with the infernal cigar called for attention.

"In light of the circumstances and knowing some of you may have places you need to be, we're going ahead with announcing the winners of the women's race division. Unfortunately, the men's speed race has been halted in Columbia and won't resume due to the inclement weather. From a field of six women in the two-day race, five finished. Let's give these ladies a round of applause."

It was half-hearted, knowing a sixth woman was still unaccounted for. After an awkward few seconds, the official opened an envelope.

"In spite of it being a rough day in the sky today, two of the women broke previous records for flights of five hundred miles, and the remaining three were close behind. First place, with a prize of four hundred dollars, goes to Calista Gilson of Atlanta, Georgia."

This time, the applause was hearty, Mittie included. Someone wolf whistled from the back of the hangar and yelled, "Way to go, Peach!"

Peach stepped forward. "It's been a pure delight to be here and meet all y'all. Thank you for giving women a chance to prove that, while we may not be faster or fly higher than our male counterparts, we can fly. And look pretty at the same time." More applause. More whistles.

She sashayed back to her spot among a group of her admirers.

Mittie's heart raced as Ames took her hand and gave it a soft squeeze. Bobby stood close by with Victor and Weaver. She *had* finished. That was what counted. But still, she prayed.

"In second place at fourteen minutes behind—" The single entry door to the hangar creaked, and two figures entered. The air stilled, and then a shout went up.

Marie! She made it, and she was alive. The applause was joyous as a muddy, bedraggled Marie stepped forward while a bushy-bearded man wearing a heavy barn coat trailed behind. Everyone wanted to know what happened, and gradually, between Marie and the farmer who'd rescued her, they heard her story.

She'd hit the line of bad weather and lost control of the rudder. She was able to make a partial recovery, but the engine stalled, and she crash-landed in an open field. Stunned but not injured as near as she could tell, Marie crawled out of the plane that had landed on its side, snapping one of the wings. She walked along a dirt road that led eventually to a farmhouse, where she found a man tending his livestock. She helped him get the animals secure in light of the impending storm.

Her face beamed as she said, "And here we are. I knew everyone would be worried, so this gentleman was kind enough to drive me over."

Mittie's eyes stung, her throat scratchy with emotion. She was immeasurably thankful that Marie had survived, but she also knew it could have been her, that the Swallow had lurched in the same wind that sent Marie plummeting to earth. And Mittie's mother would hear of the story and no doubt deliver one of her lectures about the dangers of flying and how being a teacher or a legal secretary or even the wife of a shady senator was infinitely more suitable. Lost in thought, she didn't even hear the official announce that she had come in second place—fourteen minutes behind Calista and only five minutes in front of Barb, the one Peach called Venus. Barb was a beauty, but more than that, she was a competitor. Warmth flooded Mittie's chest as she looked at each woman who'd flown. United they stood in their quest to conquer the skies. A band of sisters.

Mittie stepped forward to receive her envelope. She hadn't even heard what her prize amount was and had certainly not prepared a statement.

"Thank you all. I'm obviously not one of the ones who can fly and look pretty at the same time like my friend here, yet I'm thrilled

to be a part of this group. Someday, dear sisters, we will make aviation history."

Tears clogged her throat as she placed her fingers to her lips and
blew a kiss across the hangar where dust particles hung in the air like
glitter.

CHAPTER 16

The storm had more growl than substance, bringing only a skiff of snow and a spat of cold. Two days later, the skies were an inviting cerulean blue, and Mittie and Ames flew back to Louisville. Mittie exchanged addresses and phone numbers with the girls who'd flown in the race and promised to keep in touch. For most of them, it would most likely be spring before the weather was reliable enough to do any serious flying. Like the squirrels who stored away hickory nuts in the autumn, Mittie and her new sisters would have to rely on tucked-away memories to feed their hunger for the skies.

A reporter came out to the farm to do a story about the air rally. He took a picture of Mittie riding Gypsy and asked her about women in aviation and the impact Charles Lindbergh had made. The headline read *Former Horsewoman Trades the Saddle for the Cockpit.* He slanted the article so that it sounded as if she'd been a failure with Gypsy and had turned to flying as a consolation.

Her mother thought it was vulgar. "He makes it sound like you're desperate for a thrill. I've no idea what the women in the Louisville Ladies' Society will think. First you fall from the wing of an airplane, and now this—participating in a sport that's going to get you killed."

"Say what you will, Mother. We've been down this road so many times that the ruts are full of ruts. I would've preferred that he mention that I'd taken up aviation in addition to being a horsewoman, but it still gives credibility to women who fly. And if this thrill, as you say, is forging a new frontier, then I would think your friends would rally around that, if not for themselves, then for their daughters and granddaughters."

"My friends are genteel women who believe a woman's place is beside a man, conducting herself in a ladylike manner for noble causes."

"I admire your passion, Mother, the way you've always taken care of our family and worked tirelessly helping the flood victims over in Mississippi, but I see a future where aviators can come to the aid of their fellow man within hours, not days or weeks. And just think: in a year or two, when Iris starts having little ones, we could fly down to Birmingham in two shakes."

"Victor isn't going to loan you his plane whenever you get a notion."

"He won't have to if I have my own plane." Just like that it popped out of her mouth. Not that she hadn't thought of it often enough, but saying it to her mother was bold, even for her.

"Oh, forevermore. That's absurd. I liked it better when all you wanted to do was ride horses and do your daddy's books. Before Ames Dewberry waltzed into your life."

Mittie snapped to attention. "What does Ames have to do with this?"

Her mother sighed. "You don't know anything about him. His people. Where he's from."

"Those things are immaterial to me. We have things in common that I adore—flying, dancing, our hopes for the future."

Her mother gasped. "You're surely not planning to marry him."

"It's not a subject that's come up, but I do think I'm in love with him."

"What kind of future would that be? Skipping around the country flying airplanes is hardly what I would call putting down roots. And the man doesn't even have a job, for pity's sake."

"Not an important position, if that's what you mean. He has dreams of success with his new patent. I wouldn't be surprised if he owned his own company one day."

"And if he fails?"

"He'll try something else. Grandmother's told me that her parents thought she was crazy to follow a man who dreamed of owning a horse farm. I guess if I'm crazy for following my dreams, I've come by the trait honestly."

"Humph."

Mittie waited for the retort. She hated bickering with her mother. She should've just let her mother's opinion of the newspaper article rest and mumbled something like, "At least they spelled my name right." Now it was too late, and they were both on edge. Her mother's eyes drifted to a spot behind Mittie. "You and your daddy are so full of purpose . . ."

It slammed Mittie in the depths. This wasn't about flying or Ames or the newspaper article but about the simple fact that, after years of drifting along, Mittie had latched onto a smoldering passion. The only purpose her mother had was directing the lives of others. Her committees. Her daughters. Her husband, whose need for her had grown thin now that he was stronger.

A tear trickled down her mother's face.

Mittie's gut wrenched. How could she have not seen it? Her mother talked about knowing the right people, being an upstanding citizen, a woman who was involved in worthy causes, but it was all a façade. In reality, she was sinking into a sea of extinction, a world where she was no longer needed. If Mittie's relationship with Ames did become serious, it would be the last blow to her mother's ability to control the world around her. It was a burden

that Mittie couldn't bear. Wouldn't bear. Her mother was right—
Mittie did have purpose, and whether it was a noble cause or not,
the desire to fly was etched in her bones. And she couldn't let her
mother's emotional state thwart her. Not now that she'd made such
strides.

Deep inside, the shell of determination that encased her heart
hardened.

The mother-daughter dance they knew so well carried them
through December. When Ames had come for dinner, her mother
had been pleasant, at times charming, in spite of trying to elicit information about his family.

"Your parents? They're still in Ohio?"

"Iowa. And no, ma'am. They passed when my sister and I were
in grammar school. My grandparents raised us."

"Oh, you dear boy. How unfortunate for you."

He shrugged. "They kept clothes on our back and food in our
stomachs. Granny saw to our religious training and . . . sadly, both
she and Pawpaw have passed."

"But your sister? You're still close?"

"Like peas in a pod. Fern fusses over me every chance I get back
to visit."

"That's lovely. You'll be going there for Christmas, I would
guess."

Mittie shot her mother a look that said she was stepping over the
line. Like the accommodating soul that he was, Mittie's daddy had
stayed quiet, calmly eating his roast beef, nodding at the right times.
Mittie would do well to take a page from him.

Quickly her mother added, "I only ask because you would be
welcome to join us if you can't make it to Iowa."

"Thanks. I appreciate the invitation. Mittie said Iris would be
coming. I'm sure you're happy about that."

"We can hardly wait, isn't that right, dear?" She patted Mittie's dad on the arm.

"Absolutely. I've missed her, and I'm anxious to hear about the steel industry from Hayden as well. Nothing like getting an insider's view on the economic side."

Ames raised his eyebrows. "For your investments?"

"My banker tells me I need to diversify."

"Have you considered aviation? Not that steel isn't viable, but there was quite a show of interest when I was in St. Louis with Mittie."

"I've gathered that from the newspapers. Any particular companies you'd recommend?"

"Most are growing right now. Travel Air. Lockheed. They'll be players in the near future, I'm sure. Even Henry Ford's jumped in with the Tri-Motor he brought out last year."

"The one they call the Tin Goose?"

Ames chuckled and nodded.

Afterward, Mittie's mother, bless her heart, didn't mention the dangers of flying or the unfortunate childhood she imagined for Ames. In the tit-for-tat waltz she and her mother had engaged in, Mittie offered to write out the invitations for the baby shower they were having for Nell while Iris was home for Christmas. And she didn't even flinch when her mother suggested that she embroider a pair of lambs on a receiving blanket for the new baby. With every wobbly stitch and bloodied finger from poking herself with the needle, Mittie envisioned flying in her own plane. What kind of plane could she afford? A zippy little Swallow like Victor's or a tried-and-true Canuck like Weaver's? Someday. Someday soon.

The night before Ames left for a trip to Wichita to see another possible investor, he took her to a tavern that was known for its rustic ambience and hearty food. He looked up from the menu and said, "I'm leaving *Trixie* in your care. If you have a sunny day, you might take her up so she doesn't get rusty."

"You're sure about driving instead of flying?"

"After the storm that blew into St. Louis, I'm a little leery."

"You may rest assured that I'll handle *Trixie* with kid gloves and treat her like she's my very own." Light flickered from the kerosene lantern between them, casting shadows on the walls, bathing one side of Ames' face in light, leaving the other shadowed. Her heart skipped just looking at him. "And speaking of my very own, I'm serious about getting a plane. I was hoping you could advise me on what features would be best for competition and what one might cost."

He asked how much her daddy was willing to spend.

"I could never ask him to buy a plane. I have a small trust fund that Grandfather set up, but I don't want to use all of it, as there'll be other expenses. Competitions. Travel money. Repairs."

"I know it's none of my business, but he must've left a substantial amount."

"Not a great lot, but with what I've saved from working for Daddy, it should be enough."

He blew out a breath that riffled the raven hair on his forehead.

Mittie laughed. "Do that again. You look cute with your hair mussed like that."

"You're something else, you know that? Here I am hoping to set up a romantic moment, and you're discussing the price of airplanes and making goofball conversation about my hair."

"Sorry, but I do think it makes you look dashing. I have to agree, though, that letting me take care of *Trixie* is quite the romantic gesture."

"That was just the warm-up." He reached over and took her hand and pressed it to his lips. "Just a promise for later, okay?" He reached into his suit pocket and pulled out a thin rectangular box.

Mittie sucked in an audible breath and gave a mental sigh at the same time. *Engagement rings come in cubed boxes. Bracelets and necklaces in flat ones.* She knew she wasn't ready for the cubed box. At least not yet.

"For you, my dear." He tucked the jeweler's case in her hand and told her to open it.

There was no wrapping paper, just the caramel leather case. And inside, a gold heart-shaped locket rested on red velvet.

"It's lovely." The fine gold chain glinted in the yellow lantern light as she ran it through her fingers. "Oh look—it opens." Inside was a picture, smaller than a dime.

"The picture is Pawpaw, and the locket was Granny's. I don't have a trust fund like you—"

"I can't take this. It's your grandmother's, what you have to remember her and your grandfather by. And what about your sister. Fern, isn't that what you called her? Maybe she would like it."

"Fern's not the sentimental type. Granny would've loved you as I do. And I'd bet the moon and stars that she's smiling right now, happy for you to have her necklace."

Mittie's fingers shook. "Are you sure?"

"Never more sure of anything in my life. Here—let me help you put it on."

His fingers were warm on the back of her neck as she held her hair up for him, but the locket was cool against her chest. She leaned in close and kissed Ames on the cheek. "Thank you; it's perfect. And the kiss was just a sample of the real one I'm saving for later."

"I can't wait."

The locket grew warm, nestled near her heart.

CHAPTER 17

Iris and Hayden breezed in three days before Christmas, their antic-
ipated visit spurring Mittie's mother into a whirlwind of shopping,
decorating, and planning menus, her purpose renewed.

They arrived in a shiny late-model automobile, a cloud of dust in
its wake. When Mittie saw them coming, she flew from the house,
and yanked open the passenger-side door handle almost before Hayden rolled to a stop.

"How was your drive? I thought you'd never get here." She took
Iris' hand and pulled her from the car, their arms around each other,
both of them talking at once. Iris pulled back first and stood, arms
wide open, looking toward the house.

"Oh, how I've missed this. And you and Mother and Daddy."

"Merry Christmas, darling." Their mother joined them. More
hugs. A few tears. "Don't you look smart? What a darling dress. I
do believe married life agrees with you."

Iris smiled, her chin quivering a bit as she said thank you.
"Where's Daddy?"

"I asked Bertha to fetch him from his study." Her mother gave a
finger wave and said, "Hello, Hayden. So glad you made it."

Iris said, "Tell me: How's Daddy doing? Back still okay?"

"A twinge here and again, and no matter how many times I urge him to rest, he just ignores me. It's no secret who Mittie gets her stubbornness from."

Iris gave Mittie one of her knowing looks, one that said it would do no good to argue. And although Iris did have a glow about her and looked perfectly stunning, there were puffs, like tiny pillows, below her eyes as if she'd been crying. When their eyes met, Iris looked away quickly.

"Where should I take our things, sweetheart?" Hayden stood like a porter in his starched shirt with a leather suitcase in each hand and a parcel under each arm.

Mittie's mother said, "Here—let me help you." She relieved him of the packages and told him everything was ready in the guest room.

Iris gave a start. "Oh, I thought we'd be in my room."

"You'd have to share a bath with Mittie. I thought you'd need more privacy."

Mittie said, "What Mother means is that she wouldn't want me to see Hayden in his Skivvies."

"Good gracious, Mittie. Watch your tongue. You'll have Hayden hightailing back to Birmingham before we've even had Christmas."

Iris shrugged. "Whatever you think about the room, but honestly, I've been looking forward to sleeping in my old bed."

Hayden said, "I'm sure your mama is right, sugar. Why don't you get your hatbox and my valise from the back while we carry these things up?"

Mittie said she'd help, and when her mother and Hayden were out of earshot, Mittie edged close to her twin. "What's going on?"

Iris' eyes widened in a startling blue. "*Nothing* is going on. However do you come up with these silly notions?"

She tossed the hatbox to Iris. "It's not a notion. I can see it written on your face." She grabbed the valise and a pile of coats from the rear seat and closed the door with her hip. "Don't worry, Sis; I'll get it out of you."

Iris, though, was halfway up the walk.

It appeared that, indeed, nothing was wrong as Iris and Hayden were like lovebirds, holding hands, stealing kisses when they thought no one was watching. Mittie decided that Iris had only been weary from the trip or was an actress who had missed her calling. There was no time to dwell on it, as the next two days were filled with decorating the tree and last-minute shopping.

Mittie stewed over the obvious fact that Ames wasn't there, nor had he called in more than a week. His meeting in Wichita had turned out to be a dead end, so he was headed to Tulsa, where he'd heard that men who'd made it rich in the oil boom were turning their interests to the aviation field. Every time the telephone rang or someone came to the door, she jumped, hoping it was Ames.

The only time she ventured from the house was for her daily ride on Gypsy. Mittie stayed out longer than usual on Christmas Eve, letting Gypsy race across the hills, their hearts beating as one.

Like Iris and Hayden's. And, she had begun to think, like hers and Ames'.

Toby was ready for Mittie and Gypsy when she dismounted, and after wishing him a merry Christmas, she jammed her hands in her pockets and lifted her face to the sky. The wind roughed her cheeks as she marched back to the house that was filled with the aroma of fresh gingerbread and pine needles and Bobby York's cologne.

"Isn't it just the dearest thing for Bobby to come out and join us?" Mittie's mother intercepted Mittie on the stairs as she went to change for the luncheon her mother was having for a few close neighbors who were anxious to see Iris.

"Of course. Did you call him or did he need something?"

"He said he had some news for you, so I invited him to stay for lunch. Run along and get ready. Iris and Hayden are keeping him company until you come down."

Half an hour later, Mittie entered the parlor, where Bobby was having tea with Iris and Hayden, the three of them standing near the warmth of the fireplace. "So guess you all have been introduced."

Iris gave her a questioning look. "We've met before. At least I remember Bobby from the time we visited London. The posh party one of Daddy's friends invited us to."

"I remember no such party." Mittie turned to Bobby. "Do you remember it?"

"Vaguely. Not that I could recollect your names. It wasn't unusual for my dad to pull me along to his social gatherings, hoping that some of his interests would rub off on me." He gave a sly grin. "To no avail, I'm afraid."

Iris nodded. "Sounds like someone else I know." Her pointed look at Mittie was mischievous.

"You do me a great disservice, sweet Iris. I adore my Gypsy and everything to do with the show ring. I just love flying more."

"You and Bobby should be quite a pair, then." Honestly, Iris sounded more like her mother every day.

Mittie turned to Bobby. "Mother said you have news. Are you going to tell me or am I going to stand here all day guessing?"

Iris took Hayden's arm and said she'd like to show him the party favors they'd made for Nell's baby shower. Bless her; she always knew when to make a graceful exit.

When they'd gone, Bobby asked if she'd like some tea.

"Not right now."

"Let's sit down, then." He moved to a wingback chair and waited for her to take the one opposite before he sat down.

"It must not be good news if you're having me sit. I hope it's not

Weaver. Oh, that would be awful if he was sick or something terrible happened to him at Christmas."

He tented his fingers, letting his chin rest lightly on their tips.
"No, Weaver's tip-top as far as I know. I've just come as a mes-
senger."

Her stomach sank, a light-headedness coming over her, and she
knew it was something to do with Ames even before he continued.

"Ames stopped by this morning. Said he'd been driving all night
and needed to get home to Iowa. He picked up *Trixie* and wanted
you to know."

"He was here? In Louisville? Why didn't he call?" Her hand went
instinctively to the locket on the chain around her neck.

"He was in a bit of a dither—something about his sister taking
ill—and he needed to get in the air while the weather was amiable."

"I bet he didn't say amiable."

"Not his exact words, no, but he wanted me to give you his regrets and tell you he would call when he got there."

"Call me or the airfield?"

"You, I assume."

A mix of emotions and questions roiled in her stomach. Why
hadn't he just driven from Oklahoma to Iowa? And what if the
weather turned nasty? Bobby had no answers to her questions but
said that he, too, was sorry.

"Was he going to be here for Christmas?"

She shrugged. "Best-laid plans."

Her mother stuck her head in and said it was time for lunch.
"Everything all right?"

Mittie nodded and took Bobby's arm. "Hungry?"

Her own appetite had fled.

Ames still hadn't called when it was time to leave for the Christmas
Eve service. Candles flickered in the tiny sanctuary where Mittie

sat between Iris and her Daddy. Her thoughts were a jumble, her neck tense, but as they sang "What Child Is This?" a calm fell over her. Christmas and the Christ Child. She slipped her hand in the crook of her daddy's arm and said a silent prayer for someone she didn't know in Iowa. When they stepped out into the frosty night air, snowflakes as big as quarters fell silently from the heavens, blanketing the ground, the trees, the rooftops. The earth was hushed on a starless night, lit only by gas lampposts and the glow of a long-ago night in a lowly stable.

Mittie gazed into the sky and prayed that Ames had made it safely to his sister's side, that he wasn't grounded somewhere, alone in a strange place.

The overnight snow made it a white Christmas, but the accumulation was slight, and the day dawned with bright sunshine. Mittie's mother was elated because it meant that everyone would be able to make the drive over from Louisville, including Bobby, who she'd insisted come and share Christmas with them. Nell looked as if she'd swallowed a watermelon as she sat contentedly beside Quentin. Caroline giggled and showed Bobby how to make a Jacob's ladder with a length of string that had been knotted into a large circle. Every time he put his fingers through the wrong slot and ended up with a tangled mess, she howled with laughter and called him a silly goose. He teased her back and showed her that he could make a cup and saucer with the string, which earned him a round of applause.

The laughter was good and took Mittie's mind off the worry she had for Ames. Iris cast reassuring looks at her, telling her everything was going to be fine. It didn't feel fine, even though the air sparkled with the chatter of family gathered around the fir tree that stretched nearly to the drawing room's ceiling. Tiny candles, strings of cranberries, and satin bows graced its branches while bright packages nestled beneath them.

Bertha appeared in the doorway and motioned for Mittie. *Ames.* Her heart pounded as she followed Bertha to the ladies' parlor and, with trembling fingers, picked up the telephone and spoke into the bell. Relief rushed out when Ames said hello on the other end.

"How are you? Or maybe I should say, where are you? Did you make it?"

The telephone receiver crackled like the logs in the fireplace, but she thought she made out the word *Iowa.*

"Fern? Is she better?"

"...doing...soon...Christmas."

"I'm having trouble with the connection. Can you hear me?"

"...love...make it...wish..."

"I love you, too. Merry Christmas."

The line went dead. Had he made it? It sounded like he might have. No way to know how his sister was, but Ames sounded very much alive. Relief skated along her bones, her steps light as she went into the drawing room and joined her family in a toast. Peace on earth. Goodwill to men.

Bobby eyed her from across the room and stepped quickly to her when the toasts were finished. "Ames?"

Mittie nodded and gave him a brief report as they went into the dining room. When they were seated, Mittie's dad asked Quentin to return the blessing, and while her dad carved the turkey, Mittie's mother asked who was on the phone.

"Ames. He made it home safely. At least I think he did. We had a bad connection, and I couldn't make out much."

"What was the poor man thinking taking off in an airplane in the dead of winter?"

"His sister needed him. I'd want to be there if Iris needed me."

Iris nodded. "And I'd do the same for you. Ames must be a good man to sacrifice and be with his family when he would rather be somewhere else." She patted Hayden's hand. "Right, honey?"

Hayden answered with a tight-lipped, "Of course. Although it's rather difficult to give an opinion about someone I've never met."

"Ames was at our wedding, dear. Remember the one who wore the cream-colored suit that your mother went on about?"

"I know *who* you're talking about; I just don't believe we were introduced."

Iris gave him a half frown, like something was brewing between them. Mittie hoped it was just her imagination, but Hayden had been rather sulky all morning, now that she thought about it.

Then Hayden's face brightened. "Poor guy doesn't know what he's missing. I know I'm tickled to death to spend Christmas with all of you." He stabbed a piece of turkey with his fork. "Mrs. Humphreys, everything is right tasty."

Mittie's grandmother started to answer, then realized he was addressing Iris' mother, who said, "For pity's sake, Hayden, you're part of our family now. Please call me Sarah."

"Yes, ma'am, I'll try to remember that."

Mittie's mother asked how his family celebrated Christmas.

"We go to a lake that my family owns. We've all got cabins there."

"All?"

"My folks and both my uncles. Someday Iris and I hope to build there, too."

"That sounds lovely. So quaint and surely not your normal Southern tradition. You are a man of constant surprises, Hayden."

Iris nudged him. "Tell her who was going to be there this year."

Hayden scowled at Iris, then sighed and said, "The governor and his wife."

Mittie's mother's eyes widened. "Oh dear, and you had to miss that to come here. You should have said something. I'm sure Iris would've understood and wanted you to stay there."

"Not really, Mother. They were going to spend the entire time duck hunting."

"Not the entire time." Another dark look from Hayden.

"That's not the way your mother tells it."

Mittie glanced at her dad, who looked like he'd rather be duck hunting. He took a deep breath. "Evangeline, could you pass the gravy? You know, there's nobody makes giblet gravy like our Ruby."

An awkward silence ensued. Bobby turned to Quentin next to him and asked if he and Nell were planning to take the baby to England to meet his family.

"I'm afraid not. My congregation is small; there isn't much in the way of extras."

Nell rubbed a hand over her stomach and winced. "We know the Lord will provide when the time is right."

Aunt Evangeline asked if she was okay and Nell nodded, her cheeks pinking up at the attention. Mittie wasn't so sure. Perspiration bubbled along Nell's hairline.

Quentin draped his arm around Nell and said to no one in particular, "We're trying to put a bit back in case there's a financial disaster as everyone is predicting."

Hayden lifted his chin. "I wouldn't pay attention to all that babble. Steel and construction are at the highest levels they've ever been. Matter of fact, I've had Iris invest her trust fund in Wainwright Steel."

Iris looked apologetically at her grandmother. "I wanted to ask you first, but Hayden insisted, said the time was right."

Grandmother said, "Gracious, it's nothing to do with me. Your grandfather wanted you girls to have the money, to give you a little nest egg to use however you wanted."

Hayden said, "Why leave it lying around gaining a pittance of interest when it could double or triple in a few years?"

A cloudy look had settled on Iris' face. "But what if Quentin is right? I could lose it all."

"Trust me, sugar. Nothing against the reverend, but I believe my father, who's been at the helm for twenty years and knows what's going on in his own industry." Hayden looked at Mittie. "I'd be happy to set you up an account to invest your portion as well. It would certainly be a wise move."

Mittie's jaw dropped at the audacity. "How sweet of you to offer, but I've already made plans for what I'm doing with my portion. And I'm not investing in steel."

"To your peril, I would kindly suggest."

Silence fell around the table. No clattering of forks. No murmured conversations. All eyes were on Mittie.

"Mother actually gave me the idea..."

"I've no idea what you're talking about."

"Steel doesn't interest me except the part that is used for nuts and bolts and engine parts. I'm going to buy an airplane."

"Good heavens!" Mittie's mother huffed out a breath. "I thought you were trying to exasperate me when you mentioned it."

Bobby's hand slid over to Mittie's lap. He took her clammy one in his and gave it a soft squeeze. Mittie thought she saw a twinkle in her daddy's eye, but it was her grandmother who reached for her water glass and lifted it. "Good for you, darling."

Hayden had a five-year-old pouty look. Iris looked like she might cry. Caroline wiggled in her seat and asked if Mittie would take her for an airplane ride. Mittie started to answer, but from the corner of her eyes, she saw Nell clutching her abdomen, her face twisted in a look of agony. Quentin's brows were scrunched together, his arm tighter around Nell's shoulders as he whispered something inaudible.

Nell pursed her lips and blew out short breaths. She gave a weak smile and spoke softly. "I'm sure everything is fine."

Mittie's mother lifted her chin. "You poor dear. If you're not feeling well, you should go lie down. The excitement of the day has probably worn you out."

Nell nodded in agreement and pushed back her chair, but when she stood, she gasped and clung to Quentin with one hand, clutching her abdomen with the other.

General chaos erupted with everyone talking at once, telling Quentin they needed to get to the hospital, that it was too early for the baby to come, and better to be safe than sorry. And with that, Quentin took the coats Aunt Evangeline shoved at them and helped Nell into hers.

Bobby said he would drive them to the hospital so Quentin could attend to Nell. Aunt Evangeline said they would be right behind them. Caroline wailed that she wanted to go, but her mother told her they didn't let children into the hospital, and maybe Aunt Sarah would let her open a couple of gifts.

Caroline planted her hands on her hips and huffed out a big breath. "I miss all the fun." But she didn't argue.

Four hours later, Mira Josephine Bledsoe was born. "Tiny, but squalling," Quentin reported on the telephone.

Mittie's mother, teary eyed, sat between Iris and Mittie with Caroline curled up on her lap. "Josephine was my mother, the grandmother you girls never knew. What a perfectly lovely tribute."

And Mira was Nell's grandmother on her father's side. Lovely indeed.

When the house was settled that night, Mittie ran out to the barns and checked on Gypsy. The stable was quiet, the only sounds soft snorts from the horses and the rustle of straw on wood floors as the horses shifted lazily in their stalls. Gypsy lifted her head when Mittie drew near, no doubt hoping for a carrot nugget. Mittie didn't disappoint her. She rested her elbows on the ledge of the Dutch door and scratched Gypsy's muzzle, her jaw.

"Merry Christmas, girl. Sleep tight." Gypsy. The one force in Mittie's life that remained the same. Somehow, she needed that reminder.

She slipped back to the house and was crawling into bed when there was a knock on her bedroom door.

Iris. "Can I come in?"

"You sure Hayden won't mind?"

"He's already snoring."

Mittie waved her twin in, and the two of them sat cross-legged in the middle of Mittie's downy bed. Iris picked up a chenille throw pillow and twiddled with the fringe on the edge. "Just like old times." Her voice was thin, uncertain.

"Only it's not. Is everything okay with you and Hayden?"

"What makes you say that?"

"Just little clues here and there. I gathered he didn't want to come here, that he preferred duck hunting to our company."

Her eyes glistened. "You noticed."

"We all did. I mean who can compete with having your own private lake and the governor come for Christmas?"

Iris shrugged. "We did argue about that...all the way from Alabama. The governor's not actually coming until New Year's, so Hayden thought we should compromise and go back early."

"And you didn't agree?"

"Yes and no. I desperately needed to be home with all of you and have been looking forward to it for months, but I also want to be a good wife and respect my husband's wishes."

"So you had your first spat. He still seemed besotted with you if all those kisses under the mistletoe were any indication."

Iris chuckled. "We thought no one was looking. And it wasn't our first spat."

"I hope he's not mistreating you."

"Oh goodness, no. He showers me with gifts and has let me decorate the house just the way I want it. But there are times when it's not how I envisioned being married. He works all the time, goes over to his parents' and forgets to call. If I say something, he reminds me that he has to prove himself so his daddy will give him the nod for vice president." She heaved a sigh. "I miss you all more than you can imagine."

"You'll get acquainted and make hordes of friends."

"We do get scads of invitations, but I've not quite been accepted as a true Southerner, and a few have suggested that I might be a damn Yankee."

"You sound like Calista."

"Who?"

"The girl who beat me in the air race in St. Louis. A Georgia peach if there ever was one. I think I'll have a chance to beat her if I get my own plane."

"You're taking this quite serious."

"It's all I think about—that, and working on my international license so I can qualify for some of the bigger competitions."

"And Ames? Are you serious about him, too?"

Mittie reached inside her nightshirt and pulled out the locket and told Iris about it.

"I saw that earlier and meant to ask you about it. It's his grandmother's necklace, huh? I would say that was pretty serious."

"No commitments from either of us yet. Flying still tops everything."

"You might consider getting to know his family before things get too far along. Things aren't always what they seem on the surface."

"No worries there, sweet pea. With Ames, there are no mansions or houses by the lake. He only has a sister, so whatever future we have would just be the two of us."

"And us. You can't forget that you have Mother and Daddy and me."

"How could I ever forget that?"

Iris flopped back on one of the pillows. "Sometimes I wish I had your guts, your flair for the outrageous."

"Are you coming down with something? You've never said that before."

"I'm saying it now."

"Maybe you're pregnant and it's affecting your senses."

"I'm not pregnant—just a teensy bit jealous that you're going to blow your trust fund on an airplane and mine's tied up in stocks somewhere."

"I'm not blowing it. It's an investment the same as yours."

"I still think leaving it safe, even with a small amount of interest, is smarter than taking a chance."

"You don't make any sense. You say you wish you were more daring and then bemoan that you're taking a risk by investing."

"I don't think it's the money or even the risk. It's that it was one small piece of me that was mine, that if something happened to Hayden or, heaven forbid, if our marriage didn't work out, I'd have a shred to fall back on."

"Like you said, we'll always have each other."

Iris sat up. "Not if you get yourself killed in an airplane crash."

"You're starting to sound like Mother again. Go on—get back to your husband before he wakes up and finds you gone."

At breakfast the next morning, Hayden said that if he and Iris left straightaway, he might arrive at the lake in time to bag a few ducks. Iris kissed him on the cheek and said she'd be ready in an hour.

Mittie rubbed the gold locket between her thumb and forefinger. *Things aren't always what they seem.* Were Iris' words a confession or a cautionary tale?

CHAPTER 18

Ames called with news that his sister was improving, and he was waiting for clear weather to return to Louisville. It was a small consolation. Mittie busied herself with visits to Nell and Quentin and marveled along with the rest of the family at how quickly the tiny bundle named Mira had completely captured all their hearts.

On the last Monday in January, Mittie had just come in from her morning ride on Gypsy when Ames called. She held her breath, hoping he would say he was back. Instead, he was in Lincoln, Nebraska. And he had found her a plane.

"What? Nebraska? Whose plane?" Her heart raced, but it was confusing and she thought there must be something wrong with the connection.

"A single-engine Curtiss that runs like a top. I think it's just what you're looking for."

When reality began to sink in, a knot coiled in her stomach. She hadn't asked or expected Ames to take the lead on her search. Was it the nudge she needed?

Her business sense took over. "How did you happen to find it?"

"I was in Lincoln on business, talking to some of the fellas at the flying school, and heard about it."

Stay calm. Don't go flipping over something that might be a wild goose chase. Still, Ames had thought of her, and that sent goose bumps rippling down her arms.

She quizzed Ames about the plane, its track record, performance, the price—everything she could think of. It had to be a business decision, not an emotional one. She had her daddy to thank for that and her years of working among saddlebreds.

"One other question: Why is the owner selling?"

Ames chuckled. "His wife has her eye on a new house. I can pay him if you wire me the money, but we'll have to figure out how to get it to Louisville."

The operator came on the line for the one-minute warning.

"I can't buy it without testing it. What's the weather like?"

"Bright blue skies. Frosty mornings. Perfect flying weather."

"Let me do some checking here. Call me tomorrow, and I'll let you know."

"A couple of other fellas have been looking at it, and he's anxious to sell, so timing is a factor."

"See if he'll hold off until I get there." The line went dead.

Ames would call tomorrow. Either way, she needed to be prepared. She went to the bank that afternoon and got the money, and after dinner told her parents she was going to Nebraska.

Her daddy remarked that it was rather sudden.

"You know I've been anxious to do this, and it's a spectacular opportunity."

Her mother pinched her lips. "Forevermore, Mittie. What about the weather? It's so unpredictable this time of year."

She hated when her mother adopted that tone, addressing her as if she were ten years old. Mittie held her tongue. "Ames assured me the weather was fine." She gave them the details of the plane, but her daddy shook his head.

"I'm aware that you are anxious to get your own plane, but I had rather hoped you would go through Bobby York or Weaver."

"You don't think Ames knows his business?"

"I'm sure he does, but the distance concerns me, and like I said, it seems too spontaneous."

"I've already been to the bank and checked the train schedule."

"I see." Her daddy's jaw twitched. "Very well, then. You're a grown woman, and if you've made up your mind, there's no sense trying to convince you otherwise."

"I guess I'd rather hoped you would be happy for me."

She spun on her heels and left the room, tears stinging her eyes.

The next day when Ames called, she told him when she would be there the following morning. That evening, she boarded the train for the twelve-hour trip. Sleep was elusive even with the curtain drawn around her berth in the Pullman coach. As the wheels clattered on the track beneath her, she wondered if she was being rash. In the next instant, she imagined herself soaring, climbing higher as she nosed through the clouds and came out above them at heaven's footstool.

Stiff and achy, she stepped onto the platform in Lincoln and breathed in the crisp winter morning, the skies wide open.

Ames waved from the rail, and she ran to his outstretched arms. He picked her up and swung her around, then kissed her, his aftershave fresh with a hint of spice.

She leaned back and looked at him. "You must've just come from the barber." She tracked her finger along his smooth cheek, his neatly trimmed sideburns.

"Spiffed up just for you, doll." He picked up her suitcase with one hand and hailed a cab with the other. "Nance—he's the fella selling—doesn't expect us for another hour. How about some breakfast?"

"I'm too nervous to eat, but I'd love a cup of coffee."

Ames told the cab driver the name of a diner close to the Lincoln Flying School where the plane was kept. Twenty minutes later, they sat side by side in a booth, and while Ames ate, Mittie asked him to tell her again about the plane.

"You just need to see it for yourself."

"Should I change into flight gear for a test flight?"

"There's a locker room at the field." He put an arm around her and nuzzled her ear. "I can't tell you how much I've missed you."

"Me, too. And if this works out, is there any chance we might fly back together?"

"There's nothing I'd love more, but when I flew *Trixie* down here, I hadn't reckoned I'd find you a plane. All my gear is back home in Iowa." He squeezed her hand and leaned in close, his breath warm on her cheek.

Something niggled in her brain—Iris' words about getting to know Ames' family. "Wait! I have an idea. Why don't we fly to Iowa together, and I can meet your sister and see where you grew up? I'm in no rush to get back—"

He held up his hand. "Fern would love that, and so would I, but the doctor still hasn't given her clearance to be around people. The pneumonia's put quite a strain on her lungs."

"So she's still under a doctor's care?"

"For now. I'm just relieved she's made as much progress as she has."

"It's good of you to be so attentive. Is her husband able to help?"

"That lowlife? He wouldn't even if he was around. There's just Fern and Lela." He shuddered as if the subject was distasteful.

"Lela? Who's she?"

Ames' hand went to his chest. "I've not told you about Lela? Ah . . ." He took a deep breath, his lips curving into a smile. "She's my niece. Three—no, wait—four years old with big brown eyes and long eyelashes." He widened his eyes in exaggeration.

"Sounds like she got her looks from you."

Ames shook his head. "That train ride must've addled your brain."

"I don't know. I think you're pretty cute."

He drained the last of his coffee. "And with that, I think we should be on our way."

They could see the hangars of the Lincoln Flying School a few blocks away, and since they were still early, they walked, Ames carrying Mittie's bag, the bright clear morning full of promise.

Mr. Nance had clipped hair, graying at the temples, and wore coveralls with a grease rag in the back pocket. When he saw Ames, he wiped his hands on the rag and came to greet them, a curious look on his broad face.

"I see you've brought the missus."

Ames chuckled. "No, this is Mittie Humphreys, the one who's interested in buying the plane."

Mittie offered her hand. "I appreciate you waiting until I had a chance to get here."

Mr. Nance nodded, a look of puzzlement on his broad face. "You're the buyer?"

"I hope to be...after I've had a chance to try out the plane, of course. Ames tells me it flies like a dream."

He nodded toward her and turned to Ames. "Could I talk with you privately?"

"I'm sure that anything you have to say, Mittie would like to hear."

"There's been a misunderstanding. You led me to believe you were buying the plane for yourself, not..." His look soured when his eyes met Mittie's. "I'm sorry; I didn't catch your name."

"Mittie Humphreys from Louisville."

"Mr. Dewberry didn't say anything about no dame."

Ames drew in a deep breath. "You were quite eager to sell yesterday. Has someone given you a better offer?"

His jaw twitched. "I'm sorry for your trouble, miss, but the plane's no longer available."

Ames' face darkened. "What do you mean? I thought we had an understanding."

"I beg to differ. There was never any mention of selling to a woman who is young enough to be my daughter. That Earhart woman should be ashamed putting ideas into girls' heads."

Mittie felt like she'd been hit with a shovel. Who did Mr. Nance think he was? And why hadn't Ames told him she was the buyer? Her pulse pounded in her ears. *Calm down. All is not lost.*

She made a feeble attempt at chuckling. "I admire a man who has strong opinions, and I'm sure you want the best home for your plane. You no doubt wonder if I'm capable. If it's any consolation, I've been through a flying program and have a pilot's license." She walked over and looked at the plane, ran her fingers along the nose. "She's quite a beauty. I hope you'll reconsider. And I'm prepared to pay cash if that's a concern."

Mr. Nance looked from Ames to Mittie. "The plane is not for sale." He turned on the heel of heavy boots and marched toward the hangar, leaving Mittie with her mouth gaping open and fury pulsing through her.

She turned to Ames, trying to control the growl crawling up her throat. "I can't believe he would be so close-minded." The taste of acid came in her mouth. Her eyes narrowed. "Why didn't you tell him I was the buyer?"

Ames held up his hands and took a step back. "I had no idea he would be so pigheaded. He was more than eager yesterday."

"When he thought he was dealing with you . . . a man."

"I may have let on that I was the buyer. I honestly didn't think it was important. What I suspect is he had a better offer and just used you as an excuse."

Mittie gritted her teeth. "You had me come all this way and only told him half of the truth." She picked up her suitcase and walked toward the hangar.

Within seconds he was beside her. "I was only looking out for your best interests. I thought you'd be pleased. Besides..." He stopped, a scowl knitting his dark brows together.

"Besides, what?"

He gave her a sheepish look. "Look, Mr. Nance's opinion isn't all that uncommon. I've run into quite a few who share his outlook. You have to coddle people sometimes to bring them around to new ideas. I was only trying to protect you. I felt certain that once he met you, he'd have no objections."

"It looks like your brilliant plan backfired."

"You're not sore at *me*, are you?" The pleading look in his eyes almost melted her resolve.

She raised her eyebrows and looked steadily into Ames' deep brown eyes. "I'm not sure what I think. Disappointed about the plane, but upset with you, too. All this way for nothing." The heat in her face wasn't just disappointment or anger, although she did feel those things. Mr. Nance was entitled to his opinions, small-minded as they were, but the gnawing in her stomach told her she'd been foolish to have acted so impulsively, a pattern in her life she thought she'd improved on. Apparently not.

Ames tilted her chin with his index finger. "I'm sorry. Let's go somewhere and enjoy what's left of the day."

Mittie shook her head. "There's a train that leaves in two hours. I plan to be on it."

He blew out a breath and shrugged. "Have it your way. I need to be getting back home myself."

A cloud hung in the air between them, one that neither seemed to break through. Ames called a cab to take her to the station and told her he'd call. It sounded hollow.

Halfway to St. Louis, it started snowing—not big, fluffy flakes like they'd had on Christmas Eve, but blinding curtains of snow and sleet. Weather she might very well have been flying in had Mr. Nance granted her ownership of the plane. Her protection hadn't come from Ames, but from a source much greater.

She didn't need Ames Dewberry or anyone else to find her a plane. If she was going to make it in a profession ruled by men, she would have to depend on herself. And maybe a little help from above.

CHAPTER 19

Mittie told her parents the plane hadn't worked out, that she'd changed her mind. She couldn't bear to add that it was also Ames who might not be working out. *Does he really have my best interests at heart?* Her face flamed when she remembered the way she'd stormed off without giving him any credit. She thought she loved him, but was it only the lure of flying that attracted her to him? What he was willing to do for her?

She didn't have an answer, but at odd moments, her hand would go to the chain around her neck, and she would caress the locket he'd given her. They were from different worlds, which didn't concern her nearly as much as it did her mother—her mother who had once thought nothing of leaving England and moving four thousand miles away. Her spunky grandmother had bucked her patrician parents to follow the man she loved.

Ames hadn't asked her to follow him, though, only to take him as he was. Spontaneous. Full of life. Devoted to his sister and his young niece. She remembered the way kids flocked to him when he was barnstorming, his affability with them. And there was a mysterious quality that lured Mittie to him, and she knew if he walked in the door, she would leap into his arms.

She spent long hours in the barns, brushing Gypsy until her coat shone. Winter had a stranglehold on all of them, cold rainy days that made outdoor training risky with the prized horses they stabled. Mittie often joined her daddy and Rex Kline as they observed the trainers conducting exercises in the promenade area between the stalls. Rex Kline had keen intuition and was fast gaining the respect of both the employees he managed and Mittie's dad. Amid the scents of straw and horse sweat and the pine tar and neat's-foot oil that was used to doctor the horses' hooves, an air of optimism about the upcoming spring and summer shows permeated their lives. While Mittie was relieved that the success of MG Farms no longer rode on her shoulders, she was glad for the diversion and happy to lend her opinion when asked.

At night she dreamed of apple blossoms and springtime. In moments of spare time, she read and reread her aviation manuals as she prepared for the international license test and wrote letters to the other women from the St. Louis air race.

She even wrote Calista, who answered back and mentioned that she might be in Louisville in March or April and added a PS: *Any progress on your romance with Ames?*

Mittie fired back that romance was a positively Victorian notion and would interfere with her real love in this life—flying. *Brush up on your technique. I'm gunning for you.*

A week later, Calista sent a postcard. *So scared. You'll be weeping buckets the next time we race.*

At least Calista brought a chuckle. Mittie still wasn't sure she liked her, but they did have one thing in common—they both loved flying.

When Barb from Dallas sent a newspaper clipping that told of her official altitude record, Mittie ached to be among the ranks. She scrawled a note of congratulations and asked for more information.

Then overnight, it seemed, the sun came out and the temperatures soared into the sixties. Robins perched on fence posts, and tiny crocus poked through the earth. Mittie felt a new surge of energy and went to Bowman Field, hoping Weaver might let her take his plane up to get the extra hours needed to qualify for the international license. He was in a meeting, so she sauntered into the canteen to wait for him. She got a cup of coffee and looked around. There was a fresh coat of paint on the walls and a new corkboard by the cigarette machine. She took her coffee and went to see what was posted. Someone had pinned up the article about her flying in the St. Louis rally, and there was a flyer for the next Aero Club meeting. Pictures of Lindbergh and newspaper articles of his visit to Louisville. A few classified ads were tacked haphazardly along with one handwritten note.

Curtis JN-4H for sale. Hispano-Suiza V8.
Well maintained. Reasonable.

There was a daytime phone number as well as an evening one. Both local.

She scribbled down the numbers and went in search of a phone. She asked the operator to connect her to the daytime number. Mittie's palms grew damp as she waited, but then the operator said, "I'm sorry. Your party doesn't answer. May I try another number for you?"

She said she'd try again later and went to see if Weaver could see her yet.

He waved her in and asked how she'd been.

"Better now that the weather's warming up. Matter of fact, I'm simply dying to get in the air again. Any chance of getting your Canuck for a couple of hours?"

"I don't see why not. I've just had it serviced. I was thinking about going up myself but forgot I had a meeting downtown."

"If you're sure."

"You know where everything is. Have one of the boys spin the prop for you."

"Thanks." She headed out the door, then turned back. "I saw a notice in the canteen that someone's selling a Jenny 4H. Any idea who that might be?"

He gave her a lopsided grin. "Thinking of getting your own outfit?"

"It's high time, don't you think?"

"I've been wondering when you'd take the leap. And yes, I know the seller. Bobby York."

"Bobby?" The coffee she'd just swallowed sloshed in a wave of uncertainty. "He's not leaving here, is he?" Guilt crawled along her limbs. She'd not spoken to him since Christmas, although she still had his bread-and-butter note propped on her dressing table that he'd sent thanking them for Christmas dinner.

"Not if I have anything to say about it. The Aero Club's bought him a new plane for flight training. He didn't want his sitting around gathering dust."

"The Aero Club, huh?"

"They're behind the push to get a full-fledged flying school here, and they want Bobby as the director. The telephone won't stop ringing, people wanting to sign up for lessons."

"That's swell of the Aero Club and wonderful for Bobby."

"Winning combination for all of us. And his plane is still a dandy."

It was a dandy. And perfect for what she needed. And she was nearly certain Bobby York would have no objections about selling to a woman.

Mittie broached the subject with her parents that evening after they'd retired to the parlor. Her mother put a fresh Chesterfield in the silver holder and leaned over while her daddy flicked the lighter for her. She took a long drag and leaned back. "I suppose it was too much to dream that when you said you'd changed your mind, it was a permanent decision."

"The timing wasn't right for the plane in Nebraska, and like Daddy's always told me, sometimes you have to follow your instincts and walk away if you don't feel comfortable." She smiled at her dad.

"I told your mother it was only a matter of time, and the truth is, you've seemed like you've been dangling lately."

Mittie laughed. "I was hoping I'd fooled you."

"I've seen the way you worry that locket. Ames has found you another plane, then?"

"Not Ames. And he's part of the dangling you mentioned."

Her mother blew out a puff. "You haven't mentioned him in a month of Sundays. Is everything all right?"

She looked from one parent to the other. "We parted in Nebraska on rather cool turf." She told them about Mr. Nance and his reticence to sell her the plane. "I thought Ames should have been more direct with him before I made the trip. We had a misunderstanding, and I've not heard from him since."

Her daddy pulled his pipe and a pouch of tobacco from his pocket. He seemed lost in thought or trying to come up with a suitable consolation as he worked the tobacco in his fingers and then put a pinch in the bowl, packed it, added another pinch. Only when it was set the way he liked it did he look up. "He had a relative who was ill? You don't suppose he's contracted the same illness?"

"I had thought of it, but he didn't mention that his sister's pneumonia was contagious. And he looked the picture of health in Nebraska." A small knot formed in the pit of her stomach. Ames *had* been trying to please her, and her reaction had been chilly at best.

"A phone call might be warranted." He struck a match and

cupped his hand around the pipe bowl, puffing on the stem. A sweet, smoky smell curled from the pipe. "Why don't you give him a call?"

"I can't. He stays with his sister when he's home, but I don't have her number. I'm sure he's back to flying by now."

"Maybe you'll hear from him soon. So tell us—you said you wanted to talk about an airplane."

She took a deep breath. "I found out today Bobby York is selling his Jenny, the one he used for lessons."

Her mother's head shot up. "Oh, I hope the dear boy's not thinking of leaving us and going back to London."

Mittie laughed. "That was my first thought, too." She told them about the Aero Club and the possibility of a flying school. "I've not called Bobby yet. I wanted to talk to you first—something I should have done before I went to Nebraska."

Her daddy said, "You're a grown woman. You don't need our permission."

"I know I don't. I would just like your blessing."

Her mother scowled and lit another Chesterfield. "That's all I need . . . worrying about you the whole time your father and I are gone."

"Gone? Where are you going?"

"You tell her, Eli."

"There's a saddlebred meeting and a small show outside of London in April, so we're leaving a week from Friday."

"That's wonderful. Now that your back is so much better, you can make this a second honeymoon."

Her mother quirked her mouth. "I'm not sure his back is *that* much better."

"Will you go up to Yorkshire and see Uncle Spencer?"

"For what purpose? To dredge up the past?" She flicked an ash in the crystal ashtray.

The past of which they never spoke. Mittie's gut tightened. *Dobbs Lamberson.* Yes, some things were best left unspoken.

Her daddy drew on the pipe stem, but the fire had gone out. He set it aside and said, "Our trip coincides with the saddlebred show in San Francisco. Your grandmother's been looking forward to it, so I was hoping you could go along in our stead."

"Grandmother wants to go all the way to San Francisco?"

"I, for one, am not telling her no. You two will make good company for each other on the train, and I'm sure you'll enjoy being there with Gypsy."

"You can count on me, Daddy."

Her mother sighed. "All I want to count on is that you don't get yourself killed in an airplane crash."

Gypsy wasn't the only constant in Mittie's life. There was also her mother.

Mittie rose and went to her. "I'll do my best to stay alive, Mother."

At the airfield canteen, Bobby raised his sarsaparilla in a toast. "To you, Mittie, the owner of your own plane."

"And to you, for trusting me with your Jenny." Bobby took a sip and coughed, a look of surprise on his face.

Mittie turned. Ames Dewberry. Tanned and fit. Mittie's heart stopped, then started again, then skipped as Ames strolled toward them.

"Hey, doll, I thought that was your car in the lot. I was on my way to the pay phone to call you." He looked from her to Bobby. "Am I interrupting something?"

Bobby, bless him, answered. Mittie's throat had shut itself off.

"Mittie and I are just having a toast for the good things to come. Pull up a chair."

"Sounds intriguing." He winked at Mittie.

She said, "Hello, Ames. Nice tan."

"Compliments of my trip to Texas. Soon as my sister got back on her feet, I headed south for the rest of the winter." He didn't mention their spat, but then it would be untoward with Bobby sitting there.

"Barnstorming?" She'd decided to play it cool, let him direct the way the conversation went. What she wanted to do was throw her arms around his neck and kiss him. And that would have been untoward as well.

"This and that. Making a buck however I can. I'm close to a deal with a fella in Fort Worth on my air intake idea. Real close."

Bobby nodded to the woman behind the counter. "Another sarsaparilla over here." Ames reached for his wallet, but Bobby told him he'd take care of it. "I believe another celebration is in order."

The sun streamed in the window, dust motes dancing as Mittie told him about her purchase and Bobby's good news with the Aero Club. "And so I can be a real contender, Bobby's been advising me on getting my international license."

"And to think it all started at a garden party on Long Island many moons ago."

Bobby's quizzical look led to an explanation of Mrs. Benchley's party and her first airplane ride.

"I always wondered how you two met. I hate to cut this short, but I'm off to a meeting with the Aero Club. If you need me for anything, Mittie, you know where to find me." He rose and told Ames it was good to see him again.

When Bobby left, Ames leaned back. "So you bought York's plane?"

"He didn't mind selling to a female."

"I'll bet." He shoved away from the table and asked if she'd like to walk with him to the hangar to crank up his roadster.

They walked in silence, the soft breeze a curtain between them.

Finally, Mittie asked, "Why did you come back?"

"Ouch. You know how to hurt a fella, don't you?"

She didn't answer, and to his credit, he didn't put his arm around her or give her a peck on the cheek to soften her up. He let out a long sigh. "I deserved that, and then some. At first I thought I would call you right away and apologize for botching the deal in Lincoln."

Mittie held up her hand. "Part of the blame is mine. The truth is I do appreciate your effort and enthusiasm, and leaving brusquely wasn't quite fair to you."

"Guess we both have regrets. I wanted to call, but the longer I waited, the harder it was to pick up the telephone. Then I got a call from Fort Worth and thought if I could wangle a deal, I could at least come back with good news."

"It sounds good. Are you pleased with the terms?"

"Nothing's been signed, but I'm hopeful, and yes, I couldn't be happier."

"I guess you'll be heading back to Texas soon, then."

He frowned. "I will eventually, yes." He worked his mouth like he was trying to find the words. "You asked why I came back. I couldn't stop thinking about you, doll. I needed to see if you'd still want me around. You've no idea how many times I've woken at night in a cold sweat from dreaming about you."

"I've had a few of those nights myself." She took a deep breath. "And I've missed you terribly." She held out her hand for a shake. "Still friends, then?"

He clasped her hand and drew it to his lips. "I hope more than friends. I must admit, I was sweating bullets when I saw you in the canteen with York. I almost turned around and left."

"What stopped you?"

"The reflection of the gold chain around your neck. I thought if you were still wearing the locket, I had a chance."

She squeezed his hand that still held hers. "Welcome back."

CHAPTER 20

Spring 1928

Mittie would've slept in her new plane if she could have, feeling at once motherly and as possessive as a mama bear with her cub. Instead, she had the plane painted a creamy caramel color with black rimming the wings. On the side, in rich mahogany script, was the name she'd given it. *Belle. Belle of the Skies.* She thought the name had a nice ring to it, one of promise and enchantment.

Ames slipped back into her life, and Mittie wondered how she could have ever doubted him. And it was Ames who announced that a proper christening for *Belle* would be an air demonstration with the Patriots, who'd come out of winter hibernation. He scouted out a location across the river, and on a breezy day at the end of March, they did loops and stalls, end over end, flying in formation. Buster drew gasps from the onlookers with his ladder tricks and walking on air from the wing of one plane to another. The last two hours they gave airplane rides. When Mittie looked out across the sea of faces, her eyes connected with those of Bobby York. What a sly fox—sneaking in to see how she'd done in his plane. She waved to let him know she'd seen him, and when she looked again later, he was gone.

Back at Bowman Field, she and Ames headed to the canteen for a soft drink before servicing their planes and found Bobby sitting with a familiar-looking blonde. Bobby raised his chin in greeting, and the girl turned around. Calista Gilson.

Calista squealed and jumped up, gliding across the floor with open arms. "Ames! Kentucky!"

Mittie offered her hand and smiled. "Mittie, not Kentucky."

Calista pressed her fingers to her lips. "Oops, I forgot." She turned to Ames and puckered her cupid lips.

He gave her a peck on the cheek. "Hey, Peach. What are you doing here? Did you get separated from that wild bunch in Texas and lose your way?"

Mittie's head snapped to attention. "You two saw each other in Texas?"

Calista nodded and fluffed her marcel-waved bob, but it was Ames' question she answered. "I didn't get lost. I left. Cheap rats wouldn't pay me. I'm looking for a new gig and was hoping you and Lester might have something."

Ames said, "I'm sure we could work something out. Anything special you had in mind?"

She dipped her chin, her pale gray eyes wide. "I'm game for anything you are."

Ames looked around at the group. "What say we all get some grub and talk things over with Peach? The Hen's Nest okay?"

Calista linked arms with Bobby. "Do you still have that darling little foreign car?"

Bobby nodded. "If you mean the Morris, yes. Not that I consider it foreign, mind you."

Mittie said she'd meet them there, that she'd like to run by her cousin Nell's and change.

Calista winked. "I could teach you a few tricks about living out of a suitcase."

"Looks like it worked for you." She eyed Calista's pale lemon dress that hugged her like a second skin. "I'll only be a few minutes." What she really needed was a bath, a hairdresser, and a trip to a New York salon, and even then, she'd be dowdy next to Calista.

Ames gave her a quick hug. "Don't be too long. I'm starving."

An hour later, they were all crowded around a small table while Calista regaled them with a story about her close encounter with a jellyfish at the beach in Galveston. "Tell them, Ames, about the baby shark you caught."

Mittie's breath caught. "What am I missing here? Obviously, you two crossed paths in Texas, but you went to the beach?" *Together?*

Calista laughed. "Oh, didn't Ames tell you? He flew with us down by Houston. How do you think he got that gorgeous tan?"

"I see." Only she didn't. And she didn't like the jealous feeling creeping through her brought on by the familiarity between Ames and Calista.

Calista laughed. "It wasn't like we went alone, if that's what you're worried about. A whole swarm of us went together. At least the cheapskates I was with paid for my bus ticket and bought my lunch that day."

On the tiny stage, a combo was warming up with screechy brass sounds and off-key thrums on the bass—sounds that matched the medley in Mittie's chest.

Mittie had never given in to petty jealousy like some of the girls she'd known, and even now it irritated her that she'd given in to the feeling. Ames was free to go to Texas or Mars without her permission. And they'd parted at odds in Nebraska, so why did Calista feel like a burr in her britches?

When Ames walked her to her car later, he told her nothing went

on between him and Calista. "Peach is like a lost puppy trying to
find her place in the world."

"She's just so friendly. And chatty. I suppose I should be more
hospitable. Gracious, as we say in the South."

"I think Peach could use a friend."

"If she's still here when I get back from San Francisco, I'll invite
her out to the house. Maybe ask you and Bobby, too."

Ames drew her in his arms. "I'm going to miss you like the
devil."

"You're welcome to come along."

"Thanks, but the Patriots are counting on me."

And Calista. But Mittie didn't mention it.

Mittie's parents wired that they'd arrived safely in London and were
looking forward to hearing the results of the horse show in San
Francisco.

On the train ride, Mittie and her grandmother coaxed Rex Kline
and one of the horse owners into playing canasta. It didn't take
much arm-twisting with Rex, who Mittie suspected was smitten
with her grandmother.

That night in their Pullman compartment, Mittie teased her. "I
saw the way Rex kept looking at you with a twinkle in his eyes."

Her grandmother didn't even blush. "Lord-a-mercy, at my age,
I'm happy for every breath, so if the man wants to flirt with me, I'm
not going to stop him."

"So it wasn't my imagination."

Her grandmother's laugh was deep and throaty. "I've known Rex
half my life. He and his wife went to dinner with your grandfather
and me at many a horse show. If you'd been paying attention, you'd
have noticed that he comes over and eats supper with me practically
every night."

"Really? Do Mother and Daddy know this?"

"I suspect that's why they wanted you to come along on this trip—to chaperone us."

"And all this time, I thought it was so you could keep me out of trouble."

"I gave up on that long ago, sweetheart." She pulled a hairnet over her silver hair. "I just hope your young man knows what he's getting himself into."

"If you're referring to Ames, he's not my young man. I have worlds of things I want to do and accomplish before I settle into a serious relationship."

A furrow creased the space between her carefully shaped brows. "You're not playing with his affections under false pretenses, I hope."

"What do you mean?"

"Ames is accomplished and has connections that will help further your career, I would assume."

"And you think I'm using him—is that it?"

"It's crossed my mind." Her grandmother dipped her fingers in a tin of cold cream and smoothed it over her soft-lined face. "I remember you coming back from New York and the caper you had flying with him."

"I know. Everyone thought it was just Mittie being wild, the way I always was, but I think it was meant to be, that I was meant to find Ames."

Her grandmother studied an age spot on the back of her hand. "If that's the case, then I'm sure everything will work out and you'll forgive your old grandmother for fretting. It's not just your parents who worry, you know."

"Trust me—there's nothing to worry about."

Mittie stared at the ceiling long after her grandmother's soft snores filled the compartment. Was it possible that subconsciously she was using Ames for her own selfish aspirations? That she leaned on him to satisfy her hunger to learn and do and be all the things she dreamed of? Bobby York flickered in her thoughts. He'd been as much a part of her accomplishment as Ames, but it was Ames who accelerated her heart, made her weak in the knees with his kisses, and brought out the she-bear claws when Calista danced into the picture.

Her fingers went to the locket between her breasts, the smooth gold on the back, the slightly textured surface on the front. She drifted off and dreamed of looking across the supper table at Ames when their faces were creased with wrinkles and their hair had turned to silver.

At the horse show the next morning, Gypsy took first in the four-year-old class prancing and showing with confidence. She'd matured in the past year, and her performance earned her place in the five-gait championship the following afternoon. When the championship winners were announced, Mittie's heart was in her throat. Gypsy finished a remarkable second. Rex Kline said it called for a night on the town.

They feasted on *dim sum* at the Hang Ah Tea Room, tucked in an alley of Chinatown, and afterward chugged up the hill to take the cable car to the Columbia Theater. The silent film *Wings*, a wartime story featuring two pilots and the lovely Clara Bow, was showing with a full orchestra to add to the drama. Mittie dotted tears from the corners of her eyes when the credits blinked in black and white on the screen. If she could have, she would've sat through the whole movie again, but it was late, and they had an early train.

When they'd settled in the cab to return to their hotel, Rex took her grandmother's knobby hand in his. A perfect ending to a lovely trip. Mittie hoped that Gypsy's excellent work in the ring was the harbinger of things to come when Mittie took to the air.

★ ★ ★

Mittie gave her parents a report on the San Francisco show when they returned from London. Her daddy laughed and asked if Grandmother had behaved herself.

"Sweet as a lamb." She gave him a knowing wink.

"And you? What have you been up to?"

"Staying close to the stables, flying some, and going out with Ames and the Patriots in the evenings. We have a demonstration coming up the first of June, and Bobby got word about a ladies' altitude challenge in Little Rock. He thinks I'll qualify for the international license by then."

Her mother opened her mouth to say something, then paused. Her mouth widened into a smile. "It sounds wonderful, dear. I know you'll have a marvelous time."

Mittie's jaw slackened. "I expected another lecture on the perils of flying and not getting myself killed."

"Ordinarily, you would have been right to assume that, but I had quite an enlightening conversation when we were in London."

"Do tell." She looked at her daddy who shrugged as if he knew nothing.

"A wise gentleman told me that if you held a budgie in your hand too tightly, you would kill it, but if you release it and it flies away, it was never yours to begin with. If it comes back, you've a friend for life."

"That's lovely . . . and so poetic. Who was this wise man?"

"Robert York."

"Bobby's dad? I didn't know you saw him."

"We had a lovely dinner."

It was no mystery who Robert York was talking about. She wondered if he and Bobby had argued over his choice of aviation and that his dad was hopeful that Bobby would return and do something more to his liking. A spidery thread tingled along her spine, a realization that his father's gain would be a great loss to her.

Her daddy cleared his throat. "Good man, Robert York. So where is this demonstration you mentioned?"

"Memphis."

"Sarah, we've not been to Memphis in a while. Why don't we go and find out what all the fuss is about?"

Her mother put her hand to her chest. "Now darlin', let's not get carried away."

CHAPTER 21

The Memphis event got off on a bad leg. A bird flew into Lester's propeller on takeoff outside of Nashville, delaying him and Shorty and Buster. When Ames, Calista, and Mittie arrived at the small hangar on the outskirts of Memphis, the owner asked for the payment to use his facility up front.

Ames clapped him on the back. "Hey, you know how this is. We've spent all our operating funds on the adverts and fuel to get here. I'd be happy to pay you after the first day's gate."

The man crossed his arms and shook his head. "I got burned by the last outfit that went through here." He looked at their three planes. "I thought there were five of you."

Ames explained that the other two would be in later.

"Money for all five up front or you'll have to leave."

Ames puffed out his cheeks. "Give me a minute while we talk."

He took Mittie and Calista aside. "He's got us over a barrel. The others won't know where to find us if we go into the city airfield, and if we cancel, word will spread. We won't be able to fly within a hundred miles of here. I'm open to suggestions."

Calista waved away a fly. "Don't look at me. I'm broke until after this show." They both looked at Mittie.

Ames said, "I hate to ask you, doll. I thought everything was square. And I know you're excited because your parents are coming to see you."

"Mother would be relieved if we cancelled, but we've given our word that we would put on a show. And we will."

Mittie strolled over to the owner of the hangar and asked what the fee was, then dug in her pants pocket for her coin purse and paid the man.

"Thank you kindly. I'll need a fuel deposit, too. Fifty dollars."

She pursed her lips and handed him two twenties and a ten.

By dusk, Lester and Shorty had still not arrived, so Ames called a taxi for Mittie and Calista. "Your folks are expecting you. I'll spend the night here with the planes."

Mittie and Calista collected their things from their baggage compartments. Ames draped an arm around Mittie. "I don't know what I'd do without you, doll. Tell your folks I'm sorry I didn't make it to dinner."

"They'll understand."

The upsets of the day had put Calista on edge, too, and when she and Mittie arrived at the Peabody Hotel, she took one look and said, "I can't afford to stay in a swanky place like this."

"Don't worry—we're sharing a room, and it's taken care of."

The porter showed them to their room and opened their suitcases. Mittie gave him a tip and told Calista they needed to hurry. "I told Daddy we'd meet them for dinner at eight."

Mittie peeled off her clothes and bathed first. She twisted her hair into a knot on top of her head and fastened a simple headpiece with a cluster of pearls and smoky glass at the center. A quick touch-up of her cheeks from a rouge pot and she was ready. "Your turn."

After her bath, Calista slipped into a slim-fitting angular striped black and white dress. She blinked eyelashes still wet with paste mascara. "So Daddy Moneybags is picking up the tab, then?"

"He is, but don't you dare call him that. It's the first time they've come to watch me fly, so I want everything to go according to Hoyle."

"I'll be on my best behavior." She cocked one hip and gave a fake grin.

The waiter showed them to the table where her parents were waiting. "You've heard me talk about Calista, but I'm not sure you've met." She made the introductions.

Mittie's mother had a strained look, her eyes drooping at the corners. "We're so pleased to meet you. And I must say, that dress is simply darling. Not from one of our Louisville shops, is it?"

"This? Oh, it's just some glad rag I picked up at a church rummage sale."

"Aren't you clever? I'll remember that next time someone asks me a pointed question. My apologies, dear, for prying. Please, girls, have a seat."

Mittie's daddy pulled out the chair for Calista. "I do believe I detect a Georgia accent."

Mittie held her breath and hoped Calista didn't go into her spiel about those damn Yankees again, but she just nodded and said, "Yes, sir. Atlanta."

Mittie's dad pulled his watch from his vest pocket. "Ames must be delayed."

"Oh, fiddle, Daddy. I forgot. He's not coming. He wanted me to convey his regrets, and honestly, the night before a show, he's always got a lot on his mind."

"Sounds like the saddlebred business." He took his seat and signaled for the waiter, who brought sweet tea and presented menus. After they'd ordered, Mittie's dad asked, "And you'll be flying as well, Calista?"

"Mittie and I have a routine we're doing, yes, but in a crowd like this, my specialty is wing walking. It's quite the thrill."

"I'm sure." Mittie's mother took a sip of water. "It's just so dangerous." She gave a weak smile; Mittie knew she was trying valiantly not to say more.

Calista laughed. "That's what we want everyone to think, Mrs. Humphreys. It adds to the excitement."

"Wouldn't it be just as effective if you were in a harness of some sort to keep you from plummeting to the earth if something happened?"

"Oh no. That's what makes people love it, seeing me out there just free as a bird. You'll see tomorrow."

Mittie's mother had turned as white as a frog's belly, and Mittie patted her hand and told her it was okay, that she didn't have to watch. When the meal came, her mother nibbled at her pork cutlet for a few minutes, then folded her napkin and rose. "I've developed the most horrendous headache. I think I'll go lie down."

"Would you like me to come with you, Mother?"

"I'll be fine. You'll want to stay and have dessert." She kissed Mittie's cheek. "Good night, dear."

When she left, Mittie shrugged and told Calista that her flying was difficult for her mother.

"Mine didn't like it at first, but she came around."

"How did you convince her?"

"I send her a twenty-dollar bill every time I do a show. Works like a charm."

There weren't enough twenty-dollar bills in circulation that would take away Sarah Humphreys' disdain for Mittie's flying.

Lester, Shorty, and Buster didn't arrive until it was time for the show to start. Ames and Calista had given airplane rides while Mittie circulated through the crowd, hoping to find her parents. She still hadn't found them when Ames grabbed the megaphone and told everyone to get ready to be amazed by the daring feats of the Patriots and the Belles of the Sky.

Disappointment at not finding her parents contracted Mittie's chest as she waved to the crowd and slid into the cockpit. She and Calista were first up on the agenda with synchronized triple rolls followed by spirals and stalls from Ames and the Patriots. Halfway through, Mittie landed and taxied to the side to watch Calista and Buster's wing walking, ladder climbing, and heart-stopping feats. Calista had done a quick change in the cockpit of her plane and emerged in the gauzy white dress that Ames said made her look like an angel. Mittie sat up on the side of *Belle* for a better view and looked again for her parents.

She spotted them along the rope. Front row. Her daddy had his arm around her mother, their faces curious but sober. Mittie whispered a prayer and watched as Calista floated from the top wing of Lester's plane to that of Shorty's. Free as a bird.

When they finished and it was time for the airplane rides, her daddy was already in line. And beside him was her mother. Panic rose in Mittie's throat. She took a deep breath and sauntered over to them.

"Did you enjoy the show?"

Her daddy's grin was as wide as *Belle*'s wings. "I'll say this, sugar—I had no idea this many people were interested in airplanes. You were a marvel to watch."

Her mother nodded, her face frozen in a half smile.

"Looks like you're in line for a ride. Who's first?"

Her mother stepped forward. "Me. If I die, I won't have to watch your father go up."

"You're not going to die, Mother. And I promise, nothing fancy. Just up, look at the scenery, and back down." She guided her mother toward the plane. She grabbed a helmet and strapped it on her mother. "Okay, now step up on the wing." She coaxed her gently. Her mother looked down, her hand flying to her lips.

"Mittie, I don't think I can do this."

"You'll never know until you try. Now comes the tricky part—climbing into the cockpit gracefully. After that, it's as simple as pie. I'll stand behind you so no one can see you if your dress hikes up."

Once in the cockpit with her shoulder harness secure, her mother gripped the wheel so fiercely that Mittie was afraid she would rip it from the shaft.

"Relax. Here, hold onto this." She handed her a canvas canteen. "Squeeze this all you want." Goggles adjusted. "Hey, you look pretty ducky."

Her mother's expression hadn't changed, but all the color was gone from her face. Mittie hopped in the cockpit before her mother had a chance to change her mind. She taxied, slowly at first, but when they hit the first bump, her mother let out a bloodcurdling scream.

Mittie eased up and rolled the plane to the far edge of the pasture. She couldn't do this. Her mother was terrified and to take her up in the air might very well kill her. Mittie throttled down and pulled to a stop, hopped out, and leaned over her mother's seat.

Terror-filled eyes met hers. "What? What are you doing? Do you want people to think I'm a coward, that I'm the only person here who isn't thrilled to bits over a silly airplane ride?" Her mother's shoulders shook, her breaths short, eyes wide.

"Mother, look at me." She did. "Tell me—why are you so afraid?"

A slow shake of her head, eyes downcast.

"We're not leaving this field until you tell me." Mittie hated the motherly tone her voice carried.

"Take me back, and I'll tell you. Not here."

Mittie taxied back and helped her mother out, then told the on-lookers her fuel was low and she wouldn't be giving any more rides. Her mother flipped her hair and said to the crowd, "If that don't

beat all. My first chance to ride in an airplane and it's out of gas."
She hooked her hand in the crook of Mittie's daddy's arm, and the
two of them ambled off into the crowd.

Mittie begged off from going out to eat with Ames and the rest
of the gang that evening, saying she promised to spend time with
her parents. In their hotel room, Mittie crossed her arms and looked
at her mother. "You said you'd tell me."

Her mother stepped back and lowered herself onto the settee.
She closed her eyes, her lips trembling. Her eyelids fluttered open,
her gaze unfocused as she spoke. "I'm terrified of heights...Every
time I think of you flying off in that airplane, that despicable face
pops into my head."

"Whose face?"

Sarah's spine stiffened. "His. My murderous father. Our house,
that cold gray mansion whose walls hold more secrets than the pyra-
mids of Egypt, sat up on a ridge. Mama always cautioned us about
not getting too close, said we'd fall to our death. What she didn't
know was that once when I mouthed off to Papa, he yanked me up
and carried me outside."

Daddy dropped down beside Mittie's mother and slipped an arm
around her. "It's all right, Sarah."

Her mother continued, her voice faraway. "I screamed that I was
sorry, but he took me to the ridge and dangled me over the edge.
'Do you know what happens to little girls who sass their papas?' His
voice—" She shuddered, her small frame looking like it might swallow her. "I still remember that voice. Syrupy, like he was asking if
I'd like to go for a pony ride. 'Open your eyes, darling, and look.'
I opened them, the earth at the bottom a million miles away." Her
breaths came in gasps. "I couldn't look, but still he held me under my arms and swung me back and forth. Back and forth." Tears
streamed down her face, her shoulders now shaking as sobs escaped
her throat.

Mittie knelt before her and took her mother's hands. "I'm sorry, Mother. I didn't know."

"How could you? I've never told a living soul. I thought I could manage the fear if I faced it and went up in the plane...but it's no use."

"I won't ask you to." She laid her head in her mother's lap, her own eyes damp with tears. They sat there, the three of them, no words necessary, the only sound the ticking of her daddy's pocket watch.

CHAPTER 22

Mittie's mother, the one she'd always thought of as fearless, didn't mention the incident again. Like the other wounds they carried, it was written on their hearts and sealed. The measure of peace Mittie gained from knowing it wasn't something she'd done to conjure up her mother's disdain for flying was overshadowed by a deep sorrow for the past her mother had endured—a past that had given her the strength of iron. Whether she was still opposed to Mittie's flying or not, her mother had truly given up the fight over the inevitable. Mittie was born to fly.

Her mother hugged her the day she left for Little Rock and the altitude challenge. It was enough. Ames and the Patriots had traveled north for another air show, so Mittie and Calista went alone. They talked about going down to Hot Springs to take in the waters but changed their minds and walked along the banks of the Arkansas River and ate supper at a sidewalk café.

The challenge day dawned glorious. An announcer at the Little Rock airfield welcomed the Fédération Aéronautique Internationale–certified observers whose verification was necessary for official records. Mittie's international license had arrived by post just in time and would qualify her to be a record holder if she was fortunate enough to break the women's altitude record set two weeks before. When Mittie's name was announced, the crowd roared—not for her, she knew, but because they'd come in hopes of witnessing history.

Not a breath of air stirred as Mittie strapped on her helmet, waved toward the bleachers, and waited for the okay from the official to crawl into the cockpit. Ames had coached her the evening before on the telephone, talked of decreased air density with the warmer temperatures, the high humidity Little Rock was known for, and going for the best rate of climb.

Calista waved from her spot in front of the bleachers where she stood with one of the FAI-certified observers. Mittie did the final run-up, secured her goggles, and taxied. She prayed that *Belle* wouldn't let her down. At three thousand feet, Mittie leveled the plane momentarily and decreased the air-to-fuel ratio, then nosed back up. Five thousand feet. Eight thousand. Ten—a record for her, but Bobby had assured her the plane could go at least twelve. She adjusted the fuel mixture again and pulled back on the stick. At eleven thousand feet, her eyes stung; no amount of blinking was enough to bring relief to the gritty surface beneath her eyelids. Her lungs craved air, but when she inhaled, it was as if they could only hold a thimbleful. Eleven six. *Just four hundred more. Come on,* Belle. *You can do it.*

The engine sputtered. She checked the gauges. Nothing out of line. She gave one more pull, but eleven seven was the most she could do. She pursed her lips, her breaths short and shallow, her muscles twitching, and eased the stick forward for the descent.

Her official recording was 11,724 feet—a new light-aircraft women's record.

An hour later, Calista flew 11,920 feet and won the competition. That evening, Mittie and Calista walked along the river again arm in arm. Warriors together.

★ ★ ★

Ames called when they returned to Kentucky and congratulated Mittie and said he wished he'd been there to see it.

"I wish you could have, too. So, are you back? Wanna come out for dinner?"

"We're still up north. Folks up here are going crazy over the shows. We're going into Ohio this weekend. Could I interest you and Calista in a little circus fun?"

"It's very tempting, but I'm going with Mother and Daddy to the St. Louis horse show in July. There's always plenty to do to get ready, and this year we're taking Gypsy and horses for three of our owners."

"Sometimes I think I'm competing with a four-legged creature."

"You're both pretty magnificent." Her fingers worried the locket around her neck. "I just had a keen idea. Why don't you go with us? You've not seen Gypsy in the ring, and she's almost as graceful as Buster up on the wings."

"Now who's tempting who? What are the dates?"

She told him and added, "I'd love it if you could come."

Ames returned two days before Mittie was due to leave. Just barely. *Trixie's* engine had a knock and needed to be replaced. "It'll cost most of what I made in Ohio for the parts."

"Can it wait until we get back?"

"No, the new one's arriving tomorrow, and I'll need *Trixie* after the horse show. Don't worry—I'm still coming. I'll just drive the roadster."

As promised, Ames arrived in St. Louis in time for an early dinner at the elegant Union Station Hotel the evening before the show.

"Daddy's gone to a saddlebred board meeting, so I told him we'd go to the arena and check on the horses. I hope you don't mind."

"Sounds good. I'll drive."

When they arrived at the arena, the stalls were bustling with activity—grooms scurrying with buckets of water and spreading sweet-smelling straw to bed the horses. Sweat shone on the grooms' faces, shirts clinging to their backs in the humidity.

While walking toward the MG Farms stalls, she said, "Gypsy's in top form, and we've brought a pretty little sorrel stallion that shows great promise." They found Toby brushing Gypsy, and Ames asked if he could give it a try. He handed his jacket to Mittie and rolled up his sleeves. He made long strokes along Gypsy's sides, the muscles in his forearm strong and rippling.

Mittie draped Ames' jacket over her arm, and when she did, an envelope fluttered to the ground. She scooped it up and put it in her handbag for safekeeping, then offered a carrot nugget to Gypsy. After she made sure Toby and the grooms had all they needed, she and Ames strolled arm in arm toward the car. She asked how the engine replacement had gone, and he told her he'd found a couple of other things that needed work as well.

"*Trixie's* good as new. Think you'll be ready to do some flying when we get back?" They'd come to the car and Ames leaned against it, a banana moon dangling from the sky above him.

She nestled against his chest. "As a matter of fact, Bobby's been scouting some competitions for Calista and me to enter. He's had a few ideas that we're going to talk about next week."

His muscles tensed. "I'm sure York has plenty of ideas. I've seen the way he looks at you."

Mittie stepped back and wrinkled her nose. "Ames Dewberry, I do believe you're jealous. And you needn't be. Calista's the one who's sweet on him."

"Peach is sweet on every man that waltzes into the room."

"You know this from experience?"

"She's not my type. I prefer my dolls to have long legs and a dark mane that I can run my fingers through." His fingers grazed her cheek, then raked through her hair, sending a tingle up her spine.

"You've just described Gypsy."

His lips drew close. "Two beauties. But there's only one I want to do this with." His mouth found hers, the taste of him like summer wine. Her arms slipped around his waist, his body firm and warm and delicious.

Ames planted kisses on her lips, her cheek, her neck. A group of rowdy grooms passed on the other side of the car, breaking the spell. Ames gave her a last kiss on the forehead and said they'd better get back.

When they returned, Mittie told Ames she'd meet him for breakfast if he'd like. He agreed and walked with her to the elevator. While waiting, she remembered the envelope and pulled it from her handbag.

"I nearly forgot. This fell from your jacket back at the arena." She held it out. It was addressed to him in a feminine script. "Looks like a letter from a girlfriend."

"Now who's jealous?" He reached to take the envelope, but she held on to it, teasing him and holding it up like she was trying to read through the paper. The return address was Red Gulch, Iowa. And the name Fern Danner.

"Ah, your sister?" She handed it over to him. "How's she doing?"

"Fair to middlin'."

"That doesn't sound particularly good."

"It's Lela who's ailing now. Scarlet fever."

"Oh no! That's quite serious."

"She's over the worst of it, but Fern hasn't been able to work, and they're behind on their rent. She wrote to tell me they got an eviction notice."

"How dreadful. Do you need to go up there and help them out?"

"I don't have the money. I just spent all my spare change on *Trixie*."

The elevator doors clanged open. They told the operator their floor, and when they reached Mittie's room, she'd made a decision. "How much is the back rent? I could loan you the money. I can't imagine having a sick child and losing your home."

Ames ran his fingers through his hair, his face lined with worry. "I can't ask you to do that. I just feel so danged helpless."

"Let's just call it my good deed for the summer. I'll go to a bank here in the morning and get the money."

"You'd do that, doll?"

"Of course, I would. It's the right thing to do."

Ames pulled her into his arms for an encore kiss. She slipped the key into the lock, the taste of his lips lingering long after she'd closed the door and turned out the light.

Mittie declined her mother's invitation to go shopping with her and two of the owners' wives so she could go to the bank. She gave Ames the money and told him she'd promised to get to the arena early. "Do you mind wiring the money and meeting me later?"

"No. And I don't know how I can ever thank you."

"It's your family. You don't have to thank me."

Mittie found her dad in the convening area reserved for owners and trainers and their guests. She chitchatted with them until Ames arrived and her dad introduced him. "Ames is the aeronautical mastermind of a new engine."

"Only a small part of it, sir. Just a modification, really, a new twist on the carburetor to increase efficiency."

One of the men perked up. "I've quite an interest in aviation myself. I've had my own plane a couple of years. Humphreys, you ought to get one for yourself. One of those Tri-Motors would get you and the family to the association meetings and shows in style."

"I'm not the flier in the family. Mittie is."

One of the men asked what she flew.

"A Curtiss Jenny. I've just returned from an altitude challenge in Little Rock, dipping my toes into competition."

"Can't pick up the newspaper nowadays without reading about some daredevil trying a new stunt or setting a record."

Her daddy told them he'd been to watch her fly. "I think Mittie has a great future ahead of her."

The subject drifted to the upcoming presidential election and whether Hoover had the spine to shake things up and equalize salaries for the average person. They discussed the pros and cons, and then one of the owners said, "I've been meaning to tell you, Humphreys, a fella over in Oldham County's trying to undercut your stable prices."

"Doesn't surprise me. I could do it for less, too, if I went with inferior feed and didn't keep my barns weathertight. A well-looked-after animal will get more wins in the ring."

"Right you are. Just thought you ought to know their stable is recruiting. I had a phone call a couple of weeks ago."

"Anyone I might know? I like to keep abreast of the competition, you know."

"Lamberson Farms. Fella named Ogilvie called me. Their offer sounded quite attractive."

Mittie's stomach did a twist. Buck Lamberson just wouldn't quit. Her daddy hesitated, like he was chewing on a response, so Mittie said, "We do know both of them, and there's no doubt they have some fine animals. And I think I can speak for Daddy when I say that I appreciate your telling us."

"Mittie's right. We like to keep honest communication with our owners. I do hope you'll wait until after tomorrow night's championship before you consider their offer."

"Absolutely."

"Come; let's see if we can find our seats. You kids come along whenever you'd like."

Mittie nodded and turned to Ames. "Gypsy's not until the third class, but I like to spend time with her before she shows and also see if Toby needs anything. Why don't you come with me?"

"You run along. I need to call Fern. She didn't answer earlier, and I wanted to let her know I'd wired the money. Besides, I don't want my presence to be a distraction for you."

She gave him directions to their seats and went to the holding area, a little distracted herself by the news that Buck Lamberson was recruiting. April Showers and Gingersnap were both entered in events, and Mittie was curious to see how they'd fared since she'd seen them almost a year ago. She was relieved when she didn't bump into either Mr. Lamberson or Ogilvie and found Toby calm and Gypsy with a gleam in her eye. When the call to mount was given, Mittie wished them well and hurried to the grandstand.

Mittie slid into the seat next to her dad. "Has Ames made it yet?"

"I thought he was with you."

"He needed to make a phone call. I went to check on Gypsy. She's ready."

"As am I."

Moments later, Mittie's mother and the two owners' wives hurried into the box.

One of the ladies, a buxom woman wearing a hat large enough to be a small parachute, leaned over and whispered to Mittie, "Your mother knows the most marvelous shops. You should have come with us."

"Maybe next time. I'm glad it was enjoyable." There really was no one better than her mother at being in charge of a shopping trip. Mittie stretched her neck, looking over the crowd for Ames.

The woman asked if they'd missed anything.

"No, we have a horse in the upcoming five-gait. The three-year-old class with your stallion is right after. They were moving to the holding area when I was back there a few minutes ago."

The organ music started and the horses were announced. Gypsy was third to enter and received a hearty round of applause. Mittie never tired of watching the horses being put through their paces and mentally calculating—trying to outguess—what the judges would say. They made up their minds quickly. Gypsy won the class. And Ames had missed it.

When the stallion class entered, the woman in the hat giggled and grabbed her husband's hand. "Isn't this exciting, Henry?"

And it was. Toby sat tall in the seat of the cutback saddle guiding the sorrel stallion. The horse was magnificent and strutted like a peacock in mating season. He easily won his class, and his owners left to celebrate in the Owner's Club. Mittie's dad, though, thought they should watch the next event to see what Gypsy might be up against if she qualified for the championship.

The mares trotted out one by one, but it was the fifth horse that made Mittie gasp—April Showers. If the sorrel was a peacock, she was a haggard chicken. Mittie could scarcely believe it was the same horse that had won the World's Championship at the Kentucky State Fair. Her coat was dull, and her gait erratic. At first, it looked like it took all her effort to keep her head erect. Then she perked up, overcompensating, her movements energetic but jerky. The gentleman riding her had a strained look on his face as well, trying to coax April Showers but clearly failing.

Mittie was afraid to look at her daddy, but she knew he must have had the same sick feeling in his stomach as she did. Lamberson had lured Mr. Ford's horse away from them and then ruined her. Disgust blanketed Mittie.

A striking dapple mare won the class, and April Showers came in next to last, ahead of a horse that had skeletal ribs and a limp. It was a good evening for MG Farms, but when Ames slid into the seat next to her and asked what he'd missed, tears sprang to Mittie's eyes. She didn't know if they were for April Showers or because Ames had missed the show.

Mittie hovered around the stables the following morning, jittery over the possibility of seeing April Showers' owner and what words of consolation she could possibly offer. Ames, too, seemed on edge, not his usual carefree self. He'd finally talked to his sister and apologized for missing the performance the day before, but Mittie suspected he was also uncomfortable being thrust into the horse world. Gypsy's win the day before qualified her for the championship round, but it wasn't until later that evening, so Mittie asked Ames if he'd like to get away from the arena for a while.

Ames suggested going to see *The Patsy*, a movie someone had recommended to him. It was a comedy, and it felt good to laugh and hold hands with Ames in the theater. They took a long walk along the banks of the Mississippi River afterward and stopped in a coffee shop for a sandwich. It was nearly time for the championship show when they got back to the arena, just enough time to slip into their seats before the organ music and pageantry began.

The air was electric as the horses began their entry. The sorrel stallion won quite an ovation, and Mittie's heart swelled at the honor of having two horses from MG Farms in the championship. A win for either one would be a feather in her dad's cap. Three other horses entered and made their singular lap. Mittie tucked her hand into Ames' and asked if he was enjoying the show.

"I had no idea there was such pomp and circumstance."

"Just wait for the one in Louisville. It's even better." She turned her attention to the ring and watched for Gypsy. Her breath quickened, palms sweaty as she waited. And waited. Still, Gypsy didn't appear.

"Ladies and gentlemen, let's give a hand for this year's championship judges."

Mittie nudged her daddy and asked where Gypsy was. He shrugged.

The show steward approached the judging tables in the center of the ring and whispered something to the announcer. "Here you have it—a fine field of horses. Enjoy the show."

Unease crawled from the pit of Mittie's stomach to her throat. She looked around for Rex and saw him hustling toward the exit. Her dad, too, was on his feet.

Mittie whispered to Ames, "Stay here. I'm going with Daddy."

"What's going on?"

"That's what I intend to find out."

She matched her dad's determined stride as they clipped down the steps and hurried toward the holding area, which swarmed with people. Mittie's dad elbowed his way through and nearly bumped into Rex, who said, "The steward says Gypsy didn't show. Let's go to the stall."

Mittie turned and ran, panic rising in her chest. *Stay calm.* There had to be a perfectly reasonable explanation Toby hadn't brought Gypsy to the ring. Guilt riddled her. She'd opted to be with Ames rather than come down for her usual preshow check with Toby. Mittie shoved through a knot of people blocking the path to the stall area, adrenaline pumping through her. The door to the stall was open, and inside she found Toby, bareheaded but dressed in his black tails, kneeling in front of Gypsy. He held a towel to her knee that was splotched with scarlet.

Mittie bit her knuckles and dropped beside him. "What happened?"

Toby looked up, his eyes wide. "She's been cut."

"Nicked or something deeper?"

"Deep. She faltered...almost went down...I'm sorry."

"Where did it happen? Here? On the way to the holding pens?"

Toby nodded, his eyes darting quickly from side to side. "I waited for you to come, like you always do, Miz Mittie. When the final call for the horses came, I had to hurry, but there was people and horses and carts and buggies coming and going after the harness show. Next thing I know, Gypsy knuckled and . . . and blood was dripping."

"You should have called for help."

"I shore enough did. Couple of fellas helped me bring her back. 'Tweren't more than a couple hunnert feet."

Shouts bounced through the air. Her daddy yelling for the veterinary service. Rex telling people to get back. Bile rose in Mittie's throat. The air swirled with dust and sweat. A glistening string of drool from Gypsy's lips landed on Mittie's cheek. She rose, encircling Gypsy's neck, their cheeks touching. Through a veil of tears, she watched as her daddy took over. The show veterinarian shone a flashlight at the gaping flesh of Gypsy's knee and asked for water. As water mixed with blood, washing the area, the tangled fibers of tendon shone through. Mittie didn't need to hear his diagnosis. She knew. Gypsy's career was over. She would never compete in the ring again.

In the distance, frolicking trills of organ music played for the crowd, notes running up and down the scale, the *bum-bum-bum* of chords building to a feverish pitch. The champion would be announced soon, but Mittie's only thoughts were for her beloved Gypsy, and the weight of it felt as if her chest had been crushed.

CHAPTER 23

Late Summer 1928

Nothing could be done to repair Gypsy's injury, the tendon fibers too frayed to hold sutures. The veterinarian cleaned and bandaged it and recommended further treatment when they got back to MG Farms. The vet shook his head. "What a shame. A horse like this damaged in her prime."

Mittie's dad and Rex Kline surmised, along with the show officials, that it was probably a sharp object—a file or blade sticking out from an equipment trolley that the grooms were using to pack up and go home. They searched the area for the offending object but found nothing, and no one reported seeing it happen. It was merely an unfortunate accident.

Mittie recoiled when her daddy used the word. If only she'd gone to the stall as she always did, Toby wouldn't have been in a hurry. She might have even led Gypsy herself as she sometimes did. She'd failed Gypsy and her daddy.

The familiar shame shrouded her. If only she'd been more responsible, Dobbs Lamberson wouldn't be a cripple for life. If only.

Ames tried to console her, but his touch was like a hot coal. How could he know what it was like to have a living creature that you'd been with since she'd drawn her first breath now broken, her future forever ruined? And when he suggested that she ride back to Louisville in his roadster, she declined. She would be in the rail car with Gypsy. She owed her that bit of comfort.

Gypsy was seen by their veterinarian when they arrived back at MG Farms. He cleaned the wound and verified that the tendon fibers were too frayed to hold a suture. He carefully stitched the torn external flap of skin to hold everything in place and put on a heavy bandage that would protect the knee and give extra support.

"It's going to be a long process, and I don't want to get your hopes up, but with an extensor tendon injury, internal healing is possible. In rare instances, the fibers have been known to knit themselves back together. We can only wait and see at this point." He gave Gypsy a tetanus injection and gave Mittie instructions for her care: rest in the stall with walking exercise four times a day to keep her limber and promote circulation to the wound. "Gypsy's lucky to have you. I know you'll take good care of the girl."

"Gypsy can count on me."

The next day a bouquet that covered half the dining room table arrived from the owners of the sorrel stallion. Their horse had won the championship. It was a small victory for what had been a terrible day.

Routine returned to MG Farms with preparations for the World's Championship show in Louisville coming in September, but unease stirred in Mittie's bones. Three, four, a dozen times a day she went to Gypsy, checked her dressing, brushed her coat, and led her up and down the promenade area of the barn for her exercise. But the fire was gone, Gypsy's eyes dull, the limp more pronounced.

One day as she combed the mats from Gypsy's mane and whispered sweet words of encouragement, she looked up and there was Ames, forearms propped on the Dutch door, watching her.

"Hey, how long have you been standing there?"

"Long enough to know that I've got an uphill climb before you pay that much attention to me."

She walked over and offered him her cheek. "Try me."

He pecked her on the cheek and said, "Carry on. It's mesmerizing to watch you."

"I'm nearly finished. What brings you out?"

"It's been almost two weeks. You're never in the house when I call, and it's been so long since *Belle* has seen you that her bolts are starting to rust."

"It's not been that long."

"It has, doll."

"I'm sorry. I didn't think I could leave Gypsy. And I've not stopped thinking about your sister and Lela. Are they all right?"

"Much better. Fern went back to work, and they are very appreciative of your help."

"I'm glad." Mittie gave Gypsy a pat on the hindquarters. "Can you stay for dinner tonight? Mother's gone on and on about how you entertained her and the owners' wives in St. Louis."

"Good to know that at least some women still find me charming."

Mittie wiped her hands on a towel and opened the stall door. "I know I've been preoccupied with Gypsy. Her old spunk is gone, withering more each day, it seems."

"I'm sure it's just a matter of time. I believe what you need is a night out. Come away with me. Let's go somewhere, just the two of us."

"Can you wait while I get dolled up?"

An hour later she found Ames with her dad, who waved her into his study. "Ames has just told me he got the final go-ahead from Fort Worth on his engine modification." He clapped him on the back. "Proud of you, son."

"That's wonderful news, Ames."

"I was going to surprise you this evening, but I'm glad I got to tell your dad, too." He offered his hand to her dad. "And once again, let me offer my condolences about Gypsy. I know it's got Mittie torn up, and I'm hoping that not all is lost."

"Time will tell, but thank you for your sentiments. You kids staying around for dinner?"

"We're going into town, Daddy."

"Have fun."

It was a beautiful evening; they drove along the river and had a quiet dinner at the rooftop restaurant of the Brown Hotel. Stars above, the glow of Louisville below. Ames beside her only added to the warmth that nestled under Mittie's ribs.

Ames took the last bite of his Hot Brown and said, "I really would like it if you came back on the circuit with us. They've hired a couple of new mechanics out at Bowman, so it's getting harder and harder to pick up odd jobs when I'm not barnstorming."

"It's very tempting, but I can't. Not now."

"Because of Gypsy?"

"You saw her. She's not herself, and she keeps declining."

"Aren't you a flat tire!"

"I'm only being realistic. If I left and something happened, I would never forgive myself."

"What about you and me, doll? Your flying? Your big plans to set records? Madame Earhart's already flown the Atlantic, but she hasn't done it solo, and you won't either sitting in a barn stall."

"I know that. And I'm not giving up. Sometimes life intervenes and you have to do the right thing."

The warm breath of August that had enveloped them earlier was now stifling. She knew Ames was right, but she also had the feeling he was asking her to make a choice about him. For now, staying with Gypsy was the only choice she was willing to make.

During dessert and coffee, Ames brooded, and when he took her home, their kisses were short, perfunctory. When she invited him in, he declined. "I need to round up my gear. We're all leaving tomorrow. I'm not sure when we'll be back."

"Call me."

"Sure thing." His tone didn't give her much promise.

August turned into September. Ames sent a postcard from Virginia, another from Pennsylvania. He called once to tell her the first engine with his modification had come off the assembly line. A jazz song filtered across the telephone wires along with Calista's tinkling laugh. Longing for Ames and blue skies wrapped its fingers around her heart.

Ames said they'd be back at Bowman Field by late October. Mittie hoped that she could last that long.

The next day the vet paid his weekly call to check on Gypsy.

"The wound has healed, and I'm beginning to feel tension in the joint, which makes me think the tendon is also knitting back together. There's no physical reason for the melancholy you've noticed. Have you tried riding her?"

"I wasn't sure she could handle the extra weight, not with the limp still there."

"Why don't you give it a try? Could be she's feeling like she's let you down, not doing what she was born to do. Performance horses have that in their genes, I'm inclined to think. Just take it easy."

The idea terrified Mittie. She couldn't handle another disaster, but when her daddy agreed that it was worth trying, she and Toby saddled Gypsy in the stall and led her into the promenade area. Mittie stroked Gypsy's neck, spoke words of encouragement to her, and mounted. Gypsy's ears twitched, and Mittie thought she felt a shudder of excitement beneath her.

They stayed in the barn that day, her daddy watching from a distance, nodding and keeping an eye on Gypsy's injured knee. The next day they ventured out into the sunshine. Gypsy reared her head and sniffed the air, then dutifully walked between the pens of the paddock. The limp remained, but it didn't worsen. Day by day, they lengthened the time Mittie was astride, Gypsy's muscles growing stronger, her eyes now gleaming. It was time to let Gypsy take the lead.

A gentle September breeze tickled the air the day Mittie took Gypsy onto the hills beyond the paddock. Gypsy cocked her head as if asking for permission. Mittie let the reins go slack and held her breath. Gypsy lifted one foot, then another, and began to trot. Slow, but sure. Mittie didn't let her go too fast nor stay out too long, but Gypsy had done better than Mittie ever imagined.

"Someday, my friend. Someday." She spoke the words to Gypsy, but they were for her, too. It was time for Mittie to also take the lead.

She called Weaver as soon as she got back to the house and asked if he'd have someone service *Belle*, that it was a beautiful day for a flight.

When she got to the airfield, it was Bobby who met her in the hangar.

"Gosh, I didn't mean for Weaver to send you out to get the plane ready."

"I had some spare time, and all I did was top off the fuel tanks. She's been running like a top."

"So you've spun the prop a few times to keep her from getting rusty?"

"No, once a week or so I've taken her up. I wanted to keep her ready for you. I knew it was just a matter of time."

"You are the bee's knees, Bobby York. How can I ever thank you?"

"How about letting me ride along and going to dinner with me tonight?"

"I'd love that."

"Then grab a helmet and let's go."

Slipping into the cockpit was like putting on her favorite slippers. Loops. Stalls. Soaring. She lifted her chin and filled her lungs. Home at last.

Bobby asked her again about dinner as they walked back to the terminal.

"I'll need time to get ready. Why don't you come out to the farm and say hello to Mother and Daddy while I change?"

"It sounds lovely, but you're dressed fine for what I had in mind. I need to pick up a few things in the office, and then we'll go." He raised hopeful eyebrows.

"You're very persuasive, you know." Her curiosity was getting the better of her. "I'll call Mother and tell her not to expect me."

Bobby held the door of his Morris for her. Odd, but all this time, she hadn't ridden in it. Calista had always beat her to it. Bobby slid behind the wheel.

"So where is this place where I can show up like this and not get thrown out for improper dress code?"

"You'll see." He drove toward town, past Churchill Downs and the University of Louisville into the heart of the residential area where Victorian and Gothic mansions lined the streets.

"This is St. James Place. Victor Booth lives near here. Is that where you're taking me?"

He shook his head and turned onto a narrow street that led to one of the courts the neighborhood was known for. The homes here were closer together, but their iron gates and front gardens gave them a certain charm. He stopped the car before they got to the pedestrian-only court and said, "Here we are." He didn't give her time to answer—just hopped out, ran around the car, and opened the door for her. With his hand at the small of her back, he led her up the walk and then up the steps to a gray stone house with

220   CARLA STEWART

window boxes. She felt like she did when she was little and she
and Iris played the blindfold game. They'd take turns leading each
other around in the house or outdoors, and you couldn't remove
your blindfold until you'd guessed where you were. Only now Mittie didn't wear a blindfold, and she still had no idea where she was.

Bobby produced a key and opened a door that led into an
entry hall. Walk-up apartments. Luxurious ones. A tingle rippled up
and down her spine. Going to a gentleman's apartment unchaper-
oned would have her mother's friends' tongues wagging. Something
about that was titillating. Dangerous and risqué, but she doubted
Bobby had any sort of romantic intentions. Before she stepped
across the threshold, she glanced over her shoulder to see if anyone
had seen them. The street was empty.

"My place is up two flights. I hope it's all right that I brought you
here."

"I had no idea this is where you lived."

"You never asked."

His drawing room was furnished with a pair of burgundy Queen
Anne sofas, a hunter green wingback chair, and Persian rugs scattered across polished oak floors. The scent of cinnamon and something hearty filled the air.

"It's wonderful." And it was apparent his flight instructor's salary
didn't begin to cover the lease.

"There are certain advantages to being the son of Robert York."

"Who is quite a lovely man, according to Mother and Daddy."

"Without a doubt. Come—let's see what's for dinner."

She followed him into the kitchen where a potpie rested atop the
wood-burning stove and next to it, a bowl of steaming cinnamon
apples.

"Let me guess. You also have a cook and a butler."

He laughed. "Nothing as fancy as that. Just a woman who comes
in and straightens up after me and leaves something for my dinner.

She's done well tonight, I see. Shall we eat in the dining room or here at the breakfast table?"

"I'm rather fond of cozy suppers, so in here is fine. What can I do?"

He pointed to the cupboard where the china was, and while she set the table, he took a wedge of cheddar from the Kelvinator, disappeared into a pantry, and came back with a loaf of crusty bread and a bottle of sherry. "Wine would be more to my liking, but it's rather tricky to come by."

"Actually, I'd prefer water. I'm always parched after flying."

"Water it is." He filled two glasses and pulled the chair for her to sit. Then he brought the potpie to the table and joined her. "Shall I say grace or would you like to?"

"Why don't you?"

It was a simple blessing, one her mother often said.

"You are a man of surprises, Bobby York. Thanks for inviting me."

"And thank you for accepting. I did have an ulterior motive."

"I'm not that kind of girl." She wrinkled her nose at him.

"And for that I'm grateful. It is a proposition of sorts, though."

"I'm listening."

"The Aero Club has everything worked out with the flying school. We'll start the first class in January."

"That's wonderful."

"We had hoped to start sooner, but there's a lot of office work, and I'm still doing private lessons. What we need is help organizing the office. Victor and I both thought of you since you've had experience with managing the farm."

Mittie swallowed hard. "I don't even know what to say. I'm flattered that you would ask, but I'm still green when it comes to aviation."

"You're more experienced than most, and you're quite sharp.

Trust me—after a few classes, I've learned that not everyone is cut out for this."

"What about my flying? Going to competitions?"

"That would be part of the job. What better advertising for the school than to have one of our own contending for records and promoting aviation? We'd be your sponsor and pick up expenses, of course. Sponsorship seems to be quite the trend nowadays."

A team. Like in the saddlebred business. Or as her daddy always said, "Behind every champion is a well-oiled machine."

"It sounds too good to be true. And you know what they say . . ."

"If it sounds too good, it probably is. All I'm asking is for you to think about it."

"Thanks." Another thought interrupted. *Ames. The Patriots.* "I have promised Ames I'd be back on the barnstorming circuit soon. I hate to give my word and not keep it."

Bobby stiffened, his eyebrows lifting a hair. "I assumed you knew."

"Knew what?"

He let out a slow breath. "Okay, guess I've just put my nose where it doesn't belong."

"Stop with your stupid British manners and spit it out. Assumed I knew what?"

"The group broke up a couple of weeks ago."

"What? I just talked to Ames two nights ago. I've had postcards—"

He held up his hand. "Wait." He rose and went to the front of the apartment and came back with a piece of yellow paper, which he handed her.

Western Union. From San Antonio, Texas. Ames said they were in Illinois.

"Go on; open it."

It was dated the week before.

GROUP BUSTED UP STOP BE IN LOU NEXT WEEK STOP LOVE,
PEACH

A million thoughts zipped through Mittie's head. What came out
of her mouth was, "About that job—when do I start?"

"Next Monday okay?"

"Perfect. Now, if I could, I'd love that glass of sherry."

CHAPTER 24

There had to be a perfectly logical explanation why Ames hadn't mentioned breaking up with the Patriots. It could simply be Calista being melodramatic. It wasn't the first group of barnstormers she'd left. But what were they doing in San Antonio? Ames would call in due time, and she would find out the truth from him.

Mittie discussed Bobby's offer with her parents the next morning. "I realized today when I took the plane up how much I'd missed it."

Her daddy said, "Your dedication to Gypsy has been exemplary. I've never known anyone who was as focused as you are with your girl."

"She's going to be fine. I'm not sure about showing in the ring, but when I took her out in the west meadow yesterday, I could feel something different, like she was releasing me to get back to what I love."

Her mother made a small sigh. "How was dear Bobby?"

"Quite well, actually. Did you know he lives over in the courts off St. James?"

"As a matter of fact, I did. He called asking for a recommendation a few weeks after he arrived. I gave him the number of someone in the Women's League. So you went to his place?" Her eyebrows were raised, not with shock at Mittie risking her reputation, but with mirth.

She told them about the meal, his housekeeper.

"It sounds lovely, dear. I had hoped you and Bobby would hit it off one day."

Mittie laughed. "Your way of asking if this was a date? No, Mother. It was strictly business, and Bobby was a perfect gentleman, nothing romantic between us."

"That's too bad. Once you've been hurt, it must be hard to risk your heart again."

Mittie's dad scowled. "Sarah, it's not your place—"

"I'm sure you're right, dear." She waved a hand at Mittie. "I'm glad you had a good time. When does the job start?"

"Next Monday. But back up. What were you saying about Bobby and risking his heart?"

Her mother looked at her daddy. "If she's going to be working with Bobby, then she should know more about him, don't you think?"

"I think if Bobby wanted Mittie to know, he would tell her."

"You men have such a different way of viewing things. Would either of you care for another cup of coffee?"

Mittie put down her napkin. "Not for me. I'm going to check on Gypsy, and then I'm off to Bowman Field again."

"Send Bobby our love."

Mittie was curious about what her mother was talking about. She was equally sure Bobby wasn't one to share his secrets. So what were they? A marriage in London that ended badly? Or perhaps he'd disappointed his parents by turning down the suitable wife they'd picked out for him. Maybe that's why he'd stayed in the States—he needed to keep a meddling mother at bay. He wouldn't be the only one.

★ ★ ★

Monday morning came quickly with no news from Ames over the weekend. Perhaps it wasn't just the Patriots he was abandoning, but her as well. If he'd had a change of heart about her, the least he could do was tell her. The possibility of surprising her by coming into town was more his style, but even that was beginning to feel remote.

Bobby agreed to her coming in at ten, giving her time to exercise Gypsy. When she changed from her riding clothes into the navy and white pinstripe dress she thought would be suitable for office work, her fingers went automatically to the locket around her neck. Pearls were a better accessory. She unfastened the clasp on the chain and dropped the locket into the top drawer of her bureau, put on a strand of pearls and a bit of lipstick, and headed to Bowman Field.

Bobby peeked out from a stack of boxes and waved her in. "Sorry about the mess. Weaver's letting us have materials delivered here until the new building is finished. Just a few more weeks and we'll have this moved over."

"It doesn't look like you're quite ready for me."

"Actually, there's plenty to do." He handed her a stack of invoices. "I'd like you to go over these and get them logged into the ledger. Then, we have the plans from a few other schools aero clubs have started. You can read over them and look at the blueprints for our layout and start visualizing what we're doing."

"Nothing like getting in at the ground level."

"That's what we thought. In the meantime, I have three private lessons and an errand to tend to, so I won't be around. Just lock up when you need to leave."

He picked up his flight jacket. "By the way, thanks."

Mittie looked at the havoc in the room. "You're welcome, I think."

"Have you heard from Ames?"

"Not yet. How about Calista? Any word?"

"She came in last night. She's resting up over at my place."

"Your place?" Mittie recoiled, unable to reel in the image of Bobby and Calista at his apartment. Proper, respectable Bobby who wouldn't risk his heart, if Mittie's mother was to be believed?

He nodded. "Poor girl fell asleep on my davenport."

"It's all right. You don't have to explain."

Bobby opened his mouth to say something, then snapped it shut. "Ah, you thought Calista and I, that we..." He held up his hand. "Don't answer. I can see it on your face. Truth be told, I'm worried about her."

"She's not ill, I hope."

"She's not, but her mother is. Cancer, and it doesn't sound very hopeful."

"I'm so sorry. I just assumed..."

Bobby shrugged. "We all do that sometimes. When I couldn't rouse her, I covered her with a blanket and took a hotel room for myself. She's better this morning, but fretful. Fragile, I'd say. I'm taking her to the train station for the five o'clock to Atlanta."

"Why doesn't she fly?"

"Her plane's acting up, so she asked to leave it here until I can take a look at it."

Mittie wanted to march over to St. James Place and quiz Calista about the Patriots, but the soft look on Bobby's face when he spoke of Calista stopped her.

Instead, she told Bobby to give Calista her regards and went to work.

By the end of the week, Mittie had a good idea of what the inventory was and had made suggestions for the classroom and the office in the new building, which was on a tract of land Victor Booth owned adjacent to the airfield. She'd filled out forms and typed up new ones to send to a printer. Now there was nothing to do but wait until everything was moved. Every afternoon, she quit at three, changed clothes, and took *Belle* up for a spin, hoping each time she came in for a landing that *Trixie* would have magically appeared with Ames on board. Each time disappointment bit at her heart.

October came and went without a word from Ames. Mittie's hopes had grown thin on his returning at all when he called on a rainy evening in the middle of November. He was stranded in Arizona, his plane broken down, and he'd spent a week in the desert waiting for parts.

"The last I heard you were in Illinois. Or was it Texas?"

"Actually we went to San Antonio for a flying gig and then I went to Fort Worth to check with the manufacturer. How's Gypsy?"

"Worlds better. I'm back in the saddle and have her up to a canter."

"Sounds like you missed your calling. Maybe you should have been a nurse."

"I'm not squeamish, but it's never really appealed to me, either."

The operator interrupted. "One minute."

"Ames, we have a lot to talk about. You said you'd be back in October, but now it's nearly Thanksgiving."

"Trust me, doll, I miss you like the dickens. I'd have come straight to Louisville after Fort Worth, but then I heard about a new opportunity in California. It sounds like it could be quite lucrative with a new plant and all, so I thought I'd investigate it before I come to spend Christmas with you."

"How about writing to me? Explaining why you and the Patriots broke up, why you're not where you say you are?"

"It's all simple to explain—"

The line went dead.

Mittie wanted to scream. She knew nothing more about the Patriots than she did before he called. At least this time he wasn't in a dance club with music and the sound of laughter in the background.

It *was* simple. She and Ames had been on shaky ground for months. She wouldn't waste any more time fretting over him until he explained, and it had better be good.

The next day Bobby told her he was leaving in two days for New York and then sailing to England for Christmas.

"Mum and Dad have been after me to come for a visit, and once the school opens, there won't be time. I'm sorry I'll miss moving to the new building, but Victor's got things under control."

He offered his hand for a shake and then drew it back. "How about this instead?" He drew her into his arms, a warm, friendly hug. "I'm going to miss you."

Mittie's throat grew thick. "Hurry back, Bobby York. Or should I say boss?"

He laughed and said, "Take care."

And then he was gone.

Two days before Christmas, Mittie was helping her mother hang a balsam wreath on the door when a ruby-colored automobile turned in their long drive. Her mother asked if she was expecting company. Only Ames, an illusion that had dimmed as December had marched on without a word from him. Dust kicked up behind the vehicle, and then there he was, Ames springing from the car and popping a fedora on his head at the same time. Mittie's breath caught.

She would not race to greet him. She couldn't if she had wanted to; her legs had turned to jelly at the sight of him.

"Hey, doll! I told you I'd make it!"

His arms encircled her, crushing her, the scent of his cologne like a summer breeze. She inhaled and gave him only a half-hearted hug in return before she stepped back. "Yes, you made it." Her chin quivered as did her knees and elbows and everything in between, but the knot in her chest told her to wait before she threw her affections at his feet.

Ames nodded toward her mother. "Hello, Mrs. Humphreys. That wreath's a beauty."

"Why, thank you." She collected stray bits of wire and balsam twigs. "I'll leave you young people to yourselves. Mittie, don't forget we have the food baskets to deliver at three o'clock."

"I've not forgotten. Maybe Ames can help us."

Her mother disappeared into the house, leaving Mittie and Ames alone. Mittie wrapped her arms around herself to ward off the chill in the air, but more to keep herself from thrashing her arms at Ames and demanding answers to her questions.

"Hey, doll, you gonna invite me in or would you like to go for a drive in my new buggy? The heater's not much, but I have a blanket you can throw over your legs."

"A drive, I think. Let me grab my things." She went in, grabbed her blue fox coat, and told her mother she was going with Ames.

"Don't forget the food baskets."

"I won't."

Ames was behind the wheel of the car—a Model A, he told her—its motor purring. "Fresh off the assembly line. People are snapping them up like crackerjacks in California."

"You drove all the way from California?"

"Only way to get here and see you. It's been a long trip." He did have a weariness about him, a scruff of beard on his chin.

"What about *Trixie*? The Patriots? You've never told me what happened with them. You could have at least written to let me know where you were."

"Letters have never been my strong suit."

"Along with a few other things, it would seem."

"Look, can we just go somewhere?"

"Just start driving. Maybe we can stop at the diner in Rigby."

He let out the clutch and turned toward the drive. "How's Gypsy?"

"I told you she was doing much better."

"Still playing nursemaid?"

"When necessary. So where did you leave your plane?"

"I sold it. The last repairs wiped me out. I couldn't see how I would get back with no money for fuel, and flying over the mountains in December didn't seem the best idea. I got enough for *Trixie* to buy this car and pick up a few gifts so I didn't show up empty-handed."

"I don't expect gifts. I'd rather have answers to what you've been doing the past three months and why you've left me hanging."

"You were busy with more important things. Competing with a horse is a real blast for the ego, you know." He stepped on the foot feed and careened around a curve.

"Slow down. This road has a lot of twists and turns."

"Now you're telling me how to drive?"

"I'm sorry. I'm glad you're here. Really."

"You have a funny way of showing it." He huffed out a breath, silence between them. Finally, he looked over and said, "You have a big crowd coming for Christmas?"

"Just you."

"I figured you had a slew of relatives. What about your sister?"

"They're staying in Alabama this year. We've been invited to Aunt Evangeline's for Christmas Day. And I'm sorry about *Trixie*. I know you loved that plane."

"Them's the breaks."

"Any plans for a new one?"

"Do without for now since the Patriots broke up."

"About that. Care to tell me what happened?"

He worked his jaw like he was chewing on the words he needed to say. "If you heard Peach's version, it's no wonder you think I'm scum."

"That's not what I think at all. I care about you and what you're doing, which is why it upset me when I didn't hear about the Patriots from you. You don't have to give me an explanation, but I'd like it if you did."

He gripped the steering wheel, taking the curve too fast again. Mittie braced her feet on the floorboard and in her side vision saw a white-faced cow step onto the road. Tires screeched as Ames jerked the wheel and plowed straight into the hulking animal.

Mittie screamed. It was like she was in a ball tumbling down a hill. Slammed to one side of the car. Then the other. Thuds. Metal crunching. Shattered glass falling like rain.

Then dead silence.

CHAPTER 25

"Ames, are you all right?" Her voice was shrill, like the cold wind that blew through the gully where they must have landed. Mittie couldn't move, trapped between the door and Ames on top of her. Ames hung like a sack of horse feed, one arm dangling at an odd angle.

Please, Lord, don't let him be dead.

She wasn't sure if she said the words or thought them, but a groan came from inside the car. It must be Ames. She squirmed to free her right arm, but it only moved a few inches. Her fingers tingled, and there was something wet on her face. The weight of Ames against her shifted.

"Ames, can you hear me?"

Another groan, then a shudder and guttural animal-like grunts, the scent of blood and fear choking her. Minutes passed. It felt like hours.

"Whoa, what happened?" His voice was foggy, but in the next instant, he was moving about, bracing himself, drawing up one knee, then throwing his leg away from her. She wasn't sure how he did it, but the weight of him lifted. She angled her head and watched him climb through the roof. Only it wasn't the roof, but the driver's side of the car, through a window whose glass was shattered, leaving jagged edges like fangs.

"Be careful. There's glass."

He peered down at her from above. "Can you move? Do you think anything is broken? Oh no. Oh God." He turned his head and retched. His face was twisted in agony when it appeared again. "Oh, doll. Your face. Your gorgeous face."

She touched her face with the arm that was now free. Wet. Sticky. Spots danced before her eyes, then the world went black.

Someone had come along right after the accident, saw the injured cow in the road, and found them. Mittie had revived in the back of the hearse that served as Rigby's ambulance with Ames beside her. Ames had a knot on his head from the steering wheel, and his left arm was fractured in two places. Mittie, miraculously, had no broken bones, the heavy fur coat cushioning her. It was ruined, of course, saturated with blood and filled with glass shards. At the Louisville hospital, a nurse held a mask that smelled like chewing gum over her face. When she awoke, her face felt like it had been stung by wasps. Mercurochrome, to prevent infection, the doctor had said, adding that it had taken an hour to pick out the glass fragments.

The worst wound, though, was the shard that pierced Mittie's heart. Her antagonistic attitude toward Ames had distracted him. His car was a total loss, she was certain—the car he'd sold his plane to buy so he could come and see her.

She asked to see him, but the nurse said he'd requested no visitors. She didn't blame him. One look at her face, and he'd thrown up. She owed him an apology and wanted to explain that she would make it up to him, no matter what it took. All of her paychecks. What little savings she still had. What she wouldn't do was ask her daddy to pay for her mistake again. Dobbs Lamberson had been enough.

Mittie was discharged the day after Christmas, and before she left, she asked her mother for a mirror.

"There'll be time to look later. The doctor says it's best that you not see it like this."

"It's my face. I'm going to see it when I walk past the hall mirror anyway."

Her mother snapped open her purse and handed Mittie her compact.

Mittie braced herself and looked into the three-inch round mirror. She burst out laughing. "It looks like I have the chicken pox. And what's that ghastly pumpkin glow?"

"The Mercurochrome. It has to wear off. And I hardly think it's funny."

"It could have been a thousand times worse. I could have jagged scars."

Her mother stretched her lips into a smile. "A small consolation." Bless her mother's heart. At least she didn't say that her marriage chances had hit an all-time low. "Come—let's get you home."

"What about Ames? I can't just leave him here. I want to see him."

"Your daddy took him to the farm this morning. Bertha's made up a cot for him in one of the bunkhouses."

"He's not a hired hand. Why not upstairs in the guest room?"

"It would be awkward, and he'll have more privacy in the bunkhouse."

"I see." But Mittie didn't. What she saw was only her mother's disapproval for Ames, his come-what-may life.

"I know what you're thinking. I offered him the guest room. He prefers the arrangements we've made."

As far away from Mittie as possible, so he didn't have to see her disfigurement. Was that it, or did he blame her for the accident? Heaviness descended, souring her mood on the ride home. That evening, she took the tray her mother brought her for dinner and asked about Ames.

"Bertha took him a tray, same as you. I'll go over tomorrow and see if he'll join us for meals in the house."

Two days later, Mittie still hadn't seen him, so when the house had settled, she bundled up, her face still resembling an orange with cloves stuck in it. He might as well see her at her worst. She slipped into the kitchen, cut two big wedges of raisin pie and a large hunk of cheddar cheese, and got a bottle of milk from the refrigerator. She assembled it all in a basket and stepped out into the night.

The moon shone behind the clouds, making the heavens a deep gray. Tiny snowflakes swirled like the snow globe on the mantel as she made her way to the last bunkhouse in the row, just single rooms strung together but each affording a bit of privacy to the grooms and trainers who occupied them. She'd seen the shanties some farm owners provided. Her heart swelled with pride that her daddy treated his employees well, that each room was warm and dry with an iron bedstead and feather mattress instead of a bedroll on the floor. Still, why would Ames prefer that to the much nicer sur-roundings of the guest room?

A soft glow shone behind the muslin curtain. Good—he was still awake. She set down the basket and rapped on the door. No answer. She knocked again, louder. And this time she heard the shuffling of feet across the wood floor. Ames opened the door, and before he could invite her in, she waltzed past him and plunked the basket on a small wooden table.

"I brought you something."

"Your housekeeper brought my supper."

"I know. I just thought you might be hungry for a snack before bedtime."

He wore a pair of her daddy's pajamas, wool socks on his feet, and his beard now covered his jaws and chin, rich and dark. It was past the prickly stage and gave him a rugged, handsome look. Her heart stirred, but she avoided his gaze, not wanting to disgust him with the pockmarks on her face.

"Thanks."

"I did think, perhaps, we could talk."

"Didn't end so well last time." He turned away from her, obviously repulsed by the way she looked.

"That's what I want to talk about. Your car. I'll make sure you get a new one."

"I don't take charity."

"It's not charity. Would you look at me? I know I'm not the beauty you once told me I was, but it's not so bad. And this horrid color has to wear off."

He glanced at her briefly, eyes squinted. "You'll have scars the rest of your life, thanks to me."

"I don't blame you. I'm as much at fault as you were for the accident. How's your arm?"

He had a plaster from his fingertips to his armpit, a slight bend at the elbow, all of it held up by a cloth tied around his neck.

"No pain, if that's what you're asking. Six weeks before I can do a blasted thing. Driving is out, even if I had a car, so you can take your sweet time on that, doll. And I couldn't hold a tool to save my life, so..." He ran his free hand along the plaster. "So I guess I am taking charity. Eating whatever is brought to me. Living in a strange room that smells of manure and kerosene."

She leaned against the doorway. "I'm sorry. I wondered if you'd be more comfortable in the guest room."

He shot her a look that said *no* and pushed the lone chair in the room toward her. "Have a seat."

"I'm fine. Why don't you sit, though?"

He sat and propped his arm on the table. "Here's the truth, doll. I was afraid to come back. You have something special with Gypsy, and I know it was because of me that you weren't with her before the show that night. My being with you jinxed it somehow. Then you wouldn't leave her side for a minute."

"I went out to dinner with you."

"You did. And I'm not sore at you. I was frustrated because I wanted you with us for the barnstorming. Instead we had to put up with Peach. She was starting to get on all of our nerves, but she's a great flier, a real crowd pleaser. In Pennsylvania, she invented some excuse about her mother being sick and needing more money. There wasn't any more to give her, but Lester and Shorty sided with her."

"Her mother *was* sick. Cancer, Bobby said."

For once he didn't sniff at the mention of Bobby's name.

"Anyhow, we all agreed to go to Texas since Peach had a friend down there who promised us a part in a big show. We got there, and there was a misunderstanding, and they only let Peach fly with them. Everyone was short-tempered, so we decided to call it quits."

"So why did you go to California?"

"There's a new plant out there. I thought it might be a good place to start over. Doll, you would love it there. Sunny every day. An ocean at your doorstep. I thought if I got a decent job, I'd convince you to come with me. Looks like I blew it again."

Mittie didn't know what to say. It all had a ring of truth to it. And she had been devoted to Gypsy at the expense of everything else in her life. She thought Ames should understand that.

"Thanks for being honest with me. When you called that night from a dance hall and didn't write, I took that as you not caring. I even thought that maybe Calista had taken my place."

"She's like a kid sister. An annoying one."

"She is a bit hard to handle sometimes. She'll be back here eventually, and I was hoping she and I could enter some more races or altitude challenges. Bobby's going to check into it when he gets back from London."

"I should have known it would have something to do with York."

A sudden thought seized her. She hadn't told Ames about her job. She wrinkled her nose. "There's more than I've told you."

"I knew it. Cool reception when I get here. And it was hard not to notice that you're no longer wearing the locket I gave you. Go ahead—break my heart now and get it over with."

"It's nothing romantic. Far from it. The Aero Club flying school, with Bobby at the helm, starts up in January. And I'm their new office manager. My relationship with Bobby is strictly professional."

"Then how can you go gallivanting off to compete?"

"The flying school will be my official sponsor. And I just might need an ace mechanic."

"Did they hire Peach, too?"

"No. I assume she's still in Atlanta with her mother, but when she's ready, I hope we can do some flying together. In the meantime, I'm gainfully employed."

Ames held out his good hand. "Welcome to the world of working stiffs."

"I actually like it. A new beginning?"

His face crinkled into a smile. "Sure thing. So what's in that basket you brought?"

"Raisin pie."

He sucked in a noisy breath. "I haven't had that since my Granny died. How did you know it was my favorite?"

"I didn't. I just brought what Ruby made. But I brought two pieces. Can I join you?"

"It would be my pleasure."

CHAPTER 26

Winter 1929

Bobby called when he made it back from London. Mittie told him there were ten students enrolled in the flying school and that she and Ames had been in an accident. Bobby asked about the details, which she gave him.

"Are you all right to come to the office?"

"I feel fine. My face is healing, but I didn't want to alarm you." It was almost miraculous what the cocoa butter and honey ointment Ruby mixed up for her had done. The Mercurochrome had faded, leaving only acne-like scars. The pancake makeup her mother bought from a theater acquaintance worked even more wonders.

"I can't tell there's anything wrong with your face," Bobby told her on the first day back.

"Just don't look too close. The doctor says to expect some minor scarring, but all in all, I was fortunate. So how was your voyage? Your parents?"

"It was a good trip—the usual holiday parties, meeting up with old chums, and a weekend in Newmarket with the horses. Lovely all around."

"I'm glad you got to go. Family is important."

"My mum seems to think so." He picked up the roster for the new class. "Two women, I see. Anyone you know?"

Mittie sighed. So much for casual chatter. "No names I recognize. Have you heard from Calista?"

"No, I wondered if you had."

"I hope she's all right. I was looking forward to us entering some other competitions in the spring." She opened the drawer of her desk and pulled out a newspaper clipping. "Here's one in Fort Worth in March. I've requested two entry forms."

He read it over. "You're anxious, aren't you?"

"You've no idea."

She *was* restless, but not nearly as itchy as Ames. He pitched in at the stables with anything he could do with one arm, and he took a renewed interest in Gypsy and watching Mittie on her morning rides. In the evenings, he asked for deeper explanations about the different gaits, which Mittie explained as they sat around the table in the bunkhouse. She watched him braid strips of leather into round harness reins, a skill Toby had taught him now that he could use the fingers at the end of the plaster. She teased him, saying her mother could teach him to embroider if he tired of the leather.

On a cold, clear day at the end of January, she asked her daddy to go with her and pick up the car she'd bought for Ames with a loan from her bank. They both agreed that it was the right thing to do.

The plaster was removed from Ames' arm the day before Valentine's, and afterward, they'd gone shopping for a new suit for Ames for the date they had planned the next evening and for his trip to Fort Worth at the end of the month.

The double-breasted suit put the swagger back in his step, and he shaved the beard that had grown out but kept the moustache, and with just a bit of wax, it curled at the ends. Dapper, indeed. He'd called for her at the house, approval in his eyes when he saw her.

Mittie, too, had gone shopping for a new gown for the evening, a red chiffon dress with rhinestone straps at the top and a slim-fitting bodice. She piled her hair on top of her head and wove a rhinestone ribbon like that at her shoulders through it.

Ames helped her with her new fox stole and offered his arm. "My car or yours?"

"Let's take yours tonight, darling. Just watch those curves."

He tweaked her nose. "I could do without that reminder."

Mittie had reserved a private dining room at the Brown Hotel, and when they arrived, Ames pulled out the chair for her, his fingers lingering on her bare shoulder, the touch of him both familiar and yet seemingly a new era—one where they were beginning to trust each other again.

They chatted throughout dinner, ordinary things they'd seen in the paper, her plans to enter the competition in Fort Worth, his excitement over going to Texas. When the last crumbs of their chocolate pie were gone, Ames reached in his pocket and pulled out a small box. Flat. Square. Wrapped in silver paper. Guilt prickled Mittie's gut. She'd not worn the chain with the locket since the day she'd dropped it in her bureau drawer. She wasn't sure why, but she thought she was waiting for something to shift in their relationship, a sign that Ames was committed to her...to them.

She bit her lip. "I'm sorry; I didn't get you a gift."

"You weren't supposed to. This dinner, the car, the clothes... they're more than I can ever repay." He placed the box in her hands, his eyes bright with the reflection of the candlelit table.

With fumbling fingers, she removed the paper. The box wasn't a jeweler's case but a simple white one, and inside, nestled on cotton wool, was an exquisite round-braided bracelet. Not leather, but silky and delicate with a silver clasp and a tiny silver ornament of a horse. Her breath caught.

"It's beautiful. Wherever did you find this?" She held out her wrist for Ames to fasten the clasp.

"Actually, I made it from the brushed hairs from Gypsy's mane and tail. I had a few conspirators working with me, though. Toby collected the hair, snipping a few extras here and there. Rex took it to a jeweler for the clasp."

Her fingers traced the smooth texture, her heart unable to take it in. The hours it must have taken. The subterfuge to keep her from finding out. Her heart was full, and the kisses they shared that evening carried the promise she'd been waiting for.

Two weeks later, Ames loaded the new Model A and left for Fort Worth. On the Saturday after he left, Mittie took *Belle* up for a long afternoon in the skies. When she touched down and taxied toward the hangar, a lithe figure with golden hair and a sway in her hips ran out to greet her. Calista had returned.

And she hadn't changed a bit. She still called Mittie "Kentucky" and batted her eyelashes when corrected and said in her sweet Georgia drawl that she'd plumb forgotten. She was rakishly thin, and when Mittie commented on it, Calista said she hadn't been able to eat a bite for months.

"Thank the good Lord, Mama's dancing with the angels now. And probably whipping up a batch of peach cobbler."

Mittie gave her a hug and told her about the accident with Ames and him staying at the farm.

Calista's eyes clouded momentarily. "That must've been cozy."

"Ames stayed in one of the bunkhouses—his choice—but it was a good time for both of us. He told me about the misunderstanding in San Antonio, but it was probably best since he needs to devote time to the company that bought his invention."

Calista twisted a stray curl around her finger. "He was only thinking of himself. I hope you do realize that."

"I guess we all do that at times." She handed Calista the application for the altitude challenge in Fort Worth. "This time I was thinking of you, though. Are you up for a little competition? Ames said he would meet us there and service both our planes."

Calista's eyes lit up. "You bet your grits, I am. Mama left me a little nest egg, so I'm not quite so strapped for cash, and I'm itching to do something. Anything. And I'll do my ever-lovin' best to keep Ames from getting riled."

She kept her promise and was cordial with Ames on the day of the challenge in Fort Worth. Calista set a personal best record, but for the first time, Mittie beat her and set a new women's record. The camaraderie among the women was everything Mittie remembered.

The time with Ames was way too short, but she and Calista had been invited to a women's air demonstration in Tulsa and had to leave the day after the competition. Ames took Mittie in his arms for a last kiss. "Don't know when I'll see you again. I'm headed to California to test some new planes that are using the engine modification. Godspeed on your flight to Tulsa."

The event in Tulsa was a serious day of fun, flying in formation with other women, the Arkansas River below them winding through lush forests speckled with brilliant fuchsia redbuds. That evening they attended a reception at the opulent Mayo Hotel where Charles Lindbergh had once stayed. Calista sugared up a reporter who took their photo, and before they left the next morning, they picked up a newspaper. Their picture was on the front page with the caption "Georgia Peach and Kentucky Beauty pair up to bring excitement to the Tulsa skies."

They had no way of knowing that a woman named Elizabeth McQueen would see that photo, and in two months, she would change their lives forever.

CHAPTER 27

Spring 1929

Iris and Hayden came for Easter the last weekend in March, and there was more than spring blooming. Iris had a little bun in the oven, and Hayden hovered over her like she was in danger of breaking.

When Iris sprang the announcement, they almost had to break out the smelling salts for Mittie's mother, who collapsed on the sofa and fanned herself for thirty minutes. She'd then risen like a phoenix and organized a shopping trip for Saturday afternoon.

They'd stopped in Nell's shop to give her the news, and while Nell showed them a line of baby bonnets that her friend Calvin Gold in New York had created, Mittie played with Mira at the back of the shop. Mira smelled of baby powder and milk breath, her hair as downy as a fluffy chick. Mittie pressed her to her chest, an odd sensation sending tingles to the tips of her toes. She shuddered, willing away the picture in her head of someday holding her own child.

Iris, though, was overjoyed at the prospect of being a mother and had been installed as the recording secretary of the Junior League of Birmingham. There weren't any late-night chats in Iris' old room, only talk of baby names and decorating the nursery of the three-story home Hayden had built for her.

Mittie and Calista signed up for a women's airspeed race in Chicago. At the end of April, Calista flew from Atlanta to Louisville so they could go together. At Chicago Municipal Airport they were given the race regulations for the ten-mile course that was laid out with pylons to serve as guides. Six laps at a maximum of three hundred feet in the air. A nice trophy for the winner and prize money for the top two finishers.

The air was electric as people gathered to watch the race and cheer for all the entrants, but mostly for a local woman who'd be flying in her first-ever race.

At noon, they lined up, engines running, and watched for the starting flag. Mittie took a deep breath, concentrating on the takeoff line six hundred feet ahead of her, the line that had to be cleared or she'd be immediately disqualified with no second chance. To her left, Calista waved.

It wasn't unlike flying with the Patriots, the planes keeping a safe distance but always within view. She banked left and rounded the first pylon, a pole with a balloon attached for easy visibility. Her instincts took over as she pushed *Belle*, urging her onward on the straightaway, keeping an eye out for the other planes. By the third lap, she'd found her groove and thought perhaps she was gaining on the plane that flew slightly above her. Adrenalin pulsed like a bass drum. Five laps done. Time for the push. She kept *Belle* at just over two hundred feet and pulled on the throttle. The wind ate at her cheeks, her mouth dry. She licked her lips to moisten them and circled the last marker. Homestretch.

When she passed the finish line, the sixth lap completed, she circled up and away from the course, nosing up to five hundred feet as required in the rules, then came in to land on the designated field.

Two planes were already there. Her heart sank. A respectable third. Calista came in fourth. No money and no trophy, but it was hard to put a value on being a part of the sisterhood of fellow pilots.

The Chicago girl came in last place, but the crowd cheered like she'd won the Kentucky Derby.

The next day Calista wanted to see the sea lions at the Lincoln Park Zoo, so they rode the "L" from their hotel and stayed until after lunch, when Calista asked Mittie what she wanted to do next.

"I've always wondered what it was like for Lindbergh to fly over the Atlantic and see nothing but water. Since that's not going to happen anytime soon, let's see what it's like over Lake Michigan." When Calista agreed, Mittie asked, "One plane or two?"

"Let's take yours. There's a clunk in my engine I want to have checked before we leave tomorrow. We can trade off so we both get a chance to enjoy the scenery."

Before they took off, Calista talked to a mechanic about *Peaches*, then donned her leather helmet and climbed into the seat in front of Mittie. A headwind gave Mittie a little trouble on takeoff, but once they were airborne, she flew north along the shoreline, then banked right, flying over waters that looked like the meringue on one of Ruby's lemon pies. When the deep blue of the lake and the horizon became one, she leaned forward and nudged Calista to take over. Mittie hung as far over the side as she could with the safety strap that held her in the seat. They rode the wind currents like a seagull, Calista tipping the right wings down, then the left. The sun glinted from the surface in iridescent shards of cobalt and emerald. A scattering of clouds above them cast shadows on the waters, as if the mighty lake was sighing, giving up its secrets.

Mittie thought of Lindbergh spending thirty-three and a half hours above water, flying in the dark, lost at times, she was sure, only the stars and a compass to guide him. Goosebumps popped out on her arms, and she sighed as Calista turned back for safe harbor.

The next morning, they left for a long day of flying, hoping
to make Louisville with just a brief stop in Indianapolis. Halfway
to Indianapolis, Mittie rubbed the ache in her neck and watched
a line of clouds forming southwest of her course. She prayed they
were slow moving or would dissipate before reaching Indiana. Instead they grew darker and closer. She dropped her altitude to have
a better view of the landscape in case she had to land quickly. When
Indianapolis came into view, a sigh of relief escaped her lips. Calista
was waiting for her on the runway with the news that the approaching storm would leave them grounded.

A knot formed in Mittie's chest, a yearning for the gentle rolling
hills of home. Instead, it was another night in a hotel.

They ordered soup and sandwiches in the hotel dining room and
picked up a Chicago paper to see if there was anything about the
air race and found a lengthy article about the growing number of
women pilots. They devoured the story, the sustenance that satisfied
their craving to fly faster, higher, harder.

Clear skies promised a smooth ride home the next morning,
the storm from the night before long gone, leaving only puddles
and clean, crisp morning air. Two other planes were in line ahead
of Mittie and Calista, and when they were well out of view,
Calista strapped on her helmet and lifted her chin. "Race you
home?"

"Why not? One last race for the road."

Calista hopped on the wing and slipped into the cockpit, the
warmed-up engine purring like a kitten. *Peaches* bumped along
the runway, sending up a spray of water from the rutted grass of
the field. And then she was airborne and winging her way home.

Mittie followed the same procedure, the taste of Kentucky sweet
on her lips as she waited for the go-ahead and swung out onto the
runway. It was rougher than she expected, the tail skid bouncing.
Steady on the rudder. You can do this.

Another bump and the tail kicked to the right, then jerked sharply left. Mittie eased back on the throttle, gaining control. Smoother now. Going for ground speed again, Mittie kept one eye on the gauges, hands engaged on the wheel. Almost there. Time to nose up. A huge bounce jarred her insides, the back of the plane fishtailing. And it felt like the rudder was jammed.

Turn around. Go back in.

But by then, she was off the ground, and she pictured *Belle's* wheels dangling like the charm on her horsehair bracelet. The plane jerked again, the tail bobbing like a rooster shaking its tail feathers. Mittie held her breath. *Belle* was twisting. Wings rocking.

A scream rose in Mittie's throat. *Rudder! Brake!*

The right wing dipped. She overcorrected and slammed into the earth sideways on *Belle's* left wing. Crumpled. Her heart raced while her brain told her to get out fast. Her fingers wouldn't work the harness strap. Dobbs Lamberson's face flashed through her brain.

No, Dobbs! Not so fast. Keep your hands on the reins. Pay attention to what you're doing.

Then the image of her daddy.

I'm sorry, Daddy! I was only trying to get him to stop.

She fought to inhale. This wasn't a carriage ride. She was an experienced pilot. *Get. Out. Of. The. Plane. Please, Lord, help me!*

The strap unlatched in her fingers, and she hoisted herself up. The acrid fumes of fuel seeped into Mittie's nose. An automobile roared down the runway toward her. She waved, then bent her knees and leapt to the ground. The impact jarred her bones, but she needed to get away. Adrenaline shot through her body. Legs churning, she ran away from the plane.

Two figures grabbed her. "Are you all right? What happened?"

She didn't answer, for at that moment a boom filled the air, and her beloved *Belle* went up in flames.

An hour later, she hadn't stopped shaking. She was alive, and for that she was grateful, but her heart felt hollow. What hadn't she noticed? What could she have done differently?

Bobby's words focused in her head. "Never chance a takeoff if you suspect something is amiss with your plane." Amiss, yes—that was the word he used. Bobby and his refined British vernacular. Something had definitely been amiss with the rudder. A malfunction of some kind? She would never know. Ashes didn't generally have much to say.

The airport manager brought her a cup of steaming hot coffee and carried a clipboard to take down information about her and the plane. He waved someone into the room. A reporter with a camera.

"I've already snapped some pictures of the wreckage. I'd like a statement from you, if I could."

How wonderful. All her mother needed was another reason to have nightmares.

He asked the same questions as the manager and asked what brought her to Indianapolis. She explained about the air race in Chicago and that she just wanted to get home.

"Air race, huh? Are you one of the women pilots the people in Chicago are crowing about? What did they call you—the Flying Flappers?"

"I've heard the term. But we're qualified the same as men and are just as capable."

"So does this signal the end of your career, miss?"

Mittie rose and looked at the reporter at eye level. "Women are only beginning to show this country what they are capable of. And no, this is not the end of my career. It's only the beginning. And you can quote me on that, sir."

CHAPTER 28

The *Louisville Ledger* carried the picture of *Belle*'s charred remains, but there was also a picture of Mittie, hair tangled, aviator helmet in hand. And they'd printed the quote she'd given. Word for word.

Her mother sighed when she saw the article, but bless her, she didn't offer any commentary. Mittie thought she detected a sparkle in her daddy's eyes, but it could have been just the light at the dinner table the day the newspaper came out. It was too soon to figure out what Mittie would do now, and she was grateful for their silence. At least she had survived and still had a job. Bobby sent a bouquet of spring flowers and called to check on her.

Ames also called and when she told him about the crash, he said, "Holy smokes!" followed by, "Sorry—poor choice of words. Are you all right?"

She assured him she was and asked how things were in California.

"Going like gangbusters. New plants opening up every day riding the wave of aviation."

And Ames was riding it with them. Happiness for him hummed along Mittie's bones.

Calista stayed the remainder of the week trying to get up the nerve to fly on to Atlanta. They both knew that not all pilots walked away from their wreckage. Mittie returned to work the following Monday, and Calista stopped by the flying school to say good-bye.

"I know we're mortal enemies in the sky, but you're not half bad, Kentucky."

"Just wait, *Peach*. I may be temporarily down and out, but I'm not finished. Not by a country mile."

"Is Bobby around?"

"He has students until noon."

"Fiddle. He told me last night he'd be in this morning. I need to tell him something."

"I'm the official secretary. I can take a message."

Calista gave her the evil eye. "It's personal. I'll call him when I get home."

Bobby stopped in when he'd finished with his students. "May I take you to lunch?"

"I'm starving, so yes—I'd love that."

As he drove to an Italian diner on Bardstown Road, Mittie told him Calista had stopped by to talk to him.

"Did she mention what it was?"

"Personal, she said." Mittie surveyed the menu, one eye on Bobby. He scowled and looked at the menu.

They ordered and made small talk until their heaping plates of pasta with rich marinara and meatballs the size of small oranges arrived. Neither seemed anxious to talk about crashing her plane. *His* plane once. Halfway through the meal, Mittie started by telling him she was sorry.

"I'm the one with regret. I should have gone over it better before you left."

"All's well that ends well. Except for not having a plane, that is."

He nodded. "I know what you mean. I've had some close calls myself."

"But you've never had one go up in flames."

"You're right about that, but I've crashed more than once."

"You're kidding. I thought you were like Zeus, lord of the skies."

"Guess I have you fooled. My flying prowess, or lack of it, is one reason I came to the States."

"I have wondered. Care to give me the details?"

"Simple, really. I was engaged to a girl in London, someone who traveled in the right circles and had the adoration of my parents. Her dad sits in the House of Lords, so you can imagine the sort of wedding it was going to be."

"The kind my mother would drool over."

"Actually Catherine was a lot like your mother. Refined and gracious. And terrified of my flying. Two days before the wedding, I crashed a small plane out in Essex. Fortunately, I walked away with only a bruised ego, but Catherine and I argued. She gave me an ultimatum—her or my bloody airplanes. You can guess which I chose."

Mittie took a deep breath. "And now you're the pariah of London."

"Something like that. My father sent me over here until things cooled down, and I decided to stay—for a while I thought, just six months, but my heart was torn. I'd fallen in love with Kentucky and someone here."

Mittie nearly choked. "Is she someone I know?"

Bobby leaned back. "Misfortune seems to be my shadow. Things don't always work out the way you hope."

Her mother's words came back to her. *It's hard to risk your heart again.* Apparently Bobby had, and it had been torn yet again. He'd gracefully sidestepped revealing who it was. Calista? Or someone else? Calista's eagerness to talk to him made Mittie think she might be the one Bobby was referring to, but Bobby didn't ordinarily talk about his interests outside of work, and for him to say this much was puzzling.

"That stinks. What about Catherine? Did you see her in London?"

"Yes. I attended her wedding. Viscount Merkley is a financier and is deathly afraid of airplanes. It's a match made in heaven."

"So you're no longer an outcast and could go back if you wanted?"

"Theoretically, yes, but I choose not to."

"I'm glad. There are surely some other things you've not taught me."

"Celestial navigation for one. There's nothing quite so spectacular as flying at night with only the stars as a guide."

"When can we start?"

"Whenever you'd like."

The promised instruction never came because exactly one week later, Mittie received an invitation from Elizabeth McQueen, president of the newly formed Women's International Association of Aeronautics, to fly in the inaugural transcontinental women's air race. In August. Just three short months away. Mittie didn't even have a plane, and the race started in California. What were the chances? *If it sounds too good to be true . . .*

She tucked the envelope in the top drawer of her bureau next to Ames' locket and went out to ride Gypsy. The hair had grown back over Gypsy's injured knee, and only a discerning eye could detect the fine scar beneath it. Mittie's fingers went automatically to her face. It would never be as smooth as it once was, but the fine blemishes were a reminder of the grace she'd been granted time and again.

Gypsy's ears twitched, and Mittie relaxed the reins, the horse's toned body gliding into a trot. Mittie's thoughts drifted like the bits of cottonwood fluff floating in the air. *California. Women's air race.* Beneath her, Gypsy picked up the pace, taking the hill with ease. Then a shift in the saddle and Gypsy arched her neck, the ambling rhythm of her hooves on the ground as she did what her breed was born to do—the magnificent rack. Mittie held her breath, thinking she'd imagined it, but there it was. One. Two. Three. Four. Each hoof in perfect time. Mittie's heart swelled with the promise that, yes, one day Gypsy would enter the ring again and hear the applause.

When they returned to the stable, she told Toby that Gypsy was ready, that her training could resume. Mittie was ready, too. She took the letter from her bureau and showed it to Bobby when he came in for lunch the next day.

"I've just heard about it. You're accepting, aren't you?"

"The only obstacle I see is finding a plane. I was hoping you had some ideas."

"I'll give Victor a call."

"I'll talk to my parents tonight. And wire Ames."

It was a mad scramble from that day forward. Mittie wired Ames at his hotel in San Diego and the next day received a reply.

ATTA GIRL STOP PLANT HERE STOP CUSTOM PLANE STOP WILL CALL DETAILS STOP AMES

Having a plane built in California made the most sense. Ames secured access to a hangar and offered to oversee building the plane. He suggested a two-seat mono-wing with adequate horsepower and safety features that Bobby agreed were excellent choices. Her dad consulted with his banker and offered to front the production costs. Almost weekly meetings followed. Her daddy. Bobby. Victor and others in the Aero Club who voted unanimously to sponsor Mittie's expenses since her dad was paying for the plane.

They worked with the organizers of the air race in Cleveland who had partnered with the National Exchange Club. The race would coincide with the Cleveland men's air race, but it was Mrs.

McQueen who was the driving force with her declaration that "Women pilots are imperative to aviation's progress."

The names of those who had accepted the invitation were circulated, and no one was surprised to see Calista's name on the list. Mittie sent her a note. *California or bust. The ultimate challenge, dear Peach.*

Calista fired back. *This flapper is ready for you.*

Production costs and tensions ran high as the heat of July bore down on them, and they tried to think of every eventuality. Mittie pored over maps, noting possible problem spots. Ames called with progress reports every few days. Mittie yearned for her dad to be on hand for the takeoff, but her mother, ever protective, was afraid the long trip would cause his back to flare up. He promised he would be at the finish line in Cleveland. Victor and Bobby, though, made plans to travel by car to California and follow the same itinerary as the women as they flew across the continent. Mittie would take the train a few days early to get used to the feel of the new plane before the race.

Finally, with every detail in place, Mittie packed for the trip. Ames called to wish her luck and that evening, she took his grandmother's locket from her drawer. She rubbed it on her cheek and slipped it around her neck.

Ames met her at the train station in Santa Monica with open arms. They took a taxicab straight to Clover Field, a sprawling airport buzzing with activity. Trucks hauling grandstands. Roped-off parking areas.

The reality of it began to sink in, and when she saw her new plane, Mittie's eyes stung with hot tears. It was a beauty. Canary yellow with two black wavy stripes down the side and the flying school's logo on either side. With the zeal of a puppy, Ames showed her all the features.

"Sweetest engine you can imagine."

"One of yours?"

"Only the best for you, doll." He kept his arm around her shoulders, kisses handy. "Want to sit in the cockpit?"

It was a perfect fit, and she was itching to fly it, but she needed to check in with the officials first and meet the other early arrivals. In the headquarters building, Mittie found the registration table and gave her information. She turned to see if she could spot any of the other pilots when a gregarious woman in blousy pants and short curly hair came up and introduced herself. "Pancho Barnes. And you must be the darling of Kentucky. Some peach from Georgia's told me all about you." *The* Pancho Barnes, one of the contestants and already famous for her outrageous behavior and wily good humor.

Mittie shook her hand. "I'm thrilled to meet you. I just got in and didn't realize Calista—the one they call Peach—was already here."

"She's around here somewhere." Pancho jerked her head and said, "Come on—I'll introduce you to some of the gals."

Mittie shrugged at Ames and asked if he wanted to tag along.

"It's your party, doll. I'll be around."

Pancho lit up a slim black cigar and said, "Was that your mechanic?"

Mittie nodded. "And my best fella."

"I figured from the way he was looking at you. Hey, Amelia, someone I'd like you to meet."

Amelia Earhart. Mittie's heart was in her throat, but Amelia was warm and welcoming as were all the others, the ones whose names were familiar from the newspapers—Ruth Elder, Louise Thaden, Bobbi Trout. They talked of the heat in the desert, the change of plans for one of the seventeen stops, and that there were more than a few men who were betting they would fail.

Pancho blew out a puff of smoke. "We're going to show 'em.

You know the race motto, don't you? 'A woman's place is in the sky.'"

Mittie caught sight of Ames in the corner of her eye. He stood, arms crossed, talking to a man in mechanic's coveralls, but his brows were scrunched together, lips pursed. When her eyes met his, he said something to the fellow and brushed past him. Mittie took that as her cue and told Pancho that the sky was where she was headed. "It's lovely to meet you all." She stepped back from the group and the chorus of "Good luck!" and told Ames she was ready. Outside the hangar, she asked who he was talking to.

"Can't recall his name, but I've seen him around."

"You didn't look too happy."

"Guess I was thinking about us getting away while there's still plenty of sunshine." He draped his arm around her shoulders and gave her a peck on the cheek just as Calista Gilson strode across the grass.

"If you two aren't the lovebirds."

"Hey, Peach. Sounds like you're jealous." Ames put his other arm around Calista.

"That's a laugh and a half." She leaned in front of Ames and looked at Mittie. "Which one is yours?"

Mittie pointed to the canary yellow plane and Calista pointed hers out—a new Brunner-Winkle Bird, pale orange with her signature "Peaches" on the side and the Roman numeral II.

Mittie's eyes widened. "It's a beauty. But can it fly?"

"Ha! We'll see in two days."

Mittie was getting itchier by the minute to get up in the air, but Calista pulled her aside and told Ames to scram, that she wanted to talk to Mittie.

"This better be short. We need to get in the air."

"Short. Not so sweet, though. Listen—there's some rumors going around about Ames."

"I hope you didn't start them."

"No. I was having a little chat with some of the mechanics yesterday. Somehow your name came up, which led to one of them saying he'd heard of you, that Ames mentioned you in a poker game. I asked how much they took him for, and they all clammed up. But it was written all over their faces."

Mittie's face grew hot, but it wasn't from the sun that was bearing down. Calista always made such a drama out of everything. "They probably clammed up so they wouldn't have to admit that he beat them. Not that I condone poker playing for anything more than match sticks, but why are you telling me this?"

"It just got me thinking that there's a lot I haven't told you, and now I'm feeling guilty after hearing that."

"What else?"

"San Antonio, for one, when the Patriots broke up. Do you know the real reason?"

Mittie glanced at Ames, who tapped his wristwatch and made a rolling motion with his hand to hurry. "Ames said it was a misunderstanding. Why are you even bringing this up now? Can't it wait?"

Calista grabbed her arm and looked her square in the eye. "Ames lost the entire cut of our San Antonio gig in a lousy club that had a little game going in the back. Every dime."

Mittie's head scrolled back to the conversation with Ames. "He said the group there wouldn't let the Patriots fly, only you."

Calista laughed as Ames came up. "It was great seeing you, too, Kentucky. May the best girl win."

"Let's get together before the start of the race, okay?"

Calista said, "Sure thing," and scampered off.

Ames asked what the big secret was. "Just telling me the latest about her love life. Let's get going."

"You know I think instead of flying just around here, you should get some experience in the desert."

"As long as I get to fly over the ocean at least once."

He outlined a plan on the map that would take them to Temecula, which had both small mountains and desert terrain. "There's no airfield, but a fella there has a makeshift runway and a fuel station. You okay with that?"

She nodded and buckled up, oriented herself again to the differences from other planes she'd flown, and studied the map one final time before takeoff.

Once they were in the air, turquoise blue water swirled below them, waves sweeping in all the way from China and dashing against the rocks. Mittie hugged the Los Angeles shoreline for a good twenty miles, soaring and dipping like she'd only dreamed, pushing the conversation with Calista to the far corners of her mind. She nosed up and headed southeast toward the desert and the parched brown hills. Two hours later, she landed on the bumpy turf Ames pointed out.

When they got out, Ames draped his arm around her shoulders. "What did you think?"

"There's more vibration than I'm used to."

"Bigger engine and more power is what you're feeling."

A couple of other things had come to her attention, too, that she hadn't noticed at first. The gauges didn't have a shiny new look to them, and the seat was a good fit, but not new. When she asked Ames about them, he shrugged. "I put the bulk of the money into the parts that would count. Aviation prices are skyrocketing with all the interest, and we were working on a short deadline."

"And I appreciate every bit of what you've done. Truly I do." She took off her helmet and shook her hair, letting it fall around her shoulders. "Jeepers, it's hot."

"Nothing like it's going to be in Arizona. That's why I wanted you to get some desert experience. Let's get a couple of rooms here and let you fly over the San Bernardino Mountains tomorrow since that's the first leg of the race."

"Bobby and Victor have already booked me a room in Santa Monica. They're coming in tonight. If we left now, we'd make it."

"You'd be flying into the sun. I think it's too risky. Are you hungry?"

"Starving."

They walked the few blocks into town where she found a pay phone and called the hotel to leave a message for Bobby and Victor that she had a change of plans. That night, they ate burritos in a cantina downtown and afterward strolled under a star-speckled sky past a Spanish mission. They ended on a high ridge that looked across miles of moonlit mountains and a vast sparse land whose mounds of prickly cactus resembled a host of porcupines. Ames pulled Mittie into his arms, his kisses warm, the rigors of the past two months melting between them. They sat on a rocky ledge where she nestled against his shoulder.

"This was a good idea, getting away from all the people. Did I ever thank you for believing in me?"

"I've always believed in you. In us. And I hope that you'll fall in love with California as I have."

"I won't be here long enough to do that, but I have been wondering if you'd heard from Lester and Shorty lately."

"What made you think of them?"

"Seeing Calista again reminded me of the good times we used to have, the poker games you guys used to play. Where are they now?"

"Can't say as I know. And I'd prefer to think only of you for now." He nibbled her ear. "Where were we?"

She didn't answer, Calista's revelation grating in her bones. A twinge of something niggled at her, and she remembered the guy in the welcome hangar that made Ames scowl. Was something brewing that made him suggest bringing her to the desert? She pulled her knees to her chest and wrapped her arms around them, gazing at the shadowy cacti, which now looked like purple and blue bruises on the desert floor.

Ames ran his hand along her cheek. "Penny for your thoughts."

"Just thinking about the race. I'd like to get to Clover Field by noon tomorrow, if that's all right."

"Sure, doll. Probably best for me, too. I'll have to catch a train back to San Diego and get the car."

"I thought you had someone helping you with that beforehand."

"Didn't work out, but you'll be busy mingling and won't even notice I'm gone."

"You're probably right. When will you get back?"

"Early evening, I hope."

They walked back to the center of town to the small flat-roofed inn where Ames gave her a lingering kiss at the door and said goodnight.

Once in the room, Mittie remembered she hadn't called her parents to tell them she'd arrived. She didn't relish going out on the street alone to the phone she'd used earlier, but the clerk had told her it was the closest one. It was past midnight in Kentucky, and she wanted to slap herself for not remembering to call earlier, but her daddy picked up right away.

"Are you all right, sugar?"

"I'm fine. It's sunny and warm here, perfect for trying out the new plane."

"Any problems?" His voice held an edge of caution.

"Not a one. I met some of the other women and am looking forward to seeing Bobby and Victor tomorrow. You have the schedule, and you know I'll call whenever I can."

"I do, sugar. The reason I ask if there were any problems is that I got an unusual call this afternoon from the assembly plant."

Mittie's neck hairs prickled. "Oh?"

"Ames cleared out his personal things and took the plane before settling up on the bill."

She glanced over her shoulder, half expecting Ames to be standing there. "Should I ask him about it?"

"I'm sure it's an oversight, but I thought you should be aware. I don't want anything to get in the way of your being in the race."

"Ames is going to San Diego to get the car tomorrow so he can follow the race, so I'm sure he'll clear things up then."

"Good enough. Your mother and I love you."

"Love you, too."

Back in the room, Mittie slipped out of her flight pants, the feel of them still sticky from the heat, and got ready for bed, uneasy and uncertain about many things.

CHAPTER 29

Mittie awoke from a heavy sleep and couldn't shake the groggy feeling or the weight of her uncertainty about Ames. More than once during breakfast, she almost mentioned her conversation with her dad, but an urgency churned in her gut to get in the air and back to Clover Field. Flying cleared her head, and they arrived just after noon to a complete transformation from only the day before. The grandstands were set up, the grounds swarming with people. Workers. Newspaper reporters with cameras. Mechanics. Men in suits and hats. Men in coveralls.

Ames sent her off alone to look for Bobby and Victor while he took the little canary plane to do some fine-tuning and ready it for the race. Mittie wove through the crowd toward the race headquarters, where it was just as frenetic inside as out with a bank of phone lines set up, wire strung everywhere. How would she ever find Bobby and Victor in such a throng?

They found her first, Bobby coming up on her right, Victor in tow. After the *good to see you, glad you made it, how's the plane* banter, Victor said, "Can't get over what a madhouse this is. Are you all set for tomorrow?"

"I will be. I've signed in and have all the instructions—just waiting on the welcome dinner tonight. Come on; you need to see the plane."

Once outside, Bobby said, "We saw Peach earlier. She's so excited I don't think her feet ever touched the ground. Quite a machine she's got."

"Gee, that's a real confidence booster."

"I didn't mean it to sound that way. I'm sure with the specs I've seen of yours that it's superb, too."

When they got to the service hangar, a mechanic approached. "You the gal from Kentucky?"

"I am, and these are my sponsors for the race."

"Fella that brought it in wanted me to give you a message. Said his ride showed up and he'd catch you later."

"Did he service the plane?"

"Can't help you there. Got my own rigging to check."

The three of them looked at each other, the bubble of anxiety that had ridden under Mittie's ribs all day now an effervescent sea. *What ride?* Ames said he was taking the train.

"Thanks, anyway." She took a deep breath and walked to her plane. "Here it is." She ran her hand along the nose. "I'll check the maintenance log and see if Ames recorded anything."

She did a leg up on the strut and retrieved the log. No fuel or oil check recorded. Bobby, though, said he'd be glad to do a thorough check, and rocked back on his heels. "Have you talked to your father?"

"Late last night. I told him I was looking forward to seeing you two today."

Victor scowled. "I wish we'd timed this a little better. Let's go somewhere so we can talk."

Once they'd found the airfield coffee shop and were seated, Victor told her a message from her dad was waiting for them when they'd arrived at their hotel, along with the one she'd left. "Seems the fellow in San Diego that rented Ames the facility and provided the workers to build the plane hasn't been paid. If it's not settled up today, he's going to file a complaint with the race officials."

"Daddy thought it was probably an oversight on Ames' part."

"He didn't want to alarm you by telling too much, but it puts all of us in a precarious position."

"Perhaps Ames is taking care of it while he's down there getting his car." Her words carried more confidence than the doubt knotted in her gut.

Bobby, silent up until now, said, "Mittie, the situation is grave. If you take the plane without clearance, there may be legal repercussions."

Her jaw tightened. "Too many things aren't adding up. First Calista, then a trip to the desert. I think Ames is avoiding someone, that he's in some kind of trouble."

"What about Calista?"

"Something she told me yesterday. Rumors that Ames might have lost some money gambling." *Her daddy's money.*

Bobby nodded. "I've suspected that before, the odd comment here and there."

The air in the room grew thin, the sick feeling in her stomach swelling. Calista knew. Bobby knew. Everyone but her. "This isn't a good time to find out that my friends have waited until now to inform me."

Bobby blew out a breath. "It was just talk. I had no proof. He lived at your farm for two months and your father vouched for him. We had hoped to talk to Ames and find out the situation from him."

"I'm open to suggestions."

Victor said, "Your father is prepared to wire the money if Ames hasn't paid by five o'clock today"—he pulled his pocket watch from his vest—"which is precisely four hours from now. Paying for services rendered is the only way to ensure your place in the race, but the decision is yours."

"I can't believe Ames would do this. It was for his benefit as well as mine."

Victor said, "Human nature is a funny thing. More than likely he thought he could double the money your dad already paid in. I imagine he's in a bit of a panic. Perhaps even desperate."

Anger coiled in her gut. Her daddy had already paid for the plane once. Now he was going to have to pay again. The truth gripped her, and she wanted to scream. How could Ames do this to her? Images flashed through her head. Nebraska and his dishonesty there with Mr. Nance. The phone calls offering excuses for why he couldn't come home. Always making it sound like he was doing things for her benefit. Her hand went to the locket. Was that a lie, too?

"Mittie." Bobby's voice came gently through her thoughts. "Your father wants this for you. He believes in you; he's told me time and again. I know it's none of my affair, but I think you want it, too. Don't let the opportunity slip from your fingers."

"It would be selfish of me to assume daddy should pay for my mistake in judging Ames' character."

"We've all been duped into trusting people who didn't deserve that honor. There are nineteen other women who are counting on you. Do it for them. And for yourself."

The yoke that bore down on her shoulders lifted. "You're right."

Victor's concern was that the factory owner who'd called was also trying to bilk them. He offered to drive to San Diego and check the validity of the claim. Rather than have her daddy wire the money directly to a stranger, Victor would collect it and carry it himself. He didn't have much time, so he hurried off, leaving Bobby to do the maintenance check on the plane and go with Mittie for a test flight.

Before Victor left, she said, "I don't know how I can ever repay you."

"Perhaps Ames will come through."

The whirlpool in her stomach told her he wouldn't.

Bobby found the source of the vibration in the plane and replaced a couple of parts before the two of them took it for a test flight. They got to the hotel with not much time to spare before the evening banquet. Mittie left a message at the desk for Calista with her room number, not sure if she would catch her. Just as Mittie put on one of the fancy frocks she'd brought, a knock sounded.

Mittie opened the door, and Calista breezed in.

"Hey, Kentucky, nice dress."

"Thanks for coming. You look gorgeous, but then you always do. About our conversation earlier—there have been developments, which I won't go into, but I have very good reason to believe you were telling me the truth about Ames and San Antonio. What I want to know is why you didn't tell me before."

"I honestly don't know. I wanted to partially get back at Ames, but then he had that wreck and you were so starry-eyed over him after he stayed at your farm, it didn't seem right. I was hoping for your sake he'd changed."

"He did seem different then, but I could also sense a restlessness in him. I thought it was to get back to his work, but now I don't know. It's like he's happiest when he's adrift."

"He's going to be adrift for sure if those guys in the hangar were right about his gambling. Is everything all right with your plane?"

"It is now. Another guy who's adrift went over it."

"You must be talking about Bobby."

Mittie nodded, a warm feeling settling in her chest.

Calista went to the mirror and fixed a smudge of her lipstick with her pinkie. "I don't mean to tell you how to run your life, but if

you'd get your head out of the clouds about Ames, I think you'd see
that our dear Bobby is pining for you."

"That's insane. You've had your eyes on Bobby since Kansas City,
and if I'm not mistaken, he's in love with you." Mittie pulled on her
long gloves and grabbed her evening bag.

"Bobby's swell, but he's not in love with me. I let that fantasy run
away with me for a while, but nothing ever clicked." She grabbed
her handbag and swiveled her hips. "All I'm going to say is that you
need to open your eyes, darlin'."

What Calista suggested about Bobby was ridiculous, of course.
She knew he was fond of her, but pining after her? Hardly. And it
wasn't something she even wanted to dwell on with the race starting
in less than a day.

Mittie was glad she hadn't mentioned anything to Ames about
her conversation with her dad. If he suspected she was aware of the
fiasco, he might stay away to save face. Her faith in him might be
shattered, but in her inmost being, she felt Ames still cherished being a part of the race. And she did want to hear his explanation. He
deserved that opportunity at least.

He still hadn't arrived by the start of the banquet hosted by the
National Exchange Club. It was a gala affair with cameramen and
other press reporters lingering about, chatting with the other girls
decked out in their finery—all except Pancho, who came in a men's
tuxedo complete with a red carnation in the lapel. The tension was
palpable, prerace jitters, but also one of camaraderie, each woman
honored to be there. And Mittie wasn't the only one who'd had a
snag in her plans. One of the women told about picking up her new
plane and suffering from carbon monoxide poisoning before touching down and having an emergency revision made to deliver fresh
air to the cockpit. One contender was still waiting for her plane to
arrive, and another hadn't even shown up yet. It was a mad scramble
for all of them, cobbled-together hopes and dreams.

When the time came to eat, the chair reserved for Ames remained empty. No one had seen him, including the garage owner in San Diego where Victor had relinquished the money and obtained a manifest of the parts and labor and a receipt. The chicken was baked dry, as was Mittie's throat, but she was determined not to let circumstances ruin her evening. As the waiters served slices of apple pie a la mode, Ames, his hair still damp from the shower, his tie slightly askew, slipped into the chair beside Mittie.

Her heart skipped. He made it. This was not a man who had deliberately set out to hurt her. *That smile.* There was a logical explanation. There had to be.

He leaned in and whispered, "Have I missed anything?"

"Not yet." Restraint from asking him a million questions tore at her insides as the welcome was given and each of the women and their sponsors were introduced.

"Mittie Humphreys, from Louisville, Kentucky, flying a custom mono-wing in the light aircraft division."

She rose and nodded, then held out her hand to indicate Bobby and Victor as her sponsors. When Calista was introduced, she gave a flirty wave, her Marcel waves framing her pixie face. Her flapper headpiece with copper-colored feathers matched her slim silky dress. When she made eye contact with Mittie, it wasn't a challenge but the look of a sister. A best friend.

When it was over, Bobby leaned in and whispered his room number. "In case you need me." She bit her lower lip, emotion welling up. She blinked twice and told him she'd see him in the morning.

She turned to Ames. "Could we go for a walk?"

"Sure, doll, but I thought you'd want to get your beauty sleep. Big day tomorrow."

"It is, isn't it? Perhaps the biggest day of my life so far." She worked to control her tone. *Stay calm.* "There's a nice breeze off the ocean. Let's enjoy it while we can." She walked across the lobby toward the glass exit doors. His shoes tapped on the marble floor as he hurried to catch up and held the door for her.

"It's a big day for me, too, and I need to get out to Clover Field early for one last look at the plane."

She strolled past a fountain and waved at a couple of the girls who were having a smoke and laughing. "It's not necessary. Bobby's already done a thorough check and serviced it."

"York? Why was he messing with it?" He grabbed her arm and stopped her.

She smiled. "Not messing, sweetie. Doing what you were supposed to do before you left."

"I'm your ace mechanic, remember? He's not familiar with the plane. I'd be surprised if he's even seen an engine like that baby has."

"He did mention that it was unusual. It took some doing, but he got rid of that vibration I noticed earlier." She didn't mean to antagonize him by mentioning Bobby, but facts were facts.

"It was one of the things I was going to fix. I sure as blue blazes don't need him tinkering with it."

"It's my plane. I assumed I could have whoever I want looking at it."

"You've certainly taken a cavalier attitude since York rolled into town."

She blew out a long breath. They'd walked far enough away that no people milled about. Time to ask the tough questions. "Ames, this has nothing to do with Bobby, but there is something we need to talk about."

He pulled her toward him, his arms around her waist. "All we need to talk about is what happens next. For you and me after the race. You know I love it here, and I've nursed the hope that you would, too."

She stiffened. How could she have been so blind? Every time

tension coiled between them, he turned on the charm, thinking that a kiss and that cow-eyed expression could melt away anything. She gripped each of his arms, removed them from around her waist, and stepped back.

"It's over between us, Ames. I know everything. Maybe not everything, but enough to know that I'm finished with your lies and your half-truths. I want to know why you gambled away my daddy's money and didn't even have the decency to tell me. If you have any desire to remain friends, then I need some straight answers."

"You know I'm always straight with you."

"Do I? Then let's start with this. Why did you take the plane from the shop in San Diego without settling up with the owner, without paying for the labor he provided?"

"It's true—I haven't settled the final payment. I've run into all kinds of snags, but I didn't want to burden you with them and distract you from what you came to do. I was only thinking of you, doll."

"Were you aware that my plane was going to be impounded because of your irresponsible action? That there would be no race for me if I didn't have a plane?"

"That's ridiculous! Where did you come up with that hooey?"

"That's immaterial, but what is important is that you have taken my daddy's money, cried about cost overruns, and then built a plane where half of the parts aren't even new."

"York. He's put you up to this. He wants the credit for whatever success you have in the race. He's been trying to squeeze me out since the minute he popped on the scene."

"No, Ames. You've squeezed yourself out. It's stupid of me that I didn't see it earlier, that I let myself be drawn in by your charm and your kisses."

"I'll make it up to you, doll. I always do." He squeaked out the words, the panic a high-tension wire that vibrated between them.

"I've no doubt you have great intentions, and if it were just me you fooled, I wouldn't be so angry. What I can't abide is that you did this to my daddy, that we trusted you." She took another step back, her arms and legs quivering.

He had no rebuke. No rebuttal. Mittie lifted her chin and saw the defeat in his stooped shoulders. Tears stung her eyes, but she said nothing more.

Ames walked to a low retaining wall of a flower bed and sat down, elbows on his knees. At last, he spoke. "You don't know what it's like growing up with a granddaddy who berated you because of your very existence, not knowing if you'd have supper from one night to the next. He was as sorry as smoke off fresh cow manure. Didn't ever make a crop. We had nothing but the shack we called home."

Mittie's heart was in her throat, but she was guarded, too. How did she know it wasn't another lie? Another attempt to gain sympathy?

"When I was fourteen, an airplane flew over the hog pen while I was doing the chores, and I knew right then that someday, I'd be in that cockpit, that those wings would take me far away where I might be somebody. I didn't even know that people like you and your family existed. I left when I was sixteen and hitchhiked to New York, which was like the other side of the moon to me. I worked in a factory in Jersey, and one night in a poker game, I won my first plane. Flying and my luck at poker took over my life. I thought I had a real chance at breaking through when I met you."

The wind had gone from Mittie's sails, too. "I hope, for your sake, that you do break through. I'm sorry you've had a rough time, but no one is immune from hurts in this life, whether you come from paupers or kings. And sometimes we have to make choices. What you chose to do with my daddy's money is inexcusable."

"I will make it up to you. You'll see."

"It's too late for that, Ames." She turned and walked slowly back up the walk, past the fountain, through the glass doors, and into the lobby with marble floors and bell captains. She squared her shoulders and pushed the button for the elevator. In her room, she peeled off her nylons and fancy dress, laid out her clothes for the next day, brushed her teeth, turned out the light, and cried herself to sleep.

CHAPTER 30

The grandstands were packed, and someone shouted that Howard Hughes and Hollywood stars were among the spectators. Dozens of photos were taken of the women pilots who would compete in the first-ever women's air derby. Twenty women were on the official roster, but at noon, just two hours before the official starting time, one girl had still not arrived but had called that she was on her way. Pancho Barnes started a petition stating that she be allowed to compete anyway. Mittie happily added her signature.

Wiley Post was the race official and would fly from stop to stop in a Lockheed Vega with the official timekeeper. He and his longtime flying buddy, Will Rogers, welcomed the girls. Mr. Rogers took a personal interest in each of them, and when he spoke to the crowd in front of the microphone, he said, "These sure are some pretty pilots. I saw one of them powdering her nose a while ago. I believe this fine event should be called the Powder Puff Derby." The crowd roared with laughter and cheers.

The lightweight aircraft participants were introduced first— Mittie and Calista among them. Amelia and Pancho both flew larger planes, which would give a decided edge with their larger-horsepower engines, so the race committee had determined early on to have two separate classes with prizes for each. But all the women would fly together. United in their mission.

Mittie went over her checklist with Bobby and Victor. Parachute. Three-day emergency food and water supply in case of going down in the mountains or being stranded in the desert. Chewing gum. Extra goggles, gloves, helmet. And two suitcases in the baggage compartment filled with ball gowns for the banquets at each of their eight overnight stops.

Action and purpose took over, leaving no time for emotional pondering, and when the call to line up was announced, Mittie shook hands with Victor, hugged Bobby, and walked tall to her bright yellow plane. Before she got in, she took one last look over her shoulder and waved at Bobby and Victor, but it was the figure that stood in the shadow of the hangar that pinched her heart. Ames. She blew a kiss into the air and hoisted herself up and into the cockpit.

The gunshot to start the race was fired in Cleveland and transmitted by radio to Clover Field. One by one the lightweight planes took off. Mittie was third in line. Calista fourth. Whatever happened now was up to Mittie. When she was airborne, she gripped the wheel and lifted her chin. She shouted into the wind, the feel of it on her cheeks intoxicating.

A short sixty-eight miles later, Mittie coasted into the San Bernardino airport for the first stop, where another crowd greeted them and rushed out on the field to see the planes and the women who flew them. When all had arrived, they were whisked to the hotel and the banquet that awaited, euphoria the tide they rode.

The day's excitement and tension had taken its toll, though, and not even Calista's chattering could keep Mittie awake once her head hit the pillow.

An hour later, shouting and banging erupted outside her door, and when she went to see what the ruckus was, a woman she recognized from the banquet said, "Get dressed. To the airfield now. All the planes have to be checked."

They were bussed to the airfield, their insides coiled with an unknown fear. The night crew had discovered that two of the women's planes had oil in the gas tanks. Bobby appeared at Mittie's side and told her he'd check hers and Calista's, that more than likely the crew was inexperienced and that it was just an unfortunate error. She could have kissed him for offering to help. Only two were found to be affected, but the next morning, rumors of sabotage circulated among their ranks.

Still, as Mittie readied for the second day of the race, confidence surged through her. The highway below led her through the high desert mountains to the oasis of Palm Springs. She consulted the map to verify when to bank right and head south. She skirted the edge of the Salton Sea, the aquamarine patch on the landscape a short respite from the vast barrenness of the desert. Heat shimmered on golden sand below, a raw beauty of its own. Joshua trees with their spiny limbs reached up from clumps of dry grass and mounds of stone. Endless miles stretched before her, a ribbon of road the guide that would take her to Calexico for a required flyover. The sun was intense, cooking her from above and from the reflection of the desert floor below. Mittie wiped a drip of sweat that trickled from beneath her leather helmet, the wind in her face that of a furnace blast. She flew low over the crowd in Calexico who came just to see the swoosh of planes go by, then nosed up and headed east toward Yuma. She ran her sandpaper tongue over her lips to moisten them, the swigs of water from her canteen inadequate to quench her thirst.

The little canary plane bucked with the wind that whipped sand up from the earth, blinding her, pelting her skin. Her eyes burned as she flew higher to avoid the sandstorm, but wherever she went, the grit and current went with her. Her shoulders ached from gripping the wheel. Her legs, too, from keeping the rudder steady. She prayed she wouldn't run into one of the other planes with the poor visibility. She prayed that her face wouldn't melt off. And she uttered a prayer of gratitude when the sand thinned into a gritty veil and the airfield at Yuma came into view.

Calista was already there and welcomed Mittie when she emerged from the cockpit. "Isn't this beastly, all this heat and ferocious sand? Amelia crashed coming in, and Bobbi flipped her plane on its back."

"No! Are they all right?"

"Amelia has a busted propeller, and they're still looking at Bobbi's plane."

Mittie tipped up her canteen, draining it, her mouth filled with grit, and together, she and Calista huddled under the wing of her little bird and waited for everyone to arrive. News spread among them that Marvel Crosson, a sweet, outgoing girl from Alaska, was having engine trouble and having a new one sent to Phoenix. Thea, who'd come all the way from Germany, received a telegram warning of sabotage.

A sense of unease wound through their ranks as Amelia's plane underwent repairs and Bobbi's plane needed more work. In quiet fear, the women took off for Phoenix, their last stop for the day. If Amelia could crash in her heavyweight plane, what fate awaited the rest of them?

Mittie made record time flying over rough terrain and its unpredictable wind patterns. It was still hot, and her lips had blisters from the heat and sun, but another kind of quiet had settled within her. Resolve to finish. To give it her all. When thoughts of Ames flickered in, she shoved them out. There would be time to think of him later.

Not a breath of air stirred when Mittie landed in Phoenix. A single cloud, maybe the size of a mattress, floated across a brilliant blue sky. The first news was that Thea from Germany had crashed shortly after takeoff in Yuma. She and her plane were no worse for the wear, but when she investigated, she found garbage stuffed in her carburetor. She cleaned it and took to the air again, arriving safely. One by one, the women arrived, but as the afternoon waned on, Marvel still hadn't come in. Was it another act of sabotage or the cranky engine Marvel was going to replace in Phoenix?

Pancho gathered the women together. "Someone is trying to stop the race. We don't know who, but if we squawk too loud, it will feed the notion that women aren't fit to fly and they'll win. I'm asking for more security. Not asking...demanding." The officials agreed to the security issue, and when reporters tried to get the women to talk about the vandalized planes, they stood firm and said the rumors were simply that—unfounded hearsay.

A chorus of ruddy-faced women with pale circles around their eyes where goggles had been sat down to another meal of baked chicken. Marvel still hadn't arrived, and search parties were activated, but no one felt like celebrating the day's winners. The only thing any of them wanted was to see the wide smile and dimpled cheeks of the girl from Alaska they'd come to regard as a kindred soul.

Tempers were short and tension as tight as a kite string the next morning when there was still no news of Marvel. Bobby checked and rechecked everything possible on Mittie's plane, and when they met for the hug they always shared before she left, he held her close. They stood facing one another, fingers clasped, his eyes as clear as the cloudless sky. Mittie broke the trance with a smile, but Bobby stepped closer and, with an oil-smudged finger, tilted her chin. He ran his tongue along his lower lip, warmth radiating between them. Her breath caught as Calista's words danced through her head. *Open your eyes, darlin'*.

For an instant she thought he would kiss her, but someone yelled, "Places, ladies!" and broke the spell. Relief zipped through her. Calista and her flippant remark had put ideas in Mittie's head that she wasn't ready to think about.

Bobby gave her a hurried hug and said, "Take care, dear Mittie."

With the wind at her back, she soared across the mountains toward Douglas, Arizona, where news of Marvel's fate awaited. Her plane had crashed in a mesquite jungle, her broken, lifeless body discovered a hundred yards away. Her parachute was half open, but both it and her plane had failed her.

Mittie had neither the heart nor the courage to call her parents and tell them what happened. After the banquet that evening, a somber time of realization that their quest was one of uncertainty and danger, Bobby asked if she would walk with him. With mountains in the distance and stars overhead, they walked in silence until they came to a small park with a gazebo in the center. Bobby sat on the second-to-last step and patted the spot beside him.

"Sweet little town, isn't it?" Mittie said as she pulled her knees up and wrapped her arms around them.

"Another fascinating part of America."

"Are you enjoying the drive with Victor?"

"Very much, but not nearly as much as what I'm doing at this moment."

"It's good to get away from the crowd for a few minutes."

Bobby stretched his legs out before him and leaned back on his elbows. "I actually had a reason for taking you away. It's been a sobering couple of days, and this morning, with Marvel still missing and you getting ready to fly across unknown territory, a feeling gripped me so strongly that I almost asked you not to go."

"We've all felt the strain and worry about Marvel. And now the terrible sadness. But we have to go on. All of us."

"I know that, but what I finally understood was what Catherine must have felt every time I flew. The fear that I might not come back. The inability to live with that fear. That's what I felt about you this morning—a mortal panic that it might be the last time I saw you laughing and twisting your hair up under your flight helmet. Or the last time I saw you teasing Peach, so full of life."

Her breath caught. A nick in her heart. "You know I have to do this."

"Yes—no matter what anyone thinks or feels, it is something you must do. And that's why, when news of Marvel came, I knew what I needed to do as well."

His words hung in the air, the chirp of a cricket nearby. Mittie held her breath, unsure of what he would say next. She turned her head, eyebrows raised, and waited.

Bobby sat back up, reached for her hand. "I know that whatever has transpired between you and Ames has probably not played its course, that there are frayed edges that need mending. I'm not trying to rush that or alter what time alone can heal. But I also can't let you go off another day without declaring my feelings for you."

The night swirled, stirred by Bobby's mention of Ames, her unexplored feelings, the pain she hadn't worked through. But a thought she couldn't quite capture also niggled.

Gently, Bobby rubbed a thumb along her finger and continued. "I love you, Mittie. I have since the day I first saw you, but I wouldn't allow myself to hurt someone again, to take the responsibility for another woman's emotions so soon after Catherine. And then you fell in love with Ames. May still be in love with him..."

The memory of Bobby saying he'd fallen in love with Kentucky and someone there slammed her chest. *Her.* He was talking about *her.*

She struggled for air and said, "I don't know what I feel for Ames. Numb. Betrayed. I suppose outraged, but you're right—I've not worked through it." And she certainly wasn't ready to fall into another man's arms. Not even one who had tugged at the corners of her heart from the moment they'd met.

"I only want you to know that when you have, I'll be waiting. I love you more than I ever thought it was possible to love another human being."

Mittie blew out a long breath, another cricket joining in the chorus. "I think it's time for me to sort out those feelings."

He rose and took her hand, pulled her up, and asked if he could kiss her. She kissed him first. A sweet, sisterly peck on the cheek.

CHAPTER 31

Two stops were scheduled before the next overnight, and as Mittie flew over the sagebrush and rocky prairies of southern New Mexico, she opened the envelope in her mind that contained the puzzle pieces of Ames. If she were cold and calculating, it would be easy. He'd taken her daddy's money and used it foolishly. He'd broken the trust between them and lied. He wasn't trustworthy. But neither was Mittie's heart. More of Ames bubbled beneath the surface of that rakishly handsome smile. The tenderness when he visited with children at barnstorming. The excitement he couldn't contain when they met after a long absence. The way he picked her up and swung her around in his strong arms. The delicately woven bracelet made from Gypsy's mane and tail. The grandfather who drank and provided no moral compass. His niece, Lela, who brought a softness to his eyes when he spoke of her.

He lied. He took Daddy's money. He skipped out on responsibility.

Like the tangled underbrush of the belly of New Mexico, her thoughts wove in and out. She screamed to the sky to give her an answer. She prayed to God Almighty to touch Ames, to make him remorseful. He was that, of course, but following through and making amends eluded him.

The wheels beneath her bounced when Mittie touched down at the border town of Columbus, New Mexico, no closer to knowing her heart than she had four days ago.

It was a quick stop and she was back in the air, back to the ponderings that left her arms numb and precipitated an ache behind the eyes. Below her white sands shifted like the sea, waves of steel blue and stark white, a dark ridge that gave way to dunes of soft gray. Shifting like the many faces of Ames. Ames the drifter. Ames the dreamer. Ames the one who made her heart dance and her knees turn to jelly. She had no future with him—of that she was sure. At least the moral compass that her parents had given her was enough to point to true north. To right and wrong. To doing the right thing when it mattered. And when it didn't. The landscape darkened with a cloud that hovered over the sand and in her heart. She consulted her map, checked the gauges, and looked for the airfield of El Paso below. To her left, the sky lit up with a jagged streak of lightning.

Giant raindrops pelted the earth like arrows as she taxied and pulled into the slot the flagman indicated. She stuffed her maps under her flight jacket and dashed for the terminal. She was next-to-the-last person to make it in, but the thunderstorm had grounded them all. They wouldn't finish the day's itinerary.

Taking advantage of the unexpected night off from the "rubber chicken" circuit, some of the women organized a trip to Juárez for a night of fun. Mittie pulled Bobby aside to tell him of the plans. "You should be a lot more worried about what happens across the border than me flying in the sky."

He laughed and told her to have a good time, that he and Victor were going to find the biggest steak in El Paso.

Calista danced on top of a table in the second cantina they visited, shaking the maracas one of the locals provided and eating up the attention. Mittie settled for feasting on rich tamales swimming in borracho beans, accompanied by ginger water laced with tequila. It was just the frivolity they needed, and as they trooped down the street, arm in arm with the heat of the desert drying their bones, the bonds that had held them together for five days strengthened. They would need it, for trouble was brewing in Texas.

At breakfast, the news was delivered that a Texas oil tycoon had demanded the air race be halted because women weren't capable of flying, and that without men for guidance, they were handicapped.

Outrage at the statement united the women even more, and a prompt rebuttal was issued by the race officials. They were off to Pecos with clear skies above them and more determination than ever. In Pecos, Blanche reported she'd had a fire in her baggage compartment and had to make an emergency landing to put it out. Since she was miles from anywhere, she had to prop her own plane to finish the trip. That day also, Pancho, who'd been their leader and biggest supporter, crashed on landing into a car that had infringed on the runway. Pancho was uninjured, but her plane was demolished, putting her out of the race.

When Mittie landed in Fort Worth, she expected Calista to greet her since she'd been ahead of her on their two touchdowns in West Texas, but the little orange plane wasn't there.

A knot twisted in Mittie's stomach that grew tighter as the day waned on. When Bobby suggested she might be lost, Mittie snapped at him. "Calista has better sense of direction than a homing pigeon. Something's happened—I just know it."

Mittie refused to leave the field and get ready for the evening banquet. Bobby sent Victor on and stayed with her, offering only the comfort of his presence. Mittie paced around the hangars outside, her eyes peeled to the west where ribbons of clouds turned fiery red and then purple, softening with the dusk into deep violet and burnt umber.

Someone shouted behind her. "Hey, Kentucky!"

Mittie turned and ran to her dusty, ragged friend, their arms entwined while Calista told her and Bobby what had happened.

"One minute everything was fine, then the engine started sputtering and the fuel gauge went to empty. I sort of panicked and started looking for a place to land, but I was over some rocky hills and there were oil derricks in every direction. I waited too long and nosed down too fast. *Peaches* landed headfirst in a yucca thicket."

"And you? Were you hurt?"

"Rattled is all."

Her flight pants were shredded, her hands scratched, but she was safe.

"Some guys from an oil rig found me walking around in a daze and gave me a lift."

"You're here—that's all that matters."

"But I'm out of the race. The plane's a total wreck."

"That stinks."

"It's up to you now, Kentucky."

Calista wore one of Mittie's dresses to the banquet that night where the other women gathered around with hugs and tears in their eyes. Back in their room, Mittie begged Calista to ride the rest of the route with her, but she refused. "This is your show now. You won't let me down, will you?"

"I'll do my best not to."

"Good, because I'll be in Cleveland, the first to welcome you."

Calista left the next morning with her team to go back to Atlanta. Their parting wrenched Mittie's heart. She would make it to Cleveland. For both of them.

Being in Fort Worth had also stirred up memories of Ames and his connections there. A desperation to sort out her conflicting feelings clawed at her bones. The skies hadn't given her the answers, and as near as she could tell, God was also silent on the issue. They touched down in Tulsa to pay homage to Wiley Post and Will

Rogers, then zipped off toward Wichita, where a huge reception for their hometown girl, Louise Thaden, awaited.

Mittie slept terribly that night and awoke feeling sluggish, but while she was packing her gear, the locket on the gold chain fell from the blouse she was folding. A shiver went through her. This was the niggling thought she'd been unable to bring to focus.

Why would Ames give her a family heirloom with the picture of a grandfather he couldn't wait to get away from? Speaking to Ames about it—even if she could—would only bring another set of excuses and lies. But there was one person who might shed some light—Ames' sister in Iowa. Now if she could only remember the name of the town where Fern and Lela lived.

All during breakfast she tried to come up with the address she'd seen on the envelope that had fallen from Ames' pocket. *Red something. Red Fork? No. Red Bend? No.*

Bobby asked if she was okay.

Red Valley? No. Red Gulch? Yes. That was it.

"Just tired. I need to make a phone call before we leave. How about I meet you in half an hour?" She finished her coffee and went to the pay telephone where she'd called her parents the night before. Hoping that she remembered correctly, she asked the operator for the number of Fern Danner in Red Gulch, Iowa, and deposited the required coins.

A woman answered on the first ring.

"Mrs. Danner?"

"Yes."

"You don't know me, but I'm acquainted with your brother, Ames."

A long pause. "Ames?"

"Yes. I have something that belongs to him and would like to return it . . . your grandmother's locket with a photo of your grandfather."

Fern snorted. "What's it look like?"

"It's heart-shaped, a little larger than a quarter, and on a gold chain."

"My grandmother had no such locket. Sounds like the one Ames was bragging about winning in a poker game. Lela had a fit over it."

A poker game. Mittie wanted to spit but instead asked, "Lela? Your little girl?"

"Who did you say this was?"

"A friend of Ames. He told me about you being sick a while back and Lela getting scarlet fever. Is she still doing all right?" She should just hang up. She found out all she needed to know. Ames had even lied about the locket, given it to her as a treasure. Some treasure.

"Is this some kind of prank?"

"No, ma'am."

"I don't know who you are or what kind of scheme you're trying to pull, but I don't have a child and never have."

Mittie's stomach cramped, her breath gone. No child. No Lela. Ames didn't have a niece with brown eyes and a smile that would light up the world. "I'm so sorry…Ames told me…." Her face flamed as if she'd been slapped.

"There's a Lela all right, but she's not my kid. She's Ames' girlfriend. They're getting hitched as soon as he gets home from California."

"Oh." No other words would come. Mittie dropped the receiver on the hook and leaned her forehead against the wall, her heart pounding. She swallowed to keep the breakfast in her stomach that threatened to come up.

"Ma'am, are you all right?"

Mittie turned to face a hotel porter. She ran clammy palms down her pant legs and forced a smile. "Yes, thank you. I'm fine. Just fine."

It all made sense now. The long absences, saying he was going to talk to investors. Not showing up for Christmas, saying his sister was ill. And the lies he must have told Lela, stringing her along. *His girlfriend? His future wife?*

Bobby asked again if she was all right when they got to the airfield. She shrugged and looked away, afraid that if her eyes met his, she would burst into tears. Ames wasn't worth crying over. After a brief touchdown in Kansas City, she flew along the Missouri River toward St. Louis. She clutched the gold locket with the photo of some poor stranger's grandfather in her hand. She kissed it and Ames good-bye, then hurled it out of the plane. She pictured the chain twisting and turning as the locket plummeted into the river to be washed into the Mississippi and out into the Gulf—out to sea where it could no longer entangle her or anyone ever again.

She shouted hallelujahs all the way to St. Louis. And if fortune was with her, Bobby would be waiting when she taxied into the terminal. It was premature to talk about whether she loved him, but with Ames behind her, she was ready to explore the possibility.

Bobby was there, and at the dinner that night, he said, "You have a glow I haven't seen in a long time. I trust your flight was good today."

"One of the best days ever. I could almost taste heaven."

"It must be something in the Missouri atmosphere. I remember you saying something similar when you flew in your first air race here."

"I do remember that. It seems a long time ago, doesn't it?" Warmth flooded her senses. Her first competition. The first time she'd met Calista and they'd huddled together, waiting while one of their own was lost. And then found. The beginning of the sisterhood of women pilots. And Bobby—he'd been there then as now, waiting patiently in the background.

The next two stops went by in a blur, and when she taxied into Columbus, Ohio, for their last overnight stop, Mittie could hardly contain the joy that filled her. Only one more day and the race would be over. History in the making.

Mittie craned her neck and scanned the welcoming spectators, trying to find Bobby. She didn't see him, but she took the time to slip out of her flight suit and smooth the wrinkles from the skirt of the frothy green dress she wore under it. She quickly donned the matching cloche, slipped on the Clara Bow shoes from her knapsack, and rose from the cockpit. Waving to the crowd with one hand, holding her dress with the other, she swung down and leapt to the ground. Her right foot landed wrong and twisted, a white-hot pain exploding in her ankle and shooting up her calf. She crumpled and fell on all fours.

A gasp went up, people swarming around her. *What happened? Can you move? Someone call for a doctor.*

Mittie winced. "I'll be fine. Just help me stand up." She took the first strong hand offered and pulled herself from the dust on one leg. She tentatively put her right foot on the ground, but it was no good, the pain excruciating. Bobby appeared at her side and between his support and that of a stranger, she hobbled to the safety of the terminal where someone put a bag of ice on the already-swollen ankle.

Victor and Bobby drove her to the nearest hospital for an exam. The X-ray was clear, nothing broken, but the doctor recommended staying off of it for two weeks and keeping it wrapped.

"Two weeks? I can't. I'm in the women's air race that ends tomorrow. I have to finish."

The doctor scowled. "I wouldn't advise it. A sprain like this can be quite debilitating."

"Is there anything you can do? A splint or plaster?"

"Plaster's not a good idea with the swelling. All I can suggest is warm Epsom salt soaks this evening and a cotton elastic bandage. See how you feel tomorrow."

Bobby and Victor thought it too dangerous, but they stopped

at a druggist and got the items the doctor suggested. And a set of crutches.

That evening, while the other girls celebrated at the banquet, Mittie sat with her foot soaking in the bathtub. And prayed the throbbing pain away.

Bobby knocked and asked if he could come in.

"Just a minute. I have to get decent." She hobbled around and threw on some clothes before letting him in.

He held out a stack of handwritten notes. "From the other girls. They want to know how you are."

"Much better. It's still swollen and it hurts to put weight on it, but I should be fine in the morning."

"I doubt it will be fine, although I admire your determination." He handed her a cotton bag. "I talked the waiters out of a bag of ice. It might help if you alternated an ice application with the hot soaks." Wrinkles of concern fanned from the corners of his eyes.

"I'm willing to try anything. I'd stand on my head if I thought it would keep me in the race."

"We can always petition to have someone fly with you."

"That would be cheating."

"But it's not worth risking your life for."

"The joy of finishing the race will be worth the risk."

"Somehow I knew that would be your stance."

"If it's any consolation, I've done a lot of thinking...about Ames...and us. I'll tell you all about it after I cross the finish line."

His lips brushed hers. "Till then. But remember—you don't have to complete the race to have my heart."

"No, I have to finish so I'll have a heart to give in return."

She sat on the bed and read each note, each word of encouragement, tears flowing as the face of each woman who'd flown above her, behind her, before her marched across her mind. Happy tears smudged the pages she held to her chest.

★ ★ ★

When portable steps were rolled to the little canary plane the next morning, a cheer went up from her fellow contestants. Mittie waved and said she'd see them all in Cleveland. With the aid of the crutches, she made it up the steps and rolled ungracefully into the cockpit. Helmet on. Goggles in place. Feet on the rudder. Her right foot throbbed beneath the tight elastic bandage as she did the run-up and checked all the gauges, waiting for the signal to take off.

The little canary hummed and bounced down the runway, each bump like a lightning bolt through her ankle. Mittie gritted her teeth, speeding onward. She nosed up until the air currents claimed her. One hundred and forty-eight miles. It was mere inches compared to the twenty-eight hundred she'd flown the last nine days.

The wind bit her cheeks and whispered its secrets to her. The ground below cradled and guided her. The sweat from her pores bathed her in sweet nectar. She was astride her beloved Gypsy, soaring, banking, headed for a distant shore. Joy wrapped its fingers around her heart and brought her safely across the finish line.

Thousands cheered—not because she was victorious in being the fastest, but because she'd been a part of something much larger than herself.

Bobby's and Victor's strong arms lifted her from the seat. She balanced on one leg and waved to the crowd, blowing kisses and blubbering like a baby. Bobby and Victor helped her down the steps and into the open arms of her daddy. Beside him stood her mother, dressed finer than the queen of England, her delicate fingers clutching a hanky and blotting the corner of one eye.

"Mother, Daddy. You're here."

Her mother sniffed back tears. "Why wouldn't we be? You're a celebrity." A photographer clicked a picture of their embrace as a reporter stepped forward, pencil poised above a notebook.

"What was it like to fly with only one usable foot on the rudder?"

Mittie looked him in the eye. "There were always two feet on the rudder, but only one was mine. The other was the spirit of my sisters in this race, the women who would fly to the moon and back to help one another. And I believe that someone much greater than all of us had a part."

"Were you ever tempted to give up?"

"It never entered my mind."

From the throng that stormed the field, Calista cut through their midst like an apparition. "I knew you'd do it, Kentucky. The drama at the end was a nice twist."

Mittie laughed. "Someone had to fill your shoes."

Bobby appeared with a wheelchair. "Your chariot, madame."

Mittie pivoted and sank onto the wooden seat, her throat thick. "You always know exactly what I need. Thank you."

Her mother raised expectant eyebrows.

Mittie shrugged and said, "Let's go and congratulate the winners."

Louise Thaden won the derby in her heavyweight Travel Air, a deserving and gracious woman whom they all had come to love. A girl named Phoebe won with her lightweight plane, the division where Mittie placed fourth. At the gala party that night, Calista whispered, "Next year, I'm gunning for you." She nailed her with a slanty-eyed look and ran off to dance with a fella who said he was a Hollywood talent agent.

Her daddy turned to Mittie's mother. "Let's show these kids how to cut a rug."

Bobby draped his arm across the back of her chair. "Guess I won't get a dance tonight."

"I'm afraid not." She leaned in close and turned her face toward his. "Will you settle for this?" She kissed him warmly on the lips as the soloist for the band sang of nothing but blue skies from now on.

CHAPTER 32

The dancing bears at the Kentucky State Fair had been replaced with an organ grinder and his pet monkey who collected tips and shiny objects from the audience, but the jugglers in clown suits, canning demonstrations, carnival rides, and sweet smell of cotton candy were still the same. The livestock barns were still a chorus of bleating and lowing and cackling, the smell that of fresh straw, lye soap, and the sharp ammonia of urine. And as always, Mittie gravitated toward the horse stalls behind the arena, where grooms ferried buckets of water, trainers led their prized horses to and from the exercise ring, and owners gathered to check out the competition.

Mittie found Toby fussing over Gypsy. She laced her fingers in Gypsy's mane and worked out a knot, her heart swollen with joy, knowing what Gypsy had overcome just to be in the ring once again. She gave her a quick pat on the rump and told Toby she'd be back later. She then hurried toward the hangar with the newest addition to the fair—the aviation exhibit. For two days, a hearty crowd had gathered to get a close-up look at the custom-built canary yellow mono-wing that had been part of history in the making. Bobby had flown the plane back from Cleveland and polished it up for the display. He and Victor, along with the Aero Club members, answered questions about the women's air race and the new advances in aviation. But today, the hangar was closed until noon in preparation for Mittie's first public appearance.

She ran her tongue over her lips to moisten them, more nervous than she'd been at the starting line in Santa Monica, California, only a few weeks before. As she drew near, she saw hordes of fairgoers milling about, waiting for the doors to open. Her heart raced at the thought of so many there to see her. Flying solo across mountains and rivers, in sandstorms and rainstorms, in staggering heat, and through unbearable sorrow seemed easier in comparison. She skirted the crowd and slipped in the side door of the hangar, where Victor greeted her.

"Ah, you're here. York's been looking for you."

"I hope I'm not late. Where is Bobby, anyway?"

He pointed to one of the demonstration booths that was set up like the classroom where Mittie had first learned of vertical and horizontal axes and aileron flaps and magneto checks. Bobby's back was turned as he tacked up a corner of a map that had come loose. She tiptoed up behind him and tapped him on the shoulder.

"Excuse me, sir, I was wondering if this is where I sign up for flying lessons."

He turned and pulled her close. "No, this is the kissing booth. Two kisses for a sixpence." He gave her two quick pecks on the lips.

"May I put those on my tab?"

"That's a free sample. And the price goes down after dark."

"Lovely. I can hardly wait." She took a deep breath. "All right. Tell me what I'm supposed to do. I'm a bundle of nerves. Have you seen all those people out there? Am I supposed to talk or just sign autographs?"

"You're going to be fine. Come—I'll show you where we're set up."

"Does my hair look all right? What about my dress?" She twirled around. "Are there any straw bits on it?"

He ignored her and led her to a table beside the plane she'd called home for nine days. Boxes of publicity photos the fair organizers had printed of her in her flight jacket and helmet lined the table. "You'll sit on this stool and greet people, sign the photos, and thank them for coming."

"So simple a trained monkey could do it, right?"

"All you have to do is smile and look lovely. Which you do, by the way. And no, there's no straw on your dress."

The doors were pulled open and the crowd was directed to form a line behind the ropes. Mittie sat poised on the stool and signed the photographs Bobby handed out as people approached. Mittie made eye contact with each person and asked for his or her name. Then she wrote a personal note, scrawled her name, and said, "Thanks for coming. So happy to meet you." After an hour, her fingers cramped and her back ached, and the line looked even longer than it had at the start.

Bobby handed her a bottle of ginger water. "Would you like to take a break?"

"Not just yet." She looked up at a gentleman in a natty suit and fedora, something about him oddly familiar.

Before she could ask for the name, the man said, "Hello, Mittie. Dobbs Lamberson."

Mittie's hand flew to her mouth, the room moving in and out of focus. She gulped in a breath. "Dobbs—why, Dobbs Lamberson. How are you?" A sweat bead bubbled above her upper lip.

"I'm swell. Never better." He turned to a stunning girl beside him with short ginger hair wearing a violet and cream sleeveless dress. "This is Martha, my fiancée. We've been following all the stories in the paper about you. We're plumb proud at what you've done."

Martha leaned in and extended her hand. "Dobbs has told me all about you, how you taught him to drive a pony cart when you were kids." She smiled sweetly. Innocently.

Mittie's head flashed a warning. Had he told her that she was the one who crippled him? Ruined his life? She held the fountain pen, poised to autograph the photo. "Did he?" was all she could squeak out.

Dobbs leaned in. "When we heard you were coming, I told Martha we had to come and see you."

"I'm honored. I truly am, and I think of you often."

Behind him, someone shouted, "We don't have all day. Let's get the line moving."

Bobby gave her a cautionary look and a surreptitious motion with his thumb to hurry them along. Mittie ignored him.

"Dobbs, I'm so sorry for the accident... for your injury. I wanted to call you—"

"We were silly, stupid kids. It wasn't your fault. It was never your fault."

"But the operations..." *The limp.*

"A rousing success." He thrust the photograph at her.

She scrawled her signature and watched as they walked away, arm in arm. She had more of a limp from a sprained ankle than he did.

Gypsy pranced her way to victory in her five-gait class the next morning, and after shaking hands with the judges, Mittie stayed to watch the next class. April Showers, whom the announcer said was from a stable in Jefferson County, looked magnificent and won handily, putting both her and Gypsy in the finals for the Five-Gait World's Championship. At dinner that night, Mittie asked her dad about the change in April Showers' stable.

"Jake Ford called and asked if we'd take his horses back, but I

didn't want to stir up a hornet's nest. I gave him a couple of rec-
ommendations, and he picked the one I would have. Gingersnap,
I'm afraid, is just not a show pony, but April Showers...she'll be a
tough one to beat in the championship."

Puzzle pieces clicked together. Show ponies, their owners, the
performances, and fans who filled arenas. A celebration of form, of
style, of running the race. Winners came and went. But love of the
sport and all that went with it made a lovely completed picture.

"What about Buck Lamberson? Any idea what happened to him?"

"The last I heard he had the stable for sale and was moving to
Montana."

"I saw Dobbs yesterday. He looks good and is engaged to a beautiful girl. All these years I've pictured him as a grotesque cripple."

"I've not seen him, but I believe he's studying to be a doctor.
Your uncle Granville might know."

Mittie sighed. She wouldn't ask; it was enough to know Dobbs
was all right, that he'd risen above the bitterness and greed of his
parents. Her heart ached a little that Ames hadn't.

The arena was packed for the saddlebred Five-Gait World's Championship, and once again, her family gathered in support of MG
Farms, her daddy, and tonight, Gypsy in her final performance. Her
last chance at the cup before she became a broodmare and would
hopefully, with her pedigree, birth future champions. It was a joint
decision between Mittie and her parents, and they'd consulted her
grandmother and Rex as well. As a five-year-old, it was time for
Gypsy to leave her youth behind and embrace the future.

Bobby held her hand gently in his, the talk between them easy.
Mittie, too, was ready to embrace her future, the one with Bobby
York beside her. Each day, her love for him had deepened. When
she'd finally thought about Calista's declaration that she should open
her eyes, Mittie's soul had been flooded with memories of Bobby.

His tenderness and quiet but reassuring manner. Always faithful and steady. She'd been blinded by her affections for Ames and not seen it, but when the veil was drawn aside, she knew Bobby was the rudder who'd been there all along. She squeezed the hand he'd placed in hers and gazed into eyes the color of the sky.

The organ music began and with it the announcement of the horses and their solo lap around the rail. April Showers. The sorrel stallion from MG Farms. A few newcomers. And Gypsy.

Gypsy was resplendent, her muscles like sculpted clay, her hooves lifting high. And as the crowd clapped and cheered, Gypsy put on the show of her life. Walk. Park trot. Canter. Rack. Slow gait. There wasn't a step she didn't make to perfection. When the judges examined the horses for conformation, Mittie tried to guess what they were thinking and the marks they were giving.

Her daddy leaned over, elbows on knees, his face unreadable. The other faithful and steady force in her life. And beside him, her mother. Perfectly coifed. Her proper black gloves. Matching handbag and shoes. The one who had swallowed her fear and finally given Mittie wings.

Mittie's grip on Bobby's hand grew tighter as the judges asked for another demonstration of the rack and slow gait. Her lungs burned from the breath she held while the judges made the eliminations. Then only Gypsy, the sorrel, and April Showers remained.

The organ played a *bum-bum-bum-bum-pa, bum-bum-bum-bum-pa* until at last, the head judge stepped forward. "This year's Five-Gait World's Championship goes to Gypsy of Morning Glory Farms."

Tears sprang to Mittie's eyes, her heart in her throat. Bobby put his arm around her shoulders, kissed her cheek, and handed her his monogrammed silk handkerchief.

She rose and went with her parents to accept the silver bowl. Unspeakable joy radiated through her as she waved to the crowd, but Bobby's face was the only one she saw. Her spirit soared.

Note to Readers

Weaving historical events into fiction is both a fascinating and challenging part of the writing process. I want to give my stories verisimilitude, but at the same time, I tremble at the mantle of portraying history accurately. *A Flying Affair* is the juncture of my imagination and a slice of the past based on the following documented historical events.

Colonel Charles Lindbergh did indeed fly the Atlantic in May 1927, a widely acclaimed feat, and in the months following, he went on a goodwill tour promoting aviation. He made an overnight stop in Louisville on August 8, 1927, landing the *Spirit of St. Louis* at Bowman Field. The conversation with Mittie Humphreys is a product of my imagination.

In an exciting decade of aviation, there were numerous events across the country. Barnstorming was generally unregulated and flight challenges sprang up frequently. The events I created were based on similar shows and events found during the research process, but none are factual until the Women's National Air Derby near the end of the book. It is based on a true event—the first Women's National Air Derby that took place in August 1929, a collaborative effort of the Cleveland Air Race officials and the National Exchange

Club. The scheduled stops, mishaps, and people mentioned are based on others' accounts of this much-heralded event. Among the women who participated were Amelia Earhart, Louise Thaden, Pancho Barnes, and Marvel Crosson, whose death was a sobering reminder of the dangers of early flight. I inserted Mittie Humphreys and Calista Gilson as two of the twenty participants for the purpose of the story without changing the outcome or historical significance of the race. I pray my portrayal pays homage to these women pioneers in aviation.

I'm so grateful for the work of Heather A. Taylor, whose meticulously researched, award-winning documentary, *Breaking through the Clouds* (2010), was invaluable to me as I crafted the scenes of the Women's Air Derby. For readers who want to learn more, I encourage you to visit www.breakingthroughtheclouds.com.

A sidenote about women in aviation: In November 1929 there were 117 licensed American female pilots. All were invited to assemble in New York to form an organization for mutual support and the advancement of aviation. Of those, 99 charter members formed The Ninety-Nines, a group that is still active today. Amelia Earhart was elected the first president with Louise Thaden as secretary.

When I first began research on *A Flying Affair*, I thought the Humphreys farm would have Thoroughbred horses trained for racing. On a research trip, I discovered the other jewel of the Kentucky equine world—the American saddlebred, considered by many as the peacock among horses. This look into the training and showing of this magnificent breed is based on my observing a training session at a modern-day saddlebred farm and the information gleaned from reading about similar shows held during the era. Creative license was taken with the actual dates and winners.

Thank you for following the fictive dream of *A Flying Affair*. I've tried to stay the course in presenting history in a way that entices and entertains. Any errors are mine.

Reading Group Guide

1. Aviation was a new frontier in the Roaring Twenties, and Mittie Humphreys' grandest dream was to fly and be part of this exciting time. Considering the era, what were some of the obstacles she faced? Would she face those same obstacles today?

2. One of Mittie's obstacles was gender bias. Do those issues still arise today? Discuss any experiences you might have had.

3. Mittie had the lifelong notion that she had to prove herself to meet her dad's approval. At the same time, she regarded Iris, her twin, as the "pretty one" who met with both her parents' approval. Do you struggle with being good enough or trying to meet the expectations of others? Do you think Mittie's dad and sister would be surprised by how Mittie felt?

4. Mittie's dream of flying was connected to Ames, who took her on her first flight. How much did the free-spirited Ames play into Mittie's own need for adventure? Have you ever been so enamored with someone that you didn't see their imperfec-

tions? How does the saying "Love is blind" apply to Mittie and Ames? Mittie and Bobby?

5. Ames gives Mittie a locket, which becomes a symbol for their relationship. Have you ever had a treasured item that later elicited negative feelings? Did you keep the item or get rid of it?

6. When Bobby is the surprise dinner guest, Mittie assumes her parents are trying to fix her up with someone they find suitable. Had Mittie met Bobby on her own, how might their relationship have developed differently?

7. Mittie's relationship with her mother is described as a "dance"—a give-and-take that keeps peace between them. Are there people in your life that you find difficult to get along with? Do you avoid them or try to work out your differences? Was Sarah's fear of Mittie's flying justified?

8. Mittie puts her dream on hold to care for Gypsy when she's injured, which showed her personal integrity and work ethic. Name a time when you've had a life interruption. Was it a time of frustration or personal growth for you?

9. The horse-showing circuit is a fraternity of sorts. How did this background prepare Mittie for flying competitions and the "sisters" she found among her fellow aviatrixes? Which matters more: winning or running the race?

10. Charles Lindbergh was a world-renowned hero after his solo flight across the Atlantic. Who are your heroes? What makes someone heroic?

Don't miss Carla Stewart's other 1920s novel,

The Hatmaker's Heart

For Nell Marchwold, bliss is seeing the transformation when someone gets a glimpse in the mirror while wearing one of her creations and feels beautiful. Nell has always strived to create hats that bring out a woman's best qualities. She knows she's fortunate to have landed a job as an apprentice designer at the prominent Oscar Fields Millinery in New York City. Yet when Nell's fresh designs begin to catch on, her boss holds her back from the limelight, claiming the stutter she's had since childhood reflects poorly on her and his salon.

But it seems Nell's gift won't be hidden by Oscar's efforts. Soon an up-and-coming fashion designer is seeking her out as a partner of his 1922 collection. The publicity leads to an opportunity for Nell to make hats in London for a royal wedding. There, she sees her childhood friend, Quentin, and an unexpected spark kindles between them. But thanks to her success, Oscar is determined to keep her. As her heart tugs in two directions, Nell must decide what she is willing to sacrifice for her dream, and what her dream truly is.